DEATH IN THE SUN

Death in the Sun

ADAM CREED

faber and faber

First published in this edition in 2012
by Faber and Faber Limited
Bloomsbury House, 74–77 Great Russell Street,
London WC1B 3DA

Typeset by Faber and Faber Limited
Printed and bound by CPI Group (UK) Ltd, Croydon, CR0 4YY

A CIP record for this book
is available from the British Library

ISBN 978-0-571-27497-0

2 4 6 8 10 9 7 5 3 1

The Alpujarras

'Fui piedra y perdí mi centro
y me arrojaron al mar
y a fuerza de mucho tiempo
mi centro vine a encontrar.'

'I was a stone and lost my centre
and was thrown into the sea
and after a very long time
I came to find my centre again.'

(Traditional song)

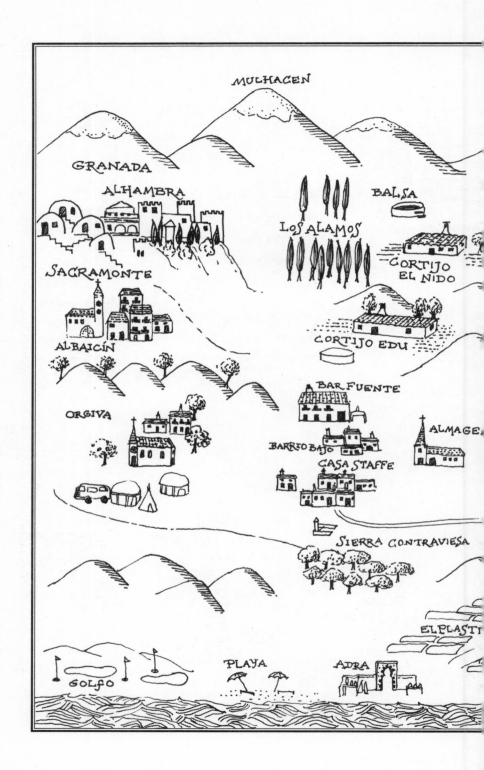

PART ONE

One

Jadus Golding pauses on the corner, finds a shadow and checks his watch. For an instant its indigo and bejewelled dial makes him feel good about himself, but then he remembers the price it came at. He looks from the time to the sky and sees a leaf, falling. The trees are heavy with leaves and he knows that if he catches the leaf, then luck will come to him. He could do with it.

He holds out his hand, spreading his fingers, then he sees Brandon, walking slow with his hands plunged deep down the front of his Sean Pauls. Jadus closes his hand into an empty fist. The leaf is on the ground.

Jadus runs a few steps, to keep Brandon in sight. He pauses when Brandon pauses to let the traffic go; crosses when Brandon crosses. They proceed in this ill-tailored tandem all the way up to Spitalfields, and all the way, the Limekiln estate comes in and out of view, like an island in a high sea. This makes his blood sluice. He is so close to Jasmine and Millie, but cannot call on his lover and their daughter.

The streets thicken and suits mix with jeans; summer frocks with *salwar kameez*. Brandon slows, turns into the entrance to the market, and stops. Jadus immediately recognises the man he is talking to, which gives him plenty cause for concern. Brandon, so long a friend, has been in hiding since he was shortlisted for the manslaughter of a nineteen-year-old student who just happened to be crossing the road in the aftermath of a job on the Seven Sisters Road – so why is he talking to a policeman?

A Cherokee Jeep slows up and Brandon nods at it, makes a circle in the air with his finger and carries on talking to DS Pulford.

As the Cherokee cruises towards him, its windows blacked out, Jadus pulls his beanie hat down. He gives the Limekiln tower a long, last look, and slopes into Flower and Dean Street, drawing shapes of what he will have to do, if Pulford doesn't get off his case.

He scrolls through his phone, sees the name is still there: *Staffe Work; Staffe Mobile.* He deletes one and then the other, but knows that this particular policeman will always be there – everywhere he goes.

Two

Slowly, he realises that he is not dead.

He is accustomed to this process but lately it has been complicated by the fact that gunshot awakens him. Birds flap up into the walnut tree, scared by Paco the Frog's automated gun crow.

The pillows are wet on his neck and the sheets are knotted around his ankles. His fever comes and goes but it has been on the wane this last week. Tomorrow, his friend Manolo is taking him to the hospital in Almería where they will, hopefully, appraise his healed wound a final time. They will chastise him for rushing his rehab, but this latest setback will be his last, he promises himself.

The ceiling is high and the poplar beams are varnished. The house martins circle in the pale morning. Beyond the fringe of silver chains, hanging by the open door to keep the mosquitoes away, the low sun is becoming brilliant. It seems that winter will never come.

Near, mules clatter down the cobbled track that runs by his rented house and into the *campo*. The sweetness of Frog's black tobacco swirls up through the leaves of the walnut tree.

He pushes himself upright in the bed and touches his soreness. It is less tender than yesterday. This time, he must let it heal completely, stay free from infection.

Frog calls to his dog and Staffe walks across his bedroom's

terracotta floor, warm already, and parts the silver chain *cortinas,* blinking. Beyond the walnut tree, wisps of cloud strand the sky and the massif of Gador is far away, between him and Almería. Tomorrow Manolo has promised him lunch at his *tío*'s bar – an Almerían institution, so he claims.

Staffe picks his phone from the crude, chestnut dressing table and looks for messages. Not a sausage. How his stomach pines for sausage, the English way.

*

A line of men lean against the thick, oak counter of Bar Fuente, arguing fiercely and banging fists. Some wear broad-rimmed straw hats, check shirts and drill trousers tied at the waist with rope; others, younger, are in blue cotton overalls and baseball caps sporting the logos of local plumbing and electrical suppliers. In front of them, on the bar, are rows of tiny white cups and saucers with ferocious coffee alongside small goblets filled to their brims with *sol y sombre* – a breakfast tipple of brandy and anis.

Staffe makes his way to the *comedor* and the locals nod and smile. He says to Consuela, 'The usual,' and she smiles sheepishly, her eyes darting to the floor. Staffe chides Frog, for setting his gun crow too early in the morning. Frog pushes back his dog-eared beret, says something indecipherable in reply, then looks Consuela up and down. She has a broad face, her bones are fine and she is taller than most of the men. She is not from these parts, but for some reason has stuck around – perhaps it has something to do with the child she has. She didn't arrive in Almagen with the child. Frog says something else at her and

6

laughs – like a frog, his big eyes bulging. She scuttles into the kitchen.

As he waits, Staffe looks at some new posters on the wall. They are handwritten in an ornate font with renditions of paintbrushes, books and musical notes as a border. The posters are all slightly different, but each advertises a final decisive meeting with the Junta to determine whether Almagen will be awarded its Cultural Academy. It has been the talk of the village. It will revitalise the place, secure its future.

Bar Fuente, like Staffe's house, is in the lower *barrio* – the oldest part of the village. The Moors built it in the sixteenth century when they were banished from Granada. Later, the village spread up the hill towards what became a main road, the *carretera*. Each *barrio* has a square and a fountain. In these parts, where the melting snow from the Sierra Nevada flows, water is priceless.

Consuela brings Staffe his *tostada* with tomato and olive oil, a glass of orange juice and *café con leche*.

'Hey, Guilli!' says Manolo, picking up a *sol y sombre,* coming to join him. As he brushes past Consuela, Frog says something and Manolo blushes.

'Guirri!' calls another.

'No, Guillermo, you idiot.' It's Manolo's joke – to shorten Guillermo, the Spanish for William, to Guilli. A *guirri* is an outsider, implicitly unwelcome. 'They're idiots,' says Manolo, plonking down a plastic bag on the floor and sitting heavily on the chair opposite Staffe, his torso broad and deep, as if he is not to scale. He nods and smiles at Staffe. His teeth are white and good, odd in these parts, but his skin is dark as stained oak and rough from the sun and the *sierra* winds. Manolo is the

7

village shepherd – El Pastor, and probably a few years younger than Staffe, but the ravages of the sun and wind make him seem older. Frog calls him a stupid goat. Someone else calls him a goat fucker. Manolo ignores them: hurt, but seeming as though he has heard it all before. The lines on his forehead deepen and his shoulders hunch an extra degree. He says, 'Tomorrow, Almería. You're still good to go?' as though apologising for something.

'Of course,' says Staffe.

Frog shouts across, 'I hear your brother is back, the one who got all the brains!'

Manolo pushes the bag towards Staffe with his foot. 'Tomatoes and peppers, from my *huerta*.' He swirls his *sol y sombra*, the goblet like a thimble in his enormous hands.

'Show my friend here your hole,' calls Frog, imploring Staffe with his wide, bulging eyes. A cluster of the men from the bar turn, urging him, and Staffe reluctantly lifts his shirt. He has done this a dozen times but he manages a smile. One of the younger men comes across, tipping back his baseball cap, crouching, prodding the baby-pink tissue of his two scars: the one between his hip and the navel has healed well but the other, between his heart and the pit of his arm, weeps, having reopened a month ago when a bigoted chump from Mecina, the next village, had started on Manolo. Staffe stepped in, and so did the chump's friends. Strong as Manolo is, they took quite a hiding.

He swallows away the memory of where the two bullets came from, how long it has been since the doctors at City Royal cheated death, saved the fugitive Jadus from becoming a murderer. It seems a lifetime ago now.

Today, he will do his physio and spend an hour brushing up on his conjugations, then he will meet his young nephew, Harry, from school. They will walk up the mountain together, to El Nido, his sister Marie's *cortijo* where she lives with the ne'er-do-well Paolo. Meanwhile, he and Manolo sit together. Slowly, the bar thins out.

Staffe says to his friend, 'Your brother? You never mentioned a brother.'

'He went away. He is barely anything to me.'

'Wouldn't it be nice, to have some family with you – especially with your father away. The family line is what we call it.'

'Some families are maybe best without a line.'

Frog bangs an empty glass on the counter, shouts something thick and fast to Consuela, who is in the kitchen. The other old goat still at the bar laughs, but Consuela looks hurt and Manolo stands, slowly.

Consuela shouts, 'No. Lolo, no!'

Manolo walks towards Frog who says, 'Sit down, you thick lump.' Manolo reaches out with a big hand and Frog's friend grabs his forearm, but Manolo gets Frog by the throat anyway, launches him into the wall with one hand around his throat. Frog's beret falls to ground and his feet twitch in the air. Manolo puts his free hand to his hip, where Staffe sees the carved handle of a knife protruding from a plaited, makeshift belt fashioned from baling twine.

Staffe shouts, 'No!' as the colour drains instantly from Frog's face. Salva, the bar owner, rushes in from the store room, throws himself at Manolo, grabbing him round the neck. But Manolo stands firm and still and Frog's feet twitch. He squeals, high pitched, like air from a balloon.

Consuela walks through the hatch at the end of the bar and puts a fine hand on Manolo's massive, taut forearm. She whispers, 'Please. Let him go. For me.'

Frog drops to the floor, like a sack of beans from a mule. Manolo returns to the table, his eyes empty and cold. He reaches for his hip and pulls his knife, cuts open a tomato and offers a slice to Staffe. 'My tomatoes are the best.' The knife has a goat's head intricately carved for its handle. Seeing Staffe looking, Manolo says in his little voice, 'I carved it myself.'

Staffe nods at the posters, says, 'You could get involved in the Academy.'

'That's not for us. This lot just want to make off with the money from the government. One man's culture, another man's crime.' He runs his blade through another tomato and Consuela brings him a plate of bread. They don't look at each other, nor exchange even pleasantries.

*

Staffe finds slim shade by the church in the middle *barrio*. He presses his back to the stone, which is warm. A couple of mothers stand by the fountain watching their young play. The bells peal and before the final ring echoes around the fringe of houses, the children rush through the arched, filigree gate of the school cloister and into the square. The mothers call out to their young but are ignored.

A nun brings a lone child to the ironwork gate. She pats him on the shoulder and points up the mountain, ushering him away. Harry looks sad and Staffe calls out to him. Harry's face lights up when he hears his name, but becomes instantly glum.

He walks towards his uncle briskly, head down. 'I can walk home on my own.'

Staffe raises a bag. 'I have tomatoes and peppers from Manolo's *huerta*.'

'His garden, you mean.' Harry walks off up the steep, narrow alley that leads to the main road. At the top of the hill, he drinks lustily from a fountain. When Staffe catches up, Harry holds his uncle's hand and they cross the Mecina road, take the goat track into the sierra.

'You don't know how lucky you are, living here,' says Staffe.

'Why can't I stay with you in the village?'

'Your mum and Paolo live up the mountain. And you have a new brother or sister about to come along.'

'There's nothing to do up there.'

'What about the baby?'

'It will only make things worse. You know how small that house is.'

Staffe wants to tell him that he will look back on these days and marvel. 'You can learn the land. And you should ask your friends up to El Nido. You could make a camp and have them to sleep over.'

Harry looks up at Staffe as if he is deciding whether to confide a secret. He says nothing.

They walk briskly for twenty minutes, Staffe suffering in the heat, but when they reach the *cortijo*, Harry runs past the building, sits on the edge of the *balsa*, a circular, concrete pond that holds water for the land, and for washing. Normally, his feet dangle in the water, but not today.

Marie is chopping peppers outside the stone *cortijo*, which has a kitchen cum living room and a small bedroom either side.

The shower is outside and the toilet is wherever takes your fancy. Paolo started on the building work with a vengeance, but as summer hotted up, his mission soon petered out into long afternoons sat on the veranda, smoking his way through his own supply and drinking the local *terrano* wine that comes by the five-litre. Marie fries the peppers, adds beaten eggs to a skillet and rustles up a *revuelta*.

They eat and drink and watch the shadowless enormity of the valley. Paolo talks about what he has planted and how it's hit and miss but next year will be better.

Staffe thinks, 'Yeah, right. *Mañana*,' but says, 'What will you do in the winter for fuel? The locals have started bringing in their wood.'

'We'll do it when it gets cooler,' says Paolo.

'Surely, when it gets cooler you'll already be needing it.'

Paolo says, 'They've thrown the towel in.'

'What?' says Staffe.

'Can't we let our lunch settle?' says Marie, gathering the dishes and looking daggers at Paolo. 'We're away from the world here. That's supposed to be the point.'

'Who's thrown the towel in?' asks Staffe.

Marie takes the dishes away and as soon as she is out of earshot, Paolo says, 'I saw it on the telly in Orgiva. It's ETA. They have stopped for good.'

Staffe watches Marie at the sink by the door, scrubbing the skillet. When she is done with the pan, she fills a bowl for the dishes, starts singing a Pretenders song. She has a beautiful voice. He says to Paolo, 'If Marie didn't want you to say anything, you shouldn't have said anything.'

'But she says you're . . .' He lets the words drift to nothing.

Staffe goes to Marie, says, 'Sing that song again. What is it?'

She removes the muslin from a cheese that Manolo had brought round last week. 'He told you, didn't he?'

'What does it matter?'

'It matters. That's the problem.'

'It will be winter soon. You can't shower outside in the winter.' He kisses her on the forehead and starts to dry the dishes.

Marie sings, 'Though you are far away, I know you'll always be near to me.' She cuts a slice of cheese, reaches out to Staffe with a piece, pops it in his mouth.

It conjures a memory.

She must see it, because she says, 'I feel it too, you know, Will. I miss them so badly. But you can't get angry – that won't do any good. And surely, if ETA are stopping – that has to be good.'

He chews on the cheese and she leans against him, rests her head on his chest, her ear pressing against his wound. He feels the pain, lets it come, thinks about the heartless bastard who killed their parents: Santi Etxebatteria, who, it seems, is allowed to see the error of his ways and put an end to bad activity. Just like that. Does that make their death even more worthless – that the cause is no longer fought? It is madness to think that way, he knows.

Marie holds up a slice of cheese, says, 'This is good. Remember when Mum would tell you off for eating it straight from the fridge?'

He smiles, remembers how his teeth would leave their imprint in the waxy cheddar, always catching him out. 'This is Manolo's cheese.'

'You were laid up when he brought it round. He came with his brother. I didn't know he has a brother,' says Marie.

'Nobody tells you anything up here,' says Staffe.

*

The setting sun catches Gador and brushes it pink and coral. Tomorrow, Manolo is going to take him towards it, but veering to the west, to where Almeria stands by the Med like a proud Moor, looking back at Africa.

Staffe rocks in his wooden chair up on the roof of his village house, puts down *Monsignor Quixote* and swirls the mint tea in its nickel pot. He pours himself another glass, thinking back to when he had only a notion of Spain.

The three of them were waiting for the last call for boarding the ferry. His father was sporting his panama hat and wore a silly Hawaiian shirt. His mother had a floral summer dress that floated from its empire line and her face was sun kissed from the hot June. Twenty-five years ago, yet sometimes it feels like never – or as if it happened to someone else. Other times, it seems like yesterday: the only thing of significance that ever touched him.

'Will,' his mother had said, 'You'll be . . .'

'All right!' he had snapped. There was a party back up in Surrey and in his pocket he was touching the joint he had rolled ready for the drive back up the A3.

'Will,' his father said, wearily. 'We know you'll be all right. But one day, you'll understand.'

'I understand now.'

'And you'll be good to Marie.'

His mother had pulled down her hat too far on her head and she tilted her face up, peered at him. He waited for her to admonish him, but she just reached out and put a finger to his lips, said, 'I don't know what I would do, if anything happened to you, Will.'

He should have said, then, that he loved her. He should have said that to his father, too. Instead, he looked up at the *Pride of Bilbao* and said, 'They're boarding.' He accepted the handshake from his father and stood limply as his mother hugged him. There were gulls in the sky and a faraway look in her eye. He waited for her to kiss him, but she didn't, she just put the palm of her hand flat to his chest and said, 'My boy.'

The next time he saw her, her freckles were gone and her eyes were closed. They had pulled a gown right up to her neck and when he looked down, there wasn't the contour you would expect. They had put her hair up, in a bun, a way she had never had it. She was all gone.

Three

Manolo stoops at the counter of the Quinta Toro, bending low so his elbow can rest on the bar. He is talking with his *tio*, Angel, and raises his hand the instant Staffe steps down from the blistering sun of Almería's market and into the dark, empty bar. His smile is frail and his eyes are soft, but he is undoubtedly pleased to see Staffe – almost as if he has been counting the moments towards a loved one's safe return.

Approaching Manolo now, Staffe sees his friend in a different kind of light. He is wearing a jacket for his trip to town and his trousers are clean with a sharp crease, his shoes shine and his skin sings from a good scrubbing. Today, his friend is almost dashing, but he is stiff, as if broom handles are stuck down the arms and legs of his clothes.

'*Papas a lo pobre*,' says Manolo, thrusting a saucerful of glistening potatoes at him. 'The best. And how are things with you?' Manolo looks at Staffe's chest, his face sad again. He holds Staffe by the shoulder as he awaits the response.

'I'm fine. The hospital said I'm fit to travel.'

'You are going home? To England?'

The consultant had told Staffe his blood had tested well but he wouldn't be able to work for at least a month, though he could travel – best not by air.

'I might go back in a couple of weeks or so.'

Manolo looks glum. 'Good for you but bad for us.' He turns

away, issues a rally of fast, blurring words and Angel glugs a glassful of wine into a goblet. Angel is older than Staffe, his forehead crinkled with lines and, unusually for a Spaniard, his head totally hairless, gleaming.

They clash drinks and Manolo tells him how long the Quinta Toro has been in the family and how proud they all are that Angel has kept it going – the old way. But the bar is empty. Its history looks spent.

Angel brings small dishes of chicken livers in rich gravy. Manolo tells Angel, 'This is my friend, the *guardia* from England.'

Staffe nods. 'Police. More like the Cuerpo Nacional, though.'

'He is a detective?' says Angel, looking suspiciously at Staffe, then Manolo.

'Maybe I should take him by Adra on our way home.'

'Why?' says Staffe.

Angel talks impossibly fast, the words blurring into one another, and as he talks, he reaches down, produces more wine and pours it lustily, the wine spilling onto the counter.

Manolo puts a finger to his temple and taps it, nodding at Angel. He says to Staffe, 'We have our own mysteries here. A murder.'

Angel leans forward, lowers his voice. 'This one is a *guirri*. It's nothing.'

'His son, Jesús, is in the Cuerpo,' says Manolo. 'He's down at the scene.'

'He's only a young puppy dog but he has seen many, many deaths already,' says Angel. 'This is no different.'

'But he told me it is the worst,' says Manolo.

'How?' says Staffe.

Angel shakes his head, which glints from the lantern lights above. He is suddenly earnest. 'I cannot betray his confidence.' He raises a finger to his lips.

'I can take you, though,' says Manolo, 'A shame not to whet your appetite.'

'You should leave Jesús to his business,' says Angel.

Staffe slides a spoonful of livers into his mouth, presses his tongue to the roof of his mouth and the livers dissolve, leave a taste of something unmistakably foreign. 'What is this spice?' he asks Angel.

'A secret,' says Angel.

And Staffe gets it. Something you seldom taste in Spain, this is star anise, a cousin of fennel and the anis liqueur they swill for breakfast.

On their way out, Manolo says, 'So, that's my *tio*.' He looks back at the bar, two large barrels out front and an ancient sign beneath a weathered, bronze bull's head. 'What did you make of him?'

'He's a proud man.'

Manolo puts his arm on Staffe's back, pats his shoulder, firmly. 'I'm pleased. I value your opinion. You know that, don't you?'

*

As they drive to Adra, Manolo's dog, Suki, constantly yaps and jumps from the foot well on to his lap and back again, but Manolo is expressionless, seems elsewhere. Staffe says, 'Is something wrong?'

'Wrong?' Manolo shrugs.

They pass a restaurant, El Marisco, on its own opposite the field of vast plastic greenhouses that spill down to the sea. The restaurant is like an oasis, with beautiful *cordobés* tiles. A line of Mercs and 4x4s are parked out front.

Waiters in starched white tunics and slicked black hair tend the great and the good with straight backs and silver service. A man at the top of the steps meets and greets. He clocks Manolo's van and waves, but Manolo ignores him.

Staffe says, 'Angel said it was a *guirri*; a *guirri* like me?'

'You shouldn't think of yourself as a *guirri*. You live here. You have family who have moved here.'

'They say if you've been a *guirri*, you're always a *guirri*.' Staffe knows that Manolo's father, the one they say is mad and lives in Granada, went to Germany. They say he found himself a beautiful wife who deserted him, destroyed him; gave him a *guirri* son. Or two. 'How do you feel?'

'I'm from Almagen. I wish I wasn't, but I am. God willing, that will be the end of it for us *Canos*.' Manolo pulls Suki onto his lap, fusses with the dog's fluffy white head. For a moment, disregarding the scale of him, Manolo looks free as a boy.

Staffe wants to ask Manolo if his mother went off and took his younger brother with her – the brother he has never mentioned. He waits for Manolo to say something.

'You have your sister and your Arri. It's a good family to have.'

'I'll tell you about my family one day.'

Manolo puts a hand under Suki's body, lifts her up and kisses the top of her head. He places her down, gently, between himself and Staffe. 'It's all right, Guilli. I know about your parents. I'm very sorry.' He stops the van.

Plastic greenhouses are everywhere, some the size of football pitches. This is intensive farming on an epic scale. Some of the greenhouses are new, but most are decrepit: dirty plastic sheets full of holes and tied to rusting metal frames. The sand blows up from the track and as he gets out of the van, Staffe can smell that they are near the sea. He looks into one of the greenhouses where the soil is like dust and sprinklers lie like snakes amongst the canes. He can't recall ever having told Manolo about his parents, but doesn't ask, instead says, 'What grows here?'

'Whatever you want. Whenever you want it. But the land is shit. Not like my *huerta* with my goats' shit and the sierra water.'

'Where is Jesús?'

Manolo points down a narrow track between the plastic structures. 'You had best be quick.'

'You're not coming?'

'I need to collect something.'

Once he is out of Manolo's battered grey van, the heat intensifies – shimmering off the plastic sheets; even with his sunglasses on, Staffe has to squint against the glare. A chemical smell of unnatural nutrients mixes with the ozone. Staffe walks past a chest-high drum that says 'NitroFos'. He goes deep between the giant enclosures and here and there, Moroccans mooch in ones and twos: some in hooded *burnous*, others in garish nylon track suits. Some exude menace, watching him carefully.

When Staffe looks back for Manolo's van, a Moroccan, crouched on his haunches and wearing a hemp *burnous,* dyed yellow and blue, is staring at him. The hood is down and his eyes are heavy as pebbles. His shaven head is smooth as wet rocks and black as a bible. As he turns a corner, he senses that the man stands. Turning, he sees Manolo standing beside the Moroccan, holding an empty, hessian sack. Manolo ushers Staffe on with a flutter of the fingers and crouches beside the Moroccan.

Once Staffe is right in amongst the plastic, there are no points of reference. The sun is immediately above, and even mighty Gador is nowhere to be seen. He keeps checking for the sea, sees a thin, blue strip of it every now and again as he works his way left and forward, right and forward, all the time committing his moves to memory.

Staffe discerns human noise: a crackle of radio. He follows the sounds, coming from within a plastic-sheeted greenhouse right down near the sea. By its entrance, a Cuerpo Nacional officer leans against a quad bike. He is strapped up with a revolver and a lethal truncheon. His uniform is blue and he is handsome with slicked hair and bright eyes, his skin the colour of walnut. He gives Staffe a lingering look, not blinking. When Staffe gets to within six feet, the policeman says, 'Stop!'

'Where is the beach?' Staffe asks.

The policeman laughs. 'Beach? This is no beach.'

Staffe walks by, stands on the low shelf of scrub overlooking thirty metres of sand and wooden pallets and tin cans. Shopping bags flutter in the breeze. If life was this beach, you'd top yourself. He turns, 'You're right,' trying to see into the ramshackle greenhouse. Inside, makeshift pinboards have been erected and an enormously fat man with a rush of curly brown hair walks slowly around a penned area, peering at the ground. His shirt is stained dark with sweat all down its back and in patches beneath each arm, the size of dinner plates. 'What happened?'

The young *cuerpo* says, 'You shouldn't be here.'

'What are they growing?'

'Strawberries, but not any more. Are you German?'

'Are you Jesús? You have a look of your father – Angel. He's a friend of mine.'

'My father doesn't care for Germans.'

'I'm English.'

Jesús's lip curls, as if Staffe had said, 'I'm a war criminal.'

Staffe takes a step closer, trying to see the subject of attention inside the greenhouse.

Jesús puts a hand to his hip, rubs his thumb against the butt of his revolver, poking from its holster. 'Stop!'

The fat man looks up, makes his way wearily to the entrance. 'Who is he, Jesús?'

Staffe says, 'I have a house in the Alpujarras.'

'You're no *Alpujarreño*. Your Spanish is too clean.' The two men laugh.

'What happened?'

'You must go.' The fat man reaches behind him, pulls out a radio. 'Jesús, take him away.'

Staffe jumps away from Jesús and waves his hands in front of his face, shouts, 'Wasp! Wasp! I'm allergic. I'm allergic!'

The fat man and Jesús each take a step back and Staffe carves great swipes in the air at the imaginary wasp, focusing on the scene behind the fat man. The head and shoulders of a fair-haired man stick up from a hole in the ground. His skin is swollen, bloodied and torn, and his nose is askew. Staffe thinks an eye socket is lower than it ought to be.

Jesús walks towards Staffe, grabs his arm, leads him away from the entrance, and as they go, Staffe says, 'Is it a bad one?'

'It'll be in the papers tomorrow.'

'Don't worry. I know how it goes. I'm in the police in England.'

Jesús wipes his mouth. 'Like I said, read it in the papers.'

'I could hear it straight from the journalist. There's no law against that, is there?'

'Why would you bother?' Jesús looks at him and for an instant, Staffe thinks the policeman might expect a convincing response.

'You've been in those mountains. There's nothing to do if you haven't got a mule.' He laughs. 'It can't do any harm.'

Jesús sighs. 'How do you know my father?'

'Manolo Cano, your *primo*, is my best friend here in Spain. Tell me about the journalist. Like you say, it'll be in the papers tomorrow.'

Jesús lowers his voice. 'He's with *La Lente*.' He looks over his shoulder. 'Now, you need to get yourself back to the hills.'

Staffe makes his way back through the plastic-sheeted greenhouses and all the time, he feels watched. He turns quickly, thinks he sees the blur of a darting body. A dog, perhaps. He stops dead, listens hard and thinks he can hear a scuttle. Maybe a snake.

He walks on as softly as he can, through the dust, and eventually spots the drum of NitroFos, close to where Manolo parked the van. He looks around. No Manolo, nor his van. 'Manolo!' he calls, peering all around. Twenty metres away, the African in the blue and yellow *burnous* is still on his haunches and staring right at Staffe.

Staffe beckons the African to stand, but he stays put, looking anxious, putting his hands together, as if in prayer, rocking back and forth, moving his lips but saying nothing.

'Have you seen a man – my friend, the one with the grey van?'

He shakes his head vociferously, looking at his black feet on the white stones.

Staffe stands over him. 'What happened here?'

The African man cowers and clamps a hand over his own mouth.

'Tell me.'

The man removes the hand and says a word with his mouth, but no sound comes.

'You are . . . ?' Staffe has forgotten the Spanish word for 'mute' but the man nods.

Staffe sits alongside and motions over his shoulder with his thumb, towards the sea. 'What did happen?'

The man pokes a finger into the dust. He works his finger round and round until a hole the size of a fist is made. He reaches into his *burnous* and pulls out a bottle of water. He puts his open fist into the hole and pours the water into his hand. The hole grows dark but the water soon disappears and the soil is light again.

'My friend?'

The man shakes his head and draws a flattened palm slowly across his own throat.

'What!' Staffe stands, thinking about the fair-haired, beaten man with his head and shoulders planted in the Almería dust. The doctors prescribed against this.

'Guilli! Guilli! We have to go.'

Turning, Staffe sees Manolo trudge from between a couple of greenhouses. 'Where were you?'

Manolo holds up an old sack of seed, barely a quarter full. 'The finest pepper seeds in all Andalucia,' he laughs, weakly. 'Now, we must go – quick.'

They drive fast, a different way that doesn't take them back past El Marisco. Bordering an enormous, verdant gap amongst the plastic, between the motorway and the Med, signs for 'GOLF TROPICAL' have been defaced into the aerosol words of 'GUERRA GOLFO'.

'Golf war?' says Staffe.

'There's only so much water,' says Manolo. 'Some people think it's better to use it for food than for golf. Damn fools.' Manolo is agitated and chomps away on a mouthful of sunflower seeds, spitting the soft shells out of the window. After a while, he says, 'So, did you see anything?'

'I got a glimpse of the victim. He was in a terrible state.'

Manolo looks ahead, squinting at the signs for the *autopista*. 'What did he look like?'

'Fair hair. That's all you could say. The rest of him was a bloody mess.'

Four

Staffe leans against the ancient, wrought balcony of his room in Almería's Hotel Catedral, watches two young gypsy boys kick a football against the massive sand-coloured stones of the cathedral's façade. Old couples promenade through the *plaza* in their Sunday best. The sun is low but the evening is sultry and the merest breath of the Med comes up from Almería's port.

A couple of hours ago, he waved off troubled Manolo and asked the receptionist in the hotel if she could help him catch up with an old friend of his who writes for *La Lente*. 'He uses a pseudonym these days, though,' Staffe had told the receptionist. 'I don't know what name he goes by, but I know he's covering a murder down on the coast.'

The receptionist embraced the challenge, phoning *La Lente* and coming up with the name Gutiérrez. Raúl Gutiérrez.

'That story isn't even out, yet,' Gutiérrez had said when Staffe called.

'What I know won't affect the story you are running tomorrow, but it could lead to something bigger,' Staffe had said.

'This story's big enough, don't you worry.'

'Murder always is.'

'Who are you?'

'I am police.'

'You talk shit.'

'Did you interview the African?' asks Staffe.

'Which African?'

'He is mute, but he saw it all.'

'Nobody saw it, and anyway, this is my story.'

'Stories of murder aren't yours or mine. They belong to the dead and their families and whoever might be next. Can you meet me? Café Tanger, at eight o'clock.'

'You sound quite intent, Señor Wagstaffe.'

Staffe had tried to recall when he might have let slip his name to Raúl Gutiérrez. He was quite sure he hadn't. He hung up, knowing that he really had no business with this killing. But if Gutiérrez showed up, maybe that was a sign. If he didn't, he would let it lie: have a good dinner and slide between crisp linen sheets and get a bus tomorrow, back to the hills. Mind his own.

Now, making his way down through the hotel then walking down Calle Real, he feels bubbles of air trap in his belly; a slow rush in his loins. As the cranes of the port come into view and the sun catches the tops of the buildings, he feels kind of weightless. Every so often, he sees the battered face of the fair *guirri*, his shoulders like a dead tree stump in the ground.

What will he do if Gutiérrez doesn't show?

Since his wound was re-treated, Staffe has grown a little stronger every day. But for all those weeks, he has dreaded going back to London and the Force – a little more each day.

Jadus Golding had looked him in the eye and pulled the trigger, rather than go back to jail.

Staffe had done everything he knew to help Jadus get clean. He invested his faith in a young man who had been a criminal since before he went to school. Now, he doesn't know what he will be if he can't go back to the Force, but he knows that a policeman needs one thing above all else. Forget courage and method and intelligence. If you lack judgement, your days are numbered. That night, his judgement had failed him.

*

In Café Tanger, a Muslim affair, he orders a mint tea, looks out towards the port. On the other side of the glass, Moroccan men sit in rows, facing Africa and stirring their tea, passing the hookah pipe.

'Señor Wagstaffe.'

Staffe turns, jolted by the sound of his own name. 'Señor Gutiérrez?'

Raúl Gutiérrez nods and lights a black cigarette.

'Do you want tea?'

Gutiérrez shakes his head, sucks on his smoke. 'You are a long way from home, Inspector. A long way indeed from your Leadengate home.' Raúl sits down. He is fiftyish and clean as a whistling dandy, dressed for the ladies, Staffe thinks, and oozing expensive cologne.

'You've done some homework,' says Staffe, wondering what Gutiérrez has gleaned in the hours since they spoke. He thinks about asking Raúl how he knew his name, but decides to keep that card close.

'And you, too. Now, tell me about your new African friend.'

'How do you know he is a new friend?'

'Information is my life. It is like the sun and water. Without it, I can't live.' Gutiérrez motions to the waiter, asks for water. 'You nearly died. You should be more careful.' When the water comes, Gutiérrez waits for the waiter to turn away and takes out a quarter bottle of J&B.

Staffe looks anxiously around.

Gutiérrez says, 'I don't mind Africans, but we are in Spain and if I want to drink whisky in my own country, I will. They know what is what. I don't know why you said to meet here.'

'The victim was in a hell of a state,' says Staffe.

Gutiérrez drinks half his whisky in one, theatrically opening his eyes wide and blowing out his cheeks, smiling. 'You saw nothing.'

'In England, a crime scene like that would be crawling with journalists, but you've got an exclusive – right?'

'You should concentrate on your convalescence.'

The waiter comes across to the table and speaks rapidly to Gutiérrez, clearly angry. He scoops up the whisky bottle and curses.

Gutiérrez calls the waiter a 'fucking infidel', and a group of four young Moroccans appear from what must be the kitchen at the far end of the café. Two of them hold chef's knives and all of them smile, as if Gutiérrez might be a big enough shit to make their day. The four youths slowly advance and Staffe holds up his hands. 'I apologise for my friend. We shall leave.' He puts down a five-euro note and ushers Raúl Gutiérrez up by the lapel.

Raúl Gutiérrez says, 'There's a proper place round the corner. Come on. I'm buying.'

Casa Joaquín is one block back from the waterfront and populated by men between forty and fifty-five, all with their hair slicked back, picking at seafood and drinking *copas* of *manzanilla*. They stand in clusters and talk passionately about the red shrimp of Almería, the anchovies and the clams. Most seem to know Gutiérrez, who has two glasses plonked down for him on the counter where a space is made.

'I suggest you get me drunk, Inspector. My tongue loosens. And I might even get to talking about Santi Etxebatteria.'

'What!'

'It seems I can be all kinds of uses to you, but what can you do for me?'

Staffe spears an anchovy, lets the salt make a delicious film in his mouth. He calls for two more *copas*, still reeling at the sound of the name of the man who murdered his parents.

'There were only three English killed. It might have been a long time ago, but it's a big thing in Spain, still. Paul and Enid Wagstaffe. They lie heavy on our conscience, like the memories of our two boys on yours.'

'Omagh,' says Staffe.

Gutiérrez clinks his glass against Staffe's, says, 'I think you have nothing. In which case, let's get drunk and tomorrow you can be on your way back to Almagen.'

Staffe sips his *manzanilla*, considers the fact that he hadn't told Gutiérrez he is living in Almagen. He leans close to Raúl, whispers, 'He was killed with water, right?'

Raúl's eyes flicker and he smiles. 'What exactly did your African friend say?'

'He drew me a pretty picture. Maybe I should see what you say in your newspaper and then I'll know how deep you are in the Cuerpo's pocket.'

'And why should you care, Inspector Wagstaffe?'

He guesses that Raúl has built a career on people underestimating him, thinking he is some played-out libertine. He finishes the sherry and looks at the fish and crustaceans on ice behind the bar. 'There must be a dozen tapas to be had here.'

'To loosen my tongue?'

Staffe thinks to himself, that's not on the menu. Not to-night.

Raúl must see this because he puts an arm around Staffe's shoulder. His breath is malty as he says, 'We're going to get on fine, the two of us. I just know it.' He slaps Staffe hard on the back and laughs. Behind the eyes, though, Staffe sees something familiar, glinting in the dark. Raúl is afraid.

*

Pulford watches Brandon Latymer leave Pearl's. B-Lat, which is what Brandon goes by, swaggers out of the caff with his hips low and his jeans halfway down his thighs and as he walks past the window, he winks at Pulford and taps his chest, twice, to signify that he is carrying and there is nothing that an officer of the law can do about it – not when you take into account the shenanigans that Pulford is requesting Brandon to per-form; even though he is supposedly in hiding from the likes of Pulford, on account of a hit and run up on the Seven Sisters Road.

DS David Pulford puts his head in his hands and sighs, heavy and long. His conscience will wrestle with B-Lat's guilt later, when he has brought Jadus Golding to justice. He pushes his mug away and leaves enough money to cover his tea and Brandon's can of Nurishment. He feels as though this goose chase is getting away from him and he takes another look at the warrant for arrest he had just shown Brandon.

Of all Jadus Golding's e.Gang, B-Lat has most to lose by not fingering Jadus for the shooting of Staffe. Brandon wants his warrant for arrest for the hit and run withdrawn, on account of a new alibi he has discovered. Pulford told him he couldn't do that, but he would help him remain at large. Brandon had said, 'You must be a pussy, letting people like us take pops at police. He was your boss, right?' He laughed. 'Proper pussy.'

'I'll have you and your brother for manslaughter.'

'And these conversations? You want that in the open?'

'You couldn't prove anything.'

'Not according to my barrister.'

'You're talking to your barrister!'

That was when Brandon had got up, looking down on Pulford. 'You know, they say police was on the Seven Sisters that night I was supposed to have mowed that poor boy down.'

Pulford knows where Brandon parked his Cherokee Jeep and he will know exactly where it will go, from now until whenever he finds the tracker. The device is unauthorised. In the eyes of the law it doesn't exist, but if things work out, it won't be necessary in any court of law.

On his way to the Limekiln, Pulford remembers the first time Staffe took him to Pearl's. They had ribs, rice and peas, and corn bread. It wasn't Pulford's bag, but Staffe loved it.

Staffe's Peugeot is parked up in the Limekiln car park and Pulford sits on its bonnet, looks up at Jasmine Cash's flat. He waits ten minutes until she finally comes out on the deck, young Millie on her hip. She shouts down for him to 'Fuck off', which makes him ashamed because he knows Staffe really liked Jasmine. But Pulford figures that if Jadus knows he is harassing his girlfriend, he might come out of the shadows. Also, the more Jadus thinks it's not safe to call on them in their own home the more he will want to.

Pulford gets in the car, starts it up and swings out onto the East Road. He makes his way up Columbia Road, seeing on the small monitor down by his gearstick that Brandon is making his way out on the Roman Road towards Stratford. He reaffirms the ethics of his approach, his faith in the many ways the goodness of the law can manifest itself.

Five

Staffe reads Raúl Gutiérrez's article, which made the front page of *La Lente*. He can ascribe sense to most of the words. He has been topping up his Spanish, layering new lumps of nouns and verbs onto his faded memories of the foreign language. Recently, propped up in bed with only cicadas and the slow arc of the sun for distraction, the language has become increasingly clear.

He drains the last bottle of soft drink from the minibar and douses his head in cold water again. Last night, he and Raúl went to a *peña* way out at the top of the Avenida Garcia Lorca, and after the flamenco, they drank with a guitarist friend of Raúl's and went back to Gutiérrez's place – an apartment somewhere near Casa Joaquín – but the *cubatas* had taken their toll and Staffe had fallen asleep. He was awakened rudely early by the sound of Raúl's snoring – kicking at his temples like a stableful of mules. At dawn, he made his way back to the Hotel Catedral, picked up a morning edition of *La Lente*.

He reads Gutiérrez's story one more time.

GANG EXECUTION IN THE PLASTIC
But Who Will Pay the Real Price?
Yesterday Almería saw another example of what happens when money and drugs come together.
A foreigner was discovered dead in the intensive farming green-

houses on the coast between Adra and Roquetas del Mar. Tourists on all-inclusive holidays played in the sea and relaxed by swimming pools drinking cuba libres as a man was viciously murdered. Police are certain the death is related to the importation of drugs from Morocco.

The dead man is a white northern European and police say that several witnesses saw a group of black men behaving suspiciously in the plastic shortly before the estimated time of the killing.

The price we ordinary people will pay for this terrible industry that is staining the city and province of Almería is that people will choose to go elsewhere for their holidays. It is imperative that we drive these greedy criminals back where they came from – to save our jobs and conserve the tradition of our unique Andalusian way of life.

Drug use amongst the young in Spain is already a problem and we must make it as difficult as we can for our youth to acquire these narcotics. As for the death of another trafficker or dealer – do we really care?

RAÚL GUTIÉRREZ

Staffe tosses the paper into his case and makes his way down to reception where he orders a two-litre bottle of water and asks them to find out what time the buses leave for the Alpujarras.

As he waits, he considers what Raúl might be up to. His story couldn't have been written any better by the Comisario of police himself – if he wanted a free-for-all on drug trafficking. And he wouldn't want to be a Moroccan, trapped down there in the plastic on twenty euros a day and taking the blame for all bad things that pass.

'There is a bus at twelve-thirty but you have to change at Ugijar. Would you like a taxi to the station, Señor Wagstaffe?'

'Yes.' The way he feels now, dehydrated and sweating, he thinks he wouldn't care if he never clapped eyes on Gutiérrez ever again. Then he recalls that the journalist knew about Santi Etxebatteria. The bile rises.

'Guilli!'

Staffe looks around, seeking out Manolo, wondering what would have brought his friend back to collect him. He scans the Plaza Catedral for his grey van, but sees nothing.

'Guilli!' The call is from a table outside the hotel. Gutiérrez is clean shaven and wearing a crisp, lemon shirt and pressed, sun-bleached jeans. His hair is slicked back and he tips Coca-Cola into a tumbler of amber-coloured spirit. He clinks the ice and says, 'Something for the ditch, before we drive to the mountains.'

'The mountains?' Staffe swigs from his bottle of water, plonks it on Raúl's table. Fat beads of sweat pop on his scalp.

'Like we said last night. It is years since I was in Almagen, when that English artist died. You know all about him, I suppose.'

'Hugo Barrington?' says Staffe.

'It'll be good to go back there.'

'I read your article.'

Gutiérrez twirls the ice in his glass and drinks it down, taking his time. He regards the finished drink. 'My car is just there.' He points at a red Alfa Spyder, the hood down.

Staffe contemplates having to wait in Ugijar for two hours for his connection. He watches as Gutiérrez swigs his drink and walks jauntily to the Alfa. Staffe joins him, says, 'So, you know Almagen.'

'I've got *primos* in Mecina. Up in the hills, one old goat gets a flea and they all scratch. Yes, I know Almagen all right.'

'Don't you have to follow up on your story?'

'The *comisario* will call me when they get their man.'

'You're in his pocket.'

'I'm in no one's pocket, Guilli.' He gets in, revs the car and raises his voice. 'A journalist works with what he's got. If they change the music, you dance a different dance.' The engine noise subsides and the sound of 'This Is The One' rushes forth. 'I love the Stone Roses. Such a shame their spirit was slain by a million paper cuts. The damned law! Now, will you please get in.'

Staffe climbs in and reaches for his seat belt, but Raúl taps him on the arm, says, 'No seat belts, not in my car – they're killers. A man needs to be able to get out of a tight situation.'

They roar off and by the time they are driving down Calle Real towards the port and passing Casa Joaquín, Raúl is joining in with 'I Am the Resurrection'.

*

Manolo sits on the steps outside Bar Fuente, drinking gin and Fanta orange. He is due to go up the mountain for another stint with his flock. The goats spend their summers high in the sierra, it being too hot in the village; Manolo works to a rota of two weeks up the mountain and one week back in the village. His father, Rubio, used to spend the whole summer up the mountain with the goats, until one year he didn't come down.

37

They say his brain fried. Now, he lives with the nuns and the mad in Granada. When villagers talk of Rubio, they lower their voices.

Raúl parks the Alfa, in the shade of plane trees in the *plazeta*, and slaps Manolo on the shoulder as he goes into the bar, calling him a goat fucker. Manolo looks into his *cubata*, sheepish. Staffe thinks that perhaps Manolo doesn't care for such fancy Dans.

Staffe orders mint tea and Gutiérrez calls him a ladyboy. Frog calls across to Gutiérrez, 'You're the ladyboy, you old dandy!'

Gutiérrez squints and says, 'Frog? Is that you? Frog!'

Frog laughs, like a frog, comes across to Raúl, hitting him on the arm with a rolled copy of *La Lente* and muttering indecipherable dialect. He says to Staffe, 'Just another dead foreigner – is that all they can come up with?' He throws down the paper and calls out, 'That's his story.' He grabs Raúl by the ear. 'What have we done to deserve a bastard journalist amongst us? Aren't there enough lies in this village?'

Raúl says, 'I have no pen.' He pulls out his pockets and says, 'See! I'm not armed. You're safe.'

'It doesn't matter, the shepherd can't read anyway. He talks goat,' says Frog.

Everybody laughs and Manolo looks ashamed, says, 'I'm going up the mountain, where there's beasts I can trust.'

'He loves his beasts!' scoffs Frog.

'There's nothing wrong with a goat,' says Raúl.

'If your wife is out of action, but that's no problem for him.'

Raúl orders up a round in the twirl of a finger. 'The goats, they're in my blood, too. My grandfather was the shepherd in Mecina. I'd go up the mountain with him in summer.'

Manolo grabs his hand, says, 'They're ladies' hands.'

'Ladyboys,' says Frog. 'You should have taken the flock.'

'And go mad?' says Raúl, looking at Manolo. He realises he has said the wrong thing. 'I'm sorry.'

'None of you have seen a day's work,' says Manolo. 'Doing the devil's work is all you can do – writing his lies for him.'

Gutiérrez takes out his wallet, slams it on the bar, shouts, 'How much have you got? I'll prove it. I know more about goats than you ever will. It's in my blood, I tell you.'

'Prove it, then,' says Frog. 'Go up the mountain with him.'

Staffe says, 'I'm going home. I need to sleep.' He puts a twenty euro down and Manolo picks it up, stuffs it down the neck of Staffe's shirt. As he leaves, Manolo follows him and in the privacy of the square, he whispers, 'Tell me, Guilli. When you went to the plastic, what exactly did you see?'

'I told you, he was in a hell of a state.'

'Is there something you're not telling me?' Manolo clicks his fingers and Suki runs to him, jumping, and Manolo scoops her up in one giant hand. He stands tall, his shoulders square, for once, and the blocks the sun from Staffe, who can't see his friend's face properly, being in the shade. In a deeper, stronger voice, Manolo says, 'You should tell me, you know. There is nothing to fear from me.'

Staffe says, 'I told you what I know. Ask your friend Raúl what went on. He knows more than he writes, wouldn't you say?'

*

39

Staffe drifts off with the window open and in the fringe of his sleep, he dreams the dry rattle of Manolo's *moto* is driving into his bedroom.

He jolts from sleep and walks unsteadily to his balcony, sees Manolo's Bultaco Sherpa – a classic, competition trail bike but now clearly straining at every joint of its vintage red frame as it plies along the narrow road towards the cemetery. Behind, Raúl follows in the Alfa, with Suki in the front seat, jumping up and down.

*

Yousef removes the cardamom pod from the flame and places it on the large stone with the rest of the pods. He takes the smaller stone, rubs it on the larger, the roasted pods between. He makes slow circles, as he does four times each day, between prayers. The aroma overcomes everything else. It transports him to Moulay Idriss, to his family. He has no letterbox and they have no telephone. He scrapes the cardamom essence from the stones with the blade of his knife, places it in the small pot of warm milk, adds honey and takes a mouthful which ought to scorch him but doesn't. He tips back his head and gargles. His throat makes a noise. The words in his mind bubble, float to air with hundreds of bursting pods of sound.

He was turned away from work this morning. Even though he got there at six-thirty, the sun still beneath the serrated horizon of the Cabo de Gata, the lorry was already loaded up. The foreman watched Yousef walk all the way down from the *carretera*, called him a lazy son of a whore; told him he shouldn't sleep so much.

Sleep has always come too easily for Yousef. He turns from the world readily. But for three days now, he has struggled to find dreams. In his corrugated house, three metres by three metres, he lies out flat and straight on a bed of reeds, distilling the sound of the sea's surf. The water washes over the beach. The water was lifted high by a hand.

Another hand had taken the man's broken head, tugged it viciously, by the hair. Yousef knew he should have turned his back. Crouching, peering beneath the plastic of the greenhouse, he watched in spite of himself.

The buried man was up to his neck in the earth, and even though he couldn't resist, they tied a strap to his head, tethering it to a stake so his mouth faced the sky. Then they shoved the bottle into his mouth and emptied it into him, refilling the bottle from the drum of NitroFos. They carried on filling him up with more water, even though the man seemed quite motionless. If they poured so much water like that, would it be like being trapped inside the sea? And then they stopped. Perhaps it was he who disturbed them, stopped them finishing whatever it was they had started.

But it was a day and a half before the police came in all their numbers, their wiry *comisario* in tow. And a day later, he saw that *guirri*. He made a re-creation for him and thinks now that he was a fool for that. In the end, all he did was make his re-creation with a hole in the earth and an open fist and a bottle of water.

He knows how to find the stranger. His sad friend in the grey van who bought seeds told him, and Yousef knows Almagen is two days' hard walk. He hears the gypsies talk of how lush it is up there, because of how the Moors taught the Spanish to make orchards from dust. The gypsies would walk from Adra to Al-magen and steal tomatoes and beans, beg for eggs. If they went near the goats, they would be shot.

When he was home in Moulay, he would look at the map, seeing El Andalus stashed like treasure at the bottom of Spain. He had believed everything he heard in Moulay about the wealth that was here; about it being a promised land, once theirs. It had been good to believe.

His mind tumbles, free, and he sleeps.

Six

'Like a London bus,' says Marie. Her hair is tied up in a scarf and she is wearing blue workmen's overalls. 'Don't see you for a week and then . . .'

'Very funny,' says Staffe. 'You look like one of those women from the town hall, sweeping the square.'

'What is it with that? Why can't the men lift a finger in this bloody village?'

'Where's Harry?'

'Playing with Rubén, down at his house.'

'He has a friend?'

'Of course he has a friend. He's got too many friends. Some days he's not home until after supper.'

Staffe doesn't know what to say. Surely, at his age, Harry shouldn't be left to such devices, practically feral down in the village whilst Marie and Paolo lounge around up here on the mountain. 'Where's Paolo?'

Marie nods up the sierra. High above them, Mulhacen's snowy peak juts up, like a smear of toothpaste against the azure and cloudless sky. 'He put some Thai basil down. Reckons the sun won't be too strong by the time they come through. The restaurants in Orgiva have said they will take it.'

Staffe looks through the telescope that Marie keeps on the veranda. It had been their father's. He watches Paolo toiling away with a roll-up in his mouth. He works with a hand tool in his right hand and a bucket of goat shit in his left. When he has done a row, he goes back and substitutes the bucket of shit for a bucket of water. He scoops the water with a cupped hand, his back bent double. His smile is unerring.

'You thought he'd fuck up,' says Marie. 'Didn't you? Well, I had my suspicions too, if I'm honest. All we have to worry about is the water.'

'There is plenty of water. You should get six hours every eight days, according to your deeds.'

'There's something wrong. The *balsa*'s low.'

'Do you want me to look at it?'

'Paolo says he'll sort it out. Don't tread on his toes.'

Staffe turns away from the telescope, reaches out for his sister and pulls her close. 'I'm pleased for you, I really am. Believe me, there's nothing would make me happier than to be wrong.'

'About Paolo?'

Staffe nods, but he is thinking also about Harry.

'Oh, Will.' She holds him close. 'You're going to stay, aren't you?' She squeezes him extra tight.

'What's wrong?'

'Nothing's wrong.'

'I know you, Marie, and something's wrong.' He holds her by the arms, leans away and weighs her up – deep in the eyes.

She shrugs. 'It's nothing. Just, when you were poorly, a few weeks ago – I thought someone was nosing around up here. That's all. Just me being stupid.'

'I can't stick around doing nothing for ever.'

'Someone tried to kill you, for God's sake! You've got all that rent from your properties. You don't need to go back to London and the damned Force.' She stands back from him, holding his hands and looks him up and down. 'I have a friend. You should meet her.'

'Marie!' He lets go of her hands. 'I'll find my own woman. All in good time.'

'You already have, but you let her slip. You're hopeless.'

He goes back to the telescope and scans the mountainside, tracking the edge of the high pine forest, down to the Rio Mecina's gorge, and he follows it to Manolo's stone-built *cortijo*. Out front, beneath his iron spit, he has built a fire but not set it. Hanging in the doorway of the *cortijo* is a goat, gutted; about to become *choto*.

There is no sign of Manolo, or Raúl, so he scans the mountain again, looking for Manolo's flock. 'Have you seen Manolo?'

'He passed by with some *burracho*.'

'A smartish kind of a fellow? Slicked hair and an expensive shirt?'

'In a girl's car. Stank of cologne.'

'That's Raúl. He's a reporter.'

'Oh shit!'

'What's wrong?'

'Nothing. Just, he seemed familiar.'

'Spanish men of a certain age all look the same, don't you think?' says Staffe, laughing, 'The waning libido; a last lunge in their loins.'

'You're right!'

'Where did they go?'

'Up towards Jackson's place. Manolo must have gone up there – there's nothing else between Jackson's and the other side of the pass, but it's a good two hours walk from here. You'd

45

best set off now, while there's still light – if that's what you want?'

'I came to see you, though.'

She goes to her brother, hugs him and says, 'I know you, Will. You're up to something. But don't forget – you're supposed to be taking it easy.'

'He knows about mum and dad,' whispers Staffe, into Marie's hair. He whispers it softly, half hoping she won't hear. She tenses up but says nothing, squeezes him a little tighter, and he says, 'And you're worried about someone sniffing around. What's going on, Marie?'

Her arms and shoulders are rigid, like mortise and tenon. She says, 'I've seen him before. I'm sure I have.'

*

It is dusk and he finishes the last of his water. At this altitude, it is already cold and only the peaks are getting the sun. He has no sweater and nothing to eat. His wounds are sore and he has left his medicine in the village, way down below in a crease of the mountains. The Med is a thin ribbon of blue, between the wide spread of plastic farming and the reddening sky. In this light, the plastic looks like salt flats, all the way from Adra to Almería. You can see Africa on a good day. Today is a good day and the clouds are low over the Rif.

The goat track takes him into a dark copse of chestnut trees. He can hear water, thinks he can also hear the scurry of animals. The locals tell terrible tales of the scorpions up here in the sierra and in the cool he suspects his fever might be coming back. He shouldn't have drunk so much with Raúl yesterday. Was it only

46

yesterday? The track swirls back on itself and he hears howling. This high, any dogs would be wild.

And then the track ends. He stands on a promontory, over-looking a waterfall. The thin river trickles twenty metres or so down into a pool. He squints, discerns – on the banks of the pool, perching on boulders – Raúl and Manolo with a man he has never seen before. It must be Jackson Roberts, the American: a wild old war vet; so they say. Staffe breathes deep, fills his chest with air and opens his mouth.

His body wants to call out, but he thinks twice. Raúl dangles his legs above the pool of wild water and Manolo is messing with his dog, Suki. The third man, fussing with a fire, calls out in an American accent, 'You should have brought your fucking goat, man.'

Staffe climbs down towards the pool, holding onto the trunks of small, clinging trees, obscured from the men below but still able to hear them.

Manolo says, 'You are the host. It is your party.'

The American drawls, 'We can eat dog. We did in Vietnam.'

'Korea's where they eat dog,' says Raúl, who turns to Manolo. 'How can we trust anything this shit tells us?'

'You're drunk,' says the American, who has a thick wad of hair, light brown but with streaks of gold. The jaw is strong. His bare-chested torso is lean, the pecs and abdomen well defined. All that gives away a life of decadence are his rosy, bloodshot eyes, the deep, treacly voice and the scrawn of his neck.

Jackson stands over Raúl, rests a foot on the journalist's shoulder, who grips the edge of the rock. 'Why would I lie? You're the journalist.'

47

'That article is shit, that's for sure,' says Manolo. He sounds morose and lies back, pulling Suki towards him, resting the animal on his chest. 'I'm hungry.'

'You should have brought that goat,' says Jackson.

'Why would I feed you, after all you have done?'

'I have *chorizo*,' says Roberts. 'And the beans are in. I'll make a *fabada*.'

'And I'll tend the bar,' says Raúl.

'I'm going home,' says Manolo.

'No!' says Raúl. 'It's dark. We're stuck for the night.'

They trundle off, muttering, and every now and again Raúl laughs. Roberts drawls into the night, but all the way, there's not a peep out of Manolo as they make their way to Jackson Roberts's *cortijo*, set low in a sheltered dell beneath a ridge which the locals call Silla Montar, the Saddle.

Staffe follows and sits above the *cortijo* until he can smell burning thyme. Plumes of smoke rise from the chimney. The sounds from inside are muffled and he looks down the mountain to the twinkling lights of Almagen and Mecina, like scattered stars. His wounds pinch, and he muses upon what secrets an all-seeing eye might witness from somewhere like here. It is completely dark now, and getting cold. Time to brace himself and go in.

Seven

Jackson Roberts nestles up to the fireplace on a low, wicker-seated rocking chair. Every now and again, he leans right forward and stirs the pot on the fire. The rest of the time, he rolls and smokes cigarettes – every other one a modest spliff.

Manolo is in the corner, his vast frame hunched in a dining chair and quiet now that he has finished berating Staffe for coming here – risking his health by walking all this way in his condition. Tonight, in Manolo's brooding silence, Staffe senses deep disquiet.

Raúl cannot keep still. He tops up everyone's drinks and mooches out onto the terrace and back again, waxing lyrical about how good the country life is; how this reminds him of when his father and uncles taught him to play cards and drink whisky in their *cortijo*s. Raúl catches Staffe's eye as he goes back out onto the terrace. 'You'll never see a night sky like the ones up here. Come.'

Staffe follows Raúl outside and together, they look up into the dark, star-speckled sky. Gradually, new stars begin to appear as their eyes adjust. The journalist says, lowering his voice, 'There's something I think you should know.'

The door opens and light spills onto the terrace from inside the *cortijo*, dimming their view of the universe, Jackson appears, lighting up a spliff. 'Where's your family *cortijo*, then, Raúl?'

'The other side of the Rio Mecina.'

Jackson offers the spliff around and Staffe declines, but Raúl tokes heartily and often, giving Staffe a resigned look, as if to say his disclosure can wait a while. They finish the spliff and they all go back inside, Staffe saying to Jackson, 'It's good of you to put me up for the night.'

'You're Marie's brother, right? How could I not?' says Jackson.

'I hadn't guessed it would be so desolate up here. They could declare war out there and you'd never know.'

'Not tonight,' says Jackson, laughing quietly to himself.

'This place could tell some stories, I bet.' Staffe looks at an oil canvas hung on the undressed stone wall that leads into one of the bedrooms. It is a landscape, hued of red and yellow and in the middle distance, two hunters walk away. A woman and another man remain behind. 'You sell them?'

'Never.' Jackson's sculpted features warp in the fire-glow flicker. The only other light is from a church candle on the bleached wooden table made from planks of chestnut wood, and a paraffin light hanging in the doorway to the terrace. 'It's for private consumption.'

'Tell him who the woman is,' says Raúl.

Staffe sees Manolo shoot Jackson a hateful look.

'It's from a long time ago,' says Jackson.

'When there were two artists in the village,' says Raúl.

'I'm no artist,' says Jackson.

Manolo says, 'He was never one of us.'

Staffe catches up with what they are talking about. 'Barrington?' he says.

'They fucked our women and told the world lies. They don't know one thing about us.' Manolo finishes his glass of whisky, turns on Jackson. 'You paint like him. Why so much red? Are you a commie?'

Raúl says, 'I don't care what you say, but Barrington could paint. He turned out some shit, but his best stuff . . . That's how history will judge him.'

Staffe returns to the painting, looks at it hard.

'That's private,' says Roberts, leaving his fire and offering round a plate of *empanadas*.

'It has humanity,' says Staffe. The painting appears to be a landscape, but almost lost in the folds of thick oil, the woman is clearly forlorn. Larger, in the foreground, a man carves a piece of wood in the shade of pines. Staffe pops an *empanada* in his mouth.

'Come and sit down.' Jackson looks back – long and hard at Manolo, his smile gone.

'This is amazing,' says Staffe, savouring the *empanada*.

'Made them myself.'

'Who is the man carving?' says Staffe, running his tongue along his teeth, putting his finger on the taste: star anise amongst the filling inside the flaky pastry.

'My father,' murmurs Manolo.

'It could be anyone,' says Jackson.

'What about your mother, Manolo? Still gone?' says Raúl. 'That was a fatal unsuitability.'

'You don't know how much he loved her. He couldn't be without her,' says Manolo.

'Fatal?' says Staffe.

'A figure of speech,' says Raúl. 'You never met Barrington?'

'I know he did his bit in the war,' says Staffe. 'Joined the

International Brigade when he was seventeen. That says something about the man.'

'It was a war and he was drawn to it,' says Manolo. 'It wasn't his war, though. And yes,' he looks daggers at Jackson Roberts, 'Mother is still gone.'

Staffe wants to ask if that is why Rubio went mad. Instead, he says, fearing for his friend's state of mind, 'People don't talk about the war. I thought it was taboo.'

'We buried it. Buried it deep,' says Raúl.

'I can tell you plenty,' says Manolo.

'Not tonight,' says Raúl, replenishing Manolo's glass, and whispering to Staffe, 'We have to talk, later – it's worse than I thought.'

'Worse?'

Jackson interrupts. Stirring the pot, he says, 'Fuck the stuff of life and the stuff of art.' He stands up. 'Now, let's stuff our faces.' He lifts the lid from the earthenware pot with his bare hands and a cloud of steam bellows from the hearth. 'Now bring your bowls.'

The *fabada* is thick and unctuous and pitted with chunks of *chorizo* the size of your thumb. The burnt spice of paprika oozes and the stew is blazing hot, all the way from the mouth to the belly. Each of his guests blows out with puffed cheeks and Jackson brings out a quart jug of the local wine – cloudy amber. 'I put a few chillies in.'

And the wine flows.

'I heard they had a way of killing in the war,' says Staffe. It is a vague memory, from an article he read once about the war as they fought it up in the Basque Country. 'They would bury a man in the earth – up to his neck and . . .' As he talks, he remembers the African in the blue and yellow *burnous,* with no tongue to tell his tale. He closes his eyes, can see the African pouring the water into his open palm.

'Go on,' says Raúl.

'They would fill him with water.'

'I thought we weren't talking about the war,' says Jackson.

Manolo leans back from the table. He leans further and further back, grips the table as if to prevent himself from falling. 'It was the fucking Communists who did that. The good guys did that. Ha!'

'Your father would be too young to have fought in the war,' says Staffe, to Manolo. 'Like mine. They're a lost generation, the men who never got to become heroes.'

'His war was with poverty. He went to Germany. That's where he found my mother. He fought for her.' Manolo drinks his wine down in one and it goes to his eyes.

Raúl says, 'I heard your brother is back. Does he see your mother?'

Manolo looks at Raúl quizzically, as if struggling to choose which reply to administer, but it seems that drink might have defeated him.

Jackson says, 'Let's get you to bed.' He comes across, puts an arm around Manolo and helps him to his feet.

Raúl nods to Staffe, indicating that they should go outside and they leave Jackson and Manolo to it, both looking to the stars as they stand on the terrace. Up here, cloudless and with no light for miles and miles, the universe seems bigger.

Staffe says, 'You said it was worse than you thought.'

'I don't know how much to tell you.' Raúl plants a heavy hand on Staffe's shoulder.

'Tell me everything.'

'Once you've been told, that's it. There's no going back.'

'Was it a war killing?'

Raúl shakes his head. 'He was . . .'

Inside the *cortijo*, something breaks. A plate or a bottle, and Manolo shouts out that Jackson is a cunt and that he is going to kill him.

'He was what?' says Staffe. 'Tell me who was killed down there.'

'No!' comes the cry from inside the *cortijo*. It is Jackson.

Raúl says, 'I was going to say, he was already dead. They didn't drown him.'

'No! Don't!' shouts Jackson.

'We should go in,' says Raúl. 'Manolo has a dreadful temper.'

'Tell me what happened down there in the greenhouse. Who was killed?'

'Later,' says Raúl rushing back into the *cortijo*, calling, 'Manolo! Stop!'

'Already dead?' says Staffe, following Raúl, seeing that Manolo has Jackson Roberts pushed up against the fireplace. The flames from the fire are catching his trousers and his eyes bulge.

'Let go of him!' shouts Raúl, grabbing Manolo, but he makes no impression. Manolo's shoulders aren't hunched; they are broad like before and he has both of his thick-fingered hands around Jackson's throat. Staffe tries to help Raúl pull Manolo off, but there is no chance. Jackson looks at him, pleadingly. Another twenty seconds and he will be dead, for sure. Staffe looks around the room, smelling the burning cloth of Jackson's trousers. Picking up the pot, he empties the remains of the *fabada* onto the floor and holds the pot high, advancing quickly and bringing it down, as viciously as he dares, onto his friend's head.

The sound of the pan on skull is hollow and it rings out, through the commotion. Manolo turns to look at Staffe, his hands still on Jackson's throat, and Staffe thinks if he hits him again any harder, he might crack Manolo's skull.

'It's all right,' says Manolo. 'I don't want him dead.' He relaxes his grip and Jackson gulps for air. Manolo's eyes hood down and he wavers, unsteady on his feet. 'Really. I don't want him dead. Far from it.'

Jackson bends double, coughing and cursing as Staffe and Raúl lead Manolo back to his chair, ease him down before his legs give way.

'Are you all right?' says Staffe.

Jackson nods, quite vociferously. 'It was nothing. Let's forget it. Come on, let's have a drink and then get to bed.'

Staffe clears the table and sweeps up the spilled *fabada*. By the time he is done, Manolo is asleep in his chair with a sad look on his downturned face, his arms hugging his big torso and Suki burrowed into the crook of his neck.

As he puts a blanket over his friend, Staffe catches Jackson taking down the landscape painting, placing it against the wall in the other room. 'I never liked the fucking thing,' he says.

Staffe notices Manolo's knife on the floor by the fireplace. He picks it up and runs his fingers all around the intricate carvings of the goat's head and horns. You'd think he would have had enough of goats.

The three of them sit up, drinking and talking about Barrington and all the while, Staffe waits for Jackson to leave, but instead he bunks down on the sofa. 'You take the bed in the other room.'

'No, it's your bed. I came uninvited.'

'I insist. As a guest, the least you can do is accept my hospitality. I won't take "no" for an answer.'

'Go on,' says Raúl, on the verge of sleep in his chair. 'We'll talk tomorrow. You can buy me lunch – in Fuente.'

And with that, Staffe retires. He sleeps deep; so deep that not even Raúl's snoring wakes him.

Eight

Staffe sits on the slate rim of the stone trough outside Jackson's *cortijo*. He dips his feet into the icy water and the shorn edge of the slate cuts into the backs of his thighs. The sun is just up and, five thousand feet high, a chill from the night still clings.

He thinks about last night and what Raúl had said to him about things being worse than he thought. He cups his balls with one hand, edges himself off the slate with the other, sliding into the trough and it catches all his breath. He gasps, can't help but whoop at the cold.

Lying in the trough, he soon becomes numb and for the first time in months, he cannot feel his wounds. He runs a thumb over his scar tissue and presses, can feel it a little, and he realises he has left his medication down at his house. Woozy, and almost in a trance, he sees the events of the past two days quite clearly, but he doesn't believe it – not as presented to him.

His fingers and toes are all gone to prune by the time he gets out. Staffe had hoped Raúl would rise early and join him outside, tell him what happened down in the greenhouse, which for some reason he is intent on keeping secret from Jackson, and maybe Manolo, too. But as he gathers his clothes, a chorus of deep snoring comes from the comatose *cortijo*, where Jackson sleeps alongside Raúl. Every now and then, Raúl snorts like a pig, just like he did the other night at his place in Almería. Staffe smiles to himself and makes his way down the mountain, wondering what more Raúl will have to say to him today when they meet for lunch in Bar Fuente. By the time he crosses the lateral track that runs to Mecina, he can see the old boys coming up the mountain, to tend their water. The *campo* is pitted with *cortijos*, like single bricks of Lego, and if you listen closely, even though they are still half a mile away, you can hear the old boys talking to each other, hundreds of yards apart.

In his first weeks in Almagen, before the wounds reopened and became infected, Staffe would come up here to spend a day with Edu. Edu runs the tiny Museo de Almagen, which is three small rooms above the *ayuntamiento* near Harry's school. It opens Tuesday afternoons, saint's day mornings for an hour after the *misa* and by appointment. When he's not overrun with museum duties, proud Edu tries to stay off the local alcofilth by busying himself at his *cortijo* just above the village. He lives alone and always has, they say, and Staffe can't quite work him out. He is from good stock, but is a loafer with a penchant for the Russian girls down on the coast. Above all, Edu is bitter.

'You should choose your company more wisely,' says Edu as Staffe approaches. His skin is tight and his eyes are bright. His nostrils are flared and his face has something of the baby about it even though he must be into his sixties. Life seems to have taken it easier on Edu than on most of the locals. He once confided to Staffe that his father did rather well under Franco. Rumours have it that his sister once had a thing for Barrington.

On the terrace, Edu pours coffee into shot glasses on an upturned plastic beer crate. 'I saw you coming down the mountain. There's only one person up that way.'

'I was with Gutiérrez. Do you know him?'

'I know plenty Gutiérrez.'

'Raúl. He's a journalist.'

'Aah.' Edu drinks his coffee down in one and turns away, fussing with his vine. It is trained over an iron frame to give shelter. 'I don't know what's wrong with these leaves. I need them bigger.'

'He's from Mecina, this Gutiérrez.'

'And fancies himself as a little emperor. But you don't get to be a little emperor without first being a big prick.'

'That's Edu's Law?' laughs Staffe.

'Edu's Law. I like that.'

'You must remember him, when he lived up here.'

'His mother was left stranded when her husband went to Germany. He went for work and money and got so much he never came back. Raúl was left with all the mouths to feed and he took them all down to Almería. This place was always too small for him if you ask me.' Edu goes back to his vine and curses. 'You know, it doesn't do to mix. People here should stay here. I'm sorry, Guilli, but . . . These shoots aren't good enough. The shade is ruined. Ruined to hell.'

'How would Gutiérrez know the American?'

'Tell me about your wounds. Are you recovered?'

'And how would the American know Barrington?'

'Anybody would think you are the Guardia,' laughs Edu. 'All your questions.'

'He's a good host.'

'I've known him thirty years and not so much as a glass of *terrano* from the cocksucker.'

'Thirty years!'

'What's that?' Edu raises his eyebrows, purses his lips.

'Jackson Roberts has been here thirty years?'

'Maybe more. Since Vietnam. But quiet, please. I can hear something.'

An engine is roaring, but Staffe can't see where. Edu clambers up the small *bancale* to the bean field which stretches away up to the Mecina track.

'Son of a whore!' shouts Edu.

Beyond the beans, a cloud of dust plumes up, curving away to the left, but the sound seems to be coming straight at the house. The engine roar gets louder and louder and the partridges, caged at the back of the *cortijo*, start flapping and squawking, then a blur of red whooshes through the sound of the engine and is gone, leaving an imprint of the sound of 'She Bangs the Drums'.

'Stone Roses,' says Staffe.

'What?'

The dust comes across onto the terrace and the engine noise fades, but when it is gone, the sound of music remains, like a tattoo.

'Gutiérrez,' says Staffe.

'What?'

'That was his music. His car. But where does that track lead?'

'He'll have to go down to the bridge. There's only one road across the Rio Mecina, but he knows that. He'll be going to his family's *cortijo*. They were shepherds. It's in the blood, you know. Up and down the mountain like cock-sucking goats.'

'Like Manolo?'

'That family!'

'You don't like Manolo?' Staffe looks away from the diminishing cloud of dust, the engine roar now distant in the folds of the sierra. 'Why is that, Edu?'

'People should know their station.'

'They say his father went crazy up in the mountains, living with goats and his brain frying in the sun.'

'Rubio? He went away and he came back with that woman. That's what sent him mad.'

'A fatal unsuitability,' says Staffe.

'Fatal?'

'A figure of speech.' Staffe drinks his coffee, and the two of them look across the sierra to the clouds thrown up by the car. 'You didn't get on with Rubio either?'

'A man should be able to control his heart.'

Edu looks up at the sun and dabs his forehead with a handkerchief. 'This summer never ends. We need rain for the land. Look at my *balsa*.' He points towards the circular, concrete water reserve which is three-quarters empty. 'I have to tend to my beans.'

'Rubio couldn't control his heart? What about his wife?'

Edu looks at Staffe the way a kind-hearted man with empty pockets would regard a beggar. 'You worry me, with all the questions. People here – they're not going to like it. Here, the past stays where it is.'

Staffe wonders if he should ask Edu about Marie's water, but he decides against it. Instead, he says, 'It looks as if you'll be getting your Academy.'

'No Academy of mine. They're all cunts – after money and not minding if they have to whore their history to someone else's culture.'

'But the Academy will honour the village's traditions. It will help secure its future. Tourists will come.'

'It'll be all about that bastard Barrington, and nothing about our way of life.'

'But it's going to happen, isn't it?'

'Not if we can help it. We're all right the way we are. Hey! If you want some real Spanish culture, you should come to my *matanza* – fuck the foreign painters. Wednesday, at nine sharp and bring some of your fancy whisky.'

*

Manolo puts his finger into her ear and Suki moans. She moves her head in a small figure of eight to get his finger just where she wants it and she gives off a long sigh of satisfaction. Then she licks Manolo and unplugs herself from him, jumps off the seat of his Bultaco and gambols up the hillside, but she soon runs out of steam. She's getting on now and he remembers how he and his father came by her. She filled the gap left by Astrid.

The gap Astrid left had grown with time. She had disappeared before and, to begin with, this time seemed no different. It was autumn; the time she liked to go to Morocco. If she wanted winter, she'd never have left Germany, she said. So Octobers were for Tangier and Chefchouen. But this time she didn't take Barrington because he was dying and Jackson remained, and her son, his brother, Agustín was already in Germany – reclaimed, it seems, by his and Manolo's grandparents. Manolo never went, nor Rubio. They had the goats.

He can see Africa now, like a strip of lean in the fat of the *tocino* ham. He should have insisted on going with his mother;

things might have been different. Astrid might be here now and his father not with the nuns in the madhouse. At the very least, he might understand more why she abandoned them.

He thinks, how strange that Agustín should have come back. But then, not strange at all. He had to come back some time, but all he could talk about was Astrid and where she might be. Indeed, he seemed preoccupied with the notion that their mother was dead, which meant that Manolo couldn't take him to see Rubio because, of all the things in his small world that Rubio can't bear, it's talk of Astrid.

Manolo knows that you can love someone too much. He knows that it is better to not be with someone than to love them too much, to make it impossible for them to live alongside you.

He looks across to his goats and knows they will be just fine. The winter was wet and there is plenty to go at, still, on the mountain. It's Suki he worries about. And himself. He fears it is in his blood. He thinks of Astrid, who fawned on him and Agustín, telling them constantly that she loved them, but who would leave at the drop of a beret. Agustín disappeared, too, until he came back – brought running by death. Their maternal grandfather was dying in a foreign land, and his brother had come running, looking for mummy. That's not how it should be.

Manolo looks up at his herd. Suki wants to be off, to tend them, but he doesn't want her up the mountain alone, not with the wild dogs, so he picks her up and holds her tight. In the distance, he thinks he can hear music. Or a siren. Perhaps he is going mad.

Harry follows Rubén and the other boys down into the lower *barrio*. During his special Spanish lessons, when the nun leant over him, supervising the changing of a word and smelling of ham fat, he saw his uncle Will walk past the school and through the Plaza de Iglesia. Now, free, he is intent upon demonstrating to his uncle that he is getting on just fine with the village boys. However, Gracia is standing by the alleyway that leads to his uncle's house.

Rubén shouts, 'Arri! Are you going to play dolls with your girlfriend?'

Harry's Spanish is good enough to get the gist, not quite good enough to make a riposte.

Gracia looks at him with her big, surprised eyes. She has got her hair down and it is sun-kissed by the long summer. Harry feels funny in his stomach when he sees Gracia, especially when she has changed out of her school uniform, wearing her floaty, primrose dress that her mother fashioned from offcuts. The other children poke fun at her for having home-made clothes. This dress comes to her knees and has thin straps that show her shoulders, brown as almond shells.

'Don't listen to them, Arri,' she calls. 'I was going for a walk, along the Ruta Barrington.'

'A walk! Maybe today he will kiss her,' calls Rubén, and the boys run down the hill to the water troughs, laughing.

Beyond the sound of the boys running away, Harry hears a siren from the top of the village – the Guardia or a fire engine, perhaps. There have been fires up in the sierra this summer and he knows from his teachers not to leave bottles when they go

64

into the *campo*. They magnify the sun and tinder the scorched grass.

He follows the boys down to the troughs, but Gracia runs up to him and tugs at the hem of his shirt. 'Show me your treasures, Arri.'

'I showed them last week.'

She giggles, says, 'I love the way you talk. Say it in English.'

He sits under the walnut tree. If he were to climb it, and were he light enough not to break its bough, he could make his way onto the balcony of his uncle's bedroom. He says, in English, 'Let's go along the *ruta*.'

Gracia smiles and sits next to him, puts her hand into his pocket and pulls out his leather pouch. It used to be a pencil case, but now it is a museum of the life he left behind.

She unzips the pouch and places it in the primrose canopy of her lap. One by one she removes: a fifty-pence piece; a picture of Harry and his best friend, Conor, taken as they plunged into the water on the log flume at Thorpe Park; the ticket from when his uncle took him to see Orient play Arsenal in the FA Cup; his Disneyland pass with its image of Mickey in front of the enchanted castle – that was the treat when his mum and Paolo told him he was going to have a sister. And finally, the item that Gracia likes best and which makes her big eyes go bigger still and her cherub mouth hang open in awe: the folded Polaroid image of his baby sister in shades of black and white within his mother's belly.

Gracia whispers, 'Miracle.'

Harry is troubled because he doesn't like the picture. He knows, for sure, that he should.

The boys shout up to Harry but he can't understand what

they say. Gracia looks up at him and says they should go. She seems sad and holds his hand, tugs him to come the opposite way to the boys, and says, 'When your sister comes, I will call her my *prima*. I'll take her for walks and when she is old enough, I will teach her Spanish and how to make *papas a lo pobre*.'

'We won't be here that long,' says Harry, certain he can't stand to be in Spain for much longer. But it would break his heart to not see Gracia ever again. He squeezes her hand.

'I love you, Arri.'

'Don't be stupid.'

*

Staffe watches Harry walk off down the Ruta Barrington. The route descends into the valley bottom, passing through almonds and olives, down to where the oranges are happy to thrive. It was here long before Barrington.

He is on his roof, sitting on the very edge in an old deck-chair, reading *Monsignor Quixote* with a stick of *chorizo* and a stump of the dry village bread. He washes it down with a swig of *sin alcohol* beer and looks across the rooftops to where Gracia's mother, Consuela, is laying out peppers on wire racks, to dry in the sun. She had been watching the two children, too, and she catches Staffe's eye.

Staffe waves, smiles and calls, '*Hola!*'

She raises a hand, but is tight-lipped.

Consuela brings up Gracia alone. Nobody talks about where Gracia came from or where the father went, but the other women of the village pay her only the most cursory pleasantries. When the fish man comes up in his van from Motril, she stands alone at the back until the queue has gone, and buys a euro's worth of *boquerones*. He puts in a couple of sardines, *gratis*, and she accepts them, ashamed at the charity. It doesn't help that she works for Salva in Bar Fuente. That's a man's world and Consuela has fine features and a flat stomach. They say Salva is so supremely endowed, that his wife could take no more. It is why she disappeared in the night and he is alone and had to take on Consuela for his kitchen. None of which aids Consuela's cause. Some say she is the one who should disappear.

Consuela turns away, towards a row of cars. Staffe registers the noise, too, and looks towards the cemetery, where he sees flashing blue lights: one, two and a third. Then a fourth. The Guardia's 4x4s race up the track. There can't be more than four police Land Rovers in the whole valley, and they are all whooshing up towards the lower *barrio*.

All across the rooftops, people hang off their balconies beholding the commotion. Consuela has a hand to her mouth, leaning right off her roof as Harry and Gracia come running up the track after the police cars.

*

The villagers pack along one side of the bridge, a rickety affair made from blue metal railings sunk into concrete ballasts. The lights from the Guardia 4X4s are still flashing and there is also a squad car from the Cuerpo. On the other side of the *barranco*, which the bridge spans, Manolo sits on his haunches, looking sad beside his red Bultaco.

Staffe clambers up the hillside and edges towards the ravine, looking down into the *barranco*. In the bottom, its nose plunged head first and its stylish rear end facing the sky, is a red Alfa Spyder. Staffe catches his breath, murmurs, 'Raúl.' He feels weak in the knees, sick in the pit of his stomach.

Round and round, stuck in a groove, the sound of 'I am the Resurrection' wheels away in the mountain air, but the Cuerpo officer reaches into the car and cuts the music dead. Then he cuts Raúl's seat-belt webbing, begins to pull him free.

On the Mecina side of the bridge, an ambulance parks up. Its back doors swing open. On the bridge, the fire brigade have set up a winch and they are lowering a metal-framed, canvas stretcher into the dry river bed. Staffe watches their every move as they lift out Raúl, the tattered lemon shreds of his shirt drenched with blood all down his back.

He knows that if he hadn't visited the murder scene in Almería, Raúl wouldn't be in the bottom of this *barranco* being manhandled by two *guardia*.

The *guardia* heave him onto the stretcher and attach the hook of the hoist to the cradle. The firemen on the bridge wind the winch and Gutiérrez rises slowly. Higher and higher, he sways in the air and the villagers gasp, mutter. As he reaches the bridge, an untarnished silence descends. There is no wind; no birdsong. The canvas stretcher is soaked in blood and from its middle, a drip of blood falls, and then another, like sap.

A policeman in a blue suit – as opposed to the green of the Guardia Civil, who oversee the law in the countryside – points from the bridge to where Staffe is sitting, beckons him. As Staffe makes his way slowly down the hillside, he sees that the officer must be Cuerpo Nacional – unusual in these parts. The officer is short and wiry with a long, *bandido* moustache.

'You are the *guirri*,' says the Cuerpo officer.

'I am English,' says Staffe.

'He was a friend of yours?'

'Not really.'

'I hear that you are police, in England.'

'This is a holiday.'

'Not convalescence?' The Cuerpo has a laurel insignia on his tunic and Staffe thinks that might make him a *comisario*. His holster is impossibly shiny and his moustache jet black, though the groomed slicks of hair beneath his peaked cap are grey. He smokes a Cohiba cigar with its familiar black and gold band. Its deep, sweet tar smells of success, hard won. He looks up at Staffe and over his shoulder as he says, 'We know this man. He came up from Almería and he was drunk. You were with him and as a policeman you should do better.'

'*Do* better? This is not my fault.'

The officer lowers his voice. 'He was drunk as a monkey and they're telling me this was a stupid accident.' The officer extends his hand to Staffe, shakes it with a limp action. 'I am Sanchez. Come on, we should get out of their way. Come onto the bridge with me.'

Staffe looks again at the insignia on Sanchez's uniform. '*Comisario.*' He follows Sanchez.

'Some crazy circle of life, up here in the mountains. I should know.'

'You're from up here?'

'You could say that. It seems the place never lets you go. There's always some kind of mess needs clearing up.' The officer smooths down his sleeves and nods to his driver, who starts the car.

Together, they look over the bridge. Way down below, Staffe sees a red rag. When he looks more closely, he sees it is a duster, patches of yellow making it look like the Spanish flag. A blood-soaked duster, he thinks. He looks away from the rag, but thinks the Comisario may have seen him.

Sanchez says, 'Good luck with becoming an uncle. Up here in the Alpujarras, it's one big family – but you're best off out of it.'

'How do you know about me?'

'We attend to strangers, Inspector Wagstaffe. And take my advice.' Sanchez looks down from the bridge, towards where the bloody rag flutters in a strawberry bush in the dry river bed. 'Forget what you think you might have seen. It's better that you leave,' and Sanchez ushers Staffe away, watches him all the way up the road, back to the village.

When Staffe gets to the last bend, where the bridge is about to disappear from sight in the tight curves that must have done for Raúl, he sees a red motorbike weave up the hillside. He waves, thinking it is Manolo, but it isn't him. Manolo is above the bridge, still, with Suki. The other red motorbike belongs to Jackson Roberts who rides it fast and sure, away from the ravine that took Raúl Gutiérrez.

*

For the first time in her life, Suki has a strap around her neck. Manolo ties it tight and puts a lead to it. He will make a gift of her to Gracia. That girl will surely know how to care properly. It's in her blood.

He is on the high side of the ravine and the rest of the village are all on the other side, with the police cars, ambulance and the fire engine. They begin to disperse. Consuela looks up at him and he thinks she smiles, but she looks quickly away and he feels lost. He wants to touch her and he is sure he never will. The sadness feels like a memory he won't ever be able to lose.

When she is all the way gone from his sight, not looking back even once, Manolo follows. He ties Suki to the drainpipe that runs down from the roof he sometimes sees her on, hanging her washing, drying her peppers, looking across the valley towards the sea. Sometimes, he hears her sing. It saddens him so, the beauty of everything she is.

He walks quickly away, out of the village along the *acequia* and all the way across the sierra to the Silla Montar. He is going over the top and down into Granada, into the past to make things right before any more harm is visited upon him, the remnants of his family, and the people he loves.

Above Edu's *cortijo,* he pauses, watches Edu coming across the *campo* from the direction of Mecina. In all the years he has patrolled these mountains, tending his father's flock, Manolo has never seen Edu on his land. Stretched out on his terrace, bottles littered at his feet – yes, but never striding his land the way he is now. He drinks water from his *bota* and waits for Edu to come close enough to speak, which he does, and Manolo turns his back, continues on his way. Once Edu stops calling him, Manolo's thoughts turn to his English friend; what he might be made of. Manolo can't help thinking he might come up short.

PART TWO

Nine

DS Pulford isn't sure where he is. These last few months he has been doubling his shifts: official, and not. He rubs his eyes, thinks for a moment he is upside down, but he is on the sofa. He is still wearing his clothes and the sun is just up. It is twenty to five. Two nights running, he hasn't made it to the bedroom. Sometimes, he doesn't know if he's taking work home, or the other way round.

Immigrant labour gangs have reared up again in Hackney and knife crime looks as if it will never go away. The other day, they stabbed a seventeen-year-old temp on Fenchurch Street. It was her second day at work.

He thinks he has a plan; can persuade Brandon to give up the gun that Jadus Golding used on Staffe, and possibly – if a deal with the CPS can be achieved – obtain a statement, but he has to be careful. A decent defence lawyer could leave them hung to dry, and Jadus could walk – for good.

Brandon says he knows where the gun is, says he was upstairs in Cutz when it happened. But he is still insisting that his warrant for the hit and run is withdrawn before he gives anything up. If Pulford was to bring him in now that would be game over, because B-Lat's barrister says they have enough evidence that Pulford has breached procedure to ensure he never works again.

So last night, after he was done at Leadengate and after he

had been to see the poor temp down at City morgue, Pulford went and stood in the Limekiln, looking up at Jasmine's flat. She screamed at him, and some neighbours had come out and told him he was a bastard, and shouldn't he be out catching rapists. But he stood there, for maybe half an hour, until he could be sure she had called Jadus.

His phone is ringing. Somewhere. That's what must have awakened him. Dawn is pale and he rubs his eyes, knows he won't get back to sleep, so he rifles the pockets of his jacket and pulls out his phone and answers. In all these months, it is the first time he has heard the voice. 'Fucking back off,' says Jadus.

'Come out, like a man, and I won't need to keep an eye on your woman.'

'I won't tell you again.'

'Is that a threat?' says Pulford.

The line is silent. It hisses, as if expressing what Jadus could say – that he has shot a copper before and if he's in for a penny he may as well go down for tuppence. Jadus doesn't say anything.

'I saw a man going in there, Jadus. I suppose she's got to find the rent, now you're not working.'

'I'll fucking . . .'

'Yes?'

The line hisses again.

'We should meet, Jadus.'

'Maybe we will. But you won't see me coming.'

And the line is dead.

*

76

'How did you know Raúl?' asks Pepa. She is late twenties but has a hoarse voice, drags on a cigarette between mouthfuls of coffee. Like many of the people at Raúl's funeral, she works for *La Lente*.

'A chance encounter. He showed me Almería, took me to a *peña* on the Avenida Lorca.' Staffe shades his eyes from the setting sun. They are in El Marisco, barely half a mile from where they buried the victim in Raúl's last ever story.

'He liked his flamenco, that's for sure,' says Pepa.

'And his Stone Roses.'

'Aah. I got him into them, but he preferred drink and women. Did he show you those, too?'

Staffe cannot see her eyes behind the over-sized Prada shades. He says, 'I heard they didn't have a post-mortem.'

Pepa raises her glasses, gives Staffe a quizzical stare. 'The coroner's verdict was clear.'

Staffe wonders what else Raúl was going to tell him about the killing amongst the plastic. He looks across at a defaced sign for Golfo Tropical, says, 'It seems like some people aren't too keen on recreation round here.'

'They're attached to their water. It's kind of important. They don't need it wasted on golf courses.' Pepa finishes her Cacique rum. 'There are a couple of things of mine up at his place. I need to go.'

'I could give you a hand,' says Staffe.

She lowers her sunglasses. 'I bet you could. But first, tell me what you want.'

'I don't ...'

'Then I will go alone.'

The maître d' hovers. Staffe thinks he knows him, or maybe

vice versa. 'There was a murder Raúl was covering.' Both Staffe and Pepa instinctively look towards the plastic, the sea beyond. 'He knew a friend of mine.'

'Is that how you met Raúl?'

'Not exactly.'

'Do you believe in the small world?'

Staffe shakes his head. 'And what is worse, he knew a man I would like to see dead.'

'Ahaa. In our worlds, we have to be suspicious of such coincidences.' Pepa takes off her glasses and lays them on the table. She says, 'Can you promise me, on whatever is holy in your life, that if there is a story in what you are snooping for, you come to me?'

'I'm not snooping.'

'Promise?'

He nods, watches Pepa pull a bunch of keys from her pocket. As she spins them on her finger, he thinks she is probably trouble. Nonetheless, he goes with her.

*

Pepa lies on Raúl's bed, stares at his ceiling. 'I'd like a few minutes,' she says.

Staffe says, 'I'll check out the view.' He climbs the steep, stone steps onto the roof and from the terrace he can just make out the canopy above the etched window of Casa Joaquín – where he and Raúl shared *manzanilla* and the red shrimp of Almería just the other evening. He can see the port; the other way, across the rooftops and beyond the Cathedral, stands the Alcazar.

After a while, Staffe thinks he can hear crying from below, but when Pepa eventually emerges onto the roof, she is dry-eyed and carrying a holdall, emblazoned with 'Feria de Almería 2011'. 'I've got what I came for.'

They go down into the apartment and Staffe notices a large, carved door they haven't been through. He tries the handle but it is locked. 'What's this?' he says.

'He wasn't born here. It was a start from nothing. Did you know that?'

'His father went to Germany.'

'He loved it so much here: his bulls and his *peñas*. And he could sail. God! He could sail, but all that's ash now. Just ash.' She reaches up to the lintel above the door and pulls down a key. 'You can go in.'

The door is made from chestnut, intricately carved. It is heavier than any of the other doors, as if to an entire house. Staffe pushes it open and listens to it creak. There are large, leaded windows on either side of the room. One window has a desk beneath it, the other a sofa and as Staffe approaches the desk, he can see that he is above the alleyway that leads down to Joaquín's. Now, he can work out where he is. There is a bridge that spans the alley, from one building to the next. This is the bridge. He leans over the desk, presses his nose to the window and sees people on their *paseo*, linking arms, eating ice-cream cornets.

There is nothing on the desk, save the last few copies of *La Lente*, an ashtray brimming with cigar stubs and a notebook. Staffe flicks through the notebook and sees nothing to catch the eye, save the words: '*Etxebatteria. Cabeza. Toro.*' The name of his parents' killer. Head. Bull.

Staffe sits at the desk and opens and closes the drawers. Most are empty. On one wall is a large tapestry and a bull's head, grandly mounted. On the other wall, the door is surrounded mainly by photographs of matadors, some signed 'To Raúl', with scrawled quips and fond messages. There is a photograph of a young Raúl with an old Manolito – Almería's most famous killer of bulls. There is also a watercolour of an Alpujarran village, with a *tinao* in the foreground, and beneath a torn poster from the *corrida* of the 1989 *feria* is a familiar swirl of colours. It is a small painting, in the artist's early style, depicting the high sierra with pine trees and a snow-capped mountain. In the mid-distance is the Silla Montar, above Almagen. It is an original: signed Barrington.

Pepa appears by his side, smelling of soap; a hint of perfume.

Staffe asks, 'Did he ever talk to you about the mountains, or his village?'

'You're fond of your questions. I went out with a policeman once. It was a curse.'

'Charming. Raúl claimed to dislike Barrington, but he has one of his paintings.'

'It's a painting of his part of the world, and not exactly a bad investment. Besides,' Pepa turns to look at the painting, 'it's hardly one of his finest pieces.'

'Could you could take me to his office?'

'All that is left of him is his work – his finished work.'

'What about his sources?'

'He would have absolutely no records of his sources. Raúl was meticulous, but anything he needed, he kept in his head.' She prods her temple with her forefinger. 'If you want to know

Raúl, you have to read his work.' She laughs and finishes her coffee. 'It's exactly what he would want.'

'And where can I find his work? Buried in a vault somewhere, rotting?'

'We were once a third world country, but not any more. The owners of the paper commissioned an electronic archive two years ago. All editorial, news and feature articles are available online, provided you have the authority.'

'How far back does it go?' Staffe asks.

But she is gone, holding a tissue to her nose.

*

The man grips the African firmly by the forearm. The African's blue and yellow *burnous* now has smears of blood on one of the arms and at the hip. 'Is this him?'

From the window of Café Tanger, they watch the Englishman and the woman from *La Lente* walk away.

'Well!' says the man. 'Is it him?'

The African bows his head, nods.

'And what did you tell him?'

The African shakes his head.

'You're coming with me. We're not done yet.'

Behind the counter, two Moroccans stand, passive. They want to intervene, but know better. He is not to be messed with, they know. In this land, there are battles you cannot win.

*

The plastic greenhouses are golden; translucent in the dusk sun. Staffe asks the taxi driver to stop by the NitroFos drum.

'Here?' says Pepa. She is wearing her dark suit from the funeral, and Prada shades. Staffe strides ahead, wending left and then right and soon they are lost amongst the plastic. He pauses where the African in the *burnous* had been and Pepa catches up, her heels snagging in the dirt. 'Was it here?'

'There was a man. A Moroccan, as black as the peak of a *cuerpo*'s cap. I spoke to him.'

'And what did he say?'

'Nothing. But he showed me water, being poured into a man, I think.'

In a clearing, between two sorry-looking plastic sheds, two Moroccans sit on their haunches outside a hut made with corrugated roof pieces and pallets. One of them is in a Chicago Bulls vest and the other is bare-chested and wearing towelling jogging bottoms. They look stoned and stare at the ground as Staffe approaches. He says, 'There is a man who wears a blue and yellow *burnous*. Where is he?'

The men seem worried and shake their heads without looking up.

'I can help him.'

They shake their heads again.

Pepa goes into her handbag and pulls out a small block of resin – maybe a spliff or two shy of an eighth. She holds it out to them, says, 'He's right. We can help him.'

The men look at each other and one of them says, 'You police? You can't trap us.'

Pepa pulls out her press card, shows it to them. 'We're not police. Just tell us and we are gone. You'll never see us again.'

'You got anything more?' says the one in the Bulls vest. He casts a lazy smile towards Pepa and the sun catches a ruby stud in his left ear.

Pepa puts the resin away, says, 'You missed out.'

'No.' He holds out his hand. 'You mean Yousef. Now give it to me.'

Pepa hands him the resin.

The man with the Bulls vest and the ruby stud inspects it and stands up, walks away and when he is twenty metres away, he pulls out a knife. It is a small, old penknife, but he looks as if he could stick you with it. He says, 'They beat him. Then they took him away.'

'Who took him?'

'Who do you think?'

'The police?'

'Not police. But something close. You can tell when people are beyond the law.'

Ten

Staffe hangs up the phone. Because of what happened to his parents, he never completed his degree, but he kept in touch with a couple of his friends from Merton College. A few years ago, he bumped into David Grice, a short-lived best friend. They went for a pint and Grice had told him there was a Gaudy coming up and that he was on the committee and could get Will on the list, if he would come.

At the Gaudy, Staffe had talked to Jasper Newton who knew all about his parents. Jasper's specialism is Spain and in particular its Civil War. The following week, he had called Jasper to talk more about ETA, Santi Etxebatteria, and their real levels of activity.

This morning, five years on, he called Jasper again – to enquire about methods and rituals of torture.

Jasper described several types of torture, leading to execution, and Staffe's stomach slowly turned, and turned, until the professor's supply of the horrific was exhausted.

'Did you ever hear of anybody being buried and made to drink?'

'Aah. The Caligula,' Newton had said. 'Caligula liked to seal off the route for a man's piss. He'd use twine and then pour water into his victims until the bladder bloated and bloated and finally burst. Well, the Spanish weren't as cruel as all that, but what they would do, to extract information, was bury a man, usually kneeling, up to his neck in the earth, and then pour water into him. It would be fast and furious and the man would feel like he was drowning.'

'It sounds like waterboarding.'

'This was the real thing. They would put a peg in the earth and use their belts to hold the poor man's head back so his face pointed to the sky. It is just one of many . . .' He had paused; said nothing more.

*

Staffe is shown through the small *comedor* of the Quinta Toro. There are two besuited fifty-year-old men at the bar, swigging brandy as if it is nothing to be ashamed of at eleven in the morning.

The room is adorned head to toe with bullfighting posters and photographs, including one of Angel, the bar's owner, shaking hands with King Juan Carlos. Otherwise, the place is empty.

Jesús, the young officer who was at the plastic greenhouse, is in his father's tiny office which has crates of beer and boxes of broad beans and sacks of potatoes stacked high. He stubs out a cigarette and immediately lights another, says, 'You come asking about him and three days later, he is in the ground.'

Staffe sits on a beer barrel on the opposite side of the room to Jesús. 'I don't believe in chance. There is a reason why people do things; a reason for everything that happens. That's all that we do, as police. We find out why.'

'He was drunk.'

'The dead man in the plastic was tortured, wasn't he?'

'Tortured?' Jesús's eyes are wide. He stubs out his cigarette on the floor.

'I'll bet there was a peg in the ground. Tell me, Jesús – am I right? And were there marks on his forehead?'

'I was standing guard, outside. That's all.'

'Did you cut the rope that held him – or was it a belt? And did you have to dig him out of there? Did you lay him out and make it look as if he had just taken a little too much heroin?'

Jesús leans forward and sighs heavily. 'What's it to you?'

'Was he dead before they put him in the ground?'

According to Manolo, Jesús got his job in the Guardia because of who his father is, because of this place. Knowing where his *papas a lo pobre* are sautéed, the young man isn't talking. He says it by leaving.

*

From her desk, Pepa can see the castellated towers of the Alcazar. She thinks about the history, wonders if she did the best thing coming to the city, when her family wanted her to stay in Gabo. She looks down at her notes on the latest batch of demolition orders. Her instructions from the chief of the newspaper are to shame the outgoing mayor. She is to report how preposterous it is that these demolitions, urbanisations bought off-plan and principally by the English, are being pushed through.

Her door swings open. Her chief chews violently on his nicotine gum, holds his head high, pince-nez balanced on the bridge of his nose. 'I saw you at the funeral, Pepa. And I saw you leave. Where did you go with your new friend?'

'I think he likes me. That's all.' She says this knowing he doesn't; that, or he is a cold fish.

'You know Raúl was a fine man.' The Chief glazes over, looks wistfully at the Alcazar. 'He could be a fine man, when he allowed it. And he was a friend.' He pulls up a chair. 'His reputation is his legacy. It's all he leaves behind and we must protect him now. Now it's too late. There is no story here. Do you understand?'

Pepa has to look away, such is the intensity of the way he looks at her.

'The *feria* is coming and there's no space for new copy. We have to report the *casetas* and the *corrida*. You know how it is.'

'You mean we shut up.'

'Raúl's demise leaves a vacancy. It will be advertised, of course. But I expect you to apply and I expect your application to be strong. We mourn, we move on. New life shoots up from beneath. That's nature.'

*

Staffe pulls up by the bridge on the Mecina road in his hire car – a Cinquecento. Squeezing himself in at the Atesa depot, he had chuckled to himself, wondering if, in any estimation, he could be a Quijote. He doesn't know what he is tilting at, for sure. As soon as he left the coastal plain, the Fiat began to struggle on the mountain passes. This car, quite appropriately, is more donkey than horse-powered.

He eases himself out of the tiny vehicle and two workmen, resting in the shade of an olive tree, interrupt their lunch of ham and beer to laugh at him. The workmen have been tasked with repairing the bridge; the police tape has already been taken down, bundled up beneath the idling cement mixer.

The bridge railings comprise a five-centimetre metal tubing frame, painted blue and stuck into a knee-high concrete base. Staffe approaches the bridge and is confused. The men appear to be working at its wrong end – the eastern, Mecina end. Raúl had breached the bridge at its western end – that is to say, on the Almagen side.

Staffe peers down into the ravine, looks for the blood-soaked rag, colours of the Spanish flag, but he can't see it. It was directly below the bridge, not twenty yards from the crashed car – but now it is gone.

One of the men stands up and strolls up to Staffe, holding his *bocadillo* of ham like a club. 'You can't stand there.'

'Is this a new accident?' Staffe points at their handiwork.

The man shrugs. 'You can't stand there.'

Staffe thinks it odd that the men are repairing damage which presents no threat to the motorist, while at the other end of the bridge is a gaping hole that any car could easily go sailing through, the bridge being on a tight, downhill bend. 'The accident was at the other end, right?' He peers over the bridge into the *barranco*. The dry bed of the Rio Mecina is sixty feet below and Raúl's Alfa Spyder is still down there, its red boot pointing towards Almagen.

'You can't stand there!'

Raúl could only have gone into the *barranco* on his way out of the village, but the damage at the other end of the bridge suggests that perhaps another vehicle had come at him. 'Was there a car coming the other way? Is that what you are repairing?'

The workman sighs.

Staffe peers back down into the *barranco*, focusing on the Alfa's bonnet – caved in on its left-hand, driver's side, from the impact with the bridge's rails. The front of the bonnet is partially crushed from the slide down the hillside into the river bed. But Staffe's curiosity is touched by something he sees on the car's right-hand wing.

He bids the workman farewell and as he goes along the bridge, he runs his hand along the blue-painted rail, shiny and smooth, but then rough, where the paint is taken away. Thin streaks of red run along the rail. He pauses, watches the workman return to his lunch. For three metres before the breach that the men are working on, the paint is scratched from the bridge's two rails.

Just before he gets to where his Cinquecento is parked, Staffe darts down the side of the bridge and clambers down the *barranco*. The workmen shout at him, but he doubts they will bother to follow. The brambles scratch his arms as he grabs them to stop himself from tumbling and he has to throw himself onto his back to avoid toppling over.

The sun beats down ferociously on the valley bottom and he is drenched in sweat, crouching by Raúl's Alfa. He peruses one side of the car and his suspicion is confirmed. On the car's right-hand wing, two thin strips of blue run like tramlines, where the Alfa had surely crashed into the railings – on the side the men were repairing. The wrong side.

The workmen lean over, shouting down at him. He looks up and the *barranco* now seems steeper. The bridge is a long way off.

Tilting at bloody something, he thinks, ignoring the workmens' calls and looking in the dry river bed for the blood-soaked rag, finding nothing of the sort – just the rogue bush of wild strawberries, fruit withered and dry, but with a cluster of leaves, petalled red with a smear of what could be blood, fully twenty metres from Raúl's dead car.

*

When Staffe parks up in the *plazeta*, his neighbour, Carmen, beckons him from the alley that leads to his house.

Carmen could be anywhere between forty-five and seventy. She smokes the local black tobacco as she tells him that his landlord has been to the house. He came with another man and they had entered the house despite her protestations. When she had stood in their way, the other man had laid hands on her and they had locked the door behind them so she couldn't even oversee what they were up to.

'Here,' she says, touching her shoulder as if it were a wound. 'Here, he touched me.' They said they had come to check that the water and the gas were working. 'But that man had never seen a spanner in his life. A plumber? Mother of God!'

Staffe opens the door to his house and can immediately tell someone has been in because they double-locked the door when they left – something he never does. He quickly goes up to the small studio that leads out onto the roof. As he goes through his papers, Carmen huffs and puffs behind him, the sweet black tobacco preceding her.

He checks what few documents he has, sees nothing is missing. His camera is still there, his laptop, too. But when he stands back and reappraises the position of everything, something is wrong. He sits in the corner of the studio, in the old rocking chair with the padded, hide arms. From here, he can see all of Gador. If you sit there for an hour, in the morning or evening, the big mountain constantly changes colour. It's where he sits with his laptop and when he is done, he places it on the sideboard, but when he reaches for it now – even at full stretch, it is beyond.

Someone has moved it.

He fires it up and tries to log in. As he does – about to type in the last digit of his password – he is alerted to a message. He has one remaining attempt to log in.

Carmen bends double at the top of the steep stairs, hands on knees, getting her breath and still pulling on the cigarette that hasn't left her mouth. 'Is there anything wrong?' she pants.

'No, Carmen. I remember now. I did call the landlord about the hot water for my shower. It was a couple of weeks ago, but at least he has come now.'

She looks at him as if she knows his game, goes out onto the roof terrace, and tells him he shouldn't have lavender pots up here. He should grow a vine, for shade. If he did, she could water it for him and train it. She laughs, says he will never learn how to live here properly.

Carmen pulls the dead lavender from its pot and hurls it over the walnut tree and into the *campo*. As she does it, Carmen catches the eye of Consuela, hanging her washing on the roof opposite. Carmen tuts and sits down heavily, eyes up an unopened bottle of Anís del Mono that Manolo brought once. Staffe asks if she would like a glass and she shrugs, lets him pour, tells him she can get him a cutting from a vine.

'Why don't you like Consuela, Carmen?' he says in a low voice.

'Nobody knows who the wretched child's father is. You need to choose your friends more wisely. That Manolo is no better.'

Carmen watches him plug in the dongle to his laptop and lights up another of her black cigarettes.

He taps away at the keyboard then pauses, wondering whether to 'send', going outside while he decides. He has a glass of Anís del Mono with Carmen and accepts a drag on her cigarette. It takes him back to a previous time and he returns to the computer, presses the return key and his request pings across the sky to Jasper Newton: that he might arrange an audience with his good friend and one-time comrade, Professor Peralta in the School of Military History at the University of Granada.

Staffe recharges Carmen's glass and hears a dog barking across the roofs. When he looks, he is sure he sees the tail end of Suki, tucked under Gracia's arm as she disappears through the hatch of their roof. Manolo doesn't go anywhere without his Suki.

*

Salva nods politely to Staffe as he goes into Bar Fuente. He is putting up more posters for the new Academia. Now, they propose it will be called the Academia Barrington. It will bring tourists flocking.

As Staffe works his way around the bar, the tinny clatter of conversation that normally rings off the tiles, dims quickly to an awkward silence.

When Salva brings his mint tea, Staffe asks, 'No Manolo today?'

Salva looks at him suspiciously. 'He was up the mountain with that journalist friend of yours.'

'I haven't seen him since then. He wasn't at the funeral.'

'Why would he be?' says Frog, talking around his wagging *duro* cigarette. 'He didn't really know that cunt from Almería. None of us did, you understand.'

'The Junta decide any day now,' says Salva, tapping the poster. 'It could be the making of us.'

'Our very own Academia Cultural,' says Frog – as if this is café society. 'We don't want any boats capsizing. It was you that brought that journalist here. Remember? You and your friend Manolo. That man's thick in the head.'

'He's not!'

'He's a shepherd – that's all he is, so why would he hang out with some fancy journalist from Almería? The man's off his rocker. You saw him go for me the other day. The whole fucking family is howling at the moon.'

'You're the one who's thick in the head,' says Staffe.

'It's time you fucked off back where you came from.'

Staffe stirs his tea, waiting for it to cool, and the old goats at the bar mooch off, one by one. Usually, a departure is a trigger for buffoonery and chidings as to who invited who for a drink, but today, each bill is settled singly and quietly.

When they are alone, Salva comes across to Staffe, says, in the quietest of confidences, 'You didn't hear this from me . . .'

Staffe nods.

'Manolo called round. He's gone to see his father, in a *hospedería* in Granada.'

'Which one?'

'He didn't want you to worry.'

93

'Please tell me, Salva. He's left Suki here.'

Salva looks over each shoulder again and passes his wedding finger across his pursed lips. 'Our Lady of Mercy, in the Albaicín.'

Staffe drinks his tea, feels the potion settle his stomach. He says, 'Not everybody wants this Cultural Academy. Is that right?'

'If they know what's good for the village, they'll want it.'

'I was talking to Edu before. He says it's a bad thing.'

'Well, Edu has his own crops to harvest.'

Salva goes into the kitchen and Staffe calls Professor Peralta at the School of Military History to confirm their meeting. He feels the tug of Granada, remembers what Jasper Newton had said of his *compadre*. 'Old Peralta, he likes to lift the carpet, blow all the dirt out where it can be seen.'

Eleven

Marie is cooking peppers on a barbecue outside El Nido beneath a bamboo canopy. She has put on a few kilos, over and above the baby, and her eyes are bright. Staffe thinks she suits the colour of her skin and her hair is shiny, brushed all the way through and longer now. She looks reborn.

Harry sits at the head of the table, in Paolo's absence, poking away at his hand-held virtuality. His brow is thick and his mouth set rigid.

'Put that thing down, Harry,' says Marie. She fills Staffe's glass with half wine, half water. 'Those blasted games. That machine makes him so uptight.'

Staffe whispers, 'He's doing all right, in the real world.'

'Shut up, you two!' Harry slams down his device and stares at his uncle.

'Come here and apologise.' Marie pats her lap and beckons her petulant son but Harry stamps from the table. As he goes, he shouts, 'Why can't we live in a proper house!'

'Oh my,' says Marie. 'I think he's worried about the new one.' She taps her swollen tummy and smiles at her brother. 'I don't know why – we've involved him all along. He knows what's going on.'

Staffe thinks, Jesús, no wonder he's playing up – telling him what's going on in *there*.

95

'What did you mean about him doing all right in the real world?'

Staffe ponders whether to tell her about Gracia, and how the boys tease Harry and shut him out. 'Nothing, just he's got friends in the village.' He breaks off a chunk of bread, dips it in the thick *salmorejo* that Marie has made from tomatoes and garlic, olive oil and stale bread.

'Go on.'

'What do you mean?'

'I know you, Will. There's something else you want to say.'

'Did you ever think about getting a house in the village – for winter? It would be closer to Harry's friends. And when the baby comes, it might suit to have proper facilities.'

'And everything we left behind in England. We could get Sky TV, too!'

'That's not what I said.'

'We came to be in the mountains; close to nature.'

'And while you're in the mountains, Paolo is in Orgiva – right?'

'He's gone to get seeds. They're cheap down there. And Jackson gave him a lift. It saves on petrol.'

Staffe bites his tongue. 'I'm sorry. I think you're doing great.' He leans across, holds her hand.

'I'm glad you're here. It's good for Harry. He adores you. I don't know what was wrong with him earlier.' Staffe returns to his *salmorejo* and Marie goes back to the fire, turns her peppers. 'So, you're off to Granada,' she calls. 'Can you bring me some saffron from the market. And hey! You drive carefully. Did you hear about that nonsense the other day? A man killed himself on the Mecina road. That damned bridge.'

'Killed himself?'

'He was blind drunk, apparently.'

'It was that fellow who came up with Manolo the other day.'

'My God, no!'

'You said you'd seen him up here. What exactly happened when he came before?'

'He was with Manolo, messing about in the woods, I think. We were in the meadow, bringing in the tobacco.' She winks at her brother, miming the dragging upon a joint.

He looks past her, to the woods.

*

Orgiva is half way to Granada on the Guadalfeo river. It is a beautiful town with a grand church and a seven-eye bridge, nestling in a delta. Less than a century ago, it was a barbed front line between Franco and the Communists. Peace came, and with it, hippies from northern Europe. They sought what they couldn't get at home and turned it into a shitty corner of Amsterdam.

The Dragon Bar is down a side street off the *rambla* where the market is held. You can find it with your eyes shut by following the sound of Bob Marley and the smell of weed. But Staffe has his eyes open, clocks Jackson and Paolo at a table in the corner where they are drinking *cubatas* with a forty-something woman with over-done kohl, a singlet top and denim mini-skirt. He reckons her tits have been done.

'Will!' says Paolo, a smile tattooed on his face but the fear of a caught man in his eyes.

The woman says, 'Hello.' Staffe thinks she sounds German.

Jackson is busy rolling a fat cigarette. This is his world: a scrawny place from when Vietnam went pear-shaped and Cream split up.

Staffe says to Jackson, 'Shouldn't you be back in the village, answering questions?'

'What do you mean?' says Paolo, slurring his words.

Jackson carries on preparing his joint. He says something in German that makes the woman look at Staffe, then laugh.

'Raúl spent the night at yours and the next morning he is dead.'

Jackson drawls, 'Maybe I could have a minute to chew the fat with our dude, here.'

The woman looks disappointed, but scoops up her drink.

'Maybe you should go, too,' says Staffe, to Paolo. 'If you don't know Raúl, this doesn't concern you.' He would willingly drag Paolo into this situation were it not for Marie and Harry and the new baby. 'And steer clear of that stray.'

The German woman turns and glares but Paolo, passing her, says something to make her move on.

Staffe says to Jackson, 'Don't the police want to talk to you?'

'You don't know anything at all about me. I'm damn sure you have a *balsa* full of preconceptions, but this isn't your country so you can take your police ways and shove them where your shit stinks.' Jackson's eyes harden, his lips retract to a thin line. His voice is lower, deeper. He leans forward, suddenly looks as if he could damage anybody. 'You've got nothing to frighten me with, you son of a bitch. And if you ever embarrass me in front of my friends, or anyone I choose to hang out with, or even someone I just want to screw – you'll rue the fucking day.'

'And you will rue the fucking day, Jackson . . .' Staffe leans

98

forward, too, his heart beating fast, thinking that maybe Jackson has a trick from Indo-Asia that could pluck his Adam's apple from his throat.

'Yes?'

'What made you invite Raúl Gutiérrez into your world?'

'Don't be so fucking dramatic, man.' Jackson leans back, takes his drink with him. He holds the glass like a weapon. 'I invited him for dinner. In fact, he invited himself for dinner. He got wasted on my whisky and then drove down the mountain, into a ditch, and killed himself. An inglorious end, but it's not my fault. It's nobody's fault.'

'He was in the village a few weeks ago. Something must have drawn him,' says Staffe.

'He's a fucking journalist. They sniff like dogs but there isn't always heat.'

'And what about Manolo? He's missing.'

'He's a fucking shepherd. It's his job to go missing. Have you checked out the goats?'

'He's not with them. His dog is in the village.'

'Me and Bobby McGee' comes on and Jackson smiles. His eyes are warm and he sips his *cubata* of whisky and coke, puts his feet up on the seat of the stool next to Staffe.

'A bit of a cliché, Jackson.'

'Maybe, but not for me. I hate the fucking song.' He blows a kiss to the girl behind the bar. She is young and slim and fresh and has a smile too dirty for her years. 'But she thinks I like it. That's why I love this place, man. It's out of time.'

'That night, up at your *cortijo*, Raúl said he was going to tell me something. Something he didn't want anyone else to know.'

99

'Maybe it was Barrington. I think he had a thing about Barrington. It was the fucking Academy, I bet.'

'What do you think about the Academy? It will bring tourists in; money and jobs.'

'It won't suit everybody. Me? I came here for the quiet life.'

'I think Raúl had something to tell me about that body down in the plastic.'

'Or maybe Santi Etxebatteria.'

'What!' says Staffe. 'What do you know about him?'

'Raúl and Manolo were talking about you.'

'Whatever it was he was going to tell me, I'll find out.'

Jackson laughs, as if he hasn't a care in all the world. 'Talking to the dead, now? Maybe you could ask Janis where she left all the drugs.'

Looking at him leaning back and dragging on his joint, Staffe thinks that maybe Jackson really does have nothing to worry about.

Jackson says, 'Look, man, I've nothing against you. I invited you into my home and we partied. I like your sister and Paolo's not so bad but I've been here forty years and I haven't a clue how this country operates, so take my advice and get yourself better. Get over what's happened.'

'I'm not like that. Someone died in that plastic.'

'You've seen what's going on down there.'

'The Golf wars?'

'Too right! You ask me, it's something to do with money. And if I'm right, it'll never get sorted out. Not in this country.'

'Money,' says Staffe. 'It's never far away.'

*

Staffe has walked past the indigo-coloured door twice. It has an iron grille, the size of his paperback. He stoops and looks through into a sloping garden of cypress trees, bougainvillea and roses which border a pedicured, well-watered lawn of deep green. It all leads up to a grand *carmen* with filigree iron balconies and finely worked wooden shutters.

He walked past the door twice because he was looking for the kind of place they would put a sectioned shepherd from the mountains: some functional, modern building built in the concrete and nasty fashion of the Generalissimo. This place, the Hospedería of Our Lady of Mercy, is the opposite.

Staffe presses the bell and when a nun, dressed in white and with an equally pale face comes to the gate, he says, though the grille, as if genuflecting and in his most proper Castellano Spanish, 'I am Guillermo Wagstaffe and I am a friend of Manolo Cano. His father is a resident and they call him Rubio.'

She nods and slides a wooden shutter across the grille.

He waits.

Ten minutes later the wooden shutter slides back to reveal the troubled face of Manolo. The nun stands behind him. Manolo seems anxious and says, 'I am visiting my father. Why do you intrude?'

'I know you and Raúl met weeks ago, up the mountain.'

'I am here to see my father, if you don't mind.'

'Why did you take me to see your *tio*, and then to the plastic?'

'I wanted you to try the *papas a lo pobre*. They are the finest. I was trying to be kind.'

'If I hadn't gone with you that day, I wouldn't have tracked down Raúl. I won't rest . . .'

'All right. All right!' Manolo says to the nun, 'It's fine, he is a family friend. I just didn't know he was coming today. He can come in – if it is acceptable to you.'

*

Rubio is writing into a leather-bound notebook at a desk by the tall window of his room, which looks over the flat-roofed, white houses of the Albaicín to the Alhambra palace. As confinements go, it's not a bad one.

The nun leaves and Rubio closes his notebook, stands – a slim, broad-shouldered, still handsome man with blond hair and the bluest eyes. He doesn't look the slightest bit mad.

He puts his notebook on a small pile of identical leather-bound notebooks, ensures the pile is perfectly straight. Looking at Staffe, he says to his son, 'Who is this foreigner you bring to my home?'

'Father!'

'I don't see anyone for years and now you bring men with you. Won't you ever get married; ever bear me a grandchild, you ladyboy?'

Staffe sits on the edge of the bed and says, 'How do you get on with the nuns?'

Rubio's eyes lighten a little and his mouth creases into a smile. 'God would never forgive me.'

'When did you ever care about God, papa?'

'You care more when you can hear the harps, believe me. But I tell you, there's a couple of nurses come round to check on me. Force to your dick.' Rubio laughs, but quickly corrects himself. 'What is it you came for?'

'Your friend, Raúl Gutiérrez.'

'I don't know any Gutiérrez.'

'He died, Rubio,' says Staffe, watching closely as Rubio's eyes blink rapidly.

With a crack in his voice, he says, 'It's sad, of course, when someone dies. Even if you don't know them.'

Staffe says, 'And Astrid? Where is your wife, Rubio?'

'Leave him!' shouts Manolo.

'Do you know a man called Jackson Roberts?' says Staffe. 'He's American.'

'Get out!' shouts Rubio. 'What are these questions?' He glares at Manolo. 'You don't visit since . . . since . . . and now you bring him! Who is he?'

A nun comes to the door, says, 'We cannot have this shouting. You must leave.'

'Rubio, tell me what Raúl was looking for in Almagen,' pleads Staffe.

Rubio shakes his head. He jigs his knee up and down and wrings his hands, turns away from Staffe and his own son, to look up to the Alhambra. A small perfection beneath God's mountains: the mountains that were Rubio's domain, until something stopped that and it passed to his son.

'Come!' insists the nun and she shows Staffe and Manolo back to the indigo door, colder than a fish this time around.

*

'What were you thinking, upsetting my papa like that? You must stop this questioning.'

'Must I, Manolo?'

They are in a *gitano* bar in the Albaicín. Staffe switches his wallet to his front pocket as they settle at the bar.

He continues, 'What is it, exactly, that you don't like about the questions?'

Manolo can't look Staffe in the eye, says nothing.

'In Jackson's *cortijo*, you told me that you knew plenty. Those were your exact words.'

'I was drunk.'

'You were afraid of something. And you still are.'

Manolo slams down his *cana* of beer. 'There is plenty you don't know about me. You don't have to know everything about everything, Guilli.'

'Raúl was going to tell me something the day he died.'

'What would life be like without secrets? You know all about secrets.'

'Yes. And I told you about my parents. Raúl knew about my parents, and Jackson Roberts.'

'Raúl's a journalist, for the love of Christ. You spend time with a journalist, what do you expect?'

'And that journalist has a Barrington on his wall. How could he afford such a thing?'

'I never knew the Englishman. I remember the funeral. It was a big thing. You want to know about Barrington, just ask your friend, Edu. He was there.'

'There?'

'At the funeral. It was a big thing. I just wish I could have been there; seen everything.'

'But Edu didn't like Barrington.'

'Secrets,' says Manolo, paying for the drinks. 'I need the toilet. And then we should leave.'

'What were you and Jackson arguing about that night in his *cortijo*?'

'I can't remember; it's a mystery to me.'

As he goes, deadly earnest, Manolo says, 'If secrets are meant to be revealed, they will be, but friends should behave like friends. Friends will do anything for each other. Anything, right?'

'Of course.'

Manolo slaps Staffe on the shoulder and smiles thinly, with sad eyes. 'Then we are friends. We all have secrets. Even friends. But I will tell you what you need to know. If I can, I will do it. And that, my friend, is a promise.'

Staffe waits at the bar and finishes his drink, busies himself with eating his *tapa* of sardines. He is getting better at leaving no flesh, just the spine and head, which the locals seem able to do by simply putting the whole fish into the mouth and immediately withdrawing it, through closed lips.

He turns to watch a young man in the corner who is singing. He has a dirty face and knotted, shoulder-length hair; wears a white shirt open to the waist and tight black jeans, high Cuban heels which he stamps on the off-beat. The barman claps out a rhythm and the young man closes his eyes, sings a *soleá*. When he is done, the singer leaves, reaching down, adjusting the fit of the long-bladed knife in his boot.

Staffe looks around for Manolo. The toilet is a tiny cubicle with room for only one person at a time. He walks across, presses the door. It swings open, empty.

Manolo is not in the bar, nor is he in the *plazeta* opposite, where a gang of heroin-thin, swarthy men have gathered, swigging from bottles of beer and sucking on joints. When he pays, Staffe asks the bartender if he saw his friend leave.

'If he left without saying goodbye, he's not your friend,' is all he says, trousering the money and nodding to the street as if to say, 'Go on, it's time you left. You're not our type'.

Outside, the evening has become night. Staffe mulls what Manolo had said about being friends and secrets being revealed; saying he will tell him what he needs to know. What might he need to know?

There are fewer people now and those who are left on the streets are local, male, and in groups of three and more. They talk closely to each other, scrawny-shouldered and hunched. They all wear the sharp boots with heels and room for more than a leg. He tries to avoid their eyes and puts his hand in his pocket, on his wallet, has the other in a fist, cocked.

He works his way left and right through the maze of narrow, winding streets, but comes full circle to the *gitano* bar, which is full now. He goes the other way down the hill and every chance he gets, he takes the steepest lane down, knowing that his hotel, the Ladrón del Agua, is on the front line to the Rio Darro, which is, surely, at the bottom of the hill.

When he gets to the church at the top of the steep streets of the Arab market, the *gitano* singer is leaning against a shut-up shop. He steps out in front of Staffe, asks him what he is looking for. Does he want coke, or is it a fuck?

'Nothing.'

'We all want something.' He reaches down.

Staffe thinks the man is going for a knife and walks quickly away. When he gets to the bottom of the next flight of steps, he turns, sees the singer is still watching him. He takes the next flight two at a time towards the lights of the Plaza Nueva just below.

The city becomes warmer the lower he gets, and in the rhythm of his footsteps on the old stone, shiny in the street-lights, he replays Manolo's words, 'Friends will do anything for each other,' all the way to the door of his hotel, which is a different world. The houseboy standing by the fountain in the *patio andaluz* is dressed as a Berber and nods respectfully, offers him a warm, wet towel, to dab away the dirt of the day.

Twelve

The Hospital Isabella is not a hospital. Its cloisters echo with learning, not suffering, for it now houses the University of Granada's Faculty of History, but this time of year, the rooms for private study looking out into the courtyard are all unused. A gnarled old man dressed in a dark suit takes Staffe up a broad staircase to meet Professor Peralta.

In his grand room, Peralta is halfway up a ladder reaching for a book from the ceiling-high cases; he waves Staffe in, asks how his friend 'The Jasper' is getting on. Staffe tells him he seemed very well when they spoke and thanks the professor for seeing him at such short notice.

Peralta turns his back and resumes the quest for his book, overreaching for the volume. Staffe thinks he is about to fall and the old man in the dark suit chides him, but the book is successfully plucked and Peralta descends, says, 'You are delving into our terrible war, so The Jasper tells me.'

'I'm afraid I am interested in the methods of killing.'

Peralta shakes his head. 'They found every way to kill a man in those insane years.' He pauses, reordering his thoughts. 'Each side was as bad as the other. Don't let anyone tell you otherwise. One lot, in the name of everything egalitarian and with *Kapital* behind them, were killing priests and raping nuns. The others sought out reds where there weren't any and executed them anyway – with the most horrible methods.'

Staffe says, 'The method I think I know is truly terrible.'

'I am putting the finishing touches to a conference next spring. For me, the integrity of the sourcing and verification must be impeccable. I have an academic deity to answer to and what you tell me may be published.'

'What I know is hearsay, I'm afraid.'

'You are asking me to be frank and honest, Señor Wagstaffe, so you must be the same.'

'All I can say is that there is a crime under investigation. The *Cuerpo* seem to have a solution, but let us imagine . . .'

'I cannot imagine, Señor.'

'Two men are dead.'

'The man in the plastic – is he one? That was a simple case of druggies killing each other. It made the papers here in Granada.'

'A simple case? I suspect not. What if he had been buried to his neck and had his head strapped back, and . . .'

'And drowned. Drowned in the earth – am I right?'

Staffe nods. 'This is what I am speculating about.'

'You said there were two dead.'

'The other is a journalist.'

'Ahaa, Gutiérrez. I never met him, but we get some of his feature articles in the Granada *La Lente*. They say he drove into a *barranco* as drunk as a monkey.'

'It was he who covered the body in the plastic story.'

'Is it to do with the Golf?'

'Tell me about the water method.'

'I have heard of such a method. The Jasper would call them "Caligulas". But they are not. That's just his Anglo-Saxon predilection. We don't obsess about the Romans the way you do. Here, those few who talk about that method, we call them *"ladrones"*. They were executions claimed in the name of war, but were really to avenge matters of life. It is such things that underline the "civil" in our civil war and precisely the abominations that make it such a terrible war – beyond the imagination.'

'The killings were over water?'

'For some, the war was a screen. Imagine, your grandfather stole land or, more importantly, water from my grandfather. My family lived destitute for three generations – and then the war comes and they are with the Nationalists. I call myself a Republican, and I take your life – and your land and my water back. I call it war, and when the war is done – the war is done. We bury the war and let the water rise, Señor Wagstaffe – we preoccupy ourselves with getting on with the peace.'

'And these crimes were committed by Fascists?'

'It depends. Certainly, once they were in the ascendancy. But everyone was tainted.'

'*Ladrones*,' muses Staffe, smiling to himself.

'You have a strange sense of humour, Señor.'

'My hotel is the Ladrón Del Agua.'

'I know it. It is for our new generation. A special place. Perhaps it bodes well.'

*

From her room, which remains precisely as she left it when she moved away from Gabo ten years ago, Pepa can see the Luna dune. It is a hundred metres high and for half her life, she wondered how the wind didn't take it. Then her brother,

Hilario, told her it is the wind that put it here; keeps it here. Soon after, her brother was taken – by the sea.

Above her bed is her prized poster of *Quadrophenia*. Hilario bought it from a website. It is signed by Pete Townshend and she looks away from it and back out to the sea, remembers her brother. She feels sad, and puts on a CD, plays 'Won't Get Fooled Again' at full blast and waits for her father to come stamping up the stairs. It is her joke, to make her less sad, and she hides behind the door, waiting for him to come storming in, shouting, 'Turn it down, turn it down,' which he does, and she jumps out from behind the door and hugs him tight, her hands clasped tight around his chest and her face snuggled into his neck.

She can smell the sea on him. He is only a small man, a fisherman who did very well from all the fancy restaurants which the village sprouted in the boom. When the peseta turned euro – a black day for all Spain, according to her father – a spanking new Mercedes had appeared in the garage and a new fishing boat was bought, kept on a stand in Motril. The Merc comes out when they go to weddings and christenings; the boat has never been in the water.

'I am so proud of you, my Pepa,' he says.

She holds her breath, daren't tell him that, for all her fancy clothes and expensive habits, she is slowly, surely, drowning in debt.

They hold each other tight for a while and her father eventually says, 'Turn it down, for your mother's sake. I don't understand all this foreign business that consumes you. Where did that come from? It breaks my heart that you are not happy to be truly Spanish.'

'I am, papa. I love Spain. I love Gabo and all my friends here.'

'But you live with the Moors in the city.'

Pepa chastises him but he knows only what he knows. Fishing for his life, he has to fear everything he doesn't know, and who knows the sea? Even this Mediterranean, a sea he has fished all his life, holds terrible depths. In these waters, and especially in winter, God can take you.

When Hilario was sixteen, and she two years younger, he had left school to learn his father's trade. They hit rocks off Agua Amarga and the boat capsized. Her father had dived and dived until he found Hilario. He brought him home and carried him into the house, across his arms like an offertory, tears stained into his salt cheeks.

Her father looks at the poster Hilario bought for her, using his first wage packet. As if it's too much for him to bear, he gives her a lingering kiss on each cheek, holds her by the shoulders and says he will see her at dinner.

Pepa returns to her papers. There is a whole list of *denuncias* relating to new building projects across Andalucia and one of them relates to a local developer who has built a four-star hotel two bays away from Gabo and right on an idyllic cove. As usual, the outgoing mayor, who granted the permissions and who is now living on Fuerteventura in a massive villa, is being shamed and the new mayor has swept in with his new brush. Pepa spends a couple of hours going through the demolition order on the new hotel, cursing the legal system. When she is done, she goes back to the list of *denuncias*. Near the top is Almagen: an order against an English couple, the Harbinsons.

Last winter, the Harbinsons' *cortijo* on the edge of the village suffered storm damage, like everyone else in the Alpujarras.

The banks of their *acequia*, which serves water for all the farms below them, had burst. As a result, many villagers had been denied their water – hence the *denuncia*. But once the town hall looked at it and visited the Harbinsons, they declared the entire smallholding illegal. As it stands, the house is set to be demolished after a final court hearing in Granada.

She looks up a contact she has at the London *Times*. Every now and again, she writes as a stringer for him and this hard-luck story of paradise gone sour could appeal. She makes the call, wondering what the English policeman will be sniffing around at, right now; what use he might be.

*

Jackson lets himself into the apartment in Realejo. When he first came to Granada, Realejo was a down-at-heel *barrio* and its Campo de Principe was filled with furtive lovers and kids scoring dope. Now, the streets are lined with trendy bars and shops selling *objets d'art*, and the *campo* is like any piazza in any proud city in the world. The food's gone downhill but the menus are in four languages.

He bought his place, which is the top floor of an eighteenth-century house next to the church of Santo Domingo, in 1985. Jackson gave six thousand bucks for it and earlier today, an agent came round to see him and sucked his teeth and banged on about *El Crisis*, finally said he would struggle to get quarter of a million for it.

The apartment has a knocked-through living room with a kitchen in one corner. On the northern side of the apartment is his old studio, though it is years since he painted. Now, whenever he comes, it is the opposite side of the building which sees the action.

Today, he feels nostalgic and unlocks the walk-in cupboard in the studio and takes out his stack of six Barringtons, lines them up along the wall, like captured soldiers. He gets a bottle of Wild Turkey and pours himself a tumbler, rolls a joint, and leans back in his Barcelona chair. He looks and drinks; looks and smokes; does it some more and remembers those bad, bad times. The best.

'You fucker, Barrington. You bad fucker,' he says as Wild Turkey slowly disappears. He fleshes out a sketch of Yolanda in pen and ink, from memory. The northern light, which he prefers, fades quickly and his thoughts turn to Manolo. Poor Manolo.

He telephones Yolanda and counts out a hundred euros for her. She has been on his back for a little extra – actually, quite a bit extra, but that is all she is getting.

While he waits, he puts on Patti Smith, full blast, and showers long and hard, one-handed. From the other, he drinks the Wild Turkey from the bottle, remembers more about the bad old days. It brings a little something to his face.

*

Yolanda is upset because Jackson doesn't want to talk. He doesn't kiss her and isn't at all charming. It takes him ages, too, and all the time she is down on him, he looks at those infernal paintings, muttering to himself.

She spits him out and takes the hundred euros he laid out. 'You don't have what I asked for?'

'That's plenty,' he says, pouring himself a glass of bourbon. 'You want some?'

'I told you, I need a little extra.'

'A little extra? Well, ask someone else.'

'And you ask someone else, you bastard!'

'I could do that.'

'They wouldn't put up with you. No one would. We're done, all done! And don't call me. Not ever!' Yolanda fixes herself and slips the money into her clothes then storms towards the door.

But Jackson blocks the doorway, holds her and says, 'Don't be like that.' Taking her by the shoulders, he turns her round, asks her which of the paintings she likes best.

'Fuck yourself.'

He digs into his trousers, on the back of the chair, and slips a fifty-euro note between her tits.

'I need more.'

'Tell me. Which is the best?"

Without hesitating, she points at the one on the end, by the window. 'That one.'

It's a seascape, with three people aboard a boat. In a tiny portion of the tempestuous canvas, there is a love story. It is, quite simply, genius – in a way which the other Barringtons are not.

'I could love you, baby,' he says. 'You know that, don't you?'

'You could *show* your appreciation.'

His dick points up at her – hard as oak. Some women have said they don't know how he does it. 'You chose right, baby. But that's all you're getting.'

'I never chose right, my whole life. You treat me right – next time.'

'It's been a funny couple days.'

When Yolanda is gone, Jackson puts Patti Smith back on and – as she swaggers through 'Redondo Beach', kind of like it's out of the corner of her mouth but also, absolutely, from the centre of her soul – Jackson carefully places the seascape love painting to one side. He puts the rest of the canvases face down all over the floor and with a hammer and chisel, one by one, he dismantles the frames at each of their four corners. It takes until halfway through side two before he has a pile of wood and a stack of canvases. The wood, he carries to the hearth and puts it with the logs that surround his wood-burning stove; the canvases, this thin pile of five Barringtons, each bearing the dead man's signature, he rolls up and secretes at the back of the cupboard.

'It's a long time till fucking winter,' he says aloud, looking at the stack of wood and flopping out on his day bed. He got the bed in Tangier on a weekend with Barrington. He laughs aloud, remembering how they stuffed twenty bricks of hashish into the mattress. 'Bad old times, you fucker,' he says, reaching across, pulling the Wild Turkey by its neck, and opens up his sketch pad. In pen and ink, he doodles around with his likeness of Yolanda, and slides slowly to a deep sleep, the monochrome her falling to ground.

*

In Staffe's room in the Ladrón del Agua, a portrait of Lorca hangs beside photographs of old Granada. Lorca, killed by the General's men in the early days of the war. Peralta had told him that when Dalí, supposedly a friend of Lorca's, heard that his friend was dead, he said, '*Olé*,' knowing that the General was set to prevail in the War. Even though he was a Communist, Salvador was planning for the peace.

He recalls something that Sylvie had said to him. Sylvie – probably the love of his life if there is such a thing; a quarter French and wholly Catholic – once said that he was an irredeemable Protestant who had to constantly strive to impose a sense of what was right, what was just. 'It has nothing to do with your job, Will,' she had said. 'That's simply a convenience for you. A pain in the arse for the rest of us. If only you could be like us. You could do your bit, fail, still see yourself as noble, and move on – get on with your life.'

It has been many months since he felt the warm press of flesh on his, and he settles for his *Monsignor Quixote* and his fellow traveller, the deposed Communist mayor: estranged, but utterly placed in his deity.

In the very first stage of sleep, he hears the book fall onto the cool floor, and visions of Manolo enter his dreams, like bleeding watercolours.

Thirteen

Manolo's *cortijo* is the summer station for the goats to escape the blistering heat. It is up by the highest spring and the first throe of pines. Behind it, the Silla Montar, mountain gateway to Granada, swoops between the two highest peaks. Far away, Staffe can hear goat bells, but otherwise, the place is deserted, and he feels ridiculous looking over his shoulder to make sure that nobody can see him as he pushes open the door to Manolo's mountain dwelling. It's a healthy instinct, perhaps.

The door swings free. There would be no point locking it and all that seems to be inside is a couple of butane bottles, flour and yeast, two pots, a knife, and a large bull whip hung above the fireplace.

Staffe checks all the corners of the main room and opens all the cupboards, then goes into the other two rooms. The first is full to waist height with chopped pine. Two mattresses take up most of the floor of the other room, and Staffe sniffs at something sweet in the air, steps over the mattresses to get to a chest under the tiny window. The chest is made from the local pine. Cleverly done, it is finished to the standards of a keen amateur and as Staffe runs his fingers over the grain, he can picture Manolo sitting in the shade of a canopy of pines, his goats grazing, chiselling joints and sanding them smooth.

He opens the shutters fully and sees where the smell is coming from. A goat carcass, strung up by its hind hooves and with its head seemingly twisting round to face Staffe, has been hung too long. It is past its best – good only for its hide now. He gets the knife, which has a carved handle of a goat's head – the knife Staffe has seen Manolo using. Or a perfect copy. He returns to the bedroom and upturns a log, stands on it, stretching, cutting down the goat.

When he is done, he douses himself from the outside tap and returns to the bedroom, kneels by the chest and opens it. Amongst the brightly coloured woven blankets and sundry headwear, he finds a copy of *Gulliver's Travels*. Inside, a small stack of postcards, all addressed to 'Astrid Cano' in an elegant, long and educated hand, and signed 'Your Son, Agustín'. They are postmarked Tangier, Bavaria, Chefchouen, Amsterdam, Marrakech, and London for the years 1996 to 1999. They are written in German and extremely succinct.

Staffe delves deeper into the chest, finds a few papers scattered in the bottom. The writing is scrawled and difficult to read and he sits at the table in the main room trying to translate. When he is done, he reads over what he has written in his own notebook.

As the mountain skies are blue
So are your eyes
And the snow in spring, still,
Your smile shines.
And the autumn of the cherry
Sheds its blossoms,
So my   heart bleeds.

He squints at the missing word, can't make it out. He returns the papers to the chest and rummages in the bottom to see if he has missed anything. When he gets his head right inside, he can see that there are two photographs, stuck where the side panel joints to the bottom. He pulls them out, sees a young Rubio and a dark-haired, large-featured woman with sixties lips and big hair in a short, crocheted mini-dress. She and Rubio are sitting by a river. A picnic is spread out in front of them and Rubio is holding a dark young boy with big limbs and a soft smile: clearly a young Manolo, maybe five years old. The dark-haired woman has another child on her lap: younger and frail; fair and mischievous, pouting into camera.

The second photograph shows a younger Edu and Jackson Roberts carrying a coffin. Behind them are two other figures: Rubio and someone totally obscured. In the background, Almagen's white houses slope away up the hill, like dropped cubes of sugar. A long train of people follow the coffin and, turning the photograph over, he says, 'Barrington?' There is a date of processing on the back, in faded blue ink: *21 June 1999*. He looks at the photograph again and says aloud, 'Edu?' realising that his friend claims to have had no time for the English painter. And he wonders who took the photograph.

Staffe closes the *cortijo*'s main door behind him, sets out to walk down the mountain, feeling that he has violated a privacy. Manolo's Bultaco leans against the animal shelter and Staffe wonders how far away Manolo might be by now. He listens for the sound of goats, hears nothing now.

*

Sweat drips from Paolo's nose and chin. He watches Marie all the way as she goes into the wood to get beers from the *acequia* in the woods which they use as a fridge. 'You pissed Jackson off,' he hisses, to Staffe.

Staffe says to Paolo, 'If I find you've been cheating on her with those sad hippy tarts, I'll . . .'

'I had to get a bus back. Jackson took off after you stuck your oar in.'

Marie comes back, hands them their bottles and rubs her tummy. 'Next week, so they reckon.'

'You should come down to the village and stay with me until the baby is born. Just in case.'

'We're happy up here,' says Paolo.

Marie says, 'All they can talk about in the village is that poor man who was killed. I went down with Harry today and it turned me right off – so morbid! And that cow in the bread shop was talking about Manolo. I couldn't make it out, just heard her say his name, and that curl she puts on her nasty mouth.'

'Do you ever hear them talk about Barrington?' asks Staffe.

'I get the impression the locals can't stand him. He got a couple of the girls in the way, so they say. You should ask Jackson. He must have known Barrington.'

'What about Edu? I heard he had a sister who had a thing for Barrington,' says Staffe.

'A thing for him? She had his child.'

'What!'

'That's what I heard in the doctor's surgery. She's not so well.' Marie shakes her head and puts the palms of her hands flat to her tummy. 'I'm so excited. So pleased you'll be here when the baby comes.'

'Will you?' says Paolo. 'I thought you were better. Isn't that why you went to Almería?

'I'm sticking around,' says Staffe, thinking about Edu, uncle to Barrington's bastard child, and when Marie goes up to the *balsa* behind the *cortijo*, calling Harry to come for something to eat, he says, 'Jackson knew Barrington all right. He carried the coffin at his funeral.'

'It was probably because they were both *guirris.*' Paolo looks at Staffe from the corner of his hooded, dopey eye. 'A fellow *guirri* – when all you want is to get away from them.'

'Are you fed up of me being around, Paolo?'

'I didn't know you were so interested in art.'

'Paintings record history.'

'They decorate walls.'

Up by the *balsa*, Marie hugs Harry. He rests his face on her swell. The sun dapples them, in a way Camille Pissarro might relate to.

Staffe says, 'It strikes me that Barrington is like the war round here. Nobody wants to talk about him.'

Paolo laughs. 'You can take the policeman out of the station . . .'

'Just tell me what you know, Paolo. We're family, for God's sake.'

'I can assure you, in all the years I've known Jackson . . .' Paolo lets his words drift.

A long plume of dust way below catches their eye. Ahead of it, a small red car kicks up the dust. It stops outside a *cortijo*. 'Whose place is that?'

'Some English. The Harbinsons. Not our cup of Darjeeling,' says Paolo and he chuckles to himself again. 'They're in deep shit. Gonna have to tear the play-house down, so everyone says. It's illegal.'

Staffe churns over what Paolo said earlier. 'In all the years I've known Jackson . . .' How would Paolo have known Jackson before he came out here? Did Jackson find this *cortijo* for Paolo? Why would it suit Jackson to have Paolo here? He goes across to the telescope at the end of the terrace, turns it on the small red car.

Beneath, at the Harbinsons', a young, dark-haired woman with over-sized sunglasses knocks on the door, seems to get no joy. Pepa paces around the property and stands on the edge of a deep ravine, where a crop terrace has collapsed. She starts punching away at her mobile phone.

By the time Staffe gets back to the table, Marie has come back and she and Paolo are having a row. It hushes. Marie says, 'We should ask Will.'

'No!'

'It's my land, too. And he put the money up.'

'Why do you undermine me?' says Paolo.

Marie says, 'The water in the *balsa* is low again. Too low.'

'But you're entitled.' says Staffe.

'It's not coming through properly.'

Staffe says, 'You think someone's up to no good?'

'No way!' says Paolo. 'In any case, there's a stream runs through the wood and it only needs a short channel to get it to the *balsa*. I could fill up and then shut it off again.'

'Isn't that illegal?'

'We're entitled. You said it yourself.'

'You can't touch the water,' says Harry through the grilled window of his tiny bedroom. 'Rubén's father is chief of the water. They'll kill you. The water belongs to the village and to God.'

'In that order,' says Marie.

Fourteen

Frog and the rest of the old goats at the bar stare at Pepa. She is distinctly not of the village, with her shiny, black hair and glossy make-up; her tailored suit and stiletto heels.

She and Staffe are at a table by the unlit fire in Bar Fuente's *comedor*, sharing plates of clams in saffron and sautéed squid with cumin.

'Have you got hold of the coroner's report for Raúl yet?' he says, softly.

'I'm here to check on a *denuncia*, for a series on the demolitions. You might be having one here.'

'Aah, the English.'

'You know about them?'

'I saw you at their *cortijo*.'

'How?'

'What about the coroner's report on the body in the plastic?'

'You know these English?'

'The Harbinsons?' He nods sagely. 'I need to see a photo of that body in the plastic.'

'I have my notes on Raúl's death.' She delves into her bag, produces an A5 notebook, and shifts her chair to his side of the table. Finding the page, she reads her shorthand to him, as quiet as if they were lovers. 'The deceased suffered a heart attack which might have caused the crash, but more probably the crash precipitated the heart attack.'

'Did he have any other injuries, not consistent with the crash?'

'Why do you ask that?'

Staffe will not tell her about the two breaches of the bridge, nor the bloodied rag. Not yet. 'I have a suspicious nature, that's all.'

'He had a cut to the head and his skull was fractured to the rear. The coroner said it was certainly caused by the crash.'

'The coroner said "certainly"?'

Pepa refers to her notes. 'That precise word.'

'You'll have spoken to coroners many times, Pepa. In England, "certain" is a word you have to drag from them.'

'And here, too, usually. And another thing is odd. It's the same coroner for Raúl's death as it is for the corpse in the plastic.'

'This is beginning to smell quite bad,' says Staffe. 'There would be blood inside the car if his head injuries were caused by the crash.'

'There is no mention in the police report.'

'How happy are you with the investigations into the death of your colleague?'

'There's no doubt he was full of drink.' She leans forward, whispers, 'Are you suggesting that something happened to Raúl before the crash?'

'Later, I'll show you the car.' As Staffe says this, Quesada, the local Guardia captain, comes in. Staffe lowers his voice. 'Raúl was used to driving full of drink, wasn't he?'

Salva pours Quesada a long drink of Pacharán, without needing to be asked. The old goats suck up to him and he holds his head high, his Roman nose raised and his greying moustache meticulously waxed. This is a man who squeezes the last drop from his rank, wears his *brigada*'s emblem with considerable might.

Pepa says, 'These roads are dangerous. He didn't know them.'

'He knew them all right.'

Pepa says, 'I'm not sure this is a road I can go down.'

'Can you let me have the code, to get into *La Lente*'s archive?'

Quesada makes his way around the bar, almost to within earshot. From where they sit, Staffe can already smell Quesada's cologne. He recognises it as 4711.

Pepa hands Staffe a slip of paper. 'You'll tell me everything you discover?'

'Of course.'

'Now tell me about the English living up the mountain.'

'Is that really why you came?'

'Why else would I?'

'All I know is that they are called the Harbinsons and their days here are numbered, but of course I can discover more. They live just below my sister.'

'You didn't tell me your sister lives here.'

Quesada waves at Staffe. 'Wait here for a moment.' He goes across to Quesada, shakes his hand, and tells him that there is someone he would like to introduce: a colleague of the murdered journalist.

'Murdered?' says Quesada.

'I'm sorry. My Spanish could improve.'

Quesada pulls up a chair, unable to keep his eyes off Pepa.

'Pepa and I were talking about the English artist, Barrington.'

Pepa raises her eyebrows, quickly nods. 'Did he ever get up to any nonsense, Brigada?'

'Barrington?'

'You would have been a young man,' says Pepa. 'But you were stationed in Almagen when he was here, building quite a career, I think.'

Quesada is flattered to be known by the beautiful young woman and Staffe leans back, admires her work. On the hoof, she continues, 'I'm here to do a piece on Barrington. He would have been ninety this September, so the English papers are hot for him. Very hot.' She puckers her mouth. 'I could do with all the help I can get – from someone who knew him. It's the real him that I want to uncover. Something new.'

'We could start with his funeral,' says Staffe.

'I don't recall,' says Quesada, trying to make a poker face, but his jaw slips a little. 'It was a long time ago.'

*

Pepa drives fast up through the narrow and winding, steep Almagen streets and Staffe reaches for his seat belt. She taps his arm, says, 'Not in Spain. We don't wear those things.' She laughs. 'If you don't like my driving, you can walk.'

Staffe leaves the seat belt where it is, watches the village flash by, thinking about Raúl.

Pepa puts on the CD player and 'Won't Get Fooled Again' blasts out. Staffe reaches forward, turns it down, says, 'They had to cut Raúl's seat belt.'

'What?'

'Down the *barranco*, they had to cut through his seat belt to get him out.'

'No way. Raul never wore a belt.' Pepa turns onto the *car-*

retera without slowing and speeds along, switchbacks onto the mountain track.

'That's what I thought. But I know what I saw.' He turns the music back up, says, 'Do you have any Stone Roses? For old times' sake.'

'Sure.' She pulls a CD out of her glove compartment and he looks at the list of tracks, puts on 'She Bangs the Drums'.

'This is my favourite.'

'He was playing this the last time I saw him.' Staffe looks at the CD sleeve and Pepa swerves left and right as she powers up the track, avoiding the worst of the boulders and potholes.

By the time they get to the Harbinsons', 'She Bangs the Drums' is still playing.

Each side of the Harbinsons' front door, roses struggle into the bleaching sun. Atop the flat roof is a satellite dish the size of their ailing front lawn.

Staffe raps the door with two heavy police knocks. Within, a dog yaps and sets off another and when the woman of the house opens the door, the dogs run out, one a Yorkshire terrier, the other a bulldog. The woman has puffy, cried-out eyes but her hair is done just so and she is wearing a silk kaftan. 'Sandra Harbinson.' She has a South London twang, somewhere between Bromley and Croydon is Staffe's guess. 'Are you from the Junta?'

'I'm from the village,' says Staffe.

'You're English! How lovely.'

'And this is my friend, Pepa. She's a journalist. She's interested in your case.'

'We can't afford to upset anyone. But come in.'

Sandra leads them into the lounge, which is small, but with

a forty-two-inch television. In front of it, glued to a frozen picture of *The Weakest Link,* is a white-haired man in a striped cotton shirt and polyester trousers. He says, 'I had it a minute ago.'

With four of them in the room, there is barely space to move.

'Terry, this is an Englishman from the village. He's new. His friend is a journalist.'

Terry doesn't turn round, just says, 'You've not come to knock us down, then.' He says it with no irony, just a soft seam of relief.

Sandra sits them at the drop-leaf dining table and begins to tell the story of the *denuncia* and the demolition order and as she does, her eyes turn red and her lips tremble, but she doesn't cry. 'We're at the point now, where there's nothing left to lose. It's all gone on lawyers and architects. Terry does a bit of decorating for the English but they have no money now, what with the euro and everything.'

Terry says, without turning round, 'And the house is still bloody illegal and falling down.'

'He gets frustrated.'

A car roars by on the track above them and Pepa says, 'Can I look at the *barranco?*'

'Branco?'

'The ditch that breached.'

'You won't paint us in a bad light, will you, my love?'

'I promise not to. My article will say that the demolitions are preposterous and need to be stopped.'

'Go on then.'

Staffe says, 'You hear the cars on this track quite clearly.'

'There aren't many. Just people going up to their cor-tee-yoes.'

'What about the other day? It would have been Thursday, there was a commotion early in the morning.'

'That fella who died?'

'Don't you say anything, Sand,' says Terry.

Sandra whispers, 'He says not to say anything, but I didn't see anything, just something on the bridge.'

'A car?'

'You can see it from our front, but my eyes aren't good.'

'There was another car on the bridge?' says Pepa.

'I don't know. But it was red, whatever it was. Then Terry called me in.'

Staffe stands, remembers Gutiérrez driving up the track, behind Manolo's red Bultaco.

'Is that what made him crash?' says Sandra Harbinson – and Terry suggests that Staffe and Pepa leave.

*

Staffe looks up from the bridge where Raúl perished. Sure enough, he can just see the Harbinsons' *cortijo* between the chestnut trees. 'How are you getting on?' he asks Pepa.

She taps her computer notebook and says, 'Like I thought, your friend Quesada was in the Guardia when Barrington was here. Then he moved away for a while.'

'Where to?'

Pepa hands him the notebook, puts a red nail to the downloaded article on her screen.

Staffe reads it twice, taking in every detail. 'So he went all the way to *teniente* on his watch here in sleepy old Almagen. That's some progress.'

In 1990, Quesada, lance-corporal, had acquired information about a shipment of Ecstasy pills which was being brought across from Morocco on a pleasure craft, into the marina at Aguadulce. Quesada had been steadfast in refusing to disclose his source and the court eventually respected his right to protect his information. Shortly after, three traffickers were convicted and Quesada was promoted to sergeant. Thereafter, he continued to be a favoured son within the Guardia Civil.

'Guess who wrote the article,' asks Pepa.

'Don't tell me. Raúl Gutiérrez.' Between the lines of his piece, Raúl suggested Quesada must have had a dubious relationship with dealers up in the mountains. 'Our friend Quesada got fat on some local misfortunes and now he's sitting pretty.' Staffe hands back the computer and they walk towards the breach which the workmen had repaired. 'I saw a rag down below the bridge. A blood-stained rag, and it disappeared.'

'But Raúl died inside the car.'

'Wearing his seat belt.' Staffe stops, closes his eyes, remembers what he heard the day Raul died. 'I am the Resurrection', going round and round, then cut dead by the policeman who cut through Raúl's seat belt.

'What track is "I am the Resurrection"?'

'It's the last song.'

'And "She Bangs the Drums"?'

'Second track.'

'There's half an hour between the two.' He looks up at the Harbinsons', back down to the bridge. 'From Edu's to here – that's not going to take more than ten minutes.'

Silent for a while – they each think about Raul and his car and his music, and Staffe contemplates the plight of the English. Earlier, before he met with Pepa, Staffe popped into CasaSol, the local estate agents.

CasaSol had overseen the sale of Paolo and Marie's land. It had been owned by four siblings who now live in Malaga, Andorra and Madrid, and they had held out and held out for the best possible price and it nearly sold a year earlier, but at the last moment, an American had stepped in and made a better offer.

'Jackson Roberts?' Staffe had said.

'How do you know? He didn't buy it in the end,' said the estate agent. 'I knew the first time I saw him he didn't have the money.'

'Did he seem at all desperate?' Staffe had said.

The estate agent had looked at him quite quizzically, said, 'Yes, actually. How did you know?'

'I didn't,' Staffe said. Now, he looks at Pepa and wonders how much of his sister's affairs he wants to disclose to a journalist. He points at the bridge, where the workmen repaired it. 'Just there. See the new concrete?'

'It's not big enough for a car to get through.'

'No. But there was a collision.' Staffe strokes the railings where the blue paint is grazed. 'It was Raúl's car. That missing paint is on his car. We can go down and I'll show you.'

'Show me what?' says Pepa, peering into the *barranco*.

Staffe looks down. There is no car in the *barranco*. When he looks up, towards the Harbinsons' house, an immaculately coiffured man with a Roman nose and waxed moustache is looking down on them. Staffe nudges Pepa, who waves up at the man.

Quesada waves back, then shuffles off.

Staffe says, 'We need to find that car, and we need to speak to the coroner.'

'I can't do that.'

'And we need a photograph of that dead man in the plastic.'

'My editor told me to steer clear of Raúl's death.'

'I know somebody we might be able to persuade. His name is Jesús.'

Fifteen

Staffe sifts through Raúl's articles in *La Lente*'s web archive. From his computer in Almería's Hotel Catedral, he searches a year either side of Quesada's Ecstasy bust, but there is no further mention of Quesada, nor does it seem that Raúl took a particular interest in the Alpujarras. Quesada's career had been newsworthy once, and only once.

He changes the search within the range of articles written by Raúl Gutiérrez from 'Quesada, Almagen', to 'Quesada, Barrington'. The programme only runs by year, so each time he has to go back and forth, but each time, the outcome is 'o results for your search'. Before long, he has drawn a complete blank, having come up to present day and gone all the way back to when the digitalisation of copy had started.

Next, he tries the same with 'Jackson Roberts, Almagen', and gets nothing, but then he tries 'Jackson Roberts, Hugo Barrington'. He gets '2 results for your search'.

The first is a routine report of the opening of an art exhibition in San José, thirty miles or so down the coast near Gabo. Beneath the headline 'San José on the International Stage' is a précis of the main contributors, a brief biography of the English painter, and a photograph, in which Barrington is a lean figure with waif shoulders but a strong jaw and narrow eyes. His hair is full and long for a man of his age and swept back. Beside him is Jackson Roberts, in a baggy-shouldered suit with a T-shirt beneath. He has what became known at the time as 'designer stubble' and a ponytail; is strikingly handsome. His arm is around Barrington. The two seem totally at ease. Alongside them is a large-featured, dark-haired woman with her arm around Jackson. At the other end of the foursome, like an awkward bookend, is Francisco 'Rubio' Cano.

The photograph is described by Gutiérrez thus: 'The English painter with fellow artist, the American Jackson Roberts, and their friends Rubio Cano and his wife Astrid.' Staffe prints off a copy of the photograph.

The second result is a report on Barrington's funeral. The funeral took place in his 'beloved' Almagen. Jackson Roberts is again pictured and again has Rubio at his side, this time without the coffin. They both seem somehow distracted, amongst a crowd of people at the cemetery. Staffe squints at the computer screen, but can see no sign of Edu or Manolo, or Astrid. He also examines the image, of a long trail of people behind the coffin on the track up to the cemetery. In the background, beneath a walnut tree, stands Quesada. Again, he prints.

Staffe tries *La Lente*'s search facility for 'Astrid Cano' and comes up empty.

He closes down the tabs from all his searches and the *La Lente* home page reverts to a collage of its latest edition, flagging an imminent report of the full police statement on the 'dead druggie in the plastic'. Across the bottom of the screen, the tickertape tells Staffe that the dead man is a thirty-eight-year-old Danish male called Jens Hansen who has a history of minor drug charges. He has no permanent address in either

Denmark or Spain and the police have tried and failed to find any family to inform.

*

Marie can't remember the last time the baby kicked, but she can feel it's coming. She can also sense Harry growing ever more distant. Today, she drove down into the village to meet him from school. Whilst Gracia and her friends swarmed around, asking about the baby, Marie waited for Harry to come to her. She watched Rueben and his friends go off without saying a word to him, and she watched him watch them go. She wanted to take him to them and make them like him. Instead, Gracia tried to hold his hand and he had shrugged her away, came to his mother. She gave him lunch up at El Nido and then he took his gaming device and walked off, traversing the mountain.

All day, Paolo has been up in their wood. When they went to release their water from its reserve into the *balsa* this morning, nothing came. The *balsa* is empty.

Marie knows the baby will bring a new centre to their life and she tries to picture what it will be like. She is tired, but lately sleep has been hard to find, with the baby bearing down on her and last night, she went out onto the veranda and looked for the moon. She could have sworn she heard something in the wood. She told Paolo and he said she was imagining things.

Will had bought her a gross of nappies, but Paolo said you can't get rid of them, they don't degrade. She also has a pulveriser for when the baby wants more than her tit; and a pushchair. Paolo built a cot and spent weeks sanding it smooth. This is the extent of her preparations for the baby and now she gets a panicky feeling: that there is a whole host of things she has stupidly overlooked, but she realises the only thing that is utterly essential is the water. She looks across the mountain, and Harry is nowhere to be seen. She looks down towards the village, feels afraid.

She walks past the *balsa* and into Los Alamos. The stream is on the far side of the wood and she expects to hear Paolo digging or dragging rocks, but there is no sign of movement; as she becomes aware of the silence, she stops moving, lightens her breathing, takes one careful step after another – almost as if she is spying. Why would she do that? She should call him.

But she doesn't.

Her eyes adjust to the dim light of the canopy; a faint rustle brushes the poplar leaves, and when it is spent, the wood is dead quiet again. There are no cicadas up here, unlike in the village.

As she takes small steps, a low sound emerges: in the heart of the wood, somebody moans. Marie thinks she sees a body hunched on a rock and she edges closer. Within a dozen smaller paces, she slows even more, seeing that the hunched figure is Paolo.

Marie keeps a wide berth, going higher so she can see exactly what is happening, and as she does, she finds herself above him. He has his back to her, which is what she wants in order to be able to see what he is doing, with whom, but all she can see is that his head is in his hands, his fingers busy in his hair, and now the moaning morphs into an utterance. And another. It sounds like 'fuck'. Over and again, he says, 'Fuck.'

She edges a couple of paces closer, determined not to be discovered until she knows what he is up to. She holds her breath, sees that he is looking down and to his right. Beyond him, and making its way to his feet, a thin trickle of water glimmers. She takes a final step, to be sure.

He has dug a channel, to divert the stream water to their *balsa*. Marie puts a hand to her mouth, gasps.

At his feet, in the channel, is a skeleton: the skull and shoulders embedded in the bank of the channel. The head seems to be looking at him. With its bone pressed to the earth in that manner, at that angle, the skeleton seems to be sitting up, begging.

Marie crouches down, sits on the stump of a felled tree. She presses the palm of one hand to the lump of the baby she carries. The other clasps her mouth and she wonders how this will affect her. Eventually, Paolo stands and covers the skull and shoulders with branches and twigs then moves off, into the light.

She goes to the skeleton, removes the branches. The head is curiously small and white as chalk, the shoulders thin and sharp. She thinks she can detect flesh where the pit of the arm ought to be and she feels sick. The baby kicks and she gasps.

Paolo calls her name, far away. She wants to scream. The baby kicks again, which she thinks must surely be a sign, but her head rules her belly and she resolves to keep quiet about this. Let him show his hand. As she retraces her steps, something gold flutters in the undergrowth. She bends, picks up a paper band of black and gold and puts it in the pocket of her elasticated jeans.

Marie scuttles across from the top of the wood to the goat shed behind the *balsa*, takes a milk jug, and works her way down. As she does, she sees Harry sloping across the sierra, his head down, like Christmas didn't show up.

She sees Paolo, too. He has the telescope trained on her and she arranges the muscles of her face into a smile and jiggles the milk jug at him. Paolo waves back, comes to meet her.

'How did you get on with your water?' she asks, her heart beating hard.

'Where were you?'

'Getting some milk. I think the goat is off.'

'I got the milk this morning.'

'No wonder I came up dry.'

'I told you I did it. We had a conversation.'

'Tell me about the water.'

'It'll take a day or so.'

'But you can do it?'

He steps close and holds her by the hips, feels her swollen tummy against him and whispers, 'Trust me, baby.'

Over his shoulder, a disconsolate Harry stomps onto the terrace. 'My batteries died.' And in a filthy *Alpujarreño* accent, he shouts, 'This whole place is dead, sons of whores.'

Sixteen

Staffe identifies his quarry, steps into the fat man's path, saying, 'Amodor Piquet?'

'Who the hell are you?' says Piquet, outside the coroner's office down by Almería port. Piquet is the same height as Staffe, but with a bulging sack of a belly and a rush of curly brown hair.

'I saw you down in the plastic where the Dane, Hansen, was murdered.'

'You didn't.'

'And I knew Raúl Gutiérrez.'

'So?'

'There wasn't much blood in the car.'

'Of course there was.'

'Raúl's car hit the other side of the bridge. Explain that.'

'Who do you think you are?' Piquet pushes past Staffe.

'Hansen was no run-of-the-mill drug killing. They say there is antagonism, down in the plastic. The farmers aren't getting their water; not since the golf courses.'

Piquet is out of breath from the short walk to his car. 'I am a busy man.'

'Strange, then, that they allocate you such disparate bodies to pronounce upon. Why are you assigned to a car crash in Almagen?'

'If you have anything to say, talk to the *comisario*.'

'Sanchez? Actually, I want to see the police reports and the autopsy photograph of the Dane. Can that be arranged?' Staffe takes out his wallet.

'Go fuck yourself.'

'I have friends in the press.'

'Believe me, you don't want to see those photographs. And there's no way we would ever let them get out. You wouldn't believe the state that poor bastard was in. It's a miracle we got an ID.'

'But you did. And the farmers still have no water. And up the road they charge a hundred and fifty for a round of golf.'

'All I can do is assign a cause. It is a pure truth, not like yours. They don't afford me the luxury of speculation. I can't flash my badge and bully people.'

Staffe steps aside, pocketing the new truth: Piquet knows he is police. How could he know that, when Staffe didn't get as far as showing his warrant card? As Piquet gets into his car, Staffe says, 'Is it true that the Dane was dead before they buried him?'

Piquet looks up at Staffe, his mouth open. He starts up the car and says, 'You have proof?'

'You have the proof.'

'Precisely.'

*

Pepa is in the tiny *comedor* at the back of the Quinta Toro with Angel, the father of Jesús. He plies her with chicken livers in a rich, thick gravy with its hint of star anise.

She says, 'You must be proud of Jesús.'

'He is a bright boy. He will do well, but he could have had this.' Angel places a hand on his shiny pate and gestures around him. 'The way I had it from my father. Perhaps some day, if he does the right thing, it will be his. And there for *his* children.'

Pepa thinks of the way her brother, Hilario, followed his father into the sea. She looks around, thinks the Quinta Toro might not be quite what it was. There was a time when there'd be six staff on the go. Now, Angel seems to be managing with just one woman to help him in the kitchen.

'There is something you wish Jesús to do?' says Angel.

'You know Manolo is missing?'

Angel shrugs. 'He's an independent one.'

'You heard about the journalist who died?'

'Of course – it was in Manolo's village.' Angel stops himself dead in his tracks. His eyebrows come to meet each other. 'He was drunk, they say.'

'He was a friend of mine.'

'My God.' Angel stares into nothing. 'I'm sorry.'

'I'm not convinced my friend Raúl died the way the police say.'

'But that was up in the mountains. Jesús is in Almería.'

'You're his father, Angel. Can't you ask him to help me? Your nephew is missing. Sometimes, two plus two is four.'

'That Dane, Hansen, who died in the plastic was a druggie. Bad things come to people like that. My Jesús didn't join the force to save lost souls. No good will come of this.' He stands. 'But if Manolo is missing . . .' He looks at his phone, clicks a button, and says, 'I'll tell Jesús. But now, I must get on.'

As Pepa goes, she can still taste the chicken livers. She will be back for more, some other day. In the meantime, she calls the Cuerpo headquarters, not content to wait and see if Angel bothers to trouble his son.

Staffe shades his eyes from the high sun and makes his way up the alleyway to Raúl's flat, looks up at the room which bridges each side of the small street. What a place for a journalist to write about the world, looming above it like that, its people passing beneath.

His phone rings and he sees it is Marie. His heart stops for a moment. 'Is it the baby?' he says.

'I've seen something,' whispers Marie. 'Can you come?'

'I'm in Almería.'

The line falls silent.

'What is it?' he says.

Marie whispers so quietly he can almost feel her breath. 'Can you come tonight?'

'I'll try.'

'You must. But call first. I'll make sure Paolo isn't here. I can send him to the village.'

'What's he done? I'll . . .'

'Nothing, Will. I don't think it's him.'

'Tell me what it is.'

'It's a body, Will.'

'What!'

'I have to go.'

He stares at the phone, sees she has gone. He tries to call her back but as he waits for the connection, someone comes out of Raúl's building and he holds the door for them. It is a woman with a pushchair. He fusses over the baby, waves them off, and sidles in, stealing up the stairs. On the first floor landing, he reaches up to the lintel, feels for a key, pulls down the plum.

Staffe lets himself in quickly because someone is coming in through the main door. Their steps echo up the stone stairwell and he reaches up, replaces the key and holds his breath. Inside, he goes straight to the study and draws the curtains closed, checking as he does that nobody in the street can see.

*

Jesús is at the police compound up the coast on the road out towards Gabo. He looks at the red Alfa and immediately sees the two blue stripes on the passenger side that the journalist had mentioned. He has seen the photographs of the bridge up in the mountains, knows that anyone who cared could glean that the car must have hit the bridge on the opposite side and at the wrong end from where it had breached the bridge and plunged into the *barranco*.

'What you up to?' says a mechanic in overalls, ambling towards him with a cigarette stuck in the corner of his mouth. He wipes a spanner on his thigh and looks at the tool, then at Jesús. 'I'm going to crush that thing. We've stripped it for parts.

The wheels are off the Alfa and Jesús sees they've had the radio and the steering wheel.

'I said, what you up to?'

Jesús wonders what he is up to, but the Englishman is his uncle's friend, and now his uncle is missing. Last night, his father had sat in his chair rocking back and forth, looking at photographs of the family, some with Manolo as a boy. When he was done, Angel had said, 'Jesús. You have to take care of this. For the family,' and he had gone to bed, leaving Jesús to leaf through the album. He had forgotten what his father looked like with hair.

Jesús has masses of strong, wavy hair and he wondered what his toll will be.

'I need to look in the car.' The window on the driver's side is smashed and Jesús pokes his head in, jags of glass just inches beneath his throat. There is no splatter of dried blood on the pillar, where Raúl's head would have impacted and no significant blood projections on the passenger seat, roof or dashboard consistent with the amount of blood that soaked Raul's tattered shirt. 'Did you clean this up? Was there more blood than this when it first came to you?'

'I wasn't told anybody would be round snooping.'

'I only want to know the car's condition.'

The mechanic taps the spanner against his leg.

Jesús says, 'You were told to get rid of this car quick, right?'

The mechanic smiles, takes a step closer.

Jesús backs away, tips his cap, says, 'It's all right. I've seen what I came for.' He turns his back and walks away, but as he gets into his car, the man with the spanner is onto the phone. Jesús sighs, wonders what he has allowed himself to become involved in.

He drives away, watching the mechanic fade in his rear-view mirror. Ahead of him, a few hundred yards away, the journalist waits. As he approaches, she raises her sunglasses, perches them in her hair. Her hair is glossy black and the breeze blows it across her face. She brushes it away and when she sees it is him, he could swear her eyes light up. It makes him fluttery in the stomach. But what should he tell her?

Jesús drops the glove compartment and puts the police report and the photograph of Hansen, the battered Dane, away.

'What did you see?' asks Pepa. She rests her bottom on the bonnet of his car and crosses her legs at the ankle.

'Nothing new, I'm afraid.'

'Were they pleased to see you?'

'They're only interested in what they can get for a wooden steering wheel.'

'You didn't stick around for long.'

He wants to ask if she would come to dinner with him. He wonders what her words might sound like, soft in his ear – further down the line. 'The car has been scrapped.'

'And what about the police report on Raúl?'

'What about the report?' She has a dimple on the top of her cheek, like the slash a baker puts in his dough.

He shakes his head. 'I don't know anything about you.'

'I'm a journalist. You will never be named. Not ever.'

'I should know more.' He shifts his weight from one foot to the other.

'So take me for dinner.'

'You'll come out with me?'

'Do you think I should trust a policeman? Especially a shy one.'

'I'm not shy.'

'Then you're deceiving me.' She stands up, reaches into the back pocket of her skirt, and pushes a piece of paper into his chest, presses her fingers on him as she says, 'Call me and we can talk properly, but bring the report, and a photo of the Dane, if you can.'

When she is gone, he gets the report from the glove compartment, reads it again. Gutiérrez's clothes were stained with significant spatterings of blood, yet there was very little blood on the fabric and frame of the car. He knows this because it was on the first report he read, but not the final, official report to which the coroner referred in his ultimate declaration.

And as for Piquet's declarations, Jesús looked at the report for the other body – the Dane in the plastic. The man had a dislocated jaw, broken nose and a fractured eye socket. Six of his ribs were cracked.

Jesús thinks twice, concerned at the transparency of *when* the coroner's report claims things happened.

On 15 August – the day of the *fiesta* of the Virgin of the Sea – the Dane's body was found and Jesús was called down to the plastic. Most of his colleagues were on annual leave, or tied up on *fiesta* duties. Fortunately – or not – he was close by, having attended a family dinner not a mile from where the Dane died, but it was not until the early hours of the 17th that the body was eventually removed from the plastic and taken to the Coroner. Jesús's instructions even when he arrived at the scene shortly after the ambulance, had been clear. Under no circumstances at all was the body to be interfered with until Comisario Sanchez had come back from Majorca. Sanchez was holidaying with his family and he got the first available flight. But that didn't stop the coroner dating his report '15 August'.

*

Staffe scrutinises the Barrington on Raúl's wall. From the little he has managed to learn, it hails from Barrington's middle period: still figurative, but experimenting with colour – not as much as in his later works.

He thinks that this painting might have been painted

around 1980, when Raúl would have been a junior reporter. Even then, Barrington was a known artist and his work was collectable. The painting would have cost him many months' salary. Of course, he could have inherited some money. Or he could have received it as a gift – were he an acquaintance, or something more.

Staffe sits in Raúl's chair, at the desk from where you can see the top of the colonial façade of the Maritime Building. He looks for something he might have missed last time. The desk is Dutch and the oak is light, the patina beautifully deep and unblemished. It is a desk that has been loved. He pulls out the top drawer and it slides easily, comes all the way out, banging into his shins. A ream of blank paper falls to the floor and Staffe curses, then something else hits him. The drawer is too short.

He runs his hand along the desk, the way you might a lover's shoulder in their sleep. He places the top drawer carefully on the floor. Then he pulls the bottom drawer all the way out and places it upon the top drawer. The bottom drawer is six inches longer.

Staffe stretches, takes a firm hold of the lips of either side of the writing surface, and heaves the top of the desk from its pedestals. He twists, places it on the floor, and feels a tweak in his side, rubs it, looking down on the frame of the desk, seeing what he wants.

To the rear of the top drawer is a secret compartment. He slides his hand in and feels around, but there is nothing there. He leans right over and squints into the dark void, sees an unevenness in the surface and runs his hand along again. His fingers snag and he takes a grip, yanks away a cardboard folder which was taped to the back of the front surface of the void.

Staffe holds his breath as he opens the folder, removes a series of photographs. One, he has seen before, it is the image from the exhibition with Roberts and Barrington, Rubio and the beautiful, dark Astrid. There is another picture of her alone, her eyes heavy and her smile far away. She is wearing a *burnous* and there are mountains behind, a sugar-cube village nestled into the fold of a mountain which could almost be the Alpujarras – except the houses are painted the lightest indigo. Clearly, it is North Africa.

In another photograph, Rubio and Jackson Roberts stand with a matching pair of Bultaco scrambling bikes, the red petrol tanks faded by the years. In the background, Barrington looks on from beneath a wide-brimmed, straw hat.

He flicks through, pulling out a photocopy of a marriage certificate, between Francisco Cano and Astrid Hesse in Hannover, 1973, and the certification of Manolo Cano, son of Astrid and Francisco. Why would Raúl have gone to such lengths to secrete public documents?

There is a noise in the hallway below, or maybe on the stairs. There are more papers and he flicks through them quickly, not even time for his heart to flutter as he sees cuttings which cover the death of his parents and the flight of Santi Etxebatteria. Such a random clutch of articles, with only one thing to bring them together.

Quickly and quietly, he returns the drawers to the carcass and lifts the writing surface back onto the pedestals.

The outside door to the apartment creaks. Then it is silent. He thinks it must be Pepa. She would be wary, entering Raúl's apartment. He could call her name, but what would he gain? A piece of paper lies on the floor. He must have dropped it and he picks it up – a folded and sealed document with a Germanic lexicon, saying '*Letzter Wille und Testament von Gustav Hesse*'. He quickly opens the window and reaches down, feeling for a gap in the flashing where the roof tiles meet the stone ledge of the window. He shoves the document into the gap as firmly as he can and closes the window as the door handle turns.

Staffe dashes behind the door, holds his breath, pressing his back to the wall. The door unclicks, then a whole wall of darkness comes straight at him, fast, his nose cracking, his legs giving way. He sinks to his knees and the door bashes into him again, cracking the side of his head.

The heavy door swings mightily into him again, and again. His chest seizes. The floor rises to meet him and the door catches him full on the skull. Before the lights go out completely, the scent of cologne.

Seventeen

Staffe blinks and his eyelids scratch the lens of his eyes. When he squeezes his eyes shut, then opens them again, rings of yellow project onto what he thinks must be a blindfold.

He smells cologne, says, 'Quesada? Quesada, is it you?'

There is no reply and he pushes himself up so he is sitting and shuffles back, feeling what might be a wall against his shoulders, then his back. It is cold and he feels his bare chest with his hand. He hears water running and then his breath is taken completely away as the water is thrown onto him. 'Bastards!' he shouts, then a slap across his face and a woman shouting, 'Shut up!' She has a husk to her voice and he thinks it might be familiar.

'Pepa?' he says, quietly. 'Is it you?'

The woman laughs, says nothing but someone takes a hold of his hair. A profound, dull weight presses on his chest. He twists and they pull him flat to the floor, holding his legs, then an excruciating pain to his heart.

He shouts, can't stop himself, and realises they have something pressed to the thin scar tissue that is taut and fresh over his wound. They press harder and he bites back on the scream.

'You shouldn't be here,' says the woman.

'What did you find?' says a man. He can't place the voice.

They press his scar tissue harder until he can't bear it. He struggles to breathe, thinks he is going to faint, then loud in his ear, 'You let this lie, Guilli. We *know* you.'

And he passes out.

*

He can see. A patch of sky above is brilliantly blue and he can smell ozone. He is swelteringly hot and his chest is sticky. He blinks his eyes and forces himself up, sees that he is nude save his boxer shorts. His chest is brown and flaking with dried blood. 'Bastards,' he says, flinching, seeing that his wound is weeping. Looking around, he is surrounded by the plastic of a large, dilapidated greenhouse. Beside him, a hole has been dug in the ground – big enough to fit a kneeling man.

Staffe senses someone is present and he looks around. There is an opening in the plastic that gives onto the scrubland sloping down to the dirty beach. Between him and the opening is the African in his *burnous*. It is blue and yellow and he is black and blue. One of his eyes is swollen. He is shaking and his nose is askew.

He remembers what the two Moroccans had said about this man: that nothing could hurt him. Staffe stands, staggers across to the man in the *burnous*, says, 'Who was it?'

The African shakes his head.

Staffe moves closer to the African, but from behind him, the tall Moroccan in the Bulls vest shouts, 'Stay away from him.' He strides across to Staffe, a machete hanging by his leg. He takes hold of Staffe and pulls him away. The sun glints off a ruby stud in the youth's ear.

In his home, made from pallets and corrugated sheets, the

153

Bulls youth gives Staffe a pair of torn, purple flannel track-suit bottoms. Staffe's mind spins to the phone call he had from his sister. Her number would be the last call in his phone. His device surely in the hands of people who had practically plucked at his heart. 'I need a phone. Do you have a phone?' he says to the Bulls youth.

'I don't have much credit.'

'Just one call. Please.'

The Bulls youth shakes his head.

Staffe forces a look of *c'est la vie*, thanks the Bulls youth for the trousers, and holds out his hand. The Bulls youth takes it and they shake, his machete still hanging loose and Staffe sees a glimmer of humanity in this man's eyes and clinches that moment, biting his lip against the pain and with the three middle fingers of his free hand, he jabs the Bulls youth in the throat, thrusts his knee into the balls, just missing the blade of the machete, hearing it fall, watching the Bulls youth bend double. He puts a foot on his throat, reaches down, puts his hand into the youth's pocket, and says, 'Sorry. I really am sorry. I will compensate you.'

He takes the man's wallet and phone and machete, then ties him to the iron stove that has been made from old truck wheels welded together. Staffe says, 'Really, I'm sorry, but I have no choice. Really, I don't.'

Then he thinks of Marie, up in the mountains with another body.

*

Pepa grimaces as she dabs the iodine-soaked lint into Staffe's reopened wound. His bottom lip is white from the continued biting. He gasps, looks as if he might faint again, and she says, 'I think it's clean, but we need to get you to the hospital.'

Staffe looks at the phone he took from the Bulls youth. He feels a stab of guilt, then a slow wave of fear. Marie still hasn't responded to his calls and texts. He says to Pepa, 'Where were you today?'

'Who are you calling?' she says, folding the lint so she has a clean corner, pouring more iodine.

'They won't answer.' He waits for her to look up. 'Like you.'

'I told you before. I was with the young policeman.'

'And what did he have for you?'

'Something is wrong.'

'What?'

'I don't know. Something to do with the police report. He won't show it me, but I'm sure he has a copy.'

'You have good relations with the police.'

'It's a thin line. They are cautious of me – you must know that.'

'I know a journalist can be a friend as well as an enemy. So, is there anything you haven't told me?'

'No!'

Staffe takes her hand. 'How would they have known I was at Raúl's?'

Pepa pulls her hand away and gives the lint to Staffe. She goes to her wardrobe and picks out the biggest blouse she has, throws it to him. 'I don't like what you're implying.'

'She sounded like you.'

'Who sounded like me?'

Staffe tries to weigh Pepa up. Today, she looks different: her hair is tied back; tight, three-quarter jeans; a crisp, white T-shirt and no make-up; a sheen on her neck and shoulders from the relentless heat. He thinks that here and now, she appears to be too young, too demure, to do what he fears she is capable of. He says, 'There was a woman.'

'Ask Jesús where I was.'

'How long were you with him?'

'You're a cocksucker.'

'I only said there was a woman.'

'You said she sounded like me. What's that supposed to mean?'

'I'll go.' He puts on the shirt.

Pepa laughs.

'What's wrong?'

'You look like someone from the fair.' She opens the door to her wardrobe and his image angles back towards him – his purple track-suit bottoms and Pepa's lemon shirt with the buttons popping; white flip-flops and two days stubble, bruising to his eyes. 'A proper *chorizo*.' She puts a hand on his forearm. 'Let me take you to the hospital.'

'I have to go back to Almagen.'

'Why?'

'I can't say.'

'Is that what the phone calls are about?'

'They're personal.'

'I'll take you.'

'Don't you have work to do?'

'I'm doing it. My chief will blame me if anything happens to blacken Raúl's name. I have to stay on top of this.'

'Cover it up, you mean.'

Pepa lets his comment slide, shakes her hair loose and tilts her head, brushing hard without the slightest grimace. 'The English papers want the Barrington story. I can tie it into the demolitions, too. It will be a nice syndication fee for *La Lente*. As you know, they have a piece of me.'

Staffe sits on the bed. He wants to sleep. The prospect of having to get a bus back up to the mountains, jostling with stinking men drinking rough wine and chomping on *bocadillos de jamón* doesn't appeal.

'I'll pack,' says Pepa, tossing her hairbrush onto the bed. 'Feel free to use it,' she smiles, going into her bathroom.

The cliché about enemies being kept close strikes him, so he calls through to the bathroom, 'When I get back, I need to be alone. For a few hours.'

'I can amuse myself.' She pops her head out. 'And in the morning, we'll get you to the local medico.'

He puts his hand to his heart and remembers Jadus Golding. Sometimes, you trust people and it cuts you. But if you can't trust anyone – what becomes of the world, and us in it? 'Fine,' he says. 'And thank you.'

She looks at him with wide, sad eyes.

Staffe leans back, wonders if things can ever be the same, since Jadus Golding unloaded two bullets into his body. He closes his eyes, pictures his office in Leadengate, and Pulford and Pennington, Josie too. He's not sure he can remember what she looks like: her nose, the line of her jaw, the fall of her hair, and the sound of her voice. But you can't take people apart like that.

The pictures fade to nothing. Next thing he knows, he jolts

in his sleep and then Pepa is tapping him gently on the shoulder. He says, 'Josie?' feels something in his heart.

Pepa says, with a husk in her voice, 'Who's Josie?'

Staffe rubs his eyes.

'Let's go,' she says in a low, foreign tongue.

*

As Staffe rounds the track below the Los Alamos woods, he loses sight of Marie's *cortijo*. His new phone vibrates and he opens it up, sees it is a text from Marie.

dont go 2 house + dont call me. Keep left + low + come 2 wood on yr left. U will b watchd.

He wants to call her, ask if she is all right and has anybody been to see her, but he does as he is told, his heart racing, and when he gets into the shade of the wood, he leans against a tree and wipes his sodden brow, lets his eyes adjust to the dark of the canopy.

Staffe hears a whistle and tries to locate it. He hears it again and peers at where he thinks it is coming from. Something moves and he walks slowly, wary of where he treads. Soon, about fifty metres away, he discerns the shape of his sister. He stops dead. She is crouching.

He moves higher, trying to glean whether she is on her own or whether she has company, but in his anxiety he takes his eye off the ground, steps on a dead branch and it cracks, high and loud, and he ducks, instinctively, squats in the parched undergrowth. Marie stands and he holds his breath. She raises an arm and he waits to see if anyone else shows their hand. She takes a step forward, coming towards him and he goes to meet her, not caring now if it is a trap. What else can he do?

'Are you alone?' he says.

'Kind of.'

'What do you mean?'

Marie steps right up to him, puts her head to his chest, which makes him wince but he swallows the pain as she begins to talk, her voice vibrating against his wound. 'I don't know why I thought something good could happen to me. Such an idiot, chasing this bloody stupid dream. That's all it is – a pipe dream.'

'What's happened?'

'I told you there was a body. It's buried in the earth, like he was standing up.'

'My God.'

Marie pulls away. 'What happened to you, Will?' She places a finger to his bruised face. 'Who did this to you?'

'A stupid fight.'

She regards him intently, notices the petal of blood on his fresh shirt. 'And what's this?' She puts a hand on his heart.

A pinch of pain utters, like a semitone. 'Does Paolo know about the body?'

She nods.

'He told you about it?'

Marie shakes her head, her lip trembling. 'No, I saw him looking at it but he said nothing to me about it. What's become of us, Will?'

'Is he at the house?'

She shakes her head again, on the verge of tears. 'I think he might be with Jackson. The police are watching the house. I saw them.'

'Is it Quesada?'

'I don't know. I told you, I heard someone out here the other night. What will you do, Will?'

'Show me the body.'

Marie leads the way and watches as her brother picks at the soil around the bones. He does it for the best part of an hour, with just one finger and when he is done, he sits opposite the skeleton, just looking at it. The look on his face is familiar to Marie. A look from the past, another country.

Eventually, Staffe takes his stolen phone out of his pocket, comes to her and she says, 'You're feeling the rush, aren't you?'

'Rush?'

'You get off on this. That rush of the chase – but it could be us being chased.'

'That's why we have to take control,' he says, calling Professor Peralta. He tells him what they have found and that he hasn't told the Guardia Civil, but it's only a matter of time before they know.

'We must preserve the authenticity of the site. I have friends in the Cuerpo Nacional here in Granada. I'll be there in the morning. And I'll have company.'

When Staffe hangs up, he is unsure as to whether he has taken a step towards the truth or – holding Marie's hand as they go slowly in the deepening dusk to the *cortijo* – not.

Eighteen

Pepa looks out through the window of what used to be the animal quarters at the bottom of Staffe's house. The room she is staying in is mainly below ground and its window affords a view of the forelocks of the neighbouring mules as they are loaded up for the trip down to the *campo*.

She hears Staffe ease his front door closed and wonders where he is going at this hour, but she has her own agenda and his absence suits her fine. She watches the frayed hems of his jeans *fandango* between the mules.

Manolo has been gone four days now and Staffe checks his friend's front door. Satisfied that nobody is home, and checking around him to make sure he is not seen, he backtracks and clambers up onto the track along the back of Manolo's house, which nestles into a slope and from here, he can see onto the terrace at the back. It is where Manolo dries his peppers; his clothes, too. The wall at the back of the house is old, unrendered, and pitted with eroded stone.

Staffe sticks his boot into a hole in the blockwork and lifts himself off the ground, reaching for another crack with his hand, and then another for his free boot. Two more moves and he feels the lip of the flat roof. As he stretches, he feels a zag of pain across his chest. He hauls himself up onto the roof, scratching his stomach and hooking his leg up over the slate edging and onto the mud and shale roof.

From here, he can see across the roofs and terraces of his neighbours. He picks out his own, thinks he sees something on his terrace. Could it be Pepa? When he had left, there was no sign of life from her.

Staffe steps carefully between the racks of drying peppers on the roof – propped up with rocks to make the best angle to the sun – and tests the hatch that leads into the house. It is closed from inside, but through its gauze he can see it is only held by a flimsy hook into an eye, so he puts his boot to the frame and the hatch swings inward.

He goes in backwards, feeling with his feet for stairs that lead down. There are no windows in this room and it is cool, dark. The smell of *jamón* and fried peppers is ingrained; sweet and deep.

The house is sparely furnished, with nothing on the walls in the hall and stairwell. Throughout, the tiled floors are highly polished. The place is brilliantly clean and as Staffe enters the main salon, he is astonished to see a fully loaded bookcase of novels and reference books.

A fine shotgun leans against the bookshelf and Staffe takes it in hand, breaks it, sees it is unloaded and he snaps it back, weighing it up for balance. When he lines up the sights, something feels wrong. Perhaps it is not as fine a weapon as it appears. He places the stock on the floor again and rests the barrel against the bookcase, then sits in an armchair draped in a brightly coloured, woven throw. It is the only chair in a room not furnished for company.

He regards the books on Manolo's shelves. Lorca and Cervantes are here, and a giant, two-volume Collins Spanish–English dictionary. Amongst the prints on the walls is a framed certificate from the convent school in Mecina.

Staffe stands, inspects the certificate, sees that Manolo had passed his *obligatoria* with distinction, gaining a *bachillerato* scholarship to the College of the Sacred Heart in Granada. From everything that Staffe knows about Manolo, he never attended Sacred Heart. He considers what he knows, for sure, about Manolo: how he came to be his friend. Certainly, the first meeting was at Manolo's instigation – coming across to him, asking him about his background and soon discussing the English police he knew from the television, offering him drink after drink and producing proudly from a pocket his own, home-made black pudding. The friendship was truly cemented when Staffe had defended his new friend in that fight in Mecina.

He looks across to the Bargueno desk, a beautifully carved chest on high, turned legs. He pulls down the wooden leaf to reveal a three-tiered bank of small drawers. In the left-hand drawer on the bottom row, Staffe removes an elegantly written invitation, embossed in gold leaf, inviting Manolo Cano to the funeral of Gustav Hesse.

Gustav Hesse? The name is familiar. It is the same as on the document Staffe had concealed in Raúl's roof. Manolo invited to the funeral, and Raúl hiding a copy of the last will and testament, of Gustav Hesse.

*

As soon as Pepa saw Staffe disappear through the hatch into Manolo's house, she descended swiftly from his terrace and left, walking quickly along the edge of the lower *barrio*. She kept her head down and made her way along the *acequia* in accordance with the instructions she was given. The spiky reeds along the irrigation channel scratched her legs and twice she nearly fell, cursing aloud.

Where the *acequeia* curves down and away towards the *campo*, Pepa makes an arc, through the olive grove, back into the village. Sure enough, a large house with a grand portal stands high, fitting the description. It has no number. The doorway is neoclassical and out of place, cracked down its plinth; the entire façade is flaked away. On the top floor, the rusted balcony sports fresh geraniums – the only clue that it may not be derelict.

Again, as instructed, Pepa knocks once and waits; then knocks twice and steps back, looking up. A key descends, lowered on baling twine from the ironwork balcony.

She lets herself in, smells cured, sweet animal fat, and the in-grained pall of burnt wood and thyme. She climbs the eroded, stone stairs.

'To the top!' calls Immaculada.

'I'm coming,' responds Pepa, and by the first landing, the mustiness has diminished. The stairwell becomes lighter and the house floods with the smell of fresh flowers. The walls are hung with woollen rugs and Moorish plates.

'Here!' calls Immaculada and Pepa gets her breath, looks around, following the light into an *acotea* where the old woman is rocking in a chair by the opening which looks across the wide valley to the Contraviesa mountains. To the left, Mount Gador reigns, like an autocrat.

'You're a skinny little thing,' says Immaculada.

Pepa puts down her bag and instinctively dips into the side pocket for her notebook and pen.

'No,' says Immaculada, placing her hands slowly to her head, running them deliberately around her face. 'Nothing official. Not ever, you hear. This is purely for your understanding.'

Pepa nods, replaces the tools of her trade.

Immaculada is extremely thin and her hair is white and thick. Her eyes are watery but they glimmer. She is dressed in black – not the way the village widows dress but in a pinafore top and linen trousers. 'I have made *gazpacho*. You will take some?'

'Yes, please,' says Pepa, taken aback. She thought Immaculada would be living up here in some kind of squalor – a woman in mourning, withdrawing into a dark past. Looking out of the *acotea*, she sees how verdant the *campo* is, despite the long, scorching summer. When Immaculada returns with the *gazpacho*, Pepa says, 'You have a wonderful view.'

Immaculada puts the tray down. 'Of the future and the past.' She hands Pepa a tumbler of the chilled soup and breathes heavily. 'Hugo is out there.' She says 'Hugo' like 'You-go', and points to a V-shape in the landscape where the sea comes and goes. 'This lot' – she stabs a thumb over her shoulder – 'they live in the past. I don't shy away from my future. I know what happens beyond this valley. Spain is new and the world is bigger than it ever was.'

'Did he show you that?'

Immaculada smiles. 'He showed me everything.'

A landscape painting hangs on the wall. The frame is splintered and the canvas is bleached by the weather. Pepa recognises the period it is from and knows that, whilst it is not the very best Barrington painted, were it well conserved it could fetch sufficient to buy an apartment in Gabo or San José and maybe enough left over to keep a maid.

'It's a beautiful painting. Were you together then?'

'We were always together. And never. He needed space, and I never liked it up there or that awful Tangier.'

'Up where?'

'In those *cortijos*. That's a man's world.'

'Did you go to Tangier?'

'I went once.'

'With your daughter?'

Immaculada's eyes glaze over and she looks up towards Gador. 'His later work, I'm not so sure about. They say it is magical. So magical it disappeared.'

'I don't understand.'

'For a foreign market. He said he was painting one for me, but it never materialised. He never lied to me. Not once. I knew everything he was up to when he and Rubio went off.'

'It would be worth a fortune, if there was another painting. A last Barrington,' Pepa ventures.

'For what purpose? I won't be here for ever.'

'What about your daughter? She is your one and only?'

'The first and last, poor thing. I devoted myself entirely.'

'To your daughter?'

Immaculada smiles, with sadness in her glimmering eyes. 'When you say "no" all your life – that is a pure love. And Guadalupe is a pure love. His legacy.'

Pepa wants to ask about Barrington's other lovers, wants to know how he coped with being so adored. Instead, she says, 'You must love Guadalupe very much.'

'I am not a good mother. In fact, I am something of a bad witch when it comes to family.'

'Your father was mayor.'

'He deserved better than the children he got.'

'Your brother, Edu, didn't get on with Hugo?'

'Edu was too busy trying to fill my father's shoes to give Hugo a chance.'

'He wants to be mayor?'

'He thinks sitting under a tree with an olive net and a bottle will do it. The things we crave can be our greatest curse and he blamed Hugo for his own failings.'

'Perhaps Edu was being protective. You know what brothers can be like.'

'He was ashamed of me and I'm sure he still is. Sometimes I think it's because he couldn't find a love of his own, he tried to destroy mine. But you came to talk about Hugo. Did he do something terrible? What made you come now?' Immaculada plays with her crucifix, which is white gold and like a tiny Modigliani – a wiry Jesús nailed to his cross. She seems to drift away, to another place. 'Hugo didn't believe. The only bad thing he ever did was to question that. I think he might have been a little jealous of my faith.' She dabs her eye with the cuff of her pinafore top. 'So I forgive him.'

'For what?'

Immaculada purses her lips and sets her jaw, looks straight at Pepa. 'I stopped believing for a while. A short while, but that's when everything went wrong. I have made my peace.' She drinks her *gazpacho* in small swallows, keeping her mouth to the lip of the terracotta tumbler and slowly tipping it higher and higher. She deliberately sets down the tumbler on an inlaid, Moroccan coffee table, wipes her mouth with the back of her index finger, and says, 'I'm not long for the world.'

'Don't be silly,' says Pepa.

'I only hope I can be forgiven.' She hands Pepa a piece of paper, makes the pass with trembling fingers, suddenly looking weak, as if she is running out of fuel. 'You know, I remember Raúl. I would have spoken to him if I could. There's not many you can trust. I hope you are the same, and I will never see my name in black and white.'

Pepa says, 'All I want is to find out how he died.'

'I remember him as a boy. He was the head of the house as a young man when his father abandoned them.' Immaculada coughs and her eyes water. 'Pass me those.' She points to a blister pack of pills. 'Give me two and go.'

'Can I get you some help?'

'God bless you. No.'

Pepa rinses out the tumbler in the makeshift kitchen and fills it with water. She waits with Immaculada until she has swallowed her tablets down. It takes several attempts and when she is done, Pepa takes back the tumbler. 'Before I go, could I ask what first drew you to Hugo.'

Immaculada's mouth spreads almost into a smile. 'When he was there, the world wasn't. It was worth it.'

'Worth it?'

'When he was away, I was empty.'

'He was a good father?'

'Guadalupe was his gift.' Immaculada looks down into her lap, as if she might have something to be ashamed of. 'A gift to me, too. You know where to find her now, so you must ask Lupe what a father he was.' She beckons Pepa with a wavering finger, signifying it is time to go. 'Whatever she says, I don't want to know.'

Pepa kisses Immaculada on the forehead.

'What we feel – ' she puts her hand on her breast '– chooses us. We can't help it.'

'You stayed here after he died. I bet they didn't make it easy for you.'

'In all my life, I was touched by one man. Just him. Not many of them can say that.'

'You could have made a new life.'

'Some things, you don't change.'

'But Guadalupe moved away. You could have gone with her.'

'My place is here. It always was.' Her eyes close.

Pepa waits for the sleep to gain depth, then removes Immaculada's shoes, lays a shawl across her lap, and leaves, reading the note she gave her, knowing exactly where to find Guadalupe.

Nineteen

Professor Peralta's battered yellow Seat Bocanegra is parked up outside the *hostal* on the Mecina road. He calls to Staffe, 'Climb in!'

The car is airless and stiflingly hot. Staffe asks, 'Where is your friend from the Cuerpo?'

Peralta prods a thumb over his right shoulder. On the back seat, from within a bundle of blankets, a mop of unruly brown hair emerges, then a tortured face. 'He has bad guts and drinks too much and he has the temerity to blame it on your mountain roads. This is Cortes. Would you believe he is an inspector in our esteemed Cuerpo Nacional, and a fine scholar in his time. Now, merely a common drunk.'

'Fuck off, prof,' says Cortes, pulling the blankets back over his head.

Peralta spins the wheels, veering off onto the dirt track, kicking up high, red dust. After ten minutes of switchback driving and cursing from beneath the blankets, Staffe points to the wood. Peralta screeches to a halt, jabs Cortes where his head appears to be, and says, 'Get your tools out, you drunken cunt. We're here!'

Cortes gets out, shakes himself down, slicks back his hair, and applies his cap. Amazingly, stood perfectly erect, Cortes now looks as though he was born to fit the uniform. The power of permacrease. He lifts open the boot and pulls out a long, silver tool case and a camera bag, which he hands to Staffe, then a shovel, which he hands to Peralta. 'Mightier than the pen,' he laughs, and they all tramp into the woods, Cortes leading, walking directly towards the site.

'You know where it is,' says Staffe. 'How?'

'Where would you plant a body in this wood?'

'As deep as you can get, and away from the stream.'

'That is why you and I are entrusted with the law.' He gives Peralta a dirty look, 'And other pricks simply fuck about with the truth of the matter.'

At the grave, Cortes chucks down his cap and his jacket, rolls up his sleeves and takes the spade from Peralta, stabbing away at the ground around the bones until he is close enough to the bone to switch to a trowel, deftly revealing the ribs. He is like an artist at an easel and is soon brushing away the earth to show three-quarters of the circumference of the bones. 'If I do any more, the bastards from the War Legacies will have my bol-locks. And there's a danger he'll collapse.'

'He?' says Staffe. 'It couldn't be a woman?'

Cortes looks closely at the skeleton. 'Do you want it to be a woman?'

Staffe considers Cortes' question, says nothing.

'It would be easier if we could appraise the pelvic bones. I can't really tell from the brow.' He leans even closer. 'It's not *too* pronounced.' He taps the small bump at the back of the skull. 'But this suggests it is a man. And we have a small fracture here. See?'

Staffe steps forward, sees a fine crack in the cranium.

'But that looks as if it happened prior to death. A few years. This looks like trabecular bone.'

171

'You mean healed?'

'I can't be sure. But look at the slope of the shoulders, the depth of the rib cage . . .' He stands, puts his hands on his hips. 'It would have to be a big woman.'

'She was tall.'

Cortes shoots Staffe a look. 'You know who this is?'

'They want it to be a war crime, but it's not.'

'Now you're doing my job for me. It's too early to say what it is.'

'It's buried vertically. Probably kneeling – to look like a *ladrones* execution?'

'Be careful, inspector.' Cortes gives Peralta a dirty look. 'There's no such thing as a *ladrones*.'

'It's entirely consistent with what is known as a *ladrones*,' says Peralta.

Cortes picks up his shovel, starts to fill in the body.

'What are you doing?' says Staffe.

Cortes says, 'It's not a war crime. So it's beyond my terms of reference.' Cortes places his forefinger on a tissue of skin beneath the skeleton's arm. 'They died a long time ago, but I don't think it's seventy years.'

When Cortes is done, Staffe asks the question again. 'How old do you think it is?'

Cortes looks over Staffe's shoulder. 'Ask him.'

Staffe turns to see the slight figure of Comisario Sanchez approaching from the southern fringe of the wood. Alongside him is Pepa. When Staffe catches her eye, she looks quickly away, lets Sanchez move ahead.

Comisario Sanchez regards Peralta and Cortes with suspicion, but when he shakes Staffe by the hand, he puts on a broad

smile. In the cool shade of the mountain copse, an aura of cologne surrounds Sanchez. It is 4711, he thinks.

'What are you doing here?' says Staffe, relaxing the pressure
of his grip within the handshake.

Sanchez smiles. He maintains his grip. 'Shouldn't I be asking
why you are here?'

'I live here.'

'On borrowed time, so people are telling me.'

'You're a long way from home, *comisario*,' says Cortes. 'But I
suppose this is a kind of homecoming for you.'

Sanchez moves away, stands over the buried body, taking in
every detail of the head and shoulders. He removes a Cohiba
cigar from its case and discards the gold and black paper ring.
Without looking up, he says, 'Cortes, if you're here, this must
be a ghost.'

'I'll write my report.'

'And I'll read it. Now cut the shit and tell me what we have
here. A ghost, right?'

Cortes says, 'We can't be sure. It might be too recent. We'll
need to test, but talking of the past, do they still welcome you
back in these parts, *comisario*, after you left in such haste?'

*

Quesada arrived soon after Sanchez called him, bringing two
guardia who have now cordoned off a twenty-metre radius
around the body. Watching the *guardia* taking over the body,
Cortes says to Sanchez, 'I see you and Quesada have made your
peace, but I still don't understand what brings you up here?'

'One of my citizens died in this village last week. And now

a body is found. I am just making sure it is coincidence; that everything is as it appears to be.' Sanchez takes two steps closer to Cortes, lowers his voice. 'This is a shameful execution from a terrible time for Spain. Unless you have evidence to prove another crime was committed, it will be documented as a ghost. Correct?'

'I will write my report,' says Cortes.

'And I will see it finds its rightful place in our body of evidence. Give my regards to your *comisario*.'

Cortes tramps off, downcast, and Peralta follows, saying to Staffe, 'Watch yourself up here – there's snakes.'

Staffe keeps his eye on them, sees Cortes toss his camera onto the passenger seat and get into the back of Peralta's Bocanegra. As they drive off, Cortes catches Staffe's eye, throws a scrunched-up ball of paper out of the car and Staffe immediately makes his way across to where it fell and plants his boot on it, waiting for Sanchez to drive past in his Jeep. Sanchez pulls up and Staffe says, 'Regardless of the truth we get, Cortes's report will make interesting reading.'

'Who do you think you are? How could you possibly get to see that report?' And with that, he drives off.

Quesada says to Staffe, 'Death seems to be following you around.'

'It's vice versa. And we're policeman. That's how it is.'

'You're no policeman. Not in my country.'

'You told me you didn't go to Barrington's funeral.'

'What makes you think I did?'

'I saw you in a photograph, watching proceedings.'

'I was in the vicinity. But I wasn't *at* the funeral,' says Quesada, turning his back, following Sanchez down the mountain.

Before the clouds of dust have dispersed, Staffe kneels down, picks up the scrunched ball of paper and makes his way up to Marie's terrace, where she and Pepa are talking.

'What was that?' Pepa asks as Staffe slumps into a deckchair.

'You came here with Sanchez,' says Staffe, straightening out the scrunched notes that Cortes had discarded.

Pepa shakes her head. 'I was on the road and he offered me a lift. I was coming here anyway.'

'On your way to a good story, hey? Will Sanchez dictate it for you – like he did to Raúl for Jens Hansen's murder story?'

'If I don't write it, somebody else will.'

'How did you know there was a body up here?'

'I didn't. Sanchez asked where your sister's *cortijo* is. What was I supposed to do – let him come here on his own, with his own devices?'

'Such a good Samaritan all of a sudden.'

'What did you pick up off the road before?'

'Nothing.'

'Those are his notes – that *cuerpo* from Granada.'

'Why were you coming up here anyway?'

'You know Barrington had an affair with a woman in the village?'

'The consensus is that there was more than one, but I presume you're talking about Edu's sister.'

'Immaculada.'

'She lives like a hermit in a big old house in the middle of the village. She won't speak to anyone.'

'Well, she spoke to me. She has a daughter, Guadalupe.'

'With Barrington?'

'And the daughter is living in Granada.'

'How the hell did you get that out of her?'

'*La Lente* is an old and trusted organ, feeding these people the truth since before Franco.'

'We can't be sure the daughter is Barrington's.'

'Immaculada is not a sentimental woman. She is bruised and she has the daughter on her conscience. I think she is dying.'

'What exactly would be on her conscience?'

'That she loves the man who shamed her – even though he didn't stand by her. That she loves him more than she loves her own daughter. That she was not a good mother.'

'And how does telling you make it any better for her?'

'I think she was rather fond of Raúl, and she is running out of time. Everyone here thinks she is a harlot and her daughter is a bastard. If she waits much longer, other people will tell her story; and his.'

'It's all right for her to say her daughter is in Granada. That's hardly a story. Granada is a big place.'

'I have an address.'

'No!'

'What's happened?' says Marie, coming out of the *cortijo* with olives and almonds and a chunk of sheep's cheese.

Pepa takes off her sunglasses. Her dark eyes glisten. 'Guilli wants me to do something, but I can't.'

The three of them eat and make small chat about the view and the end of summer. Pepa compliments Marie on the cheese and they discuss how to make *papas a lo pobre* until Paolo's truck comes rattling up the track.

'Did Edu ever mention a last Barrington?' says Pepa. 'Immaculada says he painted it for her, but it never materialised.'

Paolo stops his truck. He looks as if he might turn around

176

and go straight back down the mountain, but when the two *guardia* overseeing the body stand up, he thinks twice, gets out and walks slowly towards the house, head bowed. 'What's happened?' he asks, looking briefly at Pepa but avoiding the admonishing looks from Marie and Staffe.

'I think you know,' says Marie.

He looks across to the cordon of crime tape around the wood. 'I didn't want to worry you.'

'Not telling me is enough to make me worry. It was your idea to come and live here, remember? You're supposed to protect me from harm.'

'Did you discover the body?' asks Pepa.

'This is a family matter, if you don't mind,' says Marie, trying to be polite.

'I should go. I need to get to Granada.'

'We need to talk,' says Staffe, following Pepa down the track as Marie lays into Paolo. At the edge of the first *bancale*, Staffe says, 'You're going to Granada? We can help each other.'

'I can help you is what you mean.' Pepa looks down the mountain, picks out the track that will take her to the village. 'I'll leave your key with Salva. Thanks for putting me up.'

'Let's go together.'

'You said we could help each other. I told you about Immaculada's daughter and the last Barrington, so tell me what Cortes left for you.'

Staffe pulls out the crumpled note which Cortes threw from the car. He hands it across and Pepa reads: *This body is most definitely not a ghost from the war.*

'This brings it home,' says Pepa.

'Brings it home?'

'If Cortes is right, it brings it home that Sanchez is covering something up. You should stay here, look after your own side of things. You know Sanchez is from Mecina. He left the mountains in a hurry and nobody wants to talk about why.'

Paolo fires up his truck and Staffe says, 'We should go to Granada together.'

'I have to pack, but I'm not hanging around. I'll give you an hour and then I'm going.'

Staffe watches Pepa go down along the goat's trail that leads straight to the village, and hears Paolo coming down the main track. They look each other in the eye as the truck trundles towards Staffe and Paolo sounds the horn, doesn't slow. The track is too narrow for Paolo to steer around Staffe and Paolo hits the brakes but the wheels seize and the truck slides, lurching and kicking up large stones and Staffe has to take two quick steps back. The truck shudders and stalls, jolting a final time and scraping its bumper down Staffe's thighs. He staggers back, grimacing.

'What the fuck!' shouts Paolo.

'You really don't want to talk,' shouts Staffe. 'Why is that?'

'Get out of my way!'

The two *guardia* stir into life, are ambling down to see what is going on. 'Do you want them involved?' says Staffe, walking around the truck, climbing up into the passenger seat. Paolo lets the truck start rolling and the engine rattles up. 'Why didn't you tell Marie about the body?'

'I've given her my reasons.'

'Now tell me.'

'Why are you always sticking your nose in?'

'I spoke to the people in CasaSol. They told me Jackson Roberts found the buyer for El Nido.'

'What if he did?'

'That means you knew Jackson before you came out here.'

The track is heavily bouldered and narrow, with sharp turns and steep dips. Time and again, Paolo mounts the verge to avoid the largest of the rocks, precipitous drops on the passenger side. He does it deftly and rolls a cigarette as he goes. Staffe can't help but admire his style.

Paolo lights his roll-up, talks with it in his mouth. 'Like I said to Marie, I was worried the body would spook her. It's only a ghost from the civil war, so what's to be gained by telling her?'

'What if the body isn't what it seems?'

Paolo says nothing. They rock and roll down the hill, past Edu's *cortijo* where a pig is tethered to a post, ready for his *matanza*. Staffe twists round to see where Pepa is, picks her out, half a kilometre behind.

How odd, he thinks, that Pepa got to Immaculada, the sister of a man Staffe considered a friend, and that he knew nothing of Barrington's bastard daughter; Edu's bastard niece. He begins to think of Edu as a curator of lies, with his grand past and his idle ways and his weakness for fine wine.

When they pull up at the junction of the mountain track and the Mecina *carretera*, Staffe says, 'You know more than you're saying, Paolo. I know we'll never be best mates, but we are family. You can trust me if there's something on your mind. I wouldn't ever harm Marie.'

'Same here.'

'Tell me how you know Jackson – from before. It's best that it comes from you.'

179

Paolo flicks his cigarette out of the window and runs his hands through his hair, blows out his cheeks. 'Something strange happened.'

'Tell me.'

'You have to promise you won't tell Marie.'

'If she needs to know, you'll tell her. Right?'

Paolo looks intently at the stash in his lap as his fingers get busy. 'The *balsa* is low. We need the water and we're entitled. It's a mystery how we got cut off and it has to be foul play. It has to, but we need the water and I had to do something so I dug a trench, from the *acequeia* that runs through the wood. There's enough fall for me to get it to the *balsa* and there's no way anybody could see me doing it.'

'It doesn't pay to fool around with the water.'

'Yesterday, when I went back to finish the trench, it had changed. It had been dug another twenty metres.'

'How can you be sure?'

'I had to take it in a straight line to the *balsa* – otherwise there wouldn't have been enough fall. If you look where the trench is now, it's barely above the *balsa*.' Paolo turns, looks at Staffe. He is afraid.

Staffe recalls Marie saying she heard something in the night. 'Someone dug it to where the body is buried?'

'I can't say anything. They'd have me denounced for touching that *acequeia*.'

'So you have to keep quiet.'

'Damn right. But who the hell would do that?'

'And why?' says Staffe.

*

With the barest backward tilt of the head, Quesada summons Staffe across to his table in the *comedor* of Bar Fuente and Staffe walks past the old goats at the bar, each tutting and muttering. Be it the city of London or a mountain village in Andalucia, it doesn't pay to be seen talking to the filth.

'Your friend Sanchez has gone back to where he belongs?' says Staffe.

Quesada smiles at Staffe, puts a cigar to his mouth and sucks in his cheeks. 'Gutiérrez is a citizen of Almería. He died up here and I'm sure the *comisario* is just tying all the loose ends.'

'Gutiérrez also reported on the Dane's murder in the plastic and that was Sanchez's case. As for loose ends, that is beginning to sound like a hymn sheet you all read from.'

Quesada sighs. 'I heard today that your sister's husband is a friend of the American. Your family aren't exactly over here for the quiet life.' Quesada lowers his voice. 'I need you to understand me, Inspector Wagstaffe. It would be in your best interests, and those of your family, to purge your fascination with that body. A man drove into a *barranco*, and tongues are wagging about one of our community being missing. This isn't a good time for loose talk. You know we are waiting on the Junta's decision for our Academy. It will secure the village's future, should we succeed.'

'And I heard today that our friend the *comisario* is from Mecina. Just like Raúl.'

'The *comisario* is the *comisario*. How could I possibly gossip about such a man?'

'Forget gossip. Is there anything official about Astrid Cano and her disappearance?'

'Be careful with your digging, Inspector.'

181

'Don't worry. I'm leaving for Granada. I might go to the Corte Ingles. Tell me, what is that cologne you wear?'

'I don't.'

'You had it the other day.'

'You should try the Ladrón del Agua. A wonderful hotel.'

Staffe feels a chill at the base of his skull.

Quesada smiles. 'Forty-seven eleven is very traditional. We all wear it, some time or other.'

PART THREE

Twenty

This evening, Jadus hopes to achieve a greater degree of liberty.

He watches from a safe distance as Pulford stands in the courtyard of the Limekiln Estate. Above, Jasmine comes out, clutching Millie to her hip. She shouts down to Pulford, 'You bastard!' Jasmine is crying and Jadus can't do anything about it. Yet.

If his original crime had been allowed to run its course, he would be free now, with his family. As it is, this is intervention time.

He watches Pulford walk away and pulls his hood down an extra inch or so, feels his warm, metallic advantage against his flesh and follows the off-duty DS onto Columbia Road, going up towards Shoreditch Park. The long hot summer has died its death and it begins to drizzle again.

The sergeant sits down on one of the statues and pulls out a fag. He looks done in; blowing his cheeks and checking his watch. On the far side of the park, Hoxton way, Jadus sees what the DS is waiting for. The blacked-out Cherokee cruises up to Pulford and Jadus's heart slows. It means tonight can't be the night, but he sticks around long enough to see that it is Brandon Latymer who the copper is meeting, and he wonders how B-Lat can sail so close to the law after what happened with the hit and run up on the Seven Sisters Road. He fears there is only one answer to that question, even though they grew up in each other's cribs, have eaten from the same pot ever since.

A tramp comes up to Jadus, asks him for change and Jadus quietly tells him to go fuck himself.

'Fuck *your*self!' shouts the tramp, and the copper and B-Lat look across and Jadus has to pull down his hood another notch, walking away as naturally as he can to the cutting that plunges steeply to the Regent's Canal. He rolls as slowly as he dare, trying to change his walk so B-Lat doesn't clock him. They worked on his roll together. In theory, they are still together: every month, B-Lat coughs him two grand, still – for the time he served. Some might say it would suit B-Lat to have that debt of honour wiped.

Jadus walks along the canal and after three bridges he sits on a bench, looks left and right and up behind him. He checks the windows of the trendy, wooden-clad apartments opposite. There's nobody watching, so he takes out his spliff. It's phat and ready to go and he stretches his legs out, thinks ahead to a better day when that bastard sergeant will be behind them; when he and Jasmine are together, somewhere else. And B-Lat? He'll take care of that down the line.

He sparks up and draws in: long and holding, like someone is rubbing his temples, whispering it all away.

Cyclists come and walkers go, and all along the towpath the evening plays itself out. He looks for the moon but it is absent and he can't believe he has smoked the whole damn thing, but he has. What the fuck, he'll walk up Dalston and maybe Vicky Park, get a bus up to Stokey, right out of the way tonight. Charelle's up there and he'll be safe. They go way back.

He stands, tries to work out what bridge he's at – whether

he's gone under the New North Road yet. He can't have, so he walks on, with the canal on his right. But he's right enough because when he gets to the next bridge, it's the one before the cycle-hire caff where the canal takes a turn. The bridge is low and in the pitch dark he ducks his head, which he finds funny and his laugh echoes back at him, like someone is calling him and that makes him laugh some more.

'What the fuck's funny?'

'Hey?' says Jadus, feeling like someone has punched him below the belly.

'Nothing's funny. That's what.'

They are sitting at the empty table outside the empty caff. Jadus knows them. He looks around.

'Nobody to save you this time.'

The lights are off in the building opposite, which is offices, done up nice. He remembers when it was shit here: oil drums and shopping trolleys. Now, there's reeds by the water's edge.

The barrel of the gun glints, and they say, 'Everyone's day comes around. It's the law.'

And Jadus feels as if he's been hit below the stomach again. Only it's *in* the stomach this time. He knows the stomach is the worst place, the slowest place. And now the sound. A single shot. There's a shadow on him. He can hear the canal in the reeds but he knows the canal doesn't flow. There must be a breeze.

*

'Are you sure this is it?' says Staffe, looking up at the colonial-style building with its balconied, full-length windows, next to the church of Santo Domingo and close by the Campo de Principe.

'She has the first floor,' says Pepa, looking at the piece of paper Immaculada had given her.

'Maybe she sold a couple of daddy's paintings.'

'He never publicly acknowledged her as his own.' Pepa presses the buzzer and checks her dictaphone is charged. 'Don't freak her out. This is a lifestyle piece, pure and simple, and you are supposed to be the English journalist I'm syndicating to.'

'I know, I know.'

The door clicks open and they enter a lofty hallway. The door creaks back into its jamb and clicks softly shut. A voice curls above, bounces down the curved, stone stairwell. 'Up here!' Fresh crocuses bloom from rounded, terracotta roof tiles mounted on the wall. The place smells like a garden.

Guadalupe, daughter of Hugo Barrington, stands in the open doorway to her apartment. Behind, her world is brilliantly light and the windows are open. The bustle from the street drifts up, weaves around a jazz guitar which Staffe thinks is Joe Pass. The room is enormous and two of the walls are densely hung with primitive art and pen-and-ink cartoons from a London newspaper.

'I see you like Crichton,' says Staffe, reading one of the cartoons and laughing.

'Not my taste. But they are funny. And sad,' says Guadalupe. She is older than Staffe had imagined: in her forties, he thinks. Her hair is thick and jet black, her eyes the palest green.

'A friend of your father's?' says Pepa.

'You can put that away.' Guadalupe nods at the dictaphone. 'And sign this.'

188

Pepa takes the paper and shakes her head. 'I never surrender editorial control.'

'Surrender? An odd choice of word.' Guadalupe looks at Staffe and smiles, saying in English, 'Then you can fuck off back where you came.'

Staffe takes the paper from Pepa, says, 'It's only a piece for our Style section. I think we can live with it.' He hands the paper back to Guadalupe, says, 'I like your Summers.' He goes across to a birchwood armchair by the open window. 'It is a Summers?'

Guadalupe smiles, quite proud, appearing to lose herself in a moment.

'A gift?'

'I'm amazed she gave you my address.'

Pepa says, 'She is very weak.'

Staffe says, 'We're not here to pry into your family. But I would like to know more about the art you have, and the furniture. May I?'

She nods.

He sits in the Summers chair, says, 'Furniture tells a story, and art, too. Usually, the better the art, the more fascinating is the story. It's enough to make you consider becoming an élitist.'

Guadalupe laughs, comes towards the window, rests her bottom on the low sill and stares out towards Campo de Principe.

'Your mother must be happy with where you have ended up,' says Staffe. 'Something to show them in the village.'

'How would they know?'

'Surely you have friends from Almagen who visit?'

'They spurned me. Fuck them!' Lupe's eyes darken, as if she has seen something cruel. 'Why has mother done this now?'

189

He says, 'Perhaps she wants an acknowledgement of her relationship with your father: tacit but from afar.'

'Is that what I am – tacit and afar?' Lupe laughs.

'An Englishman abroad,' says Staffe.

'I don't feel remotely English.'

'He comes, falls in love and stays the rest of his life. And he leaves his legacy.' Staffe stands beside Lupe. 'I love your building. It's of the past; and the future, too. Like Granada. Islam in a Christian world. Do your neighbours have a similar aesthetic?'

'There's only two of us. And we think the same.'

'She has the top floor?'

'He.'

'Can I take some photographs?' says Pepa.

Lupe shrugs and Staffe mooches across to the kitchen area. As he goes, he points out a small seascape line drawing on an exposed brickwork pillar. In the flurry of ink, a boat is almost hidden amongst the waves, three people on board. In the background, the Luna dune. Pepa takes its photograph. 'This is Gabo. My father fishes it.' Pepa studies the drawing more closely then stands back. 'It's good. It's very good. It takes me back there.' She closes her eyes. 'I could swear I can smell the sea.'

Staffe recalls the photograph of Barrington and Rubio; Astrid and Jackson Roberts, all together at the exhibition in Gabo. It was a different time, but Immaculada was out of sight; Guadalupe's mother exiled in her own land.

'Who drew it?' says Staffe.

'I think you've probably got enough, haven't you?'

*

190

Staffe tokes gently on a mint hookah, feels the vapours wash through his body. It makes him see clearly. He leans back and speculates as to who Guadalupe's neighbour might be. He enjoys the hookah some more and waits, and within an hour or so, on the very perimeter of his restful gaze across the Campo de Principe, a familiar and confident gait clicks, like a camera.

The man is wiry and wears a singlet top and hipster jeans; a peaked combat cap and aviators. A man of his age should look ridiculous dressed like this, but Jackson doesn't.

Staffe counts out what he owes and walks double-time until he is three or four people behind Jackson. The pedestrian traffic is thick on Calle Molinos, but as Jackson passes slowly through, Staffe eases himself closer and by the time they pass the hardware shop that Staffe had visited earlier, for the putty, he is close enough to reach out and touch Jackson.

The shadow from the church of Santo Domingo stretches to meet them and Staffe puts his hand in his pocket, begins to work his putty. He has to step down into the road as a posse of nuns works its way in the opposite direction, towards the convent of Our Lady of Los Angeles, no doubt eager to bake that evening's batch of *magdalenas*.

Jackson's key is in the door to Guadalupe's building.

Should he wait?

He takes out the putty, watches as the large door opens. Jackson steps inside. The door is closing and Staffe sets his eyes on the door's lock, reaches out, pressing the putty into the lock. The door closes softly, not clicking.

Staffe bides his time. Waiting, he presses an ear to the thick, chestnut door. From within, he hears steps, diminishing. He counts to ten, presses open the door.

The hall is empty and he steps in, removing the putty. He can smell the linseed. He puts it in his pocket and decides to take the stairs. The door closes behind him with a click. Staffe turns, to double check.

Jackson is standing against the wall beside the door. He rubs the blade of a knife up against the grain of his three-day stubble; finings of his brown and grey face-hair sprinkle to the floor. The sound scratches the dark air. 'Why trespass?'

'I'm here to see Guadalupe.'

'You could ring the bell, like a normal person.'

'Looks like you're doing all right for yourself.' Staffe nods up to the high ceiling of the hallway.

'Come on up,' says Jackson.

'What?' says Staffe, fearing the worst now.

'I'm going to kick back. And you're going to join me.'

*

He checks his watch. It is ten minutes since the Englishman went into Roberts's building. He looks up at the windows, feeling conspicuous and seeing no sign of life. Why is he such a big lump of a man – shoulders like hams and feet as big as blades of beef? He feels the full mass of the situation he has got himself into. His father used to tell him that once you start a thing, you finish it. Manolo thinks about the way his father was before life got to him. Now, anybody meeting Rubio would consider him arrogant, obnoxious. Masks. And one of them is mad.

*

'Has it ever occurred to you that the world just might be a better place if you minded your own business?' Jackson is in a Summers chair, just like Guadalupe's in the apartment below. He prods the tip of his knife into the scallop shape of the flesh of his cheek and takes the first drag on an almighty, fully loaded joint.

'Like I said before, you have a great place here.'

'If you did your homework properly, you'd know my only dwelling in Spain is in the mountains.' Jackson hands the joint to Staffe, stands over him. 'I'd really like you to finish that fucker.'

Staffe looks at Jackson's knife, imagines what a veteran from his war might be capable of. As he did gain entry illegally, so he takes a drag, trying not to inhale and looking around the apartment. He sees an open sketch pad by the fireplace. In pen and ink, the face of a beautiful African woman looks out, holding Staffe with her almond eyes. Her hair is wild and the sketch is a study in exoticism. Just a couple of dozen masterly strokes beguiling him.

'Don't do a Clinton on me,' laughs Jackson.

'Are you and Lupe an item?' Staffe notices the top of a passport sticking out of Jackson's shirt pocket.

'I know lots of Guadalupes.'

'Tell me about you and Barrington.'

'Why should I do that?' laughs Jackson. 'You broke into my world, so finish that thing.'

Staffe takes another drag and gets a chemical hit at the back of his throat. He thinks it is probably skunk; definitely doctored. 'Quite a gang – Barrington and Rubio and Astrid. And you.'

Jackson seems to tense up.

'But Manolo's my concern.' Staffe feels his mind flit away from him. 'What kind of hold do you have over Paolo?' The dope smoothes his edges, almost to liquid. He tries to focus, but all the questions he had stored and collated morph.

Jackson stands again and places the point of the knife on the arm of Staffe's chair. With the free hand, Jackson undoes the top two buttons of Staffe's shirt and looks at the wound, trying its damnedest to heal again.

'Don't worry. I won't harm you, not if you play ball.'

'And what ball would that be?'

'I want you to leave Guadalupe alone. It's a promise I made and I don't break promises. Ever.'

'How noble.'

'You don't know me. You don't know how I feel or what I believe.'

Staffe nods. He feels gentle. 'Did you make a promise to Barrington?'

'Promises? I should have learned from my war never to make another promise. Trust can kill a man. The Spanish know that. We know its value and its power, know not to employ it, or allow ourselves not to be held by it. It's sad.'

'And love, is that a casualty of war?'

'Oh no. It teaches you to love.'

'Who did you love, Jackson?'

'I loved one woman too much. And also, maybe not enough. Sometimes I think that when you survive, the price has to be high. So high, you think it might have been better to be taken.'

Staffe says, 'I survived.'

Jackson puts his finger next to Staffe's wound, looks at it closely. 'You need to get this seen to.'

'It's OK, from what I can see of it.'

'Not everything is what you see. That's something art can teach a man. Tend your family, my friend. Your sister is having a baby. You should take more of an interest in the living.'

'Does that still have Manolo in it?' Staffe isn't quite sure what he means. His mind feels molten.

'Manolo in it?'

'You knew the body was in the woods. When you got Paolo to buy the land, you had a hold . . .' Staffe loses sight of what he wants to say.

'You feeling it?' says Jackson.

Staffe tries to clench his fists, but they're loose, as if he has just come round from the deepest sleep. 'What did you do to me?'

Jackson says, 'You'll never know Manolo's story, and that's what's best for him and all his family. I really hope you can understand that. Trust me.'

Staffe's head becomes super light and his brain feels all liquid now. His eyes are too heavy. The air in his throat washes quickly and he blinks, fast, but sleep rushes at him.

He thinks he hears banging, and somebody shouting, perhaps, but he simply can't open his eyes. He is lying flat and his muscles won't respond and after a while the commotion subsides. All is quiet and he senses Jackson, close, holding him. He smells of ham fat and wine and his words are soft, which doesn't sound like Jackson at all. 'The truth's all buried. And that's a shame,' he says, which is the last thing Staffe hears.

Twenty-one

Somewhere close, the echo of a slap.

Staffe forces his tongue from the roof of his mouth; his lips are cracked and he puts a hand to his chest, feels lint and plasters where someone has patched him up.

The walls are hung with ornately painted plates and framed pictures of swirling dancers and posing, tight-breeched *gitanos* with white blousing shirts and black, Apache hair. A jug of water on a circular table has ice floating on the top, not quite melted away, which tells him someone has been here recently.

He drinks straight from the jug and goes outside, feeling surprisingly fresh. The shadows are long, from a morning sun and he leans against the frame of the low door in the shade of fat vines. Somebody close is knocking out the heavy-hearted, Cuban-heeled rhythm for a *soleá* and he realises the slap is actually a clap. Shoeless children play with a dog-eared ball and he knows he is in Sacromonte. The cypress tips of the Generalife gardens jut the skyline.

Staffe pours the remaining water over his head and slicks back his hair. Next door, a young woman pegs out washing on the terrace, watched by her grandmother. From inside the house, the *soleá* gathers momentum. 'Whose house is this?' he says.

The young woman shakes her head. 'You go. Go now.'

'I would like to thank them, for offering me a bed.'

'They didn't offer.'

The booted beat clatters to nothing, like something disappearing on a breeze, and a long-haired *gitano* appears in the neighbouring doorway which is set into the soft Sacromonte rock. His eyes are heavy and he says, in the laziest, hoarsest Andalus, 'You must fuck off, my friend. I'd hate to have to cut you. Not in front of the children.'

The grandmother laughs. She says, 'But the children could close their eyes. And in any case, they have to learn some time.'

*

The thin road from Sacromonte into the city is quiet. Men in sports jackets and overdone cologne take coffee and read the morning *La Lente*.

The fountain in the luminescent patio of the Ladrón del Agua trickles soothingly and Staffe recognises a familiar figure at the desk, checking out it would seem. Pepa sees him as she twists to return her purse to her bag. 'Where have you been?'

'You don't know?' he says.

'I left you in that Moroccan café in the Campo de Principe.'

'I went back to Guadalupe's place.'

'I knew you were up to something.'

Yes, thinks Staffe. She knew. 'And now you are rushing off, without telling me.'

'I'm not rushing off. Quite the opposite, in fact.' She reaches for the morning edition of *La Lente* and pokes her finger at the banner. 'A day and a half, you've been gone.' She takes a step closer, sniffs him. Stands back and looks him up and down. 'Seems you've had a makeover. You're clean and your eyes aren't heavy.' She reaches out to his chest, pulls his open shirt to one side, 'And finally, you've had your dressing changed. What came over you?'

The receptionist reaches out with a folded piece of paper, says, 'Señor Wagstaffe.'

He takes the note. Reading it, he says, 'I went to see Peralta. He took me in hand.'

Pepa regards him with suspicion, says, 'Looking at you, I'd say there's been a woman involved. Is that who the note is from?'

He says, 'Let's stay just one more night.'

Pepa crosses her arms under her breasts, says, 'No way! I have to get back and file my copy on the secret life of a tongue-tied daughter of a dead painter.'

'We'll untie that tongue.'

'And how will you do that?'

'She has a lover. A very interesting lover who I'm sure she wouldn't want the world to know about. There's a *La Lente* here in Granada as well as Almería?' says Staffe.

'We share national and regional news.'

'So you know people at the office here in Granada. You can get into the archive.'

'I was there yesterday, reading up on Barrington. You know, towards the end, his style changed. He went kind of looser. It's his best stuff, they say, but there's nothing in museums and galleries from his last ten years. It was all snaffled up by the Japanese, and Americans.'

'Never to be seen. Locked away in vaults, like the wine that's never drunk.' Staffe shows Pepa the photograph of Jackson and

Barrington in the little gallery in Gabo. In the background are Rubio and his wife, the beautiful Astrid.

'Who is she?' asks Pepa, leaning across. 'She's beautiful.'

'But not around any more.'

Pepa takes the photograph, squints. 'This is the Gabo Gallery. See the bust in the corner?'

'What do you know about Astrid Cano, Pepa?'

'Nothing. Do you know her maiden name?'

'Raúl knew.' He thinks Raúl made it his business to find out everything about Astrid Cano and he wonders how much Pepa knows of what Raúl was up to. Can he trust her? He recalls the documents from Raúl's apartment. 'I think it is Hesse.'

He watches Pepa go off to *La Lente*'s Granada offices and he re-reads the note the receptionist had given him. He is to meet Professor Peralta at the university and is already late.

*

As soon as he is through feeding the spool into the projector, Peralta draws the curtains and sits beside Staffe, says, 'You have never seen this?'

'No. How did it come to be in your hands?'

'It was left in the lodge by a tramp. He stank of beer. Said he was given twenty euros to drop it off and when our porter enquired more of him, he became quite offensive. Shall we?'

The spool begins to turn, clicking. The sound of it reminds Staffe of younger times with Marie and his parents; those eager moments after the film had come back from being developed, weeks after they had got back from a summer in Cornwall or Brittany.

On screen, two figures sit at a dinner table, candle-lit and pulling faces to whoever is behind the camera. The figures are Barrington and Rubio. Barrington is wearing a flat-fronted beret, à la Falange, and Rubio is in a turban. Then the light improves and the camera turns. Carrying lanterns and naked, Jackson Roberts and Astrid walk slowly towards the camera, laughing.

There is no soundtrack, but someone must say something because Jackson and Astrid stop smiling. They lower their lanterns and each place a hand on the back of the other's neck. They move slowly into a deep, French kiss and the camera gets closer and closer. They raise their lanterns and blow out the flames, and the screen is black, then the film runs out.

'It's a shame there's no sound,' says Peralta.

'A shame we don't know who's holding the camera,' says Staffe.

'And a third shame, besides what is happening on film.'

'What's that?'

'We don't know who put it into your hands,' says Peralta.

'My hands?'

'Oh yes.' Peralta hands Staffe a bubble-wrapped envelope. It reads:

FOR SEÑOR STAFFE, c/o PROFESSOR PERALTA, DEPARTMENT OF MILITARY HISTORY, UNIVERSITY OF GRANADA.

'Let's watch it again.'

Peralta switches the spools, re-feeds, and as he waits, Staffe ruminates: whoever put the film into his hands would want to somehow damage one of the participants. Certainly, Jackson wouldn't want it to get out, and nor would Astrid or Rubio; or

Manolo – to see his mother carrying on in such a manner. And whoever arranged for the film to come into his hands knows of his acquaintance with Peralta.

The film begins its rerun and Staffe squints, leans forward. Near the end, just before the screen turns black, he says, 'There! That's it.'

'What did you see?' asks Peralta.

'Can you get us a better image of a frame?'

'We have a digital technology department, in the Screen School. Which frame do you want?'

'The instant before it goes dark. There is a face reflected in the lantern glass. I'm sure of it.'

'The cameraman?'

'Or a woman,' says Staffe. But he is pretty sure it is a man.

*

Pepa is holed up in a tiny, windowless room in the basement of the Granada offices of *La Lente*, having called in a favour from David, an editor. She worked with him on the exposure of a cokehead tennis player a couple of years ago. He is three years older than her, but is a sub-editor – which is what she should be, if she's ever going to get anywhere.

She puts down the phone to the syndications editor at *Hannoversche Allgemeine Zeitung*, known as the *HAZ*. Pepa did some work for *HAZ* during the European student games, when a German heptathlete had been drug tested. They had paid her a hundred euros for a couple of days' work, but it was all about networking she told herself. And now that chicken is roosting. She has a seven-day authorisation into their level 3 non-subscriber archive.

The 'Astrid Cano' search yields two results. One is for the marriage of Astrid Hesse to Francisco Cano, and the other is for an article run fifteen years later in which her father, Gustav, had appealed for help in finding his daughter who he hadn't seen for five years. Astrid had reportedly left her Spanish family to pursue a new life, possibly in Africa.

The article is illustrated by a picture of Astrid with her mother and father. Rubio is there, too, but he stands detached. A large child hugs his mother's leg. He looks up at her, like a cherub in a piety. In front of him, sitting cross-legged on the floor and smiling mischievously directly into camera is a smaller, fine-featured boy with fair hair. The boys are named Manolo and Agustín.

Pepa types 'Gustav Hesse' into the search facility and gets hundreds of responses. Gustav was a minor celebrity in Hannover, until he sold his publishing company to the Handelsmann empire in 1976, just a few months after his only child took her Spanish husband. Gustav netted seven million marks for his company and gradually faded from the pages of *HAZ*, apart from his plea for Astrid, and a later piece in which he was interviewed as part of a larger feature on Germany's 'disappeared'.

In that article, Gustav is pictured with his grandson, Agustín, who had returned from his commune in Tangier for his grandmother's funeral. In the photograph, outside the family home, Gustav looks dead in the eyes. Agustín smiles mischievously, again, and is wearing a Moorish-looking, collarless smock. Pepa squints, leans closer to the screen and notices that Agustín sports a tiny ruby stud in his right nostril.

She notes down: 'Tangier, nose stud. Manolo not at grandmother's funeral?' She checks the remaining articles, which report the death of Gustav Hesse just three months ago. Gustav's funeral was attended by a couple of notable authors but no immediate family. They mention specifically that his daughter, Astrid, did not attend.

Gustav's obituary cited his publishing successes and also his love of Africa. Apparently, he worked with one of his Scandinavian authors in helping build a school in Mauritania. Pepa notes down: 'Last Will and Testament?' She drags the file into her pen drive and gives up, happy with her booty.

Pepa pops upstairs to thank David.

He says, 'Tracked down any interesting cokeheads recently?' Nobody else is in the office and he comes towards her, standing too close.

'I've gone off tennis,' she says, taking a step towards him and smiling, jutting out her hip so it brushes the top of his leg.

'They say it's all about the lines, with that game.'

'Getting as close as you can.'

'Without blowing it,' he laughs.

'Can you get us close to some lines?' she says.

'To get us started,' he says, picking his jacket from off the back of his chair and placing the flat of his hand on the flesh below Pepa's hip, guiding her out, down the back stairs.

Twenty-two

Staffe describes the woman in Jackson's sketch. 'She has wild hair and almond eyes. She's African, and she is beautiful.'

The barman shrugs, but Staffe can tell he knows her. He puts a twenty on the bar. In this particular corner of town, twenty euros gets you all kinds of places, and it's sufficient to elicit a name. The barman takes the twenty and nods outside. He whispers, 'Yolanda. She'll be by.'

Bar BonBon is in the Campo de Principe. It is a lingering reminder of what the *barrio* used to be like – hippies mix with *gitanos* and South American whores. Money passes in furtive exchanges and you can almost hear broken promises snapping in the air. As the barman suggested, Staffe takes his Tanqueray outside. It comes half and half with tonic over a large handful of ice cubes. He feels better than he has in a long time and he wonders why Jackson doped him the way he did. And who tended his wounds?

The evening *paseo* is under way. Lovers, young and old, walk arm in arm; entire families meander into the square, chatting amongst themselves and with each other. You don't get this in Blighty and Staffe contemplates how he might surrender to the pull of being closer to Marie and Harry, and the new baby, too, but that gets him thinking about Sylvie – for the first time in weeks.

There is a hole in the heart of him that was made the day

his parents were murdered and Sylvie could make him feel as though the hole wasn't there. But it is. The thought of returning to Leadengate brings him down. He swirls the ice in the Tanqueray, blue as a shallow sea. And then the barman scoots out, gives him two hard taps on the shoulder as he shimmies through the outside tables.

Staffe locks onto the arc of a beautiful, large-boned African woman in a tight, fishtail skirt. She has cheekbones like halved plums and large, almond eyes. She slows down and gives him a proper look, as if to say, '*You*? You think you're man enough?' He watches her go, cutting wide, slow figures of eight with her hips. He thinks what a gift Jackson has – to so deftly capture Yolanda.

As she steps down onto Calle Molinos, Yolanda gives him a final look, and he stands, follows slowly, thinking that maybe these steps he is taking now can make some kind of sense of what happened to him in London. Maybe a blessing can emerge from the blight.

Yolanda shouts up at Jackson's building, 'Jacques!' She kicks the door and steps back into the road, shouting 'Jacques!' again up at the windows.

Staffe moves into the doorway of a closed shop.

'Cocksucker!' she calls. 'Ladyboy son of a whore.' She kicks the door a final time and reaches into her bag. Looking left and right, and pushing herself against the door, she levers it open, quick as theft, and goes inside, her fishtail skirt fanning the air behind her, as if covering tracks.

Staffe moves quickly, crossing Molinos in between the slowly moving cars. He is slowed up by the *paseo* and by the time he gets to the door, Yolanda is gone. But the door is slightly ajar – the lock broken and the jamb of the frame splintered.

He waits outside, to give her time to start doing what she is doing. As he waits, his heart beats time and a half. After five minutes, he goes in, quickly climbing the stairs past the doorway to Guadalupe's apartment. When he gets to the apartment above, he pushes open the door. He can smell turps, hears a deep cursing from behind an exposed brick wall.

Edging a step further, he holds his breath – to better discern what is being said.

'Come here, you cocksucker. Damn you!'

The voice is deep and he thinks it could be a man, which isn't what he expected.

He takes another step, reaching out and standing on the pads of his toes; and then another step.

'Son of a whore!' The voice is muffled.

He is one step away and he leans forward, craning his neck to see round the brick wall. The first thing he sees is Yolanda's bottom, swaying from side to side. She is on her knees, showing her stocking tops and straining forward. 'Aaah,' she says, from the hearth.

Her shoulders are butting up against the lintel and her head is in the chimney. She makes a lunge, for whatever it is that holds such appeal. A final curse and another sigh of relief.

Yolanda sinks to her knees, twists, and sits cross-legged in the hearth, clutching a roll of something, wrapped in a blue bin liner.

'Hello,' says Staffe.

The woman looks at him, her almond eyes showing plenty

of white. 'You?' she says, bemused. 'From the square. What the hell are you doing here?'

'I ask the same question. This is my friend's place. Jackson Roberts.'

'Jacques?'

'And that is his?' Staffe points at the wrapped roll. It is two feet long and has the circumference of a rolled-up poster.

'Oh no. This is mine. And you can go fuck yourself. I'm going.'

'Stay where you are, Yolanda.' He can see she is shocked to hear her name in his mouth.

'Jacques did this for me.'

'Did he say to break into his apartment and take it from up his chimney?'

'How do I know you're a friend of Jacques?'

'He has a *cortijo*, in the Alpujarras.'

Yolanda weighs Staffe up.

'Show me,' says Staffe, nodding at the roll. 'We should do this the proper way.' He shows her his warrant card.

'That's not Cuerpo.'

'This is a cross-border investigation. And I'm working with the Cuerpo Nacional. I should really take you to them.'

Yolanda unwraps the plastic, pulls out a roll of canvas, unfurls it and holds it up.

It is a thing of great beauty, but not what you would expect, so Staffe carefully examines the signature, bottom right. It seems to be the real thing. 'You're going to have to hand that across, Yolanda.'

'No!' she pleads.

'If it's yours, it will be returned. I will give you a receipt.'

'No!' she shouts, her voice cracking.

Staffe goes into his pocket. He has a hundred-euro note and a couple of fifties. 'Here you are. It's all I've got.'

'It's worth more than that.'

The way she says it, Yolanda clearly has no idea quite how much more. Staffe rolls up the canvas and puts it in the bin bag. 'It's all you're getting. I could report you for breaking and entering.'

'What's going on?'

Staffe and Yolanda both turn round, each clearly afraid.

'What the hell are you doing in here?' says Guadalupe. Beside her is Pepa.

Yolanda snatches the money from Staffe's hand and rushes out, pushing past Guadalupe and Pepa who watch her sashay down the stairs. On the first turn, without looking, she gives them the finger.

Guadalupe hisses, 'Jackson, and his damned whores.'

Staffe picks up the canvas.

'It's time you told me exactly who you are,' says Guadalupe.

*

Downstairs in Guadalupe's flat, Staffe has a hushed word with Pepa whilst Lupe calls a locksmith to tend the broken front door. Pepa's pupils are dilated and her eyes flit rapidly around the room, avoiding him. 'What did you find out about Astrid?'

'She's loaded. At least her family is loaded.' Pepa talks mechanically, and slow. 'Her father is Gustav Hesse. He sold a publishing firm years ago and got seven million marks for it. And he has a thing for Africa.'

'Does Astrid have any siblings?'

Pepa pauses, rubs her face. She looks at him briefly, then away at the returning Lupe. 'No. It was just her. Her mother is dead.'

'My mother!' says Lupe, sitting with them in front of the fire.

'No,' says Staffe. 'Just someone we know.'

'What was going on in Jackson's place?'

'You told Jackson we came round the other day, didn't you?'

'You lied to me. I needed to know who you really are, and he put me straight. Like I said, he's always been good to me.'

'Do you really want to be tied up in this?'

'In what?'

Staffe goes to the drawing of the seascape. He saw it the other day and now he sees the point of it: a study for something greater. 'I should alert the Cuerpo and let them ask you these questions.'

'What questions?'

'I need to know about Manolo Cano, the shepherd's son – from Almagen.'

'It was Agustín Cano who was my friend.'

'Agustín?' says Pepa.

'He left the village years ago,' says Staffe.

'His grandparents wanted him to go to a German school.'

'But they didn't send Manolo?'

'The boys were very different.'

'Manolo is missing,' says Staffe.

'And Agustín?'

'He doesn't concern me.' He leans forward in his chair. 'Manolo is my friend, Lupe. That's why I'm here.'

'Did Agustín have a stud in his nose?' asks Pepa. 'A ruby.'

'What?' says Staffe.

'He was only a teenager when I last saw him,' says Guadalupe.

'But he came back,' says Staffe. 'He was in Almagen a few weeks ago, so I heard.'

'I didn't see him,' says Guadalupe, turning away, adjusting the heads of some crocuses in a vase.

'What about his mother? Astrid. Do you see her?'

'Not in a long time. But you hear things.'

'You *hear* things?'

'The villagers never understood her. They called her a witch. She would go to Tangier. I guess Rubio wasn't exotic enough for her in the end.'

'She'd go to Africa?' says Pepa. 'I know your father liked to visit Tangiers. What appeal did it hold for him?'

'If you're asking me if he went to Tangiers with Astrid, I'd have to say no.'

'I thought he had something of a reputation,' says Pepa.

'That's easily come by in a place like Almagen.'

'Was Jackson exotic enough for Astrid?' says Staffe.

'Jackson sees the world in a different light. He has a different energy. And frankly, that appealed to me, too, for a while.' Guadalupe stands. 'He's not what you might think.'

'Does he still appeal?'

'I was young when I came to Granada and I was alone. He was a damn good friend to me – he still is. Now, I really must get on and I'd appreciate it if you put a stop to these visits.'

'Then tell me, did you see your father towards the end?'

Lupe says, 'No,' holds out her hand and shakes Staffe's with a disarmingly firm grip. 'If you want to know about my father, why not talk to my uncle.'

'Edu? But he would never have anything to do with Barrington. It's a matter of pride.'

'Pride? Do you really think so? More like he couldn't make any money out of my father being with my mother.'

'Yet he carried the coffin, at your father's funeral.'

'I always thought that might have been for my mother. It was the only thing Edu ever did for her. But at least he did it. Now, are you going to leave the painting?'

'I didn't say it was a painting.'

'I'll have to tell Jackson you've absconded with it.'

'He'll know where to find me, I'm sure.'

Twenty-three

The Alquería Morayma is a restaurant set in a Granadino garden of bougainvillea and cypress trees, and named after the woman who inspired the building of the Alhambra.

'You can't push me around. Nobody ever managed that,' says Pepa as they wait for the waiter to bring their water and a bottle of Calvente.

'Manolo is missing and my family are living on a crime scene, so I have to look under every stone.'

'I've told you everything I know.'

The waiter brings their drinks and Pepa orders her food. Staffe gestures that he will have exactly the same and as they wait, Pepa recalls the story of Morayma to herself, wondering what it would be like to be truly loved.

'What makes you unhappy, Pepa?'

She looks at the Alhambra, eventually says, 'Tell me about your parents, Guilli.'

He tells the tale and when he is done, she says, 'I knew it. Mostly. But you didn't know that, so thanks for telling me.'

'How did you know?'

'I have a deep sadness, too.' And she tells him the story of Hilario, her brother who was carried home from the sea by her father, laid out dead on a table in the *comedor* of their fishing house by the harbour; and how her father has to go back into that same sea every day. And they still eat from that very table. She says, 'We're not so different, you and I.'

'No. We're not so different, but how did you know about my parents?'

'Raúl asked me to track down Santi Etxebatteria.'

'What!'

'He's been in exile ever since he did what he did.'

'But now ETA has another truce.'

'Madrid could never grant an armistice, though. Just like they can't release the prisoners and ETA are left with a war they cannot win. All the time, what they fight for gets smaller.'

'Did you find Etxebatteria?' says Staffe.

'Once he knew I was looking, he found me.'

'You met him?'

'I was about to. Then Raúl died. My chief called me off everything to do with Raúl.'

'So why are you here?' says Staffe, thinking back to the first time he met Pepa.

'I have to make sure they don't tarnish him. His reputation is all he left behind.' She takes a moment, has a sip of wine. 'I wish I'd said more to him.'

'When I said goodbye to my parents the last time, I didn't say any of the things you should say. All I could think of was a party I wanted to get back for. I just hope I've learned to be less selfish.'

The light from the lantern above catches her eye. It glistens. 'There's plenty wrong with you, but being selfish isn't a part of it.'

He laughs and they clink glasses. 'That first time we met, at

Raúl's funeral – that was no chance encounter. You snared me,' he says.

'That's not how I remember it.'

'You had your paw on my tail from the get-go.'

Pepa laughs, says, 'In that case, you'll show me the painting when we get back to the hotel.'

'Tell me what you found about Agustín.'

'And is the painting definitely a Barrington?'

'Like you've never seen.'

She swirls her glass. 'Agustín is fine-featured and fair, almost the opposite of Manolo. He left Almagen because his grand-parents wanted to school him in Germany.'

'I still don't understand why they didn't choose to take Man-olo to Germany. He's the elder.'

'Maybe Agustín was the bright one.'

'Manolo had a scholarship to college – right here in Granada, but never got to go.'

'Agustín is the spit from Rubio. What better way to establish a hold over their son-in-law: to have his son with them, the son he loved most. And the other – he gets to tend the goats.'

'Rubio wouldn't have allowed it, surely,' says Staffe.

'Gustav's company sold for seven million marks. Perhaps Ru-bio complied with their wishes for the money.'

'If that's why they ended up staying together, estranged from their son, no wonder they fell out of love,' says Staffe, thinking about the film of Jackson with Astrid. Rubio and Barrington looking on. He looks up, sees the reflection of him and Pepa, from above, in the lantern.

'It's your turn,' says Pepa. 'Tell me what else you learned today.'

'Jackson and Astrid were lovers. There is a film of the two of them together.'

'My God.'

'You mentioned Agustín had a ruby.'

'I saw a photo of him wearing a Moorish smock. He had a piercing in his nose. Something struck me about it.'

'What, precisely?'

She shrugs. 'I had a feeling it was significant. And I've been thinking about that body in your sister's wood.'

'Thinking who it is?'

'Astrid.'

Staffe nods. 'We're in deep – you know that.'

The lights on the Alhambra morph from gold to emerald, then an electric blue. Finally, the whole palace lights up, ruby red, and Pepa wonders if it could be a bad thing – to be stuck in the middle of the biggest story she has ever had; or ever will.

*

Staffe unrolls the Barrington canvas and lays it out on his bed, a cushion at each corner softly resisting its instinct to curl back up.

Pepa comes across to the bed, gasps – as if she has been touched – wraps her arms around herself, leans right over the painting, then stands back from it. 'You were right.'

'Isn't it remarkable?' he says.

'It's different from all his others. Yes. It's quite beautiful. And romantic. It's full of love.'

Through the open window, a fast, hollow flutter of castanets, then a low, guttural lament from a tortured human voice.

'We should go to a *peña*,' says Pepa.

'Raúl took me, the first time we met.'

She looks sad and Staffe can't help feeling a concern for her. He remembers how hard he lived when he was her age, making his way, sailing close to the wind.

Pepa says, 'What do you think happened to Raúl at that bridge?'

'He didn't drive straight into the *barranco*, that's for sure.'

'I didn't ask what didn't happen to him.'

'Someone stopped him crossing the bridge. I think they were there a while.'

'There was a bloody rag, you say.'

'That's gone, and the car has been crushed. We'll never know.'

'He didn't ever wear a seat belt.'

'That's not exactly proof, though.'

'I know. But let's remember him tonight. I'll take you to the best place,' she says as they stand, side by side, looking at the painting. 'Somewhere Raúl would have loved.'

Staffe says, 'Tomorrow, there's something I'd like you to do. For both of us.'

Pepa looks at him askance, raises her eyebrows.

'Rubio is in the Hospedería. It would be good if you visited. He won't talk to me.'

'You think he knows where Manolo is?'

'That might be too much to hope for. But he has a notebook he writes in. It would help if we knew what is in it.'

Pepa's eyes glisten and a smile forms. For a moment, she looks truly happy – like a child in the heart of theft. She says, 'I'll see you in the lobby in ten minutes.'

'Why do you need ten minutes?' Staffe gives her what seems to be a look of admonition.

'It's all right. This afternoon was a lapse. I only use that stuff once in a black moon.'

*

High above the road, Staffe notices the place he woke up the other day, after he had been doctored by Jackson and patched up by God knows who. The dodgy *gitano* is outside, again, strumming a guitar. His grandmother sits beside him, smoking and clapping. Pepa says, 'This is it,' and Staffe hands the driver the fare and gets out, discerning a door into the rock. Above the door, a sign says 'Cueva Bruja' – Witch's Cave.

They climb the steep steps cut into the rock and Staffe watches the taxi's red tails get small and go out. He wonders why the driver didn't turn around, go back to where the fares come from. When he turns around, the *gitano* gives him the dead eye.

Pepa is up ahead, getting them in and with each step, the *bulería* comes at him with a stronger pulse, drowning the waifish chorus from the cicadas.

Inside, the *peña* is in a series of cells, each carved from the rock and at the far end a man plays guitar, bent almost double with his cheek on the fretboard. Beside him, another claps with his eyes shut and his face scrunched. A third dances, hammering out the *bulería* with his heels and soles, sculpting beautiful shapes with his long arms and scalloped hands. First slow, then fast, a rhythm that comes from beyond the body.

At a small bar just a few feet away from the musicians, a

young girl hands him glasses of Cacique and asks for twenty euros for the door. The drinks are free, she tells him, and the girl nods at his drink for him to finish it up. As soon as he does, she recharges his glass. The young girl winks, moves away, slipping the twenty down the front of her jeans. Staffe surrenders to the night.

The *bulería* finishes, and a woman joins them, dressed in a flowing black skirt and a white blouse that ruches off the shoulder. She dances a *fandango*, and then they play a *soleá* – his favourite. That is the end of the first set and the cave fills with chatter.

Staffe is tallest by a few inches and palest by a long chalk. He wants to ask Pepa if she has any gypsy stock in her; whether she feels what they call *duende*.

Pepa says, 'You feel it. I can see.' She puts a flat palm above her tummy, beneath her breasts, not on her heart but in the centre. Perhaps that is where the soul is.

'Where are the toilets?'

'I'll show you.' She leads him through the crowd. They spur off to the right where there is only one door, saying '*Servicios*.' He pushes the door open. Inside, it is dark and he asks her where the switch is.

'Keep going. Over there. At the end.'

He sees a cord hanging from the ceiling beyond another door and he registers where it is, just before the door swings shut behind him, shutting out all light. He takes three steps, his arm extended out and high, to grab the cord. He clasps his hand shut, expecting to feel the cord, but it's not there. He flails around with his hand but he can't feel anything. He turns towards the door he came through and can see its outline from the light beyond.

Staffe thinks he'll forget about the pee and goes back, feels for the handle, pulls, readying for the flood of light, but the door is jammed. He pulls at the handle of the door again, but the handle comes off in his hand so he taps on the door and calls, 'Pepa.'

'There's no need for that.'

The voice is behind him. It is a man's voice but it sounds muffled.

Staffe pulls at the door again, begins to pound against it, but something knocks his leg from under him and he falls to the ground. His face is on the stone floor. The ground is wet and he feels a great weight on his throat and chest.

'Be still.'

He thinks the voice might be familiar.

'Manolo?' he says, but on the third syllable, as his mouth opens to say the vowel, something cold and sharp is put into his mouth.

'Don't move.' The voice is whispering now, hot and urgent in his ear and he can smell oil and garlic and peppers on the man's breath. 'Your answers are in the mountains, and by the sea. You must think about what they buried. The dead aren't what they seem, but they are your allies. They can't ever be buried. Not truly.'

Staffe wants to speak, but fears the blade of the knife in his mouth.

'Now, lie with your face to the floor. Count fifty and don't bother to look. You can't find us.'

The metal blade presses against his tongue but the pressure

on his throat and chest seems to abate. A light, rhythmic tap on the door and light floods the room. He doesn't move. The door shuts again and all is dark.

He opens his mouth wide and slowly pulls the blade from his mouth. He sits up, waits. And waits. Eventually, the light floods in again. Pepa rushes in, kneels by his side. 'What happened?'

'Where did you go? I called for you.'

'I went for a smoke.'

She smells of smoke. He wants to believe her.

'What's that?' she says.

He looks down, and his heart misses a beat. The knife's handle is hand-turned from chestnut and has the head of a goat carved into it. He has seen one just like it.

'Are you going to tell me what happened?'

'You know as much as me. Someone here doesn't like me.' But he wonders if he might be wrong about that – amongst other things.

They weave through the dense crowd, to stand at the bar where they were before. The crowd distinctly, and quite deliberately, do not look at him.

A mournful *soleá* begins. Staffe recognises the words from his night on the tiles with Gutiérrez. He says to Pepa, in English, 'I was a stone and lost my centre, and was thrown into the sea, and after a very long time, I came to find my centre again.'

'What?' she says.

'It's the song. The Soleá de Sernata. Come on. Let's go.'

As they go, the lament soars and falls, like a gull.

On the balcony in Pepa's room, looking down on the courtyard of the Ladrón del Agua, she says, 'That song. Were your parents the centre that you lost?'

'Too much happens in life for one thing to make us who we are.'

'Don't you think we are always the same, at our centre?'

He smiles at her. 'That's a good thought, but I wasn't always the kind of person I'd want to be.'

'You seem fine to me. Come inside.' Pepa goes to her wardrobe and sinks to her haunches, reaching in. 'I'm not sure I should be doing this.' Her voice resounds in the old wood and she pulls out a buff-coloured file, turns to face Staffe, standing awkwardly, looking down on her. 'Sometimes, you have to trust someone. Don't you?'

'It's one of God's cruel jokes: such a good thing as trust – he made it so dangerous.'

Pepa removes some papers from the file, tosses them on the bed. 'That's you,' she says.

Staffe sits on the edge of the bed and begins to flick through. It takes several minutes for him to absorb the content. 'How did you get all this?' he says.

'They are all public documents, from here and there. It's easy when you're in the game.'

Staffe taps one of the papers – a photocopied cutting from a Basque newspaper, the day after his parents were murdered. 'Is this Raúl's handwriting?'

Pepa nods.

He reads the date stamp on its back. 'This was taken from the archive a week before I even met him; before I went to Almería with Manolo; before there was a body in the plastic. I didn't even know I would go there or speak to Jesús and discover Raúl was covering the case.'

'There must be something to have connected you to Raúl. Or do you believe in coincidences?'

'There's a reason for everything.'

Pepa nods, sits beside him. 'Everything has a motive. Everything we do affects someone else. That's why I couldn't trust you.'

'*You* can't trust *me*!'

'Think about it. You knew Raúl before you said you did. And you brought him up to the mountains. You were there when he died.'

'I wasn't. And I didn't know him.'

'He knew you.'

'Look! This is nothing to do with me; nothing whatsoever. I went to Almería to have my wounds tended and Manolo took me to see his *tio*, Jesús's father, and we took a ride out to the sea, where the body was.'

'What would you give, to catch up with Santi Etxebatteria?'

Staffe feels his breath get trapped above his chest. He feels light in the head.

Pepa goes to her handbag, pulls out a torn scrap of paper. 'You've seen Raúl's handwriting. Now, look at this.'

'What is it?'

The paper is torn from a diary. In the space beneath the date after Raúl Gutiérrez died, and in his own hand, he was to meet Santi Etxebatteria, the man who killed Staffe's parents.

'What is Cabeza de Toro? A bull's head?' says Staffe, remembering he had seen something similar before, in Raúl's study.

'It's a place,' says Pepa. 'In Extremadura – it's the other side of nowhere. But forget it, I've checked. He's gone without trace.'

Staffe slides down, to the cool, hard floor and wraps his arms around his knees.

Pepa crouches beside him, pulls him towards her, and she holds him.

'They've got me,' he says.

'Who are *they*?'

He looks at the fragment of Raúl's diary and shakes his head, then looks up at Pepa. 'In the *peña*, they said the dead aren't what they seem. They are our allies.'

'Who knew about your parents?'

'Manolo.'

'Did you mention the name Etxebatteria to him?'

He nods again.

'And Edu?' says Pepa.

'Just them.'

'And your sister, of course. And her husband? Four people know something in a place like Almagen – you may as well have taken a quarter page in *La Lente*.'

'But it came from them. One of them.'

Twenty-four

The art historian painstakingly clips the canvas to the board, having closed the shutters to the room and finessed the lighting overhead. In this light, from this perspective, the painting takes on an even finer dimension. Pepa can feel the tow of the sea, can comprehend its horrific depths, the scale of its swell, engulfing the boat. She is amazed by the light within the painting: dawn and a new day beckoning. There is a sense of deep sorrow and foreboding. Each of the three characters is distinct. Two lovers and an outsider.

'It is definitely a Barrington,' says the historian. 'The stroke-work and the palette. They are identical to the few examples of his late work that I have witnessed. As I said, all of those late pieces are now in private collections, in Japan and America. But this is so superior. So very superior. I must know where you discovered it.'

'I cannot say,' says Staffe.

'You must tell me. This is a national treasure. Barrington became a Spanish citizen and some say he has a Spanish daughter. My God! This would keep her in pearls and fur for several lifetimes.'

'We represent the family,' says Pepa.

'Family?'

'We are investigating the provenance of this piece,' says Staffe.

The historian pleads, 'Don't you see how special it is? It tells us what we never knew, for certain, about Barrington. You cannot take it away.'

As carefully as he can, Staffe unclips the canvas from the easel. He places it flat on a table, ignores the wincing moans of the historian as he rolls it up. When they reach the door, the historian calls out, like a spurned lover, 'What do you call it?'

'Nothing, yet. Would you like to name it?'

The historian nods and seems to drift away, as if hooked on a memory. 'It must be "*La Sernata*".'

'My God,' says Pepa.

A shiver shoots through Staffe. From the nape of his neck to his Achilles heel.

'Can't you see? Him, the one standing up, he has no centre.'

*

'He has to take his medicine in fifteen minutes. That's all the time you have,' says Sister Anna.

Rubio is in his armchair between his bed and the desk beneath the window. Sister Anna whispers to Pepa, 'Watch him. He has the devil in him.' She lowers her eyes as she says it.

The minute the nun closes the door behind her, Rubio's eyes soften and he taps two cigarettes from the soft packet of Ducados, offers one to Pepa who walks towards him. He watches all the way, lights up and she bends to catch the fire. She is wearing a polka-dot mini-dress. Her legs are bare.

'I don't know you.'

'We never met, Señor Cano.'

'I would remember.'

He has all his own teeth, which is unusual for a man from his world. His hair is golden and quite long, combed back in well-behaved waves. His eyes are blue and his cheekbones are like axe heads. Were it not for the battering his skin had taken, he could pass for forty-five. She thinks he must have been a magnificently handsome young man. 'And so would I.'

'You're a friend of Manolo's, you say.'

'That's right, but I've lost track of him.'

'He should be with his goats.'

'But I'm more a friend of Tino.'

'Tino?'

'His brother – Agustín. We met in Morocco.'

'My God. You've seen Agustín?'

Pepa opens the window, flicks her cigarette out and registers the notebook on the desk. She sits on the edge of the bed, leaning towards Rubio, trailing cigarette smoke from her mouth.

He eyes her.

She crosses her legs, looks around the room, sees a line of journals on a small bookshelf in the lee of the door. 'You want anything while I'm here?'

'Is Agustín all right?'

She leans across, takes another cigarette from his packet. 'I haven't smoked black for years.'

He smiles, leans back, weaves his fingers together above his lap. 'Why are you really here? You don't seem his type.'

'I met Agustín in Chefchouen. It's where he got his nose done.' She taps her left nostril.

'He could always knock them dead, my Agustín, but I never saw the point of men having jewellery.'

'I bet you think I'm a gold-digger, don't you, Rubio? Old

man Hesse dead, and now Manolo is missing: the grandson and heir.' Pepa stands and takes a deep draw on the cigarette. 'He told me.' She walks the other side of Rubio and perches on the edge of the writing desk beneath the open window, her knees a foot apart. 'You didn't love Astrid the way she wanted?' She feels behind her for the notebook. Just inches above his eyeline, she takes its firm spine between her fingers.

Rubio tries not to stare, but fails himself.

'I loved her well enough.'

'What happened?' Pepa raises her foot, puts it on the arm of his chair.

'Have you found her?'

'Was she lost?' Pepa raises her other foot and rests it on the other arm of Rubio's chair and he gasps. 'Can she be found, Rubio?'

She flicks her wrist, releases the book through the window and into the late morning. Now, he looks her in the eye again. 'I loved her. So much.'

She calls, 'Sister!'

'Can you love someone too much?'

Pepa stands and smooths herself down. The door opens and a new, older sister comes in, sees Pepa looking demure and aghast.

They each look at Rubio, unable to resist staring at his erection. He says, to Pepa, 'I loved her too much.'

The sister is livid, says, 'Did he touch you?'

Pepa manages a faint flutter of the eyes, like a broken-winged bird.

The nun grabs Rubio by the hair on his temple and eases him out of the chair, holding him at arm's length – as if she might catch something off him. And he takes his punishment, like someone grateful for any human contact. She calls, 'Sister Anna, get a cold bath going. It's Rubio!' Then she says to Pepa, 'Stay here. I will come back and escort you out.'

The moment they are gone, Pepa rushes to the bookshelf and drops to her knees, pulls off the first volume and flicks through the pages. As she does, her heart grows heavy at what she reads. She replaces the first volume and flicks through the second. The same. And the third, then the fourth, until she hears footsteps. But already, she has the message.

As they walk down the airy, wide staircase of the Hospedería with the breeze wafting through the open windows, Pepa confesses to Sister Anna that she and Rubio had smoked. When they get outside, she insists on picking up the cigarette butts. Beneath his room, reaching into the roses, she draws blood from a thorn but she leaves the cigarette stubs, is intent only on picking up Rubio's notebook. She reaches up her dress and slips the volume into her knickers, allows herself to be led from the garden by the fragrant Sister Anna.

*

The notebook lies open on the desk in Staffe's hotel room. 'This is what he wrote in his book in his *cortijo*. I saw it,' says Staffe. Down the page's centre, with wide margins left and right, and in the neatest, swirling fountain hand, are two seven-lined stanzas and the pattern repeats across each page in the book and in each of all the many notebooks on Rubio's bookcase in the Hospedería.

'He loved her – that's for sure,' says Pepa.

228

'He still does,' says Staffe.

'Does that mean she's not dead? If she is, he can't have killed her,' says Pepa.

Staffe reads from the book, aloud.

As the mountain skies are blue
So are your eyes
And the snow in spring, still,
Your smile shines.
And the autumn of the cherry
Sheds its blossoms,
So my wretched heart bleeds.

'This isn't love,' she says. 'It's a penance.'

'And it's wretched.'

'Wretched?'

'His heart. I couldn't read it properly when I found the poem in his *cortijo*. His handwriting has improved. Maybe practice has made him perfect.' He closes the book and takes a step back, looks at her, smiling. 'He's only flesh and blood.'

'A rush of blood.'

'Did he know who you were?'

'I said I knew Agustín. I'm pretty sure Agustín is his favourite.' Pepa loses herself in a moment.

'Is something wrong?'

'I don't think money is important to Rubio.'

'It's paying for him to stay in that grand old place.'

'That's not what I meant. I don't think he'd do anything for money. I think he'd rather be poor and back with his old life. I can't work out why he is in the Hospedería.'

'Because the world has to believe he's mad.'

She nods. 'You're right. He's as horny as the bull walking down the hill. But mad? I don't think so.'

*

Cortes loosens his tie. Dirt is ingrained on the inside of his collar. He has a red mottle to his eyes, and recent drink hums off him. He is at a desk, surrounded by a bank of screens and flashy-looking hardware. There isn't a piece of paper in sight. His office is as kempt as he is dishevelled.

'I thought you'd give up the ghost,' he says.

'But it's not a ghost, is it?'

'And you know what it is, I suppose.'

Staffe places the newspaper cutting of Astrid down in front of Cortes, and for a glimmer, life shines brilliantly in Cortes's eyes; then quickly burns itself out.

'I told you, I don't think it's a woman.'

'She is tall and large-boned; German.'

Cortes picks up the photograph and lifts the lid on a scanner, plonks it face down on the glass. He taps at his keyboard and an electric-blue light glows. Cortes taps some more, says, 'A magic piece of kit. Takes all the heartache away – all the reasons to be glad you're alive. I hate the fucking thing.' He lights a cigarette. There is a 'No Smoking' sign on the wall behind him. The cigarette wiggles as he talks. 'I pick out three trig points and input just one cell whose dimension I can identify.'

With a dirty fingernail, he taps the digitised image on the screen, covered in hundreds of faint gridlines. 'These tiles are thirty centimetres.' He taps again and a lifelike image of Astrid appears, alone, with her vital statistics written beneath her, detailing her age band, her precise height and a probable weight. A list of options regarding her likeliest provenance, based on her face, limbs, shoulders and colouring. Cortes looks at the original and reads the date at the top of the newspaper, inputs the date and the data re-churns.

'Northern European, she'd be sixty if she were alive now. When this was taken, she was one metre seventy and sixty kilos.'

'Could she be the body in the forest?' says Staffe.

'You were there. I had no time to properly appraise, and I only had the rib cage and shoulders to go on, but everything I know tells me no.'

'But if you had a sample of that skin from under the skeleton's arm and I could get some hair – from a brush or from her clothes in the house in Almagen, you could run a DNA test. That would be proof.'

'You learn fast, Guirri, but I can't work on this case.'

'You could run a DNA test for me.'

Cortes shakes his head. 'My edicts come from on high. You'll have to be satisfied with speculation.'

'You can't let them write the wrong history. Isn't that what they did all those years?'

'I need authorisation to run any test. Everything is logged. So, it becomes impossible for me to help you, Guirri.'

'You'd let Comisario Sanchez impede you?'

Cortes taps at his keyboard again and turns the screen towards Staffe. 'This, I can process.'

The image of the lantern is highly pixellated. Staffe says, 'Peralta sent this to you? Can you make it bigger?'

'This is optimal. Bigger, and you see less.'

Staffe leans in. 'Sanchez?'

'An ambitious police officer in a room with the famous artist and your American; the mad shepherd and your missing woman – what a pretty picture,' he laughs.

*

Manolo is in a cave. He is cross-legged on a dirt floor, blinking up into bright lights.

'Now!' says the voice behind a video camera, mounted on a rickety tripod.

Manolo appears as if he might have been tortured. His voice cracks as he says, 'You have to find me, Guilli. For the truth, you must come home.' The metre of what he says is rigid, like an infant scholar reading from a book that is too difficult. 'Seek your past and you will find me.' The man behind the camera leans forward and hands a newspaper to Manolo who holds it up.

The paper is from two decades ago, and more. It is the front page of *La Lente*. Alongside each other, are portraits of the parents of DI Will Wagstaffe, Leadengate CID.

The lights die and from the dark, a voice says, 'He'll come.'

PART FOUR

Twenty-five

DC Josie Chancellor climbs the stairs up to the top-floor flat. Large black bin liners are piled up outside, smelling of rotted peach. She knocks on the door, tries not to breathe too deep. There's no answer but in her line, you get a knack for knowing when people are in. She knocks again, calls, 'Dave! It's Josie.'

She hears feet, padding, and the door opens away from her. Pulford looks down, rubbing his eyes.

Josie squeezes past him and opens the window that juts from the roof, overlooking the Westway. She sniffs the stale air. 'Take your bins out, why don't you?'

'Mind your own, why don't you?'

Josie looks Pulford up and down. He seems unfamiliar, kind of cut adrift. 'What have you been up to, David? You look washed out.'

He disappears into the bathroom and a tap runs. The living room is spartan. There's a Jim Thomson book on the coffee table, one espresso cup, a brimming ashtray and a stove-top coffee pot. On the dining table, two box files. When he returns, Josie says, 'I didn't know you smoked.'

'I didn't know you cared.' Pulford's hair is wet and his eyes have a little more life in them.

'Jadus Golding is dead.'

Pulford purses his lips, exhales loudly. Eventually, he says, 'Good.'

'Wouldn't you rather we had caught him?'

'Maybe it's best we didn't.'

Josie thinks she knows what he means, but lets it lie. 'Pennington wants us to go down the morgue.'

'Why? I can take your word he's dead.'

'Jasmine Cash is going down to identify the body.'

Pulford rubs his face, says, 'So?'

'He wants a woman there, to comfort her. And he wants someone to police her, too. I thought you'd want to do this.'

*

When they get to the City Morgue, Pulford lingers in the doorway on Raven Lane, pulling on a cigarette. He says to Josie, 'I might say something I'd regret. I'd best stay here.'

'Pennington wants you in there. He said you might be able to glean something. This is a murder case.'

'Not one we'll be breaking our backs to solve.'

'Eyes will be on us.'

'What?'

'It's what Pennington said. "When a cop-killer's killed, the eyes are on us".'

'He didn't kill a cop.'

'You know what I mean.' Josie slips her arm through Pulford's. 'You can control yourself, can't you, sarge?'

They go down into the basement and as they enter the pathologists' domain, the high, slender windows onto Raven Lane proffer a pale, grey light, saturated with the smell of formaldehyde.

Jasmine Cash sits in the corner of the room, hunched beside

a trolley shrouded in white linen. Her jaw is set, her mascara jagging, all dried now. Josie crouches beside her, cajoling. Pulford stays in the doorway, watching as Josie persuades Jasmine to her feet, all the time whispering that it will be over soon and there is nothing to fear. He didn't suffer.

'You don't care. You want him dead,' says Jasmine.

Pulford takes a step back.

'We don't,' says Josie. They are by the trolley now, and with one hand, Josie reaches down, takes a hold of the shroud, peels it back, holding onto Jasmine with her other arm. She feels Jasmine go weak and she clutches her in both arms. 'Is it him? Is it Jadus?'

'You killed him all right. You killed him proper, didn't you?'

Josie hugs Jasmine tight, feels the words, cold on her neck, and when they unclasp, Jasmine is staring at the empty doorway. A last time, she says, 'You killed him.'

*

Yousef sits in his foraged-asbestos home. You can hear the sea and smell the diesel fumes from the *autopista*. They overpower the ozone. He watches his two neighbours make their way to the work truck. They don't acknowledge him any more. The one in the Bulls vest says he brings bad spirits and he should keep away.

A red motorcycle pootles down the dirt track, rests up by the NitroFos drum. The rider turns off the engine and walks directly towards Yousef, beckoning him to stand. The visor is down and Yousef remembers something his mother told him about listening to people's eyes. He stays put.

'Stand!' says the rider, lifting his visor. Beneath, he is wearing sunglasses with silver, reflective lenses.

Yousef shakes his head. There comes a time when they can't harm you any more. The rider unzips his jacket, reaches inside, and Yousef readies himself. He has nothing to give so they must do what they must do.

'They say you're mute,' says the rider, smiling. He pulls out his hand from inside the jacket and the metal glints silver in the sun. The rider crouches, pushing the metal towards him and Yousef can't help but flinch. 'Take this.'

Yousef shakes his head.

The rider reaches for his back pocket, pulls something out and quickly thrusts it at Yousef's face. 'And this.' The second weapon is paper. It is four five-hundred Euro notes. It is as much cash as would pass through Yousef's pockets in a year.

The rider drops the metal into Yousef's lap. It is circular with a hole in its middle. His neighbours have them. They make music.

'You must give this to your friend the Guirri. That is all. I will take you to where he'll come.'

Yousef shakes his head, but grips the notes tightly in his weak fist. The money would buy him drugs to take his pains away. He could send enough to last his sister a year and he could still buy flour and beans and water to take him through the winter.

'You know you are going to come.'

He shakes his head again.

'When you give it him; when we know he has it, there is more. Another thousand.'

Yousef looks at the disc in his lap. He imagines his sister's

238

reaction if he could give her a thousand and his heart is glad for the first time since the shores of El Andalus rose to meet him, three long years ago.

He could go home, without shame.

The rider holds out a hand, to help him up, but Yousef shakes his head. Every bone in his body weeps as he stands of his own accord, but his soul sings.

*

Staffe and Pepa drive back to Almagen, climbing steeply on a narrow road etched lazily into the mountain. Every time a wagon thunders towards them, it takes the breath away, makes the heart stop as they veer towards the precipitous, deathly edges. Neither says a word for half an hour as they spiral higher and higher, up the spurs of the Sierra Nevada towards the top of the Ragua pass – the highest in all Spain.

Near the top, slowly approaching a clearing in the cedar woods, Pepa says, 'Let's stop,' and pulls over to the side, the car lurching to a halt, not six inches from a fall to certain death. Pepa has to get out on the driver's side. She lights up straight away, looks where they have come from – the parched Meseta. 'What a road!'

Staffe says, 'This is all about Agustín.'

'What makes you say that?'

'There are only two roads into Almagen. This might be wild and remote, but it's no place to hide. You can't go missing out here. The gene pool is too small to bury a secret. Someone must know where Agustín is.'

'Morocco is my guess.'

'Closer than that.'

Pepa says, 'The boys won't get their fortune if Astrid is still alive.'

'They'd have to prove she is dead.'

'Or otherwise.'

Staffe nods, wondering if he knows his friend Manolo at all.

*

Yousef sits in the shade of an olive tree. Up the road, he watches each vehicle that wends its way down from the top of the pass. He takes off his shoe and unfolds the four notes. He has never seen such money in his life. He replaces the notes and touches the disc beneath his *burnous*. He is sad the Guirri is in trouble, thinks he has a good heart.

A lorry comes down the steep road and a little red Cinquecento sticks out its nose, trying to get past. Yousef stands. The car fits the bill and he readies himself. The lorry's brakes squeal and it indicates left, to carry on down the main valley, towards the sea. The little red car indicates right and accelerates quickly away from the junction towards Almagen, and him. Yousef steps out, holding his arms high in the air, standing dead still in the middle of the road.

The driver's eyes go wide and the brakes squeal as the car skids. The road is not wide enough to steer round him and Yousef closes his eyes, waits for the impact.

*

'I know this man,' says Staffe. 'What the hell was he doing? He stepped out in front of my car. Why?'

Staffe places a cushion behind Yousef, so he can sit upright on the two-seater sofa beneath the window in his house.

Yousef's eyes flicker and he puts his hand into his *burnous*. His breathing is tight and he gulps at the air to fill his lungs, pulling out the disc. The young woman takes two steps back as if she is expecting a weapon. He feels his brow soften and his breathing eases.

A strange item to treasure, Staffe thinks, watching the man lean forward, wincing as he places the CD delicately upon the arm of the sofa, then kicks off the right of his *babouche* shoes and reaches into its long toe, checks a small, many-folded wad of what appears to be five-hundred euro notes. Now, the African sighs, and even though he is clearly still in great pain, a broad smile opens all the way across his thin face. He reaches for the disc and thrusts it at Staffe.

'What is he doing?' Pepa says.

'He can't speak.'

'How do you know he can't?'

'Look.'

Yousef opens his mouth wide. Pepa puts a hand to her mouth, can't help stare at the pink stem, like a segment of strange, candied fruit, jutting quietly up at the top of his throat. She says, to Staffe, 'How do you know him?'

Staffe busies himself with his laptop at the dining table. He inserts the disc, hunkers over the machine.

'Tell me, Guilli!'

'I met him down in the plastic. He saw the body.'

'And you didn't tell me?'

'It was before we met. I didn't even know Raúl then. Christ, Pepa, I told you what he told me – that they buried the Dane kneeling up and drowned him. It's all I could glean from him, and...'

Pepa grabs his sleeve with one hand, points at the screen with the other. She says, in the quietest voice, 'Look, Guilli, it's a DVD. Isn't that your friend Manolo?'

They each watch the screen.

Yousef squeezes between them, peeking at the man in the cave. He knows him – from that day the Englishman came into his world, changing everything, for ever.

Manolo looks warily to one side of the camera and a hand appears. Manolo reaches out, looks at the piece of paper he is given, then holds the paper to camera.

Staffe sees his past, held up to him, like a mirror, and gasps: his mother and father on the front page of a Spanish newspaper.

He plugs headphones in and moves the cursor over the 'PLAY' button. He taps a key on the laptop with the little finger of his other hand to pause the footage every few seconds, his face screwed up in concentration.

Pepa leaves Staffe to it, takes the African up on the roof where he stands, back perfectly straight, head high, looking across the broad valley through the gap in the Sierra Contraviesa to the V of the Mediterranean. Pepa says on a clear day you can see the Rif mountains in Africa and he nods, his eyes becoming glassy. His chin trembles and Pepa walks towards him and hugs him. He squeezes her tight – as tight as he can, she thinks – but he makes little impression.

She goes back downstairs, tells Staffe that Yousef must stay with them. When he is fit, they will go with him and make sure that he is safe and that his shelter is good for the winter.

Yousef sits cross-legged on the bottom step of the stairs. He shakes his head, gestures with clasped hands to his heart that he is grateful but must be left to his own devices. He doesn't have the language to tell them that he is going all the way home with his unbelievable bounty.

Twenty-six

The early morning rattle from inside Bar Fuente is absent today. Staffe follows Pepa and Yousef inside; only Frog and Salva are in. Upon seeing Staffe, they both frown. Staffe orders *tostadas*, coffees and glasses of fresh orange.

Frog snorts, '*Tostadas*, for a Moor?'

Salva points to a table on the far side of the *comedor*, says he will bring their breakfast across when it is ready. As Yousef and Pepa move off, Salva clamps a tight grip on Staffe's forearm, hisses, 'You shouldn't come here. Not for a while. Wait for the dust to settle.'

'What?'

'You'll lose us all a bundle,' says Frog.

'Shut up!' says Salva. Turning back to Staffe, he says, 'Every week, I have to come up with my pesetas for this place. I can't have it empty.'

'What's happened? Where is everyone?'

'Up at your friend Edu's *matanza*,' says Frog. 'Looks like you and me are the only ones not invited.'

'Salva, tell me what's happened.'

'The *mayordomos* were called up by the Junta and that ghost you dug up in your sister's wood has got everyone running scared. Our plans for the Academy are being put on hold. You should have let it stay put.'

'Fucking bad timing,' says Frog.

'Get out!' shouts Salva, grabbing Frog's half-drunk *sol y sombra*, and when Frog has gone, cursing to himself, Salva says to Staffe, 'And when you're done, Guilli, maybe you'd go, too. I have my business to consider.'

Matanzas are all-day affairs, starting at dawn and involving many men slaying a pig then drinking all day. Frog hadn't quite got it right, because Staffe is invited. The last time he had seen Edu, his friend had positively insisted that he attend.

Pepa is going to the Ayuntamiento in Mecina to use their office suite. On the way, she dropped Yousef back at the house and Staffe at the bottom of the trail up to Edu's.

As Staffe climbs the steep track, his thoughts soon return to the DVD Yousef delivered. He can replay it in his mind now, frame by frame. The running time is barely a minute, but he had pored over it for an hour and in that time, he gleaned two clues as to Manolo's whereabouts.

In the first two seconds of running time, the camera shifts, as if it was bracketed to a ball and socket tripod plate that was being adjusted. As the shot ducked, Staffe had hit 'Pause'. He missed it the first time, only got a glimpse on the third viewing, but the frozen image was certain. On the ground, maybe two feet in front of Manolo, was a pine cone. They use pine cones up in the mountains instead of firelighters. They burn just fine and cost nothing.

And at the end of the short film, Manolo had put down the newspaper, which rustled. He had sighed and a moment of silence followed, punctuated by a single strike of a cowbell, so quiet you wouldn't hear it unless you were listening for it. But Staffe was – holding his breath and with his hands clamped over the earphones. It would not have been a cow, but a goat

– a bell around its neck, should it stray from the flock. It is all Staffe needs, to restart his search for Manolo.

On the final hundred yards up to Edu's *cortijo* – pig squealing and drunks baying – he takes a hard look up the mountain to where they take goats for summer and prime fires with pine cones. He wonders if those clues had been too readily uncovered, whether it is a subtly laid trap, luring him to Manolo's *cortijo*. But he has to go, to get hold of Manolo's copy of Gustav Hesse's will, and translate it.

From the shade of a fig tree just beneath the road that Raúl Gutiérrez drove along, en route to his death, Staffe watches a pig held down on a bench at the front of Edu's *cortijo*. Each of its trotters is tied taut to iron rings. Edu is smoking a fat cigar and rolling a smouldering bushel of thyme across the pig's back, shoulders and legs, singeing the hairs.

Staffe counts thirteen men gathered around the pig, each clutching a tumbler of spirit, each with a wagging cigarette of black tobacco. The air is thick with profanity and advice; the women gather by the doorway, ready to boil up the chitterlings and make *morcilla* and *salchichas*. The men will butcher the main cuts, set about the curing of the *jamones* and the creation of *chorizo*.

Edu sharpens his knife a last time and cuts the pig's throat. Every last drop of blood is drained. One of the thirteen does the rounds, pouring hooched *aguardiente*. Edu chain-smokes his way through the butchery, employing a large-bladed knife, then a cleaver, and a saw. The women ferry the cuts inside and before long, every last bit of the pig, from its ears all the way to its trotters have been harvested. Edu stands over the remains, quite exhausted. Someone hands him a beer which he swigs down in one.

Staffe moves from out of the shade of the fig tree towards the carousing herd. One by one, as they clock him, they fall silent. He holds out his bottle of Laphroaig to Edu who stands steadfast with a cleaver in one hand, his beer bottle in the other.

Most of the men know Staffe. They would nod or say '*hola*' down in the *campo* or on a *paseo*. Now, they blank him.

'You came,' says Edu, forcing a smile.

'You told me to bring a fancy whisky.' Staffe reaches out with the bottle. 'This is the best I could do.'

'My hands are full,' says Edu, motioning with his bloody cleaver.

'He's got some nerve,' says a man Staffe doesn't know.

Staffe slowly looks each of the thirteen men in the eye. He says, steady as he can, 'What was I supposed to do – let it lie? Fill it back in and pretend it never happened?'

'You could have waited.'

'And how long were you going to wait, Edu?'

'Wait for what?'

Staffe wants to ask him about his niece and how he came to be a pall-bearer at Barrington's funeral, but he knows this is not the time. 'I'm not going to conceal the truth. I thought those days were over.' In these parts, plenty of folk got lucky from the war and its aftermath under Franco, some building a wealth first hand; others growing fat on the bacon their fathers cured – like Edu. But, again, Staffe realises this is not the time for home truths. He wonders how many of this thirteen might know already exactly what happened in those woods.

'And anyway, if discovering that body is going to jeopardise the Academy, that should suit you.'

'I don't know what you mean,' says Edu, lowering his voice.

'That's what you said. You didn't want people coming here, disturbing the way things are.'

Edu regards his one-time friend like a firework that has fizzled and not gone off. He takes a step towards him. 'I think you got me wrong.' He reaches out to Staffe, dropping his bottle. It smashes at his feet, but he keeps hold of the cleaver. With his free hand in a fist, Edu takes a final step, all the time looking Staffe in the eye; a look Staffe hasn't seen before. He brings the hand down, opening its fist and slapping the Englishman on the shoulder: heavily, decisively. 'Let's drink. Today is a day for forgetting,' says Edu, taking the Laphroaig from his English friend.

'Tomorrow, we remember,' says one of the men. One by one, the thirteen laugh, smoothly reprising their drunkenness. They forget well up here.

*

Pepa presses 'Send' and feels the tug as her copy is spirited into her editor's inbox. The story is out of the bag and has ceased to be truly hers. But this tug is not so great. This article, on Barrington's Alpujarran legacy, is the thinnest crust to the real story and she doesn't care what the editor does with it.

The clerk comes across with a glass of tea and for a while, Pepa relaxes, lets recent events ebb, flow, and soon her fingers bring up the *La Lente* archive and she types 'Wagstaffe' and 'Gutiérrez' into 'Search'. She thinks what good friends those two men might have been had they known each other better. The search is entered and to her astonishment, there is a result. No, two results.

These men, whom the Englishman swears came together entirely by chance, are united by two pieces which Raúl Gutiérrez had written. The first is from the day after the Omagh bombing by the IRA, which claimed Spanish lives. She remembers it being on the news. The piece is a double-spread feature on terrorism and the flimsiness of the Basque case for nationalism. The killing of the Spaniards in Omagh resulted in a reappraisal of ETA's activities, and the main body of Raúl's piece is an assault on the duality of these campaigns for national identity. As the IRA drew innocent Spaniards into their bloody activities, so had ETA, killing three British tourists in an attack on a restaurant in San Sebastian.

On the right-hand page, there is a picture of Paul and Enid Wagstaffe together. The father wears a panama hat, smiling straight into camera. The mother makes a faltering connection with the lens. Part of her seems to be elsewhere. Pepa thinks how much Will is like his mother.

Raúl makes a passing reference to the children: Marie, a gifted musician and William in his first year at Oxford. Both William and Marie abandoned those paths.

She clicks on the second article. Santi Etxebatteria held a junior position on a council for the Basque Nationalist party, then stood for election to the Regional Congress. He failed by a narrow minority and a month later, his cousin, Justo, died in police custody. Justo was a schoolteacher with a young family and was also a party activist. The day after Santi buried his cousin, he resigned his post on the council and retreated into the hills – to get trained.

Santi Etxebatteria's *pièce de résistance* was the Donostia bombing. Apart from the Wagstaffes and another English tourist, Santi's expertly crafted bomb killed a group of four students from Austria, an elderly couple from Burgos and two waiters, one a Spaniard from Galicia and the other an Euskadi. One of his own. A fully paid-up party member.

After Santi's day in the sun, he was never seen again. Family, party, ETA and the police all deemed him inactive; disappeared, though he was on Prime Minister Aznar's list of people to talk to after the March 2004 Madrid train bombings. Nobody knows where Santi Etxebatteria stands these days, let alone where he lies low, but for some reason, Raúl Gutiérrez seemed to have his number.

'Can I print this, please?' Pepa asks the clerk.

The clerk nods enthusiastically, eager to please. She is only twenty, and has all her life ahead. Pepa isn't even thirty, but today she feels old.

'Are you finished yet?' asks the clerk.

'One more thing,' says Pepa. 'I might be a while. Is that OK?'

The clerk beams a broad smile, says she will make more tea. It is as if she has all the time in the world.

Twenty-seven

This year's *lomo al horno* has been butchered, cooked and eaten and last year's old wine, too fermented, too damn strong, is drunk. The thirteen men have found shade, and siesta. Staffe and Edu are the last ones sitting; Edu carving off chunks of his cousin's ewe's cheese. They have it with a Contraviesa *reserva* that Staffe knows is thirty euros a pop.

He also knows Edu doesn't work and because he signs on, he has to do a bit of work on the roads when they fall into disrepair. At Christmas and *fiestas*, the council put him in a gang to erect the lights. He sells the odd bean to the co-operative, too, and he drives a brand-spanking Land Cruiser, favours Anejo rum in his *cuba libres*. Even without his visits to the Russian girls down on the coast, it doesn't add up. Staffe remembers what his bastard niece, Guadalupe, had said about Edu not having anything to do with Barrington because he couldn't make any money out of him. And how he parks the blame for where his life went wrong: the shame that was visited upon him, courtesy of Barrington.

'This is fine stuff,' says Staffe, sipping his wine respectfully.

'I know the grower. He does me a deal. It would be wasted on this lot.'

'You lead a grand life for a peasant,' Staffe jokes.

Edu laughs. 'You are a friend, Guilli. But you need to tread more carefully. The people here will forget, but you have to meet them half way.'

'You're right, Edu. Wise words. Friends and family are important.'

'The most important thing.'

'I told you about my parents, didn't I?'

'A terrible thing.'

'I told Manolo, too.' Staffe cuts off a chunk of ewe's cheese with the goat's-head knife, the one that was shoved into his mouth in Sacromonte. He offers it to Edu, off the blade.

Edu stares at the knife, says nothing and takes the cheese.

'That journalist, Raúl, who drove past here just a few minutes before he died, was going to see the man who murdered them.'

'My God, it can be a small world.'

'He tracked him down to a place in Extremadura.'

'Have some more wine.'

'You didn't tell Raúl about my parents, did you, Edu?' He takes a sip of the wine. 'I'm sorry. You didn't know him, did you? I must be getting drunk.'

Edu wraps his hand around the goat's head of the knife. 'How is Manolo? We feared he might have done something stupid.' He cuts a slab of cheese, hands it to Staffe.

'You're not exactly friends, are you?'

'We got along all right. In small villages you can know too few people. Know them too well.'

'How well did you know his mother?'

'I didn't care for the way she carried on.'

'I've heard some ripe old tales about what went on up here with Barrington and the American.' He nods up towards Jackson's *cortijo*. 'I don't suppose that reflected too well on you and the family.'

'It was nothing to do with me.'

'I suppose they kept it secret.'

'You and your secrets! Just because you don't know something doesn't make it a secret.'

'I saw Immaculada the other day.'

'She doesn't see anybody.'

'You must have hated Barrington.'

'Not at all.'

'So you have forgiven your sister?'

'It's not a question of that.'

'But you carried his coffin.'

He says, quick as light, 'Immaculada was too small to carry, so she asked me. What was I supposed to do?'

'How long is it since you have seen her? She's ill, Edu. Very ill. I know what it's like when we leave things unsaid.'

'You could have fooled me.'

'It's terrible when the words are trapped and the people who they are meant for aren't here any more. It must be like that for Rubio.'

'His wife's not dead. She was never found.'

'Found?'

'She left, that's all. She should never have come here in the first place.'

'You must wonder what happened to Astrid. Such a beautiful woman. I bet someone knows where she went.'

A car grinds up the hill, throaty.

Staffe puts down his empty glass, stands up and stretches, theatrically. 'Funny, Raúl coming up here, and planning to visit

Extremadura to see the man who killed my parents. It's strange, how things connect.'

'Maybe they are just two actions.'

'It would establish a hold over me, keep me in my place,' he laughs, 'if there was a chance I could catch up with that murderer, Etxebatteria.'

Edu looks over Staffe's shoulder and his face slips a little. The Guardia Land Rover comes to a halt and Quesada gets out, tweaking his moustache. 'Here. Have your knife back. I'm going to make coffee for this herd of old goats.'

*

Pepa is out of the loop. There is finite information in the world and this is what journalists are up against: chasing the same things as each other. Every now and again, you get a step ahead. That's what Pepa has done, but now she must look through the other end of the telescope: see what everyone else has seen while her eyes have been focused on the past.

She is reading the news agencies' feeds for the last week, and keeping a particularly keen eye on anything to do with the death of Raúl Gutiérrez and the murdered Dane.

Nothing tasty emerges. Most of the 'noise' around Almería focuses on the council's inability to borrow funds. Talk is of rubbish piling up on the streets and no *fiesta* lights at Christmas. Perhaps Pepa chose a good week to be away.

She clicks on 'Today's streaming' and waits for the files to load. The clerk smiles at her. All morning, Pepa is the only person who has been in the Ayuntamiento.

Pepa has one finger on the function key, another on 'Page

down' and the minutes fly by. She pauses briefly to read that fifty-seven minutes ago the head of the council in Roquetas del Mar called for the acceleration of legalising illegal homes. She presses her finger again and the headlines flurry.

Then her fingers pull away from the keyboard, as if they are scalded. Pepa catches her breath, double clicks on the headline, gets a one-paragraph summary.

Forty-four minutes ago, police in Mojácar reported the death of a foreigner. Unidentified, the body was washed up onto rocks between Mojácar and Garrucha. The local *brigada* said the body was handed to the police in Almería as they had received fresh intelligence about hashish trafficking from Africa and were liaising with forces all along the coast, as far as Algeciras.

Pepa asks the clerk if she can print again, and the clerk leaps into action, hovers over the printer and hands the pages to her precious client.

Going down the stairs, intent upon collecting the Englishman, Pepa considers whether she has missed the real story here: another foreign body on the coast. Narcotics are in the air, and foreigners, too. The farmers are fighting back against the golf developers. Should she be down there; not up here?

*

The clerk sits at the work station. The journalist's seat is still warm and she looks out of the window, watches her car rollick over the speed bumps, then clicks the computer's 'Print history' icon. She hits the print command and back at her own desk, Señorita Sanchez reads each of the pieces once, then calls her uncle, returning to the warm seat in the window, waiting for him to pick up.

*

'As I remember him, Agustín was everything Manolo was not,' says Quesada, accepting a glass of Laphroaig.

'You talk as if he is a thing of the past,' says Staffe.

'That boy *is* a thing of the past, as far as we are concerned. He went back to Germany to live with his grandparents. They wanted him to go to a German university. Once Rubio went to the funny farm, he was never coming back.'

'Wasn't he here a few weeks ago?'

'If he was, he behaved himself. I didn't see him.'

'What do you think happened to Astrid Cano, *brigada*?'

'She was out of her element here. She found something that suited her better.'

'And left her sons?'

'She was a strange woman.'

'Comisario Sanchez would have known her. Wasn't he in Almagen in those days?'

'He lived in Mecina, but he was based here for a while.'

'So he'd have known Raúl.'

'You should ask him about it.' Quesada smiles, as if he has won a point.

'And he left soon after Astrid disappeared.'

'People come and people go, Señor Wagstaffe.'

'Why exactly did Sanchez leave Almagen?'

'Look where he is now. That kind of ambition needs a bigger cage.'

Staffe thinks that 'cage' is a strange word to employ. He studies the unflappable, small-town Quesada. 'Was Sanchez in on the paintings, *brigada*?'

'You shouldn't ask me such things. A *comisario* "in" on something? Please. I like you, Inspector, but you shouldn't place me in such a position.'

'Barrington reinvented himself late in life and produced his best work. That would attract Astrid; and Jackson, too. Almagen must have been quite a place back then.'

'I'll tell you what I know, Inspector.'

'Please do.'

'I know Jackson Roberts trafficked drugs.'

'He gave you information, and you turned a blind eye to him and built a career . . .'

'Please!' Quesada takes a deep breath. 'How do you get on if you never listen? I said I know Roberts dealt drugs and I know your brother-in-law was here years before you paid for your sister's place. Paolo de Venuto could be in custody like that!' He clicks his fingers. 'I have a file on him this thick.' He holds his hand out, as if placing it on a child's head. 'And he's growing weed up there now and your pregnant sister knows all about it.'

'You haven't arrested him.'

'Maybe he and Jackson knew what was in those woods when Jackson got him to buy the land. Maybe you knew. But the important thing for you to understand is if I know these things, then others do, too.'

'You mean Comisario Sanchez.'

'I can't answer that,' says Quesada, closing his eyes and crossing his hands in front of his face, signalling that his patience is exhausted.

They each take another draught of the good stuff. Staffe waits, eventually says, 'With your contacts – would you be able to find out where Santi Etxebatteria is? Could you help me?'

'That's a very uncertain world you'd be entering, Inspector.' He smiles, points at Pepa, walking quickly towards him. Knowing that she comes bearing news, Quesada walks past Staffe, says under his breath. 'There's another body. Be careful, Inspector.'

Twenty-eight

Pepa is looking across the sierra through the telescope on El Nido's terrace. She breaks off to call Staffe to hurry up. 'We have to get to Mojácar.'

Inside Marie's *cortijo*, Staffe watches Harry pack his small world into a medium-sized suitcase.

'I don't see why we have to move down to the village,' says Marie.

'The baby is coming. What if there are complications?' says Staffe.

'Complications? You think I'm in danger up here, don't you? Why would I be in danger in my own home?'

Paolo sits on the edge of the bed, staring at the floor. Marie knows something is wrong because Paolo isn't high and he seems happy they're going down to the village. She says, 'Are you packing, Paolo?'

'I have things to do here. I'll follow you.'

'You have to come, Marie,' says Staffe, kneeling beside her. He wraps his arms around her. 'Please just do it. All I want is for no harm to come to any of you.'

'You're going to have to tell me what's happening, Will.'

'I can't.'

'Then I won't go.'

'I want to go!' shouts Harry.

Staffe reaches into his pocket and unfolds the printout of

Raúl's article on the Omagh and Donostia bombings. He hands it to Marie.

She gasps; puts a hand to her mouth, and slowly, her eyes become glassy and red. But she begins to smile. 'I haven't ever seen this photograph before. Mum looks like you, Will. I always thought you looked like Dad. But you were hers, weren't you?'

'Was I?'

Marie reads the piece, says quietly, so Harry can't hear, 'Gutiérrez. He's the one who died. He wrote this years ago and then he comes up to our mountain and he drives his car off a bridge. Christ, Will. And there's more, isn't there? He was up here while you were ill, I told you I'd seen him snooping. And that body in the woods. It's not from the war, is it?'

'You and Harry need to take my house until the baby is born. We'll know more soon, and everything will be all right. I promise.'

Marie wants to believe Staffe, the way you always want to believe everything your father says to you. She hugs her brother tight, says, 'I love you, Will. You know that. But it's not your promise to make, is it? You can't promise everything will be all right.' She looks at Harry, who despite everything is suddenly happy behind his eyes.

A loud knock resounds on the door.

'I have to get going,' calls Pepa. 'And I've seen goats. Up by Manolo's *cortijo*.'

'I heard bells the day before yesterday,' says Marie. 'Manolo must be back. He'll be taking them up the Silla Montar. You're practically in Granada once you get over there.'

Many years ago, Barrington convened long parties for his

London set: artists and novelists; musicians and poets. In his memoirs, he claims to have walked from Granada to Almagen in a single day with his friend and playboy, Wesley John. The second day Staffe spent in Almagen, a young, fresh-faced aspiring writer had collapsed through the doors of Bar Fuente on the stroke of midnight. He said, over and again, 'Fucking Barrington. Bastard liar.' The young writer had set off from Granada at three o'clock that morning, in the steps of Barrington. His fact was Barrington's fiction.

Staffe looks at the Silla Montar, imagines some day climbing it, ambling down into the great city – the opposite way the last Moor had come. He remembers what the Moor's wife had said when he wept salt tears at leaving his beloved Granada. 'Don't cry like a woman for what you couldn't fight for like a man.' He says to Pepa, 'I have to go up there.'

'To Manolo's *cortijo*? You think that's where they're holding him? It's probably a trap.'

'There's something up there I need to get.'

'Gustav's will? I bet it's not all that's waiting for you.'

'I have no choice. Manolo is my friend, Pepa.'

'You can't be sure of that and I can't come with you. I have to get down to Mojácar, try and get to see that new body.'

'There's no point trying to persuade him,' says Marie, hugging her brother. 'He won't be told – until it's too late.'

*

The goat bells knock out a soundtrack to the last hundred yards of Staffe's climb up to Manolo's place. Smoke rises from

261

inside the *cortijo* and two red Bultaco scrambling bikes lean against the goat shed.

Staffe needs to get his head straight before he goes in. All the way up, he has been trying to work out what enticed Raúl up here two weeks before the Dane even died in the plastic. Could it be something to do with himself and Santi Etxebatteria?

He pictures Etxebatteria buying the components for the bomb and staking out the restaurant; setting the device's timer for the precise moment his parents were murdered and then, with the smell of charred skin still thick on the Vizcaya seafront, penning his letter claiming responsibility.

Months earlier, when Etxebatteria had lost his cherry, shooting a policeman in the head at point-blank range, he sent the widow a letter, asking if he could have his bullet back. Now, wanting to rebuild his life, Etxebatteria has said he is sorry, and the idea that he is granted some kind of amnesty makes Staffe more angry than ever: to think that such a man might access the motors of repentance.

Staffe feels the bile. He wraps himself around it, keeps it safe, like a mother would her young. He looks up to the tree line. Beyond the *cortijo*, there are pines, and cones; and to the right, beneath the Silla Montar, he sees the opening to a cave. They are here.

*

Pepa is up on Staffe's roof, looking down into the valley. A couple of houses away, a pretty woman pegs out washing, a daughter at her skirts. Pepa shouts across to ask if she has seen a Moor in the village.

Consuela points into the valley, says, 'Where the almonds stop. He's by the third orange tree.'

Pepa narrows her eyes, scans the landscape. Eventually, she sees Yousef, shouts to Consuela, 'Where is he going?'

'Along the Camino Barrington.'

'Where does it lead?'

Consuela says quietly, but in such a way that the sound carries, clear as turquoise shallows, 'To the sea, of course.' Then Harry appears, starts talking to the little girl. They sit on the low wall on the edge of the roof, forty perilous feet above the narrow street below, holding hands. In a different world.

Pepa's phone chimes, indicating that she has a signal and she immediately leafs through her address book, highlighting 'Jesús'. He picks up straight away, says, 'Three guesses why you call me now.'

'Have you heard about the body down in Mojácar?' she says.

'Why else would you call?'

'You said you'd take me for dinner.'

'Bad timing,' says Jesús.

Pepa imagines somebody coming into the room he is in. 'Are you unable to talk?'

'That's right.'

Pepa constructs questions to which he can answer 'yes' or 'no'. 'Have you seen photographs of the body?'

'No.'

'But is he a foreigner and a druggie – like Jens Hansen?'

'From what I hear.'

'I'll be there about midnight.'

'I'm not sure,' he says.

'In the *parador* and then we'll go to the morgue.'

'I'm not so sure I can.'

'You've got to get me into that morgue, Jesús. You're in-volved! Manolo's your cousin. He's in danger and it's something to do with . . .'

The line falls dead. No signal.

*

Staffe knocks on the door to Manolo's *cortijo*. He does it lightly and the weaker part of him wishes the place empty. He presses his ear to the wood, hears someone being berated. He thinks it is Jackson's voice and he walks around the building, tries to peer in through the windows but the shutters are closed.

He treads lightly back to the main door and gently levers the latch. It relents easily. He steps inside and nobody is in the main room. The sounds are coming from the side room. It is defin-itely Jackson's voice. Staffe feels for the goat's head knife, runs fingers over its handle in his pocket.

Staffe recalls the last time he was here and visualises where Gustav's will is. There is a trunk in the left-hand room and he should try to retrieve it now, but he hears a louder noise.

'My God,' says Jackson.

Staffe peers into the amber-lit gloom. Jackson is sitting on the bed, his clothes covered in blood. The bed is crimson and lying across his lap is Manolo, his head in Jackson's arms and staring straight at Staffe. His tongue is hanging from his mouth, throat slit, and Staffe steps into the room, his heart ra-cing, his legs weak, his voice cracking as he says, 'What have you done, Jackson?'

'I found him like this. He was already dead when I got here.'

264

'I walked all the way here and nobody passed me. I didn't see a soul the whole time.' Staffe's legs are weak and he sinks to the floor, feels sick.

Jackson's eyes are wild, but he talks quietly, 'He had no kind of life, not really. He didn't have a chance. Not after what happened.' He gently slides his legs from underneath Manolo's body and eases him down onto the blood-drenched sheets. He stands, walks towards the chest beneath the window and picks up a knife by the tip of its blade. 'This is what did for him.'

Staffe looks on, open-mouthed as Jackson comes towards him, holding the knife by its blade. The handle is awfully familiar: a goat's head carved from wood.

Jackson says, 'You seen this before?'

'One just like it was stuffed into my mouth. That was you, wasn't it?'

'You really have it in for me, don't you?'

'If you didn't kill him, who did?'

'You're the fucking detective.' Jackson walks past Staffe into the living room and lights up a cigarette.

Staffe says, 'You know Manolo and Agustín stood to inherit a fortune. Their grandfather is dead.'

'When did I turn from being a bad sonofabitch into a goddam oracle?'

'But they would only gain if their mother is dead.'

'Which she's not.'

'So where is she? And what did she do wrong, Jackson?'

'Plenty. It was all fucked up. But I don't know where she is.'

'Didn't they bury Astrid up in Paolo's woods? Isn't that why you got him to buy the land – to keep an eye on it. You have a hold over him.'

'When you say "they", who exactly is "they"?'

'I can't say who killed her, but I know you were having an affair with her, and Rubio knew it.'

'I loved that woman, with all my heart but never quite enough. And yes, Rubio knew. But it was all right, it really was. We got along.'

'Maybe Rubio killed her. I saw a film of the four of you. Or did Manolo find out? Or Agustín?'

'Agustín?' Jackson looks ruffled.

'You were all onto a nice little number. Getting fat off the art.'

'That was Barrington's game.'

'But then he lost it. And you were left with a world-renowned artist who couldn't do it any more. But you can paint, can't you, Jackson?'

'Nice of you to say so.'

'That painting of Gador in your *cortijo*, it's one of yours. I've seen one similar.'

'There are no others like it.'

'I bumped into your friend Yolanda. She knows an interesting item when she sees it.'

Jackson walks around the table. 'Knew it, you bastard. You didn't think you could get away with just taking it, did you? I need that canvas. What you've done is theft.'

Staffe keeps an eagle eye on Jackson Roberts, puts his hand in his pocket, feels the goat's head. 'Is that why you lured me here – to get your precious canvas?'

Jackson goes into the bedroom. Staffe calls to him, 'Passing your stuff off as Barrington's is fraud.'

From here, Manolo looks as if he might be sleeping off a heavy one. In the low light, the sheets look brown.

Jackson comes back into the room, with the murder weapon. He places it heavily on the table. 'I need that painting, Wagstaffe. You're going to give it to me.'

'The last Barrington? Why don't you just knock up another?'

'Don't be a prick. He's dead.'

'What you mean is nowadays they can carbon-date when a piece was painted. Your game is up. Just one left, hey, from when he was alive. Before, there was plenty to go round. I bet you couldn't paint them quick enough.'

'You prick.'

'Was Astrid onto you?' Staffe turns, to look at dead Manolo. 'Or Manolo?'

'I didn't kill him. I got here half an hour ago and it was already done.'

'You were holding him all that time?'

Jackson, drenched in Manolo's blood, holds out his arms, like Christ. 'I saw him grow into a man. His father is a friend, for God's sake.'

'And you loved his mother. But you used him to lure me up here.' Staffe reaches into his pocket, takes a grip of his goat's-head knife.

'I didnt say that.'

'You made that film.'

Jackson sees him, shoots out a hand and grabs the handle of a bull-whip from the dresser. Staffe feels a terrible pain on his neck and in the same instant hears the clap from the whip.

The leather tail is around Staffe's throat and as he tries to pull it free with both hands, his own knife clatters to the stone floor. Jackson walks backwards, tightening the grip on Staffe's throat and Staffe has to follow, banging into the table, squealing because his windpipe is more and more constricted. Jackson stops. 'You pick up tricks in war, Inspector. Once, in Vietnam, it took a slope two shoulders and a knee before he coughed up where his best friend was. But he coughed up. So, we'll get there.' He drops the handle of the whip, takes a step forward, and gets Staffe's arm up his back. Expertly, he twists the shoulder joint to the very cusp of dislocation. 'Now, tell me your theory, my friend.'

Staffe's throat burns. 'Barrington had lost it and you tried painting one for him. It was good. He worked on them with you. To be safe, you sold them abroad – to known collectors. Barrington gave the provenance and you split the money. Enough for everyone. Then Astrid got greedy.'

'But she was a rich heiress. Remember?'

'She got greedy for you. She wanted to be with you and threatened to expose you all. Any one of you could have killed her.'

Jackson says, 'Nice theory, but you don't know she's dead, and as for that body in your sister's woods, it's a man – a ghost from the war.'

'We'll see about that, but what about Raúl? Was he onto you?'

'Where is my painting?'

'Is it the last Barrington?'

'Where is it?' Jackson has a tight grip on Staffe's bent arm. 'I'll fucking break you, man.'

'Who killed that man in the plastic . . .'

'I'll do it. Believe me.'

268

Staffe knows Jackson will do it. 'You were near the bridge when they cut Raúl out of his car. I saw you up the mountain on your motorbike. Someone stopped Raúl on that bridge and my guess is they struck him; killed him and tried to stop the blood by using a rag. They put him back in his car and belted him in.'

'I told you – I'll do it. I'll break your fucking arm.'

'Raul never wore a seat belt.' Staffe feels the squeeze. He holds his breath. He read somewhere once – or did someone tell him? – if you hold your breath, if you starve the blood and heart and brain of oxygen, and you suffer great shock, you can . . .

He closes his eyes and the weight of Jackson on him feels more distant. He hears the crunch – a gristly, softened crack, dampened by ligament. His arm falls loose. The pain is white hot and something in Staffe shuts down. He hears his name, far away, and a harsh dark descends, with Jackson saying, 'You'll never know, you'll never know . . .'

*

On the strike of ten, Pepa fires up the Cinquecento. The rolled-up canvas is on the back seat, still wrapped up in the rug. She looks around the *plazeta* a last time, wonders where Staffe has got to. But there is no time to wait for him, she has to meet Jesús.

Twenty-nine

Standing over the Englishman, Quesada mops his brow. He can see immediately, from the splay of his arm, that Inspector Wagstaffe has suffered a dislocation to his shoulder, that the pain had caused him to pass out.

The *brigada* turns Staffe onto his back, holding the arm as he does. He sits on the floor and places one boot under the Englishman's jaw and the other against his ribcage, then he takes a firm hold of the arm and pulls, slowly finding the socket with the orphaned ball of the joint. It clicks back, re-housed. Staffe grunts and his eyes flicker and his good arm shoots across, holds his bad one. And he howls.

Quesada says, 'I told you to be careful, my friend.' He hands him three 600 mg ibuprofen tablets and a glass of water and watches as Staffe warily accepts, scrutinises, then swallows them.

'Roberts did this to you?' says Quesada.

'Did you see him?'

'Were there two Bultacos here when you arrived?'

'Yes.'

'There's only one now. I think I saw him going over the top.'

'The Silla Montar? He'll kill himself!'

'We should be that lucky,' says Quesada.

'Would it suit you to have him out of the way?'

'What makes you say such a thing?'

'You had Roberts over a barrel. He was bringing drugs up from Africa but you came to an arrangement, arresting people up and down the chain. It's how you climbed the ladder.'

'We bring as much justice as we can, not thinking we can win, but aiming to lose by as little as possible.'

'Which just so happened to free Jackson to pass off his paintings as Barringtons. They made small fortunes.'

Quesada runs his thumb and forefinger down along his moustache. He smooths it in this manner a dozen times. Then he shakes his head. 'Fuck me.'

'What?'

'For years, I've tried to work out what was going on. I knew they were up to something.'

Staffe thinks, 'They?' He says, 'Astrid worked it out and tried to blackmail them. That's why they killed her.'

'You can't be sure she is dead. We've had it confirmed it's not Astrid Cano in that wood.' Quesada puts on a rubber glove and holds up the goat's-head knife. Its blade is smeared with blood. 'Thirteen people saw you with this at Edu's *matanza*. And so did I.'

'There is another one. I swear. They're identical and whoever had it killed Manolo. I saw Jackson with it.'

'I am a simple man, Inspector, so I have to look everywhere. I work slowly and I do not jump from A to C. Come with me.'

Staffe nurses his bad arm by supporting the elbow. The pain-killers are beginning to kick in, but he still feels woozy from the pain. He straightens up, feels better now that he is standing. Following Quesada into the bedroom, he is surprised that the *brigada* has turned his back, has left the knife on the table.

Once in the bedroom, Quesada goes to the far side of the

bed, careful not to disturb the sheets or any of the articles on the floor. He takes a torch from his pocket, illuminates the stone floor and beckons Staffe. He explains where Manolo must have been killed, his throat slit and left to bleed to death, face down. To the right, a strage pattern of blood, away from the main pooling of blood. They crouch, as one. Together, they softly say the word that has been spelt out, by a single finger, in Manolo's own blood: 'Edu'.

Staffe stares at the body, then at the name in blood. He says to Quesada. 'Was Edu involved? My God. He hated Barrington.'

'All he ever really had was his family's reputation. First, Barrington defiling poor Edu's sister. Then Manolo must have wanted the truth out.'

'The truth about the paintings?'

'The truth about his mother,' says Staffe. 'So he pulled my strings. Can we go through his pockets?'

Quesada hands Staffe a clutch of clear evidence bags. 'I've done it.'

Staffe examines the items: a picture of Astrid, embracing Manolo. He must have been fourteen: just before she 'went missing'. Over a thousand euros in large-denomination notes. Finally, a small roll of high-strength baling twine.

'You have seen that before?' says Quesada.

Staffe nods, remembering how the body in the plastic had been trussed into its kneeling position, the twine cutting into the neck. 'Do you know anything about the other druggie who was washed up?'

'In Mojácar?' says Quesada. He shakes his head.

'Manolo was my friend,' says Staffe, breaking down. 'I'd like a moment alone.'

Quesada takes back the evidence bags. 'A moment.'

The instant Quesada leaves, Staffe rushes into the next room. He steps over his friend's body, saying a prayer but he keeps on moving, lifting the lid on the chest and rummaging quickly for Gustav Hesse's will. It's not there. Outside, the horn toots. He empties the chest, checks again, then hears footsteps coming back into the *cortijo*. He piles everything back into the trunk and leaves, none the wiser, but knowing for certain that whatever is in that will, is worth concealing.

*

Staffe knows that Pepa will be on her way to Mojácar, and would have taken the last Barrington. He leans the red Bultaco against the gatepost of Edu's *cortijo*, watches the lights to Quesada's Land Rover dim and die. Getting out of his Land Rover, Quesada withdraws his pistol from its holster. He has a tremor in his voice when he says, 'I have never killed a man.'

'You surprise me,' says Staffe.

'Have you?'

'No.' Even with all the death that has crossed Staffe's path, he is still unable to imagine what it demands – to take a life. Save one. Save Santi Etxebatteria. So often, he has fantasised that bloody murder.

'But you'd like to? Let me warn you, my friend, Etxebatteria is not to be touched. ETA have surrendered arms and it's not the time to rattle his cage.'

Standing on the terrace, Staffe looks at Edu's door. He thinks back to the long, lazy afternoons they spent here, when Edu would tell him about his crops and the Contraviesa wine. And he thinks, too, about all the more important things that Edu never talked about: his sister; her lover – the man whose body he carried to be buried. He says to Quesada, 'Why did Edu carry Barrington's body at his funeral, if he hated him so?'

'Perhaps he was happy to see the man buried. Or maybe he did it for his sister. I prefer the second option. And he is from a proud family. His father was the mayor and his father before him. As you know, all he wanted was to be mayor himself.' Quesada lifts the latch. 'But if he was involved in some forgery scam, we'll find out.' He kicks open the door and follows the barrel of his gun into Edu's *cortijo*.

Inside, it is dark and Staffe hesitates. Two flashes light up the interior of Edu's *cortijo*. He thinks Quesada's pistol has fired twice. The sound is deafening and Staffe throws himself to the floor, screams as he jolts his bad shoulder. Quesada is breathing heavily and he fires another single shot, illuminating a body, swinging from the poplar beams above where the dining table used to be. Then the body falls. It slaps the stone floor like a beast in a butcher's back room.

Quesada flicks on the light and Staffe, prostrate on the cold floor, looks Edu in the eye. His face is blue, his eyes are open wide and his tongue is fat and black.

'You were firing at the rope,' says Staffe. 'Good shot.'

Quesada sits heavily upon a straw-seated chair and sighs. 'How the hell will I account for all this?'

*

Jesús approaches Pepa, looking over his shoulder. He says, 'They're moving the body in the morning. I don't think we'll get to see it before it goes to Almería.'

'You have to do better than that, Jesús.' Pepa leans into him, whispering. 'I think that body is your *primo*.'

'Manolo!'

She puts an arm around his shoulder, her hand on the V of hair at the nape of his neck. 'We have to find out.'

'I don't even know the people at the morgue down here,' says Jesús, his voice cracking.

Pepa keeps her hand on his neck. 'You have to try and get us in there.'

'I have to make a call first,' says Jesús, moving towards the lobby of the *parador*.

'What's wrong with your mobile?'

'A landline will be better. I don't want anybody getting their wires crossed.'

Pepa doesn't quite understand why he is being so cautious – who it is that he doesn't want to catch the scent – but she is pleased he is gone and she hastens to his car, intent. When she is done scrutinising the contents of his glove compartment, she gets the rolled-up rug from the Cinquecento's back seat and waits for him by his car. So far, she has everything she needs.

*

Staffe rubs his shoulder and looks at the Bultaco. Riding it down from Manolo's *cortijo* to Edu's had been the worst of it, surely. He pops another Ibuprofen.

'I wish I could give you a lift, but as you can imagine, I have some paperwork to get into.' Quesada walks to Staffe, slaps him on his good shoulder and wraps his big arms around him, squeezes him tight, and says, 'Thank God, we can have some peace, finally. You have done well, my friend.'

Staffe still feels sick and hollow from discovering Manolo – and now Edu. 'Pease' is the wrong world. 'We can rest once we know who exactly is buried in that wood.'

'Sometimes, in our job we have to draw a line, call something finished. When will you be back?'

'As soon as I can. I'm going to be an uncle again, don't forget.'

'I'll make sure Marie is in good shape. The *medico* is a good friend. She isn't on her own.'

'Thank you,' says Staffe. 'But there's no need.' He wraps his leg over the Bultaco's ruby-red petrol tank.

'Take it easy with that shoulder.'

Staffe kicks it into first and looks up. The moon is small tonight, but full.

'Maybe you should go in the morning.'

Staffe says nothing.

'What's wrong?'

He thinks about Yousef and the shanty where he lives. He must get some cash to give to the man with the Chicago Bulls vest. Staffe slowly lets the clutch go, pain firing up his arm.

The Bultaco's headlamp lights the trail up for fifty metres or so. He expects the darkness to swallow him up, but the headlamp shows each curve as it sneaks up. Soon, Almagen reveals itself. Far away, between the mountains and the sea, Almería's soft electric glow lights the sky.

Thirty

Jesús assures the night porter that he will procure a disability car-parking badge for his mother and the man shows Jesús and Pepa into the tiny morgue which the police use in the basement of the Immaculada hospital on the eastern fringe of Mojácar.

The porter pulls out the stretcher, says, 'You can have two minutes. They'll be coming soon to take it to Almería for autopsy.' Pepa raises her eyebrows towards Jesús. She mouths the name 'Sanchez'.

Jesús says, 'Wouldn't this normally go to the morgue in Vera?'

The porter shrugs.

With her finger and thumb, Pepa pinches the sheet covering the cadaver and slowly pulls it down, revealing the greyed, gaunt face; the soul has long since fluttered away. This is simply the casings of what used to be a life. A breath gusts away from her. She makes sure that her body is between the porter and the corpse, sneaks out her phone, raises it.

'You can't do that,' hisses Jesús.

Pepa clicks the camera. She leans towards the body, scrutinising, sees there is no piercing to the nose. But even so, she thinks, he's a dead ringer, for the images she has seen, of the Dane, Jens Hansen.

She replaces the sheet and thanks the porter, says, 'When they come to take this body, tell them it is a man called Jens

Hansen. Tell them he is from Denmark and if they don't let his parents know, they will burn in hell.' She smiles at the porter. 'Got it?'

The porter smiles back, grateful for the fact that his job has been brightened, this one night. He watches the young woman go, all the way to the stairs, and he says the name, 'Jens Hansen,' committing it to memory.

*

Staffe leans the Bultaco against the wall of Raúl's building. He looks up at the study, bridging two buildings above the alley. Staffe walks backwards until he can see the bottom ledge of the mansard window, beneath which he had stashed the package containing Gustav's will. In the moonlight, he can't see if it is still there.

To his right, the wall rises sheer, three storeys. Impossible to scale. To his left, a two-metre wall seems to give onto a small garden. The wall runs up to Raúl's building so he wheels the Bultaco to the wall. Here and there, the sounds of dogs and carousing breaks the stillness.

Staffe climbs onto the seat of the Bultaco and then onto the wall. Slowly, he balances, stands upright and walks gingerly towards Raúl's study. A metre away, his footing slips and he throws himself forward, reaching at full stretch, grabbing the downpipe that runs down past the window to Raúl's studio. It is metal and his hand slips, but snags on the lipped joint where the pipe feeds down to the street. His legs swing, night air all around him now and just the flimsiest grip, but he goes with the swing, manages to hook his ankle onto the window ledge.

Now, straining to look up, he sees the package he had stashed. His grip on the drainpipe falters, though, and his shoulder feels as if it might pop out again. He can't take the pain and the drop is twelve, fifteen feet. With a final effort, he kicks out at the package, dislodges it. His grip gives way and he tries to right himself, mid-air.

The package slides down the roof, stops on the guttering.

Staffe falls, the street rising fast to meet him, and he grabs at the wall, manages to straighten himself and his arm scrapes down the render. His feet compact as he hits the ground and he crumples onto his back, hears his body slap the cobbles and rolling to protect his shoulder. Looking up at the night, he sees the last will of Gustav seeming to flutter, as if it could fly away, whisper its secrets to the wind.

Then it falls. It floats to earth, lands on Staffe's chest.

*

The youth in the Bulls vest holds an eight-inch chef's knife and has two friends with him on the fringe of their shanty. It is the break of dawn but they seem set for business. One holds a piece of wood and the other a metal baseball bat with the tarnished lettering of 'Louisville Slugger' running its length. They form a semicircle and edge towards Staffe one pace at a time.

'I am here to repay my debt,' says Staffe. On the way, he stopped at the 24-hour Copo and picked up a prepaid mobile with fifty euros of credit. He also went to the cash point, took out a thousand euros using each of his cash cards. He put five hundred up the crack of his arse, just in case this all goes horribly wrong.

He tosses the phone, still in its thermosealed and super-sturdy plastic casing. The Bulls youth knows better this time and steps aside, lets the phone drop to the floor.

'It's real,' shouts the boy with the baseball bat. He squints at the label. 'It's got fifty credit on it!'

'He owes me more than that.'

'And I've got more than that,' says Staffe, reaching into his right pocket, pulling out four fifty-euro notes. 'I'm "sorry" for what I did the other day. But I had no choice.'

'Your honour is worth two hundred? What kind of a man are you?'

Staffe goes in his other pocket, pulls out five twenties. 'There! You've cleaned me out.'

The Bulls youth tells the other boy to get it and he scampers up to Staffe, pulls the money from his hands.

'Right,' says the Bulls youth. 'We'll soon be even.' He holds the knife out in front of him and the other two talk nervously in patois French. Staffe tries to engage the Bulls youth, but his eyes are flitting, this way and that, and then an almighty thud rings out. The youths look around and one of them screams, falls to the ground clutching his head. He is bleeding and Staffe looks all around them, quite slowly, sees Yousef on a rock above the shanty twirling a length of leather in the air. He loads another pebble into his slingshot, has a brace of partridge slung over his shoulder.

'Yousef!' calls Staffe. 'Stop!' He picks up the phone and hands it to the Bulls youth, saying, 'I'm sorry, I really am.' As he hands it to him, he checks out the ruby stud in the youth's ear, says, 'I like your jewel. Where'd you get it?'

He shrugs.

'I'd like to buy it – if I can.'

He shrugs again, holding out his hand for the other youth to hand across the three hundred.

Yousef appears at Staffe's side and he flicks the Bulls youth's ear with his sling. He does it with such deftness that the butterfly grip floats in the air.

Staffe goes into his back pocket for two hundred, says, 'And now, you really have fleeced me.' He holds it out.

The Bulls youth smiles and reaches for the money.

Staffe makes a fist, concealing the notes. 'Tell me where it came from.'

Yousef flicks him again and the Bulls youth's knife twitches. Nothing more.

'The dead body?' says Staffe.

The youth nods.

Staffe unfurls his fist and the youth takes his loot, hands over the evidence.

*

Staffe is drinking *char* in Yousef's shack when Pepa and Jesús arrive. Yousef is pleased to see Pepa, who sits cross-legged beside him. He looks at Jesús as if he is the enemy. She wraps both hands around her tea, blowing into the metal cup. 'Jesús is helping us. We know what happened, now.' She nods towards the sea and the plastic greenhouse where the murder took place.

Pepa opens an envelope and removes two ten-by-eight photographs of the dead man that Yousef and his young neighbour in the Bulls vest discovered that day a fortnight ago. 'This is him?'

Jesús says, 'Where did you get that? That's a police photograph?'

'It was in your car. I was looking for a lighter,' says Pepa. 'We agreed to share our information. Remember?' She turns to Yousef. 'Is it him? The dead man?'

Yousef nods.

Pepa places a finger on one image. The photograph is a close-up of the corpse's face: horribly bruised but it is clear from the photograph that the nose is pierced in its left nostril, but unadorned. 'There was a ruby here?'

'This ruby,' says Staffe, holding out the gem the Bulls youth had been wearing.

Yousef nods again, his mouth sad, his eyes enquiring.

She says, 'This man is called Agustín Cano.'

'No!' says Jesús. 'You can't tell who it is. Look at the state of him.'

'Why'd they kill him?' says the youth in the Bulls vest.

'You're better off not knowing,' says Staffe.

'You shouldn't have those photographs,' says Jesús.

'Surely you would have been able to see it was Agustín. Why didn't you tell me?'

Jesús says, 'I didn't know what I was dealing with, and that's the truth.'

Pepa says to Yousef, 'Will you be all right?'

'He's going home,' says the Bulls youth.

'You must travel safely.'

'He has money. He has thousands. Me? I'm going to America. That's the next stop for me.' The Bulls youth taps his chest with a clenched fist, on the 'O' of Chicago.

Pepa says to Yousef, 'Is there anything you need?'

He shakes his head, clasps her hands and slowly bows his head.

'He's going tomorrow. In a week, he will be with his family again,' says the Bulls youth.

'Why did they cut his tongue?' says Pepa.

'He talked too much, I guess. Most times, it's better to say nothing – at least in our world.'

*

Staffe travels with Pepa and Jesús back into the city, mindful that they have the Barrington. Jesús would have to work until he was a hundred to earn what the painting might fetch. A few hundred metres from the plastic, they pass the El Morisco restaurant. The maître d' is out front, smoking, chatting to a fisherman who shows his catch from a styrofoam container on the back of his pick-up. As they drive by, the maître d' raises his hand, calls, 'Jesu!' but Jesús ignores him. Staffe turns to Jesús, says, 'There's more bad news.'

'How can there be?' says Jesús.

'What are you talking about?' says Pepa.

'Last night, Manolo . . .'

'No!' says Jesús.

'He was killed in his *cortijo*.'

Jesús doesn't cry or wail, or even sniffle. Within a couple of minutes, he drives on, his jaw set. 'So, who killed Agustín, and Manolo, too? Do you have answers?'

'What would you say?' says Staffe. 'This is your jurisdiction, after all.'

'I'm in the dark, I really am,' says Jesús.

'The Cano family has been decimated. Now, only poor Rubio is left alive. We know it stems from an association with Barrington.'

Jesús says, to Staffe, 'Manolo clearly involved you. Right? He drew you in.'

Staffe says, 'It begins in the plastic. And you're right – Manolo took me to the Quinta Toro. If I hadn't gone there, I wouldn't have found you, and then Raúl and he wouldn't have come up to Almagen.'

'Raúl was already looking upon you as a story,' says Pepa.

'Santi Etxebatteria,' says Staffe.

'Just tell me! Who do you think killed Agustín?' says Jesús.

'Manolo,' says Staffe.

'What!'

'Agustín went back to Germany and Manolo's future was bright. He had a scholarship to study in Granada but he couldn't go. Agustín dropped out, just hanging around for his inheritance. But he came back and he discovered Astrid was having an affair with Jackson Roberts, and maybe he was thinking ahead to his inheritance. Rubio was emasculated by it all, and it's quite possible that he killed Astrid and ran. The others buried her the way they might have in the war – to cover it up because they were worried about the art scam they had going. But then Rubio went mad and he was institutionalised. Or they put him there to protect him.'

'And themselves,' says Pepa.

'Whatever the reasons, Manolo felt his life was destroyed. He stayed – to tend the goats and the family tradition.'

'And Agustín left to be a free spirit, travelling the world, supported by his grandparents,' says Pepa.

Staffe says, 'Agustín came back this time because his grandfather had died. It was time to make sure he got the inheritance.'

'Manolo wouldn't kill for money, though,' says Jesús.

'If Agustín was back because of the money, that would have riled him.'

'But why would Manolo leave the body like that? Why would he kill his brother in such a fashion?'

'He wanted the death to speak volumes. So he made sure that Raúl Gutiérrez was running the story. And he pulled my strings, too. He knew I'd be inquisitive. And he knew about my past. That was enough to get Raúl interested.'

'He wanted you and Raúl to uncover the past?' says Pepa. 'So he led you to the body in the woods, too?'

'It's only a theory.' Staffe turns to Jesús. 'How did you come to be on call the day the body was found?'

'It was the holidays, as you know. Sanchez called in from Palma de Mallorca. He was golfing over there and he made sure the body was held here. I had as good a chance of being pulled out here as anybody, I suppose. I'm junior, so I don't get the big holidays off. I was on call.'

'You're family. I don't believe in coincidences. If he knew what had happened and he wanted it covered up, wouldn't he arrange for you to be stationed down there? And you did cover it up.'

Jesús says, 'Believe me, I didn't know what was happening, but why would Sanchez want to cover it up?'

'He left Almagen in a hurry.'

'I checked,' says Pepa. 'He left just a month after Barrington died.'

Staffe says, 'That makes sense.'

'But what about Raúl?' says Pepa. 'Surely, Manolo wouldn't have killed him. He wanted Agustín's body to make a trail that led to Astrid's murder.'

'Exactly! And Raúl was making that trail. Of course Manolo wouldn't want Raúl to be stopped.'

'Technically, Raúl died by misadventure. There's no evidence he was murdered,' says Jesús.

'He was dead before he went into that *barranco*. We all know that,' says Staffe.

'What about Edu?' says Jesús.

'It was Edu who killed Manolo,' says Staffe. 'Manolo wrote his name in blood, just before he died.'

'Then Edu killed himself,' says Pepa.

'It's neat,' says Staffe. 'Edu did everything he could to preserve the honour of his family. And maybe he knew about the scam, passing Jackson's paintings off as Barringtons. He knew we were onto him and he couldn't bear any more shame.'

'Unless we're missing something,' continues Staffe. In articulating his theory, Staffe comes to doubt it. In his heart, he doesn't believe Manolo could kill a man. And he knows there's only so many who could have killed Agustín.

'It's a good theory,' says Jesús. 'A damn good theory, provided you believe Edu was at his tether's end; that he had to do

something to stop the world discovering what he had been involved with.'

Pepa says, 'And there's the money, of course. They must have
a fortune. The last Barrington went for a million. Imagine, if
there were other Barringtons.'

'Big money, and Raúl was onto them. Sanchez knew about
that, hence the cover-up,' says Staffe.

'So Edu was wrapped up in all that art forgery. Who'd have
thought that?' says Pepa. 'Simple paintings leading to all that
bloodshed.'

'Not paintings. Money,' says Jesús.

'I like to think it is all about honour,' says Staffe, feeling
Gustav's untranslated will, stuffed down his shirt, wondering
what Gustav Hesse did for his final spin of the wheel.

'And love,' says Pepa.

'Of course. If Manolo hadn't loved his mother so, he would
never have taken such revenge on Agustín,' says Jesús.

Pepa takes a moment. 'Is that the only love he ever knew?'

Jesús says, 'He always had a thing for that gypsy girl. They
called her Brujita.'

'The little witch,' says Pepa.

'Consuela,' says Staffe.

'Poor Manolo, he must have hated Agustín for almost all his
life.'

'That's only my theory.' Staffe thinks about the Manolo he
thought he knew. And he thinks about Manolo's father, still living and breathing through it all.

The phone bleeps and Staffe sees 'Quesada' light up his
screen. The text appears and he says, 'I have to go back.'

287

Jesús says, 'Relax. You have got to the bottom of it all. We have to celebrate.'

'The baby is coming,' says Staffe.

Thirty-one

Yousef sits cross-legged under a lemon tree watching the man come towards him. At his back, the ferry for Morocco prepares for boarding.

The man reaches out, hands Yousef the ticket then lights up a spliff, offers it to Yousef. He declines and Jackson Roberts inhales deeply before going into his pocket, giving him the final one thousand euros, saying, 'You're doing the right thing. This country's not for you. Everyone needs a home. You know, I love this country. I love it like a woman you can't trust or understand and sure as the devil pisses hell-fire she's going to cheat on you, but you love her anyway. They say you can't change your homeland. But hey! Fuck 'em.' He draws long, hard on the spliff, dragging it all the way down to its roach. His eyes glaze and for all the world he seems empty. Unrequited.

*

On the road between Almagen and Mecina, a large truck is parked up on the crown of the bend. The grass verge is broad here and shaded by eucalyptus. Two shaven-headed men perch on the tailgate, drinking from mugs and unmistakably English.

Patricia Harbinson offers the men buttered slices of malt loaf and her husband walks down the track from their *cortijo* holding a cardboard box. He calls, 'That's the last of it.'

Each of the Harbinsons is smiling. Their eyes are bright and their skin seems to sing in the dappled light.

'You lost the court case?' says Staffe.

'No,' says Patricia Harbinson. 'The oafs made us legal. They said we can stay.' She laughs.

'But it looks as if you're going?' says Staffe.

'We missed the point,' says Terry Harbinson, crossing the road and setting the box down between the two men on the tailgate. 'When you're in a fight, you don't always know what you're fighting for.'

'At least the house is legal now. We can sell it.'

'But you're going back to England?' says Staffe.

'They don't want us here,' says Patricia. For an instant, she looks sad. Then she smiles.

'Of course they don't,' says Terry. 'Whatever made us think they might?' He takes the mugs from the men and empties the dregs over the verge, into the *campo*, where the figs trees run down to the almonds. In the bottom of the valley, oranges flourish, and olive trees too. 'Come on. Let's be off.'

*

Marie screams. She is laid out on Staffe's bed and she shouts at Paolo that he is a bastard and that if she ever gets out of this alive, she will rip off his nuts and pound them to pulp. If he ever . . . ever . . . !

Staffe holds Harry close and the nephew clings onto his leg tightly, keeps saying, 'Will she be all right? Don't let her die.'

'You should go downstairs, Harry. Keep Gracia company. I'll get you when it is done.'

'No!'

The nurse's expression changes and she gets busy. Consuela is here and she dabs Marie's forehead. A breeze ruffles the room. It comes all the way from the sea and in through the branches of the walnut tree. The nurse sinks to her knees and Marie grabs Consuela's arm, screams, 'Sweet Jesús!'

The room falls quiet.

Harry gasps, lets go of his uncle's leg. In the corner of the room, Paolo has his head in his hands, rocking manically back and forth muttering some kind of mantra.

Consuela says, 'It is coming, Marie.'

The nurse says, 'It is here. It is here, now push.'

'I am!' shouts Marie.

'Push!'

'I . . .' Marie's word expires and the room is dead quiet. For one, two, three seconds you could snap the silence over your knee like a seasoned olive branch.

Marie exhales a long, loud sigh. The sigh cracks, becomes a groan. Everyone in the room looks at her, wide-eyed, holding their breath. She grunts; then she sighs – long and easy.

The nurse stands. In one expert hand, she holds a pink, blood-spattered baby, still wired to its mother by a bloody cord. The nurse tips the baby, fast as flash, and she taps its bottom with the back of her fingers. The baby, which Staffe sees is a girl, screams blue murder and everybody laughs. Marie reaches for her daughter. Holding her tight, she looks at Staffe and says, 'We're calling her Enid.'

Enid, their mother's name.

*

Quesada pours Cava into Staffe's glass. They clink their glasses at the counter while Salva looks on, smiling.

The old goats come up to Staffe and congratulate him on the birth of his new niece, and when Frog comes in, he makes his way through the crowd, says to Staffe, 'You've done well.'

'It wasn't me. It's Marie who had the baby!' he laughs.

'I mean helping to catch up with those killers. I knew all along it had nothing to do with the war. Nothing like that went on in Almagen. I knew it. So I thank you, for showing the truth.'

'Let's hope it can stand up in court.'

Quesada says, 'We'll make sure it does.'

'Well, the bastards can't wriggle off the hook, can they? They're all dead!' says Frog

'Come on! Have a drink.' Quesada hands Frog a glass and pours, then recharges Staffe's glass.

'Will you stay?' asks the Frog.

'Stay?'

'Here in Almagen.' Frog downs his Cava in one go and the bubbles make him splutter. 'The Moors came; and then the Asturians came. Then foreigners came. They brought trouble with them – but you're the kind we need. So, will you stay?'

'I think I will.'

Frog holds out his glass, to be filled again, and he tells Staffe and Quesada about how he knew all along that there was something wrong with Manolo and Edu. As he speculates as to who might inherit Manolo's flock, and what will become of Edu's *cortijo* and more importantly, his bean crop, Staffe's mind wanders. He is tired and sore. Tomorrow, he will sleep the whole day and he will think about maybe getting a bigger place.

He dwells upon the observation Frog made: how difficult it will be to gather evidence. Witnesses are dead. The perpetrators are dead. Rubio is inadmissible. But that's not his problem.

Quesada takes a hold of Staffe's elbow and leans close, talking into his ear. 'I couldn't say in front of everyone, but we had news.'

'News?'

'They found a red Bultaco this morning. It was in a ravine on the other side of the Silla Montar.'

'Jackson Roberts?'

'He made it over the top, but copped it coming down the other side.'

'A fitting end,' says Staffe, feeling a tug at his shirt. He looks down, at Harry's beaming face looking up at him. At his side is Gracia.

'Mummy wants ice cream.'

'I'll get it.'

'You don't know what she wants.'

'Raspberry,' says Staffe, crouching. 'There's plenty I know about your mum. And one for you and Gracia, too?'

The children nod and Staffe gives Harry five euros, watches him lead Gracia into the *comedor* to the ice cream fridge. They chatter about the pros and cons of each make of ice cream and look like an old couple. It makes him think what the dead must have looked like as children, choosing their ice cream: Manolo and Agustín; Edu and Raúl; Astrid; and now Jackson Roberts, so far from home.

When Harry tries to pay, Salva refuses to take his money and Harry and Gracia run into the *plazeta*. The sun shines bright and they paddle water from the fountain onto the mules and sing to the sky as they go.

Staffe takes out Gustav's will, not really wanting to know what it says, but wanting to know why Raúl had a copy, and why someone took it from Manolo's chest. He will have it translated, into something less foreign.

PART FIVE

Thirty-two

'Why didn't you tell me about Jasmine Cash?' says DCI Pennington.

Josie Chancellor's stomach slowly churns. She doesn't know what is coming, but can tell it is bad. 'What about Jasmine Cash?'

'She's never had so much of a sniff of charge sheet. She's as clean as you and me, yet Pulford has been harassing her every night for months. And now she has reported it.'

'She's obviously very upset.'

Pennington looks wearily at his constable. 'Jadus Golding had a phone. We have had it analysed and the night he died, he called DS Pulford.'

'Oh no,' says Josie, fearing the worst for Pulford.

'He's going to need all the help he can get, Chancellor. Do you understand what I'm saying?'

'Yes, sir.'

'I've been calling Staffe but there's no answer from his damned phone. Have you spoken to him at all?'

Josie shakes her head, feels doubly sad.

'You look done in. I think you should take a few days off. Maybe you need to get away.'

*

Marie has returned to El Nido with baby Enid, who is fit and strong with a shock of black hair that comes straight from Paolo. Staffe is standing amongst piles of boxes, on the floor of his studio, finally stacking his books onto the shelves, now he is here to stay.

He comes across his battered copy of Martin Amis's *Money* and leafs through to see if the old dollar bill from his first trip to New York is still there, and it is. Seeing it reminds him of when he had to pack his father's books away. After he was murdered, he and Marie decided to take them to the Oxfam shop on Esher High Street. In packing, he had checked his father's Folio Society edition of *The Gold Rush*. Tucked into its protective case, were twenty fifty-pound notes. His father would talk about 'Grand Nights', said you should always have a grand put by – to blow. And he kept it in *The Gold Rush*.

Now, Staffe thinks about what will become of Manolo's books.

'Will!' The call is from the street and followed by the fast patter of feet up the stairs. Harry appears just seconds later, panting. 'Can I stay over? Consuela has asked if I want to have supper with them and I can sleep over but you need to ask my mum.'

'Are you sure you want him overnight?' Staffe looks past Harry to Consuela, who appears on the stairs, looking coy. 'Come in. Sit down. I'm just unpacking.'

'I'm sure,' says Consuela, looking at the books. 'Manolo liked to read.'

'I'll call your mother,' says Staffe and Harry and Gracia run downstairs. Staffe says to Consuela, 'Sit down. Please.'

'I should go.'

'Manolo was fond of you, wasn't he?'

Consuela shakes her head.

'Do you think I should take his books to Rubio?'

'I would like some – for Gracia, as she grows up.'

Staffe recalls the photograph he found of Gracia, in the same chest as Gustav's will – the will that had been removed by someone and which had earlier been copied and given to Raúl. 'I'm going to his house.'

Consuela leaves, her head bowed.

On his way out, Staffe picks up Gustav's will, duly translated, which states that the fruits of all Gustav's labours would pass – not to his daughter, and thereafter to her sons – but to the people of Al Fondoukha, a village on the border between Morocco and Mauritania. It is a place he had come to love; a place where he had built a school, but where there was much, much more to do in terms of medical and water provision. Clearly, anybody aware of that will, would know nothing would flow to Manolo and Agustín.

By the time Staffe has walked through the *plazeta*, Consuela is standing by Manolo's front door. She says, 'I have a key. I cleaned for him.'

Staffe follows her into the house and smiles as he watches Consuela trail her finger along the spines of the books. He suspects she cannot read.

Consuela says, 'Manolo couldn't kill anyone, and especially not his brother. No matter how much he hated Agustín, he wouldn't harm a hair on him.' She looks at the shotgun, propped up against the fireplace. 'It was all he could do to shoot a partridge.'

Staffe picks up the gun. He feels a memory return; something vague, unformed. 'Manolo is Gracia's father, isn't he?'

'I wouldn't let him marry me. I was a fool.'

'You didn't love him?'

'I should have. For Gracia.'

Staffe raises the shotgun. 'You did the right thing.' He nestles the stock into his right shoulder but it doesn't quite fit.

Manolo's last act was to write Edu's name in blood. He did it on the floor, to the right of where he lay, face down, blood stained on the index finger of his right hand. Staffe is right-handed.

He switches the gun's stock to his left shoulder, and rather than put his right index finger on the trigger, he runs it along the barrel. The stock fits perfectly to his left shoulder. He says, 'Manolo was left-handed,' putting the index finger of his left hand to the trigger.

'So is Gracia,' says Consuela.

'Did he ever talk to you about if he died?'

'Why would he?'

'He would want Gracia to be looked after.'

'I'll look after her.'

Staffe thinks of his own father, looks at each spine on each shelf. He picks off *Love in the Time of Cholera* and looks inside. Nothing. He tries *The Trial* and comes up empty. Then he tries *Remembrance of Things Past*. It is an English translation, which strikes him as being somehow out of place.

He stands back from the bookshelves, looking not at the titles, but for something which might stick out; anything not ordinary about a bookshelf. He lets his eye be drawn, then return. Drawn again. This time, to a foreign cipher. 'Did Manolo speak German?'

Consuela crinkles her eyebrows. 'I heard him talk to a tourist once. But they were English, I think. I'm sure of it.' She laughs. 'He wore black socks with shorts. They were English, all right.'

Staffe takes down the volume of *Siddhartha*. It is in German and published by Suhrkamp. He carefully opens Hermann Hesse's novel. It is a first edition and the frontispiece is signed, 'For my wonderful grandson, From Hermann.' Beneath, a different hand has written, 'And mine, also. From Gustav.' Staffe opens his hands, the way in which a priest might hold something holy. The pages fall open, reveal a loose leaf. Staffe reads it quickly, tells Consuela it is nothing, and carefully pockets the Last Will and Testament of Gustav Hesse. Except, it is not the last. It is a prior version to the one which he had found in Raul's study and which he had translated. In this document, secreted by Manolo, all his worldly wealth is left to his grandsons, Manolo and Agustín.

With the will in his pocket, against his heart, Staffe feels the full force of the loss of his friend, Manolo – an utterly decent and proper man. He says, 'How did Manolo and Agustín get on?'

'He never spoke of Agustín.'

'But Agustín was here, a few weeks ago.'

Consuela shakes her head. She sits down on the edge of a chair and her shoulders shake. 'He couldn't hurt him. I can assure you of that.'

'I know Manolo didn't kill Agustín.' Staffe kneels in front of Consuela.

'But you said he did. That's what Quesada and the *guardia* have been saying.'

He takes her gently by the shoulders and says, softly, 'But I have to know the truth – to get to the truth.'

Consuela nods. 'Agustín and Manolo had an argument. A terrible, terrible argument. They said such awful things to each other.'

'What did they say?'

'I was upstairs, cleaning. I didn't hear it all, but Manolo said Agustín couldn't love anybody. He said he was only interested in money.'

'And Agustín?'

'He said he had seen things Manolo hadn't, that they were so different they didn't even have the same blood. He said he was going to dig up the past and prove it to the world. I remember it exactly. It made my blood cold. I knew something terrible would happen.'

'And what did Manolo say?'

'He said Agustín was only saying it for the money. And then he said the strangest thing.'

'What?'

'Manolo told Agustín that he loved him. It went quiet and I think they must have embraced. I came to the top of the stairs.' She looks up, over her shoulder. 'And Manolo said, "Leave the past alone. They will kill you – to keep it the way it is." And then Agustín left. I never saw him again.'

*

Staffe follows Consuela out of Manolo's house, sees Quesada's

Guardia Civil Land Rover outside Bar Fuente. As Consuela walks off through the *plazeta* to find Harry and Gracia, he goes in the bar, where Quesada is in the *comedor* in a cloud of cigar smoke. But it smells richer today. Comisario Sanchez is opposite Quesada, pulling on his Cohiba. Two black and gold bands sit on the table.

Quesada looks glum, but forces a smile when Staffe sits down with them.

'This is like a police canteen,' says Staffe.

'More like the United Nations,' says Quesada. He nods at Sanchez. 'And we have good news.'

'I got Cortes to run full tests on the body from the woods,' says Sanchez. 'It's no ghost from the war.'

'What made you change your mind?' says Staffe.

'It's an old man. Between seventy and eighty years old,' says Sanchez.

'A man? Did he run the DNA test?'

Sanchez shakes his head. 'It's not Astrid Cano. You'll have to abandon that theory and look elsewhere for her body. If there is a body.'

'Her father died and she didn't go to the funeral. Explain that.'

'She's in some hippy commune somewhere? Maybe she doesn't know about Gustav Hesse passing away.'

'What does it matter? We can prove Edu killed Manolo,' says Quesada. 'And Manolo must have killed Agustín. Like you say.'

Staffe says nothing. He thinks about the poor Dane, and Raúl. He knows what Sanchez and Quesada would say. A junkie tied up in something he didn't understand, and a drunk

303

driver. Cases closed. He says, 'Who is the man up in the woods?'

'We don't know,' says Quesada. 'But we are investigating, naturally.'

Sanchez says to Quesada, 'Perhaps you could leave us for a minute or two.'

The *brigada* jumps to, picking up his cigar, popping on his cap.

Sanchez watches him all the way out of the bar, says to Staffe, 'I can see that there's something on your mind.'

'I know Jens Hansen was killed in Mojácar, not down in the plastic. And I know why he was killed – to provide a false ID for Agustín Cano's corpse. And I can see that you can construct a plausible motive for Manolo killing his brother. And there is evidence for Manolo being killed by Edu, who needed to keep his name out of any investigations into the painting scam.'

'You seem to know plenty.'

'"Know" is the wrong word. I "understand" those theories.'

'So what is your problem?'

'Who is buried up in my sister's woods? Where is Astrid Cano? And how did Santi Etxebatteria come to fit into this story, *comisario*?'

'I don't think everything needs to fit all the time, do you? If it did, we'd be left with nothing to do.'

'Did you know Raúl Gutiérrez was looking into Etxebatteria?'

'That is a question for another time, I'm afraid. You know about the peace with ETA. If you ask me, Raúl had his own story in mind and Etxebatteria was only ever a device. It's time you dropped it.' Sanchez regards his cigar. 'Understand?'

'I understand what you are saying.'

'They tell me you have decided to stay on here in Almagen.'

'I must apply myself to being a doubly good uncle now. And there is so much to discover in this country of yours.'

'What, exactly, is there to discover?'

'My first bullfight, for example.'

'The Almería feria is the place to go. There's a *corrida* every day for a week. Tomorrow, it's Tomas. He's the best. And one of our own.'

'Tickets are an impossibility, they say.'

'Nothing is impossible,' says Sanchez. 'Maybe we could help each other.'

'How?'

'Tell me why you are really staying on.'

'There are more murders here.'

'Astrid Cano?'

'And Raúl Gutiérrez.'

'And the dead have to speak.'

'Exactly!' says Staffe. He tries to evaluate the *comisario*, but Sanchez's eyes are soft and unfocused. His breathing is even.

'You should definitely go to a *corrida*. Give me your number and I'll try to fix you up with some tickets.'

Staffe scribbles his number on a paper serviette. As he hands it to Sanchez, it feels like a mistake.

*

The key swings down from the *acotea* and Staffe has to jump out of the way, but even so, it still catches him on the side of the head. He could swear that he hears Immaculada chuckle to herself as he lets himself in.

He climbs the dark, dank stairwell, up into the fragrance and light of the top floor. She is dressed in a black Mao tunic and loose, black linen trousers; her thick grey hair is scooped up in a lavish bun. Her eyes are bright but her skin is loose and grey.

Immaculada says, 'This had better be good.'

'It's very kind of you to see me. I was a friend of Edu's.'

'All my life, my brother was ashamed of me. And now, it's my turn to be ashamed of him. A pity I don't give a damn.'

'I'm sorry you couldn't make it to the funeral.'

'He killed a good man. Why would I?'

'Nothing has been proven.'

'Ha! That will take years. It will see me out. Now, why are you here?' Immaculada coughs, raises a handkerchief to her mouth. Her eyes water. 'The young journalist assured me I would be pleased with the outcome.'

Staffe holds out the rolled-up rug.

'You've not come selling me rugs, have you? I had enough of that in damned Tangier.'

'Barrington took you to Tangier?'

'Only once.'

'Just the two of you?'

'The German woman came. But I didn't let you in to talk about her.'

Staffe sinks to his knees, carefully unrolling the rug. The canvas is protected by tissue and is further sandwiched by two thick sheets of cartridge paper. Staffe slowly reveals the image and stands, takes a step back, saying, 'We have called it *La Sernata*.'

'After the song?'

'That's right.'

'It's a good painting.'

'Maybe his finest?'

'*His*? It might have Hugo's signature, but this isn't his. You're here under false pretences.'

'His later works . . .'

'Take it away!'

'They say it's worth a fortune.'

'It's worth nothing to me.'

'Do you know who painted this?'

'There's nothing of Hugo in that painting. Can't you see? Hugo was loose. This brushwork is stiff, too controlled.'

Staffe kneels in front of her, meticulously rolls the painting back up, and wraps the rug around it.

'I like the rug, though,' says Immaculada.

'Did you buy rugs in Tangier?'

'We have our own rugs, here in the Alpujarras. But the rest of them did.'

'Astrid and Jackson?'

She nods.

'Aah. Was Rubio there?'

'Yes. And his *primo*. That fellow with the bar down in Almería.'

'Angel who has the Quinta Toro?'

'That's him. Thick as thieves, him and Rubio – more like brothers than cousins.'

'Did Angel ever come up here?'

'All the time. Sundays and Mondays, as I recall – when he didn't open his bar. He'd be shooting partridge up at his *cortijo*.'

'He has a *cortijo* up here?'

'Next to his *primo*'s.'

'You mean Rubio?' says Staffe.

'They built it together.'

'And when did he stop coming?'

'A long time ago.' Immaculada's brow ruffles.

'Around the time Hugo passed away?'

'I don't know. Maybe. Yes, yes, it would have been around then.'

'Was that when Astrid went missing?'

'I've said I don't want to talk about her, if you don't mind.'

Staffe tucks the rolled rug under his arm. 'You know, I spoke to Edu just a couple of days before he passed away.'

'Passed away? He was murdered.'

'He took his own life. He hanged himself.'

'Ha! I can assure you he didn't. He wouldn't dare.'

'Dare?'

'It would condemn him to an eternity of damnation. That's what he believed. It's the only thing we have in common – our belief in the Church.'

'Is that why he carried Hugo's coffin?'

Immaculada looks puzzled, as if trying to resurrect a distant memory.

'He did that for you, didn't he? Was it his way of saying sorry, for the way he was with Hugo?'

'I don't know where you get your nonsense from. I didn't want him there, but Edu insisted. And he was well in with the priest. I didn't want to make a scene, but if I'd had my way, my

brother would have been banished from the village for the funeral.'

'You're sure? Edu insisted on being there; insisted on carrying the coffin?'

'That's right.'

'I saw a photograph. There was Jackson Roberts and Rubio,
and Edu bearing Hugo's coffin.'

'I wouldn't have had any of them there, but Hugo was his
own man. And I was ill. Ill with it all, so I let them do what they
wanted.'

'And the fourth man?'

Immaculada frowns. 'You should know. You've been talking
about him.'

'Angel?'

'What a bunch of rogues.' She laughs. 'But that's probably
what Hugo would have wanted – to plant him for the next life.'

Staffe says goodbye to Immaculada, asks if he can use the
bathroom on his way out. He runs the tap and in a hand-craf-
ted medicine cabinet built into a nook in the thick wall, he
finds an ivory-backed pair of gentlemen's brushes, picks out a
handful of hair. Hugo's hair. He places it carefully in the empty
stamp-pocket of his wallet. Something for Cortes to identify.

*

Staffe pulls off the *carretera* onto a verge, just beyond the seven-
eye bridge and above Orgiva. Down below, on the banks of the
river, smoke rises from a tepee village, which is scattered like lit-
ter with tents and benders, caravans and transits. Today, they

are holding a memorial service for Jackson Roberts, but it won't be in the twin-towered church.

A circle of people have formed on the dusty meadow beside the river. They are holding hands. A guitar strums and someone gets on the bongos. Slowly a melody forms and a woman's voice emerges, singing 'Blowin' in the Wind'. Staffe looks all around, to see if anybody else is paying respects from a distance, but it appears not. Guadalupe has not come. He hoped she might, but he waits a while, watching the hippies pay their respects, managing to enjoy themselves a little along the way. The smell of hashish drifts on the breeze and within an hour the dancing begins. It's probably what Jackson would want.

He telephones Pepa, asks her to get a message to Guadalupe, to come and collect what he has for her. And he drives away, checking that the last Barrington is safely rolled up in its Moroccan rug.

Thirty-three

The maître d' shows Staffe to a table out front, beneath El Mar-isco's bamboo canopy. The sea is across the road and the plastic greenhouses are to the right, with the small shanty where Yousef had fashioned his makeshift home just beyond.

Guadalupe arrives in a newish hatchback and the maître d' receives her as if she is not unfamiliar. As they are in conversation, he scans the road, but the road is empty. Today, and all this week, the great and the good, and the bad, are in Almer-ía for the *feria*. Staffe's room at the Hotel Catedral cost double for tonight. It seems so long since he was first there.

'You found it all right,' says Staffe as Guadalupe takes her seat. She smells fine, of jasmine, and her hair is up and done.

'I've been before.'

'I popped in to Jackson's service in Orgiva yesterday. I thought you might have been there.'

'Not my scene, really. I heard it was going to be a hippy af-fair.'

'And your uncle Edu's funeral?'

'I can't shed tears for that one, I'm afraid. I don't know what that makes me.'

'I saw your mother yesterday.'

'She said.'

'You've seen her?'

'Of course. I was passing.'

'Did she tell you about *La Sernata*?'

'Is that what you're calling it?' She looks around, to see if he has brought it. The young journalist had said he would.

'Your mother was sceptical as to its provenance.'

'She has a very romantic notion of my father. You really shouldn't have shown it to her.' Guadalupe picks up the menu, looks down in a cursory way, saying, 'The red shrimp is the thing to have.'

'I fancy the turbot.' Staffe thinks of the times he has had turbot. It takes him back, not to a world of lapping sea or fishing villages, but to the wood-panelled world of the George and Vulture – the long City lunches he and Jessop would share when a case was dragged to its conclusion. 'Yes, the turbot for me.'

'Is this your treat?'

'Maybe it could be yours. Let's call it a finder's fee.'

Guadalupe looks anxious for an instant, quickly corrects herself. 'For what?'

'The last Barrington.'

'Is there such a thing?'

He takes out his phone, clicks through the commands. 'If there is, it should be yours, wouldn't you say? If your mother doesn't want it.' He turns his phone towards her, so she can see the screen. On it, an image of *La Sernata*.

'You really have it?'

'In my hotel room.'

'If I'm buying lunch, I need more than a photograph,' she laughs. 'This could be a couple of hundred euros.'

'They have some wonderful Ribera del Duero here, too.'

'In that case, I definitely need more than a photograph.'

'I have to go straight to the bullfight after this. Here.' He shows her his key card for the Hotel Catedral. 'Room seven.'

'Are you sure?'

He nods, reaching further with his hand, proffering the key. 'It's rolled up in a rug.'

'I can assure you, no matter what you might think, this will be staying in the family. It means more than money.'

The maître d' personally comes to take their order. He gives Staffe a suspicious look.

Guadalupe says, 'I'll have the red shrimp, and my friend will have the turbot. And a bottle of your Ribera.'

When the wine comes, Staffe toasts Jackson Roberts and they clink. 'You'll miss him. Good neighbours are hard to find.'

'The fool. Fancy going over the Silla Montar on a bike. You know, I suppose in a way it's good that he went like that. He used to say that once you've seen war, every peaceful day starts with a present being unwrapped.'

'He unwrapped plenty of presents is my guess.'

The maître d' sidles up, recharges their glasses and a red Bultaco rattles by, struggling under the weight of two Moroccans, one of them the Bulls youth.

*

They are finishing off the figs and Manchego cheese and Staffe tries to stop Guadalupe from paying but she insists, and as she settles the bill with the maître d', he goes inside, feeling their eyes on him all the way, so he closes the door behind him.

Through the frosted glass, he watches their outlines. He calls the bartender across, says, 'Has my friend Jesús been in?' He takes out a twenty-euro note, places it on the bar. 'Jesús of the Cuerpo.'

'Do you want a drink?' The bartender speaks perfect Spanish, but with a Romanian accent.

'Two coffees. He comes here often. Was he here the night they found the body across the road?'

The bartender looks at the twenty with a certain disdain. 'The Cuerpo? They give good custom.'

Staffe removes the twenty, replaces it with a fifty. 'This is the last time you'll see me and I'll never talk. He was here that night, wasn't he?'

The bartender checks behind him. 'Not for long, and not with police.'

Staffe slides the note across and the bartender pockets it, deft as a thief and slides it down the waistband of his apron. 'Was there a fair man with them? He had a stud in his nose. A ruby stud?'

The bartender nods, looking past Staffe towards the door.

'There was an American with them?'

'A loudmouth.' The bartender looks towards the door. 'They drank plenty, that's for sure.'

'And did it get lively?'

'A good job they were outside, round the corner.'

'Was there a man called Edu with them – an older guy?'

The bartender shakes his head.

'Or a shepherd. A big fellow called Manolo?'

The bartender shakes his head again. 'There was just the four of them.'

'Four?'

'But Jesús left early. Almost straight away and before they started eating.'

'Who was the fourth?'

'The guy from the Quinta Toro. Jesús's father.' The bartender looks past Staffe as the door opens and the maître d' comes in. He turns towards the coffee machine, says, 'I'll bring your drinks out.'

Guadalupe is all set to go when he returns, handbag on her shoulder and sunglasses pulled down. She hasn't touched her Pacharán. She says, 'I'll follow you to the hotel.'

'I ordered coffee.' Staffe takes out his ticket for the *corrida*, says, 'I have to go straight to the Plaza de Toros.'

Guadalupe scrutinises the ticket. 'You're in the sun. Get yourself a hat.' She holds onto the ticket long enough to clock precisely where he will be sitting, then hands it back.

He says, 'Don't forget. It's room seven, and keep your hands off the minibar.'

She laughs. The sun catches her hair and he glimpses a throwback to what Barrington might have seen in the young Immaculada.

'Mother said you were quite a gentleman.'

'She's a good judge.'

Guadalupe kisses him on each cheek, says, 'If I can get a room, maybe we could take a walk down to the *feria*, after your fight. You should give me your number.'

He tells her the number and they leave as the bartender brings the coffees. Like a gentleman, he lets the lady go first, and as she does, he pockets the bill, slips it into his trouser pocket, unseen. He thinks of that last supper for Agustín, with

Jackson and Angel, and Jesús, briefly. And he thinks, too, of the men who carried Barrington: half dead, half alive.

*

Pepa is dressed to the nines in her red polka-dot dress with a tight bodice and a halter neck. It flares out like 1950s America and her lips and nails are painted to match. On the table in front of her is a box, tied with ribbon and filled, no doubt, with rich fancies.

'Have you missed me?' says Staffe.

'Of course. But I'm not complaining.' She looks out of the window at the Hotel Catedral. 'So, Guadalupe's in there?'

'I gave her my room key.'

'Can you trust her with the Barrington?'

'If it's worth anything, then she's entitled to it. And if we're right – then it's worthless. What is there to lose?'

'*If* you're right.'

'And if I'm right, you'll have the story of a lifetime.'

Pepa falls silent. Her eyebrows pinch and after a minute or so, she says, 'If you're right, there'll be a few rich collectors a little less rich.'

'An influential lot,' says Staffe.

'And Jackson really will be glad he's dead!'

Staffe thinks about this and again they sit in silence.

'Should we call him?' says Pepa.

'We better had. I'm late for the bullfight already.'

Pepa blows out her cheeks. 'I don't like this one bit, you know.'

'I see you have your cakes,' says Staffe, pointing to the ribboned box.

'Did you speak to the bartender in El Marisco?'

'Jackson was there the night they killed Agustín, and so were Angel and Jesús.'

'But no Edu, or Manolo?'

He shakes his head, keeps a sharp eye on the entrance to the Hotel Catedral. The street-cleaners are hosing down the *plaza* after the mayhem of the *feria*. By day, Almería heaves with revellers, drinking sherry by the bottle at *chiringuitos* and dancing to *mariachis* and brass bands. Then, at four, a whistle is blown and everybody sleeps. Until six. Then they slowly reappear.

Staffe's heart beats ahead of itself and he can't keep his fingers and feet still. He calls for some beer.

'He's on his way,' says Pepa, clicking off her phone. 'What if they both come at once? You don't think we should go to the police?'

'Which police? He *is* police!'

'But if he's here when Guadalupe comes out of the hotel, what do we do?'

'You follow her,' says Staffe.

'Shouldn't you?'

'I can't allow you to be left on your own with Jesús?'

'But what if she leads us to him? Would you wish that on me?'

Staffe's head spins. He feels woozy.

'And what if she doesn't come out? She might be totally on the level.'

'I know!'

'You know what?' says Jesús, who has stolen in. He sidles

317

in between Staffe and Pepa, is out of uniform, but in the heat he still wears a jacket. Summer in Almería, only old men wear a jacket. Unless, perhaps, you wanted to cover up what the Americans call heat.

'My ticket,' says Staffe, 'is in the sun.'

'You're going to the *corrida*?' says Jesús. 'What section?'

Looking Jesús in the eye, Staffe sees innocence and youth, but feels his stomach clench. Despite the fact he can't trust Jesús, he tells him precisely where he will be sitting for the *corrida*. 'K section.'

'You will fry. Like a *gamba*!' he laughs.

'Don't talk to me about *gambas*,' says Staffe. He reaches into his trouser pocket, pulls out the bill for El Marisco and tosses it onto the table in front of Jesús. 'Sixty-five euros, for a plate of red shrimp.'

Jesús checks out the date on the bill, says, 'You went today?' His mouth hangs open, then he smiles. 'But they are Almería red. The best in all the world.'

'At least I didn't pay. And the service on top. The service is so good. I've only been once before. But they remembered me. They remember everything, it seems.'

Jesús's smile evaporates. He stares at the bill.

'I have to go,' says Pepa.

'But you called me,' says Jesús. 'I thought we were going out.'

Pepa sees Guadalupe walking quickly across the *plaza*, skipping out of the way of the street-cleaners with their hoses, a rolled rug under her arm. Pepa stands, kisses Jesús rapidly on either cheek. Behind his back, she makes a telephone shape with her finger and thumb to Staffe. Once outside, she breaks into a trot, clutching her polka-dot skirt, and the cake box swinging as she goes.

She catches up to Guadalupe in the Plaza Purchena. It is easy enough to keep tabs from a distance because the streets are quiet, but as Guadalupe turns up Calle Granada and Pepa follows, the streets become busier and busier. Close to the Plaza de Toros, the cafes and bars are full and people queue outside the cake shops and tobacconists. As they turn left up Avenida Vilches, the street is full of families standing in large groups and old timers getting together.

Guadalupe moves smoothly through the crowd and Pepa keeps losing sight of her, having to break into a trot whenever she gets space, brushing past women handing out cakes and street vendors selling seat cushions the colours of the flag.

'Pepa!'

She feels someone grab her arm. She turns, sees Alejandro, her *primo* from Gabo. She kisses him quickly, three times.

'Are you going to the *corrida*?'

'I have to collect my ticket. I must go!'

'We have a *merienda*. You must come under the stands after Tomas's first bull. We're in K.'

Pepa catches a glimpse of Guadalupe, looking over her shoulder, disappearing into a large crowd coming across from Avenida Federico Lorca and the Rambla. 'I'll be there. But I have to get my ticket!'

Her *primo* keeps hold of her arm, turns to his friends. 'This is my *prima*, Pepa. Isn't she beautiful!'

Pepa yanks her arm away and waves to them all as she pushes through the crowd, trying to get to the *rambla*, but now the tide of people is too thick against her and Guadalupe is gone.

She will never know where Barrington's daughter was taking his last painting with such purpose. She has her suspicions, but now Staffe will have to wait, sit like a duck, but after all this was his idea to lure them into a crowd, the only place the dead can move safely, unseen. His stupid idea.

She steps into a shop doorway and phones Staffe, to call it off. But there is no answer. Pepa goes back into her address book. She has many contacts for the *cuerpo* police, but is torn now. She points the cursor to 'Sanchez', remembering everything Staffe had accused him of. Instead, she scrolls to 'G' for *guardia* where she has only one contact. Better to call Quesada?

*

'Your father must have been busy today,' says Staffe.

'It's the *feria*. If you're not busy for the *feria*, you'd better shut the shop,' says Jesús.

'It must be tough, keeping an old place like the Quinta Toro going. The bad world moves on and the good world gets left behind.'

'Good and bad – really? Why did Pepa call me then run off like that?'

'You should take her to El Marisco.'

'What is it with El Marisco?' says Jesús. His eyes darken and he lights up his cigarette, blows out at Staffe.

'You know what it is with El Marisco, don't you, Jesús? It was a last supper for your *primo*. You were there. On hand and then later you were first on the scene when Agustín was found – to cover it up? What exactly happened? Did they go too far with their dissuasions?'

'What the fuck are you talking about?'

'Did they take Agustín into the plastic to teach him a lesson? To persuade him to back off and go back to Morocco.'

'You said Manolo killed Agustín. Why rub our faces in it? My *primo* killed my *primo* is what you said. Is that not shame enough?'

'Why would Manolo kill his brother, Jesús? You tell me.'

Jesús's eyes flit and he looks bewildered. 'Because he was jealous of Agustín's life, the favours he was given, and for the inheritance.'

'But Manolo knew there was nothing to collect.'

'What!'

'There was nothing in Gustav's will for any of the Canos. And Manolo knew it.'

'So why would anyone want to kill Agustín?'

'Agustín thought he knew where Astrid was buried. He still thought if he could prove her dead, he could get the lot.'

'But Astrid's not buried in the wood.'

'He didn't know that,' says Staffe.

'And what about the will?'

'Maybe he thought he could get hold of the latest will and destroy it. In the previous version, he and Manolo got the lot. But Raúl had a copy of the new version.'

'Raúl!' Jesús fidgets. He stubs out his cigarette. For a second, he puts a hand on his hip – the bulge beneath his jacket. The waiter comes across, takes the empty drinks and asks if they want more.

'The same again,' says Jesús.

'Not for me. Let's talk about Astrid's lover. The American's dead, too, isn't he, Jesús? *Isn't* he?'

'I thought you had a bullfight to go to.'

'It was nothing to do with the inheritance, really. Families are close down here, aren't they? But nobody trusts police. Family or not.'

'Speak for yourself.'

'And a *primo* isn't the same as a brother. A brother would know things a *primo* wouldn't.'

The waiter brings his drink and Jesús swigs lustily. 'You're talking shit. Talking shit in circles.'

'So let's take a straight line.' Staffe reaches into his pocket and Jesús flinches, puts his hand back on his hip. 'Agustín knew about the paintings and like his mother before him, he threatened to expose their scam. He needed them to help prove Astrid was dead, but they wouldn't – of course. And that's what did for him. He threatened them – just like his mother did all those years ago.'

'When?'

'I'm not sure . . .' Staffe pauses and his mind drifts, a second or so. '. . . It must have been some time around when Barrington died, I guess.'

Jesús looks away, seems to remember something.

'They were all in on it.'

'*All* in on it?' says Jesús.

'Four of them. Including your father.' Staffe stands. 'I'm going, Jesús. Don't follow me.'

'Why would I? I haven't finished my drink.'

Thirty-four

Staffe is totally hemmed in. The bench beneath is hard and his knees are tucked to his chin. He is pressed from behind and into his sides. Cigar smoke billows from left and right, and the heat is unbearable. From time to time, the crowd roars, shifts, and he can barely breathe. The band strikes up and the old woman in front turns, offers him a cake from a large oval platter.

The *picador* runs at the bull at full speed in short strides on the balls of his feet, adjusting his angle of attack as the bull moves. Just yards away, he gets the bull in his sights, raises his hands high, and vaults, planting the two sharpened *picos* into the bull's back in mid-air. The crowd whoops. The bull, confused and with seams of blood coming from the two wounds, doesn't know which way to turn. Staffe's two wounds pinch. He thinks about the ways he has been goaded in this convalescence – since Jadus Golding delivered his twin strikes to Staffe's torso.

After the kill – clumsy and protracted – the man on his right pats Staffe on the back and says, 'Now, Tomas! A son of Almería!' and Tomas takes the bull from the get-go. He teases, acts as the *picador* and takes the sword for the kill. He is tall and slender, moving like a ballet dancer with his chin to the sun, letting the bull brush the million hand-sewn lights of his suit.

Just before his kill, Tomas kisses the bull on the head and is then fast and true with the blade. The bull's legs give way and it dies immediately. The crowd gasps. Then all is silent before a mighty roar emerges. The crowd stands as one, twirling white handkerchiefs in the air, pleading with the president to award Tomas two ears. When he awards only one, they whistle and jeer, refuse to take their seats until the third bull is brought out, and all the while, some of the crowd are leaving their seats, squeezing out along the tight rows, to meet family and friends below the stands, for a *merienda*; or simply to escape the stifling heat.

Staffe's phone vibrates in his pocket and he sees it is Pepa, texting.

Understand. Having drink with my primo. No escape. Come join. Get out of the sun! Great jamón and all clear. Nothing to fear.

He calls her back, but gets no response, so he edges along the row, makes his way down into the bowels of the amphitheatre.

When he gets down below, the narrow corridor which runs around from section to section, creaks with large groups standing around drinking and picking at wondrous spreads of food, hand-held. He squeezes through, sees a youth in a sombrero which has 'FIESTAS DE GABO 2011' on its band.

'Do you know Pepa? Pepa from Gabo?'

'She's his *prima*,' says the youth, pointing to a tall man with his back to them. 'Hey, Alejandro. Alejandro! This *guirri* is looking for Pepa.'

Alejandro is fine-boned. His eyes are glassy, clearly the worse for drink and he twists away from a brace of beautiful girls. 'Where is my *prima*? Where is she!'

'Pepa told me to meet her here. She said she was with you.'

'I haven't seen her since we came in.'

'Are you joking?' Staffe looks around, checking to see if Pepa is at the bar or queuing for the toilet. 'Tell me!' He grabs Alejandro, makes a scruff of his silk shirt.

'Hey, *coño*!'

'Where is she!'

One of Alejandro's friends swings a punch at Staffe but he swerves to one side, takes a glanced blow to the head. He raises his hands. 'OK. OK! I'm sorry, but she said she was here.'

'Get yourself out of here,' says Alejandro.

'Aren't you worried about her?' Staffe has a fluttering in his gut.

Pepa's friends laugh. 'Worried? She's not in the ring, is she?'

'Pepa got in with the bulls. Oh my God!'

They laugh again.

Staffe moves away, squeezing through the crowd and double-checking his phone. He has another message, from Pepa:

Keep moving anti-clockwise. Get out of the K. We'll get you.

'We?' he says, to himself, twisting in the crowd, as it takes him, anti-clockwise, towards the J section. Ahead, there is a break in the crowd where the corridor runs into a dead-end at a wooden wall. He thinks it must be where they bring the bulls into the ring. Above, a mighty roar erupts and the stands shake. The crowd are stamping their feet and he imagines it must be someone being gored. The crowd whistles, jeers, all hell breaking free.

He feels something on his arm.

Someone is squeezing his arm, and now saying his name. 'Inspector. Inspector! Come with me.'

He turns, sees the waxed moustache and large chest of

Quesada and Staffe's heart settles down. He can feel himself unclench. Quesada is smiling.

'Where is Pepa?' says Staffe.

'The crowd is getting agitated. Something is wrong. Come on, I can get us out of here.'

'She said she was with her *primo*!' shouts Staffe, but Quesada is moving, away from the crush of people, and Staffe is shoved in the back as more people descend the stairs from the stands, even though there is nowhere to go. Someone shouts for them to go back, that there's no room, and a whole chorus of protestations ensues for the crowd to stay put in the stands.

Quesada is getting further away, his green uniform stretched tight across his broad shoulders. Staffe makes a mighty effort, grabs hold of Quesada's arm. 'Where are we going?' Quesada keeps moving until he gets to the wall, then shrugs Staffe's grip loose and taps a code into the pad at the side of a door in the wooden wall, disappearing through the portal. Staffe rushes through, too.

Others try to follow, but Quesada slams the door shut. It makes a mighty click.

Someone pounds on the door and Staffe says, 'Shouldn't we let them through?'

'Don't be stupid.'

Suddenly, Staffe feels his arm being grabbed. He feels the roughness of hessian pulled over his face and everything becomes dark. He is gripped tight by both arms, dragged along, feeling the hotness of his own breath, trapped by whatever it is they have pulled down over his head. He smells cologne.

He tries to resist, to twist from the hold he is in, but when he does, he loses balance and his feet leave the floor. All he can do is writhe in mid-air, blind to what is happening to him.

The white noise becomes deeper and the air around them trembles. He hears animals, close. He thinks it is the bray of a horse. Then a bull, snorting. The hands leave him, and for a second, he is weightless. Then his head crashes against something hard and he is horizontal. The smell of animal is overpowering now: straw, manure, a horse's coat.

'Take it off,' says a man.

Staffe's heart quickens as he recognises the timbre of the voice, then its accent. The hessian hood is pulled off his head, scratching his face. He blinks into the gloom, seeing many shapes. Many different, large, brooding shapes. A horse. A bull. A man in a *toreador*'s uniform and three others. One is Quesada. The others are two enormous handlers, clutching ropes that lead to the bull's head. The bull is in an iron pen.

As his eyes adjust, Staffe sees Pepa. She is on the floor, her feet and hands bound; beside her, the cake box.

'Too late to expound the virtues of a man minding his own,' says the man in the *toreador*'s outfit. He is clean-shaven and looks the part. He must see the surprise on Staffe's face because he says, 'I did a bit once.'

'Very Hemingway,' says Staffe.

The *toreador* take one pace towards Staffe, then another, then swings a foot to Staffe's ribs.

'Too many people know, Jackson,' wheezes Staffe.

'Not true. With you and her out of the way, our little secret stays the way it is.'

'And the last Barrington is still worth a fortune. And all the others, too. I can imagine how perilous life would become if you made a fool of those collectors.'

'Very clever.'

Staffe sits up and one of the bull-handlers says, 'When do I let it out?'

'If you kill me, that will arouse suspicion.'

'Trampled to death, trying to save your friend, the beautiful journalist? Her *primo* will attest,' says Quesada.

Amidst the smell of animal, the sweet cologne from Quesada takes him back to another dark time. 'It was you who attacked me, in Raúl's flat.'

'Not me,' says Quesada.

'I thought it was Sanchez.'

'Sanchez is no angel.'

'It was you.'

'Not me,' says Quesada.

Staffe's mind whirrs. He tries to work out who might have overpowered him in Raúl's flat. 'Angel?'

Quesada laughs; it turns into a sneer.

'And what about you never having killed a man?'

'You'll have to wait and see,' says Quesada.

'You did for Edu, and Manolo. You were in on it with Sanchez. He left you behind in Almagen to keep an eye on that body in the woods. And he took fine care of you and your career.'

'You were wrong about that body in the woods, though. Your speculations amount to nothing, Inspector.' Quesada nods to the bull-handlers.

'No!' shouts Staffe. 'There's something we all need to sort out.' He looks around. The crowd way up in the stands gasps again, then a band strikes up. He has no plan, just to try and acquire a little more time. The bull-handler pulls back the bottom bolt of the pen.

'Listen to him!' shouts Pepa.

Staffe looks at Jackson. 'Did you make that film, of Manolo?'

'No.'

'Was it all you?'

Jackson looks at Quesada. 'You overestimate me.'

'But you killed Astrid.'

'I loved her, you fool.'

'You loved her enough to kill her,' says Staffe. 'You can tell from the paintings.'

'Enough to kill her? That's a strange thing to say,' says Jackson, his eyes glazing. 'I could never harm that woman.'

The handler pulls the middle bolt across and Quesada says to the other handler, 'You'll need to get the bull riled.'

'And Raúl? You knew he was going to put me in the picture that night up in your *cortijo*, so you stopped us talking. The next day, you went for him and he drove away, but you cut him off at the bridge on your motorbike. You stopped him talking good and proper and made it look like a crash. You're good at making things look like something they're not.'

'Shut up!' says Quesada.

Staffe says, 'They know all about the last Barrington at the university.'

'It's leaving the country, you prick,' says Jackson. 'I have a buyer. It's the last!'

Pepa is on the floor, slowly adjusting her position, a flickering determination in her eyes.

The handler returns to the pen with a pair of *picos*. They are sharpened to a lethal point and adorned with baby blue ribbons on the handles. He stands on the bottom bar of the metal pen and raises the *picos* high above his head, leans forward and lunges with all his might, plunging the wooden spears into the bull's back. The bull swings its head and kicks out with its back legs, clattering the pen as two thick rivulets of blood begin to stream down the bull's back from the wounds. The horse rears up on its hind legs, then cowers into a corner of the small enclosure. 'At least let the horse out,' shouts Staffe. 'Or the bull will kill it.'

'It will do for you first.'

'You can't get away with this.'

Jackson takes a step closer.

'Whose idea was it, to make it look like a ghost?'

'Does it matter?'

'I know who the ghost is.'

'What?' says Quesada.

'And so does the *cuerpo*.'

'Bullshit,' says Jackson.

'When you think about it, who else could it be? And you did the same to Agustín. Was that an accident, too?' Staffe looks at Quesada. 'Not exactly the product of an original mind.'

'He had every chance to leave,' says Quesada.

'But he needed to prove Astrid was dead,' says Staffe. 'His own mother. And Manolo needed that, too – but not for the money. He had to know she didn't abandon him. And for that, he is dead.'

'What was done is done,' says Jackson.

Pepa turns onto her side. At the far end of the pen, a cattle prod is propped against the wall. She stretches her foot out, rests it against the base of the prod.

Jackson turns to the bull-handler, says, 'That bull's mad enough now. Come on, get against the door.'

Staffe tries to stand but Jackson takes a swift step towards him and kicks out, karate style, catching Staffe full in the chest with the sole of his boot. He pulls out his knife; his goat's-head knife.

'Stab me and your story collapses. Unless your *brigada* here can prove the bull can hold a knife.'

'I will be telling the story,' says Quesada, 'To anybody who is interested, it will look like a bull had gored you – believe me.'

'Which it will do,' says Jackson.

'You've got some pact going on,' says Staffe.

'Pact?' says Jackson.

'But any pact is only as strong as its weakest link.'

'You're full of shit.'

'Yours has survived the test of time, I'll grant you that – since Edu guessed what was going on with Barrington's painting.'

'Edu hated Barrington,' says Jackson.

'But he needed the money, and then the day Barrington died, you had no choice but to bury the truth.'

'What?'

'I can picture you all there, that day. You and Rubio, and Edu and Angel. Just like in the photograph.'

'What photograph?' says Quesada.

'You in the background and no sign of Astrid.' On the periphery of his vision, Staffe sees Pepa shift. She moves inch by inch. 'And Santi Etxebatteria? How did he fit into your plans, Jackson?'

'I'd never heard of the son-of-a-bitch until Raúl turned up like the bad penny. You have to take what you can in life.' He goes into his pocket, unfolds the newspaper article to reveal the images of Staffe's father and mother. 'You can see how it will aid matters, if this is on your person. The authorities don't want to stir the shit with ETA just now.'

Staffe's bile rises. 'Cortes and Peralta know where Astrid is.'

Jackson turns to the handler. 'Let's get this done.' He and Quesada are both by the door now and the handler reaches for the final bolt. One meaningful tug and the pen's door will swing open.

The other handler yells, 'Wait!' and edges to the door, too. The horse rears up again and Pepa pushes out with one foot and the cattle prod falls towards her. She grabs the handle, careful not to touch the two protruding metal prongs, and uncoils, reaching out with the prod, Jackson in her sights.

Jackson plants his feet wide and readies his knife, and it strikes Pepa that she has no way of knowing whether the prod is charged; and if it is charged, what kind of a shock it will inflict. Suddenly, she wishes she had stayed put.

The blade of his knife glints as he comes towards her. She steps forward, lunges. The prod is three feet long and it jabs into Jackson's chest.

He yelps, looks her in the eye and his legs give way, but he holds out a hand, supports himself from complete collapse. As he forces himself to his feet, Pepa lunges again and Jackson shudders, drops back to his knees. The knife falls to the dirt.

Staffe thinks that the charge may be running down, can see

that Jackson may revitalise and he works his way round towards the horse.

Quesada calls, 'Let the bull out!'

'No!' shouts Jackson, picking up his knife. 'I'm in the way.'

'Let the bull out!' shouts Quesada. 'That's an order.'

Staffe stands up, rushes behind the horse and grabs its tail, smacks it on the hindquarters with all his might and the horse rears up. He pushes, as hard as he can, and the horse kicks back but Staffe jumps to one side, slaps its quarters again, shouts at the top of his voice, 'Chaaarge!'

Quesada pulls out his pistol, levels it at the handler.

'No!' shouts Jackson.

Pepa lunges again, knocks Jackson back to the ground and he looks up, dazed, his strength ebbing, but he steels himself and rolls away, seeing the fear in the handler's eyes as he pulls back the bolt, the bull baying at him. The horse charges across the room towards the door and Jackson rolls again.

The gate to the pen clatters open and the bull makes its move but the horse is charging for the door. Jackson is on his feet, getting on the blind side of the horse and running for the door. The bull kicks out with its back legs, rearing round, spoiled for targets, and Quesada has no choice, he opens the door on the far side of the enclosure and runs through as light floods the room and the roar of the crowd booms down from the arena.

The bull charges for the light and the sound. It runs, choosing freedom, chasing after Quesada, the horse and Jackson. The three run along the short, high-walled tunnel and into the amphitheatre. Quesada is first into the arena, trying to get across the ring to the opposite exit but the bull catches up with him.

Tomas, calm and slow, steps in and with one, two expert wafts of his cloak, turns the escaped bull's attention away from Quesada. He steps back, supremely elegant, drawing the bull further and further away. But as he does, his own bull, the finest, fifth bull – the *quinta toro* – charges for Quesada.

First, the bull gets him in the thigh. Next, dipping its head, its horns searching out the heart, the *quinta toro* gets him in the shoulder. The crowd groans and a posse of caped *toreadors* rush out, tempting the bull away with their swishing colours of red and yellow, like so many Spanish flags in the wind. But this bull isn't for stopping. It is the finest bull.

Back beneath the stands, Jesús steals into the enclosure. He raises his gun, levels it at Pepa. She lowers the cattle prod, says, 'No, not you.'

A shot rings out.

In the arena, the fifth bull jolts. As it gores Quesada a last time – straight to the heart – it takes a bullet to its head. It stands back up, momentarily, as if milking applause, and then collapses onto the *brigada*, pressing the last gust of life from Quesada.

Jesús's finger is on the trigger, still. He has a bead on Pepa.

Staffe shouts, 'No!' and rushes at Jesús who quickly switches his aim. He looks Staffe in the eye and Staffe can see his heart is not in it.

Jesús keeps his eyes firmly on Staffe and begins to squeeze. Closing his eyes, a second shot rings out. Jesús opens his eyes. Policeman to policeman, and as if frozen in time, he and Staffe stare each other out.

Staffe reaches for his heart, waits for the pain to come. And as he waits, he sees Jesús falling away from him. It is like the way the earth shifts when a boat makes its first, slow move from port. Jesús falls further away. He staggers out, stands at the head of the tunnel. With the entire crowd on its feet and screaming, the young policeman falls to the golden floor of the ring and slowly, blood begins to flow from his shoulder. He lies on his back in the sun and smiles, feels life coursing through his veins and into the sand.

Hand on heart, Staffe turns, sees Sanchez lowering his pistol. The *comisario* walks slowly towards him and, as if a long quest has reached its end, wraps his thin arms around Staffe, like a proud father might, the smell of cigars and cologne thick and sweet, and together they walk into the ring, see Quesada being lifted onto a stretcher, a red blanket being pulled up over his face. The bull is dragged away through the sand.

'Where is Jackson?' says Staffe.

Nowhere to be seen.

Thirty-five

Guadalupe sits by her mother, dabbing her forehead with a folded, wet flannel. She dips it back into the bowl of water on the bedside table, wrings the excess and whispers that she wishes they could have spent more time together but she had to get out of Almagen as soon as she could. Immaculada smiles, thinly.

Staffe tries to imagine what it would have been like for Guadalupe, growing up here as the bastard daughter of a foreigner; her grandfather the mayor. He remembers what Pepa had told him about how much Immaculada loved Barrington. What might it mean to Immaculada, if she could be forgiven by her daughter for not loving her well enough? He cannot begin to understand what tricks it must play, if you loved a lover more than your child; especially a cheating lover.

Immaculada's eyes close and he holds his breath. For a moment he thinks she has passed away. But her shallow breasts rise and fall. Guadalupe says to him, 'I have the painting in the other room.'

'That's not what I came for,' says Staffe. 'And you should keep it.'

'Now it's not worth a bean?' she says, managing a smile. They both look at her mother, sleeping.

'You didn't know it was a forgery?'

She shakes her head.

'You knew nothing of the scam that your father and Jackson conjured up.'

'Not the slightest.'

'Your uncle Edu did.'

'He always was on my father's case.' She dips the cloth into a bowl of water, wrings it and wipes the sweat from her mother's face and neck. 'It doesn't surprise me he found a way to profit from my father's fame.'

'Jackson must have spoken about Astrid. He told me he could never harm her, and I believe him, which makes me think her death was an accident.'

'You know she is dead?'

'We will later today.'

'How?'

'Where is Jackson Roberts, Guadalupe?'

She shrugs.

'He's the only one who knows the whole truth.'

'Sometimes, shouldn't the truth just be there. Does it always have to be *known*?'

'They're going to try to prosecute Rubio Cano for his wife's murder. I don't think he did it. He was *there*; just like your truth is always *there*. But he didn't kill his wife.'

'You think Jackson did.'

'No. They both loved her too much. She was killed for money.'

'My uncle Edu?'

'Perhaps. Or Angel Cano.'

'He knew about the paintings, too?'

'Rubio cut him in, I think. That bar down in Almería was

on its last legs, but they couldn't let it go. Angel needed the money, the rest of them just wanted it.'

'So Jackson is innocent.'

'Not exactly. You can expect a visit from Sanchez. He wants to nail you.'

'Why?'

'Because he wants to nail Jackson.'

Staffe has learned a little of what it must be like to love your country too much. Perhaps Sanchez is the last generation that understands, absolutely, what there is to preserve of the old life, of the Spain Barrington discovered, then slowly uncovered – in Almagen when he fell in love with the place and one or more of its people, for all its secrets.

'What will happen to Angel?' asks Guadalupe. 'I always did like him. My father would take me to the Quinta Toro during the *fiesta*.' She laughs, an unhappy laugh. 'He would disappear off with Rubio and Angel would look after me. He fed me those livers with the star anise. You know, I never tasted anything like it since. It would get so busy in the Quinta Toro in those days. What will happen to it now?'

'Telefonica are next door. They say they'd like to expand.'

'When my father and Rubio were done, Rubio would come back into the bar and hug me. He smelled of cheap scent and his eyes would be swimming. My father wouldn't hug me. I remember, in that crowded bar, he stood all alone. He looked as if he had lost something.'

Staffe leaves Guadalupe to the belated moments of peace with her mother. He eases the large door gently closed behind him, walks down through the white, tight streets built by the Moors. Earlier, he had spoken to the Hesse family solicitor, had told him about Gustav's will, and the solicitor was delighted. He said Gustav would perhaps be able to find peace, finally.

Staffe passes through the church square. There is more than a little of the *mudejar* about the place of worship and he tries to picture the scene in Africa when they hear that foreigners are gifting them a new school; that water will come up from the dry earth. Life becomes a little less cheap. He feels gooseflesh in the hot sun, thinks also of Yousef, walking to Moulay Idriss with his euros in his *burnous*.

*

Salva has laid a large table in the *plazeta* outside Bar Fuente. Bottles of Contraviesa wine and jugs of beer are set out and everyone is sitting down already. Sanchez is at the head, out of uniform and carving extravagant slivers of Serrano, a fat Cohiba in his mouth and the smell of cologne on the warm breeze. Jesús is on his right, his arm in a sling, and Pepa his left. She is on the phone, reading from a piece of paper, presenting final amendments to her sub-editor. When they searched Quesada's *finca* above Mecina they had found the keys for an apartment in Palma Mallorca, documents for a boat in Pollensa, and offshore bank statements for a company based in Caracas.

In front of Pepa, on the table, is her dictaphone – now out of its beautifully wrapped and ribboned cake box, and containing everything that Jackson and Quesada had said down in the bowels of the Plaza de Toros.

Paolo and Marie are at the other end of the table and Frog and a smattering of old goats make up the numbers, plus the mayor, and two empty places. One is for Staffe, who is shown to his seat by Consuela, carrying baskets of bread.

'Who is the other seat for?' says Staffe.

Consuela bites her lip and hurries inside.

Frog says, 'Manolo. We're paying respects.'

'I thought you didn't like him,' says Staffe.

'There's plenty you don't understand about us, still.' Frog stands up, offering Staffe a glass of red wine. 'But you're good enough.' He raises his glass. 'To Manolo.'

Everybody stands. 'Good health, money and love.'

Salva comes out, carrying a suckling pig on a large silver platter. Consuela follows, carrying the same again, and everyone round the table begins to fuss: recharging their wine and imploring Sanchez to carve the ham faster, before the pig gets cold, but before he can, Salva calls the table to order. He leans across and picks up two plates, holds them high, bringing them down on the pair of crisped suckling pigs, and with a *rat-a-tat-tat*, he carves the pigs simultaneously using only the plates. So succulent are they, their flesh falls away and everyone round the table applauds.

Pepa finally gets off the phone and comes to Staffe, bending down and kissing him on both cheeks, lingering. She whispers, 'I have something for you.'

He feels a weight in his lap and looks down at a large, brown-paper package. It is tied in baling twine.

She says, 'It's everything Raúl had, on Santi Etxebatteria.'

As they eat, the mayor explains that the Academia Barrington will be built on the site of the old *salon* behind the church.

'The Junta don't mind about what has happened? The forgeries?'

The mayor says, 'Barrington is more famous than ever, now. They will come in their droves. To Almagen!'

Staffe looks around, at the barefooted, nut-brown children frolicking in the fountain. The ladies in black are needlepointing in small clusters, sitting on reed chairs with their feet in dust beneath the trees. The old boys are coming up from the *campo* with their donkeys. Staffe wonders what is really best for this special place.

'And you will be here? You're staying!' says Sanchez.

'I'm staying,' says Staffe.

'Of course he is,' says Marie, craning to allow Paolo to spoon the *cochinillo* into her mouth. In her lap, sleeping baby Enid.

'To the English Inspector,' says Sanchez, raising his glass.

'To strangers!' shouts the Frog and everybody drinks. They eat quickly, hoovering up the *cochinillo* and little is said for a long while as everyone tries to absorb what has happened; what is to come. Jesús is quietest of all.

Sanchez stands, re-ignites his Cohiba, taking it to the shade of the fig tree in the corner of the *plazeta*.

Staffe follows him, refuses a cigar. 'It's amazing, how this story told itself.'

'Sometimes, you find a little truth and a whole lot more reveals itself. Sometimes . . . not.'

'That's not true, and you know it. You had to dig.'

'For the truth?' says Sanchez.

'For the body. You dug a channel. You diverted the stream to the body in my sister's woods.'

'I knew something had gone on up there, it's true.'

'But you knew they did for Astrid. Is that why you were moved out to Almería?'

'I did all right out of it – I soon got ahead of Quesada.'

'Someone must have told you. They must have told you exactly where.'

'Can't we let it lie?'

Staffe shakes his head. 'That's not how we got here.'

They both look across to the table outside Salva's. Jesús struggles to light a cigarette for himself and one for Pepa. They move a little closer.

Sanchez says, 'Jesús is a fine young man. Amazing, that a son can be a better man than the father. I never thought that.'

'Will he be all right?' Staffe and Sanchez look across to Jesús, trying to put a brave face on.

'He very nearly succumbed to temptation. He thinks he betrayed his father, his whole family, but he has done the only thing a policeman can do.'

'Because you stepped in,' says Staffe.

'Let God bless him. And forgive him his loyalty.'

'It was definitely Angel who killed Agustín?'

'Angel has coughed up. He says they never meant for it to happen and they just wanted to scare Agustín, send him on his way, and then when he resisted and it went too far – they had to do what they did, to cover up who had been killed.'

'The four of them were up in the mountains the night Barrington passed away,' says Staffe.

'Astrid wanted to go to Morocco and for Jackson to go with her, and when he said no, she said she would expose them all.'

'Some of those collectors are very influential people – as you can imagine. They'd have lost a fortune.'

'On paper,' says Sanchez.

'For some people, it's only the paper that matters. So, when Astrid tried to leave, they stopped her.'

'Angel swears she fell and fractured her skull.'

'We shall see.'

They both look up the street that leads down from the church, see the priest walking slowly towards them, with Cortes and Peralta in tow.

'So they called Quesada, and it was his idea to bury her in the style of a *ladrones*?'

Sanchez nods, takes out the papers from the pocket of his jacket.

'And Quesada took care of Agustín, Edu and Manolo?'

'According to Angel. He says the idea was to pin it all on Jackson Roberts, if they ever got caught, but as soon as he knew he was losing his bar, Angel gave up the game. It's the call of history. Some hear it too loudly.'

'But Roberts killed Raúl. You'll catch up with him for that, surely?'

Sanchez smiles. 'Sometimes, the bad guy can be innocent.' He pulls out a clear plastic evidence bag from his pocket – a small cutting of cloth that looks like a blotched sample of a Spanish flag.

'Raúl's blood,' says Staffe.

'And Quesada's prints.'

'You saw the rag when I did, from the bridge.'

'I warned you not to look,' says Sanchez.

'To make sure I did!'

The priest approaches Sanchez and they each make a small bow. Sanchez delves into the inside pocket of his jacket, produces some papers which he hands to the priest, who casts his eye over them, walking towards the cemetery, followed by Cortes and Peralta; then Sanchez and Staffe. The rest of the diners follow, and slowly the villagers come out, processing slowly. The gravediggers bring up the rear, their tools slung over their shoulders like guns.

The sun beats down on the shadeless graveyard and the village stands in silence as the diggers open up the tomb, trying not to disturb the dead. It says:

Hugo Barrington
Artist
1914–1999
Much loved in a foreign land

When the corpse is exposed, Cortes steps in, carefully easing the cadaver out and resting it on the ground, uncovering the body which is preserved in a way the victim in the woods never could be.

It is, unmistakably, Astrid.

When Cortes is done, Staffe opens his wallet and hands him the pressed ball of Barrington's hair. Cortes says, 'To prove your sister doesn't live amongst ghosts?'

Staffe looks away, looks all around him, to see if they are being watched from a safe place, but the sun blinds him, so he looks back towards the village. Still, he feels the presence of Jackson Roberts, out there somewhere.

He shields his eyes and beyond the line of villagers, he sees a woman walking slowly towards him. From the way she moves, he knows her. She wears a white cotton dress that shimmers like water. Her legs are paler than he has become accustomed to and she too holds a hand to her eyes against the brilliance of the sun. Her face is obscured, but his heart skips a beat and he feels hollow in his stomach. At first, he thinks this is because of the portent she must bring. But he knows it is probably something more. For a moment, Staffe thinks he might be in dreams.

Staffe watches her all the way and although Cortes says something to him, he doesn't hear it. All the time, she gets closer.

Finally, she is in front of him, says, 'Good afternoon, sir.'

'Josie? What are you doing here?'

'It's Pulford.'

'What's happened?'

'Jadus Golding is dead.'

Staffe looks at Josie and wants to hug her, to embrace what he thinks she represents.

'Pulford had been following Golding for months and harassing Jasmine Cash. He can't account for where he was. He was the last person Golding phoned.'

'I know Pulford and I know he didn't kill Jadus Golding. He couldn't do it.'

Josie smiles, weakly, and it evaporates like spilled water in the Almagen dust.

Beyond Josie, Harry runs up from the square. He is soaking wet from playing in the washstands and Gracia runs after him, calling 'Arri! Arri!' But Harry runs straight for his uncle. Breathless, Harry says, 'What's wrong? What's happened?'

'They want me to go home, Harry.'

'You said this was home.'

'I should leave you to it, sir,' says Josie.

'No.' He puts his hand on the small of Josie's back, keeps it there as he guides her back towards the square. 'There are some friends I'd like you to meet.'

'You'll come back with me,' she says, softly, as they walk together.

He doesn't reply, just wishes they could carry on walking this way, a while longer.

Exclusive extract from the new D. I. Staffe novel
Kill And Tell
Publishing spring 2013

One

Staffe walks up the Caledonian Road, towards Pentonville prison, which skulks like an angry, Victorian giant.

Later, he will go into Leadengate, to trawl through all the interviews DS Pulford has ever conducted with any member of the e.gang, and to document all the calls his sergeant made, from home, mobile, and the office, going back through all the months between Staffe being shot and his shooter, Jadus Golding, being murdered.

A part of him wishes he could amble on, towards the sky at the end of the street, but he knows what he must do and he churns the questions he must ask his sergeant. As he does it – as if he is being whispered to, from across a Spanish desert – he touches his chest, where his scars are almost done.

*

DS Pulford is led into the visitor centre by a sneering PO who takes delight in confiscating the sergeant's clutch of books and folders. 'Bit old for school aren't you?' he says.

Pulford puts a brave face on it, sits opposite Staffe and says, 'I came straight from the library. I only get to go once a week. Today, they had a book I was after, but the choice isn't good.'

'What are you up to, David?' says Staffe.

'I'm studying for an MA.'

'I mean with these damned charges. There's talk of this having to go to trial if we don't come up with some evidence soon.'

'I've got a supervisor at UCL – one of the most eminent criminologists . . .'

'For God's sake! You need to focus.'

'That's precisely what I'm doing.'

'You didn't kill Golding,' says Staffe.

'Is that a question?' says Pulford.

'It would be good to hear you say it.'

'Do I need to?'

'Unless we can come up with some evidence, you will have to say it to a jury.'

'You're not a jury.'

'Say it.'

'I didn't do it.' Pulford says it the way a teenage boy might goad a parent.

'Christ, Pulford! This isn't a game.' Staffe looks at his Sergeant, sees that his mouth is weak. Pulford breathes deep, shakes his head and shoulders, the way you do when the body bobs up from the freezing sea. 'Are they looking after you?'

'Some of the POs are all right, but I'm a copper.' He nods at the PO who brought him in. 'That's Crawshaw. He's a bit of a twat.'

'Have they got you in isolation?'

He nods. 'But I don't want that. It makes them think you've something to be afraid of.'

'And have you? There's two members of the e.gang in here. Did you know?'

Pulford gives Staffe a withering look. Jadus Golding, whose

murder the DS stands accused, was a member of the e.gang. 'I know all right.'

'Christ, Pulford. Is there anything you can think of that you've not told us . . . that could get you out of here?'

Pulford looks away.

'There is!'

'I've told you everything I can, sir. And that's the truth.'

'The truth can't hurt you – if you're innocent?'

'Sometimes, on the Force, you only see half the story. It's the perspective we have. Do you see that?'

'Tell me what you're afraid of, Pulford.'

Pulford says nothing. His eyes say, 'Plenty.'

'There's a number you kept calling from your mobile. It's unidentifiable, but I called it the other day and we got a trig on it before they could turn it off. It was somewhere on the Atlee. These calls were all made at times you weren't on duty. Who were you phoning?'

'If I could, I would say.'

'At least tell me why you can't.'

'There is something you can do.'

'Tell me.'

Pulford hands him a piece of paper. 'Can you download me this article? They don't let us access the internet.'

'My God! How long are you planning on being in here?'

*

As soon as he sees him, Carmelo knows the time has come.

He turns away from his visitor and out of habit, calls for Jacobo to make drinks. 'Jacobo!' he calls with a trembling voice that cracks. But perhaps Jacobo isn't here. Carmelo had a nap after he telephoned Goldman and isn't sure how long ago that was. He clears his throat and shouts again; this time at the top of his voice. 'Jacobo! Come!'

Carmelo waits, listens, hears nothing and shuffles slowly across the marble floor in his carpet slippers.

'Perhaps you gave him the afternoon off,' he says smiling eagerly. 'You are perhaps too generous for your own good. For a supposedly bad man, you can sometimes have a very kind heart.'

'And you should know.'

'I know plenty.'

'You know where the drinks are kept.'

The visitor looks at the cocktail cabinet. 'The one they stripped from Mussolini's palace in Firenze. How did you lay your hands on it?'

'How the hell do you know that? I never told you that.' Carmelo is curious and a little angry, but he musters a smile. 'Help yourself to some Grappa while I'm gone. I'll just be a minute or so.'

'It's not my cup of tea.'

'It's all I have. It's how I lived so long.'

'Then maybe I should try a little.'

Carmelo turns, excuses himself. He takes the lift to his bed-room. It reminds him of his uncle's house in Palermo. Carmelo moves a little faster now he is on his own. It pays to be one step ahead.

The dressing table is all the way across in the bay window, looking over the garden. The nearest neighbour is a hundred yards away, beyond large trees that have always been here. He opens the drawer, picks up the pistol from alongside his tortoiseshell brushes. It feels heavy in his hands and he places it on the dressing table's walnut glaze.

Carmelo looks at his hands, the middle finger of his left hand cut off just above the bottom knuckle. He switches the gun to his right hand, all liver-spotted now; he thinks how much more Saint Peter might hold him to account for, had life gone another way. He used to be left-handed, but he adjusted and now he pushes out the release catch and pulls out the magazine with his right, discharging the bullets from their clip. He replaces the empty magazine and pulls on the trigger, manages it fine. The hammer clunks heavy in the lonely house. As he returns the bullets, he thanks God for the Italian marble that constitutes his floors. There will be blood, but Jacobo can mop. Together, they will wipe clean this smear of new history.

Now the day has come, now this final bit of business is demanded of him, his blood courses a little faster. It feels nostalgic and to stiffen his ardour, he thinks of the bad things his visitor wishes to pass, and rekindles all the malice which comes with that territory. He has no choice, he really doesn't. These days on earth are just a part of our scheme: a mere section for the soul.

Tomorrow, when they have erased this execution – for that is what it is – Carmelo will confess. He will confess his ancient crime. Nobody can silence him, not all these years on.

Carmelo walks quite briskly to the lift. The blood is really shifting now, across the fibres that line his arteries. The gun is heavy in one hand and Carmelo presses the G button in the lift with the index finger of his other, but steps quickly backwards, out of the lift as the doors close on the empty chamber, and instead he takes the broad, oak staircase, peeking to see if his visitor is waiting down below for the lift. He wouldn't be surprised if he was. But as Carmelo descends, coming level with the chandelier and seeing the whole of the hallway sprawling out below, he sees that the hall is empty, the door to the drawing room still closed.

He opens the door slowly, the gun behind his back and his finger on the trigger. The visitor is standing by the French windows. He half turns, sips from his grappa, saying, 'I poured you one.'

Carmelo reasserts the grip of his right hand on the pistol, wishes his house was not so grand, its rooms not so large. He doubts if he could even hit the French windows with his shot, let alone the visitor standing in front of them, so he walks to the cocktail cabinet – just five yards or so from the target. He reaches out with his left, picks up the grappa. Carmelo holds it with his thumb and three fingers, wants to be one pace closer, to make sure. He raises the glass, suddenly wanting a taste of the aquavite, its effect; and the spirit stings his lips.

His eyes water and the grappa burns Carmelo's throat. The visitor smiles, comes towards him, reaching out, and Carmelo brings the pistol from behind his back and tries to lift it. He tries to point it at his quarry but his hand is suddenly loose. The grappa really burns him now and he hears the pistol crash onto the marble and his legs give way. When his head smashes on the marble, he thinks he might blemish it.

Carmelo brings his knees to his chest and he tries to make himself sick, but he can't.

From above, he looks like a question mark on his fine marble floor. Today, there is a thin vein of red, where Carmelo's blood makes its slow course.

Acknowledgements

The places in this story are real, but the names of the places are often not. All the characters in the book are fictional, though the forenames are usually common to friends and acquaintances, so for the Guadalupes and Manolos I know, these characters are not you. My apologies if, for even a moment, you might think they are. An exception is Jackson Roberts, who is kind of real.

My thanks to the patrons of all the places in the book, such as Bar Fuente, Quinta Toro, Hotel Catedral and Ladrón del Agua, plus many others. The places in the story are your names, but not your establishments. As an example, there is a Bar Fuente in Almagen (a fictional village very closely based on a real one), but the owner is not Salva, nor is it in the lower *barrio*; and the Quinta Toro thrives.

You might say that the milieu is a collage of isolated samples of the real Alpujarras (and Almería, Granada and the Costa) cut out and stuck back together again – like a Braque or some Picassos.

The Alpujarras is truly a last outpost of what people often refer to as the real Spain. Its people eke a hard living from a land still watered by the irrigation systems designed and built by the Moors in the sixteenth century. Tourism helps the people of the Alpujarras and I would urge people to visit – but quietly, and only tell the discerning.

Adam Creed, Las Alpujarras, 2011.

Some of the books which informed the novel are:

Arthur, Max (ed.), *Fighters Against Fascism*
Brenan, Gerald, *The Face of Spain*
                South From Granada
                The Spanish Labyrinth
De Falcones, Ildefonso, *The Hand of Fatima*
Elms, Robert, *Spain*
Greene, Graham, *Monsignor Quixote*
Hemingway, Ernest, *Fiesta*
Jacobs, Michael, *Andalucia*
Junta de Andalucia, *Guide to the Alpujarras*
Kennedy, A. L., *On Bullfighting*
Lee, Laurie, *As I Walked Out One Midsummer Morning*
                A Moment of War
Nooteboom, Cees, *Roads to Santiago*
Orwell, George, *Homage to Catalonia*
Preston, Paul, *We Saw Spain Die*
                Franco: A Biography
Richardson, Paul, *Our Lady of the Sewers*
Tóibin, Colm, *Homage to Barcelona*
Tremlett, Giles, *Ghosts of Spain*
Walker, Ted, *In Spain*

Glossary

Acequia A man-made water channel which forms part of the ancient irrigation system created by the Moors.

Acotea A room with a large, unglazed opening.

Alamos Poplar trees.

Alcazar A moorish fort.

Ayuntamiento Town hall, which in rural areas is central to village life – more so than in Britain.

Bachillerato School studies from age sixteen: the baccalaureate.

Balsa A water reserve which can be any size between a paddling pool and a large pond. Crucial in conserving one's entitlement to water.

Bancale A terrace, on which crops can be grown.

Barranco A large ditch or gulley.

Barrio A neighbourhood.

Bocquerones Anchovies. Tiny fish, often pickled in vinegar, but white and silvery – unlike the tinned variety.

Brigada Sergeant (first class).

Bocadillo A sandwich (usually crusty and half the length of a baguette).

Burnous A hooded, berber cloak.

Borracho Adjective or noun, to describe a drunken state.

Cabo Lance Corporal.

Campo The countryside.

Caña A small measure of beer, say, a third of a pint.

Carretera A main road.

Casetas The bars at a *fiesta*. Sponsored by political parties each battling for affections.

Chiringuito An open-air bar. Often found on beaches, but also in cities and the mountains.

Chorizo Literally, a spicy sausage. Also a derogatory term for a badly behaved character from a poor background.

Choto Goat (meat).

Comedor Dining room.

Corral Animal quarters at the bottom of a Spanish house, oft converted into a garage or a spare room.

Corrida Bullfight.

Cortijo A small, rural building. Usually comprises a three-roomed abode within a smallholding.

Cortinas Curtains.

Cubata A mix of spirits and a soft drink. A long drink with a generous measure of alcohol.

Cuerpo The National Police Corps – more prevalent in cities (see 'Guardia').

Denuncia There is no British equivalent of this legal process in which one citizen can denounce another.

Fabada A warm, winter dish with sausages and pork and beans; a little like *cassoulet*.

Feria Like a *fiesta*, but bigger. Usually in large cities and lasting for a week and with a series of bullfights at its heart.

Fuente Fountain.

Gitano Gypsy.

Granadinos People from Granada city.

Guardia A member of the Guardia Civil, which maintains military status and was originally created to suppress discontent in rural areas. Still associated with Franco and reviled by Lorca.

Guirri An outsider. Usually derogatory.

Huerta A parcel of land upon which villagers grow produce. Akin to an allotment but privately owned and larger.

Lente (la) Lens. In this case, the name of the (fictional) regional newspaper for the city and province of Almería.

Matanza Traditional slaying of a pig and a whole day's partying whilst the beast is butchered and sausages and black pudding are made.

Merienda Picnic

Misa Mass

Mosto Grape juice, non-alcoholic, but which attracts a free tapa in traditional bars.

Nido (el) Nest (the)

Papas al pobre An Andalucian dish of potatoes and peppers, slowly fried in a small sea of olive oil.

Paseo A Spanish institution in which groups of people informally process, dressed smartly; typically between eight o'clock and ten in the evening. An everyday ritual.

Peña A club, often for aficionados of flamenco.

Plaza/plazeta A square/small square.

Primo/prima Cousin. In rural Spain, people have many dozens of *primos* living in the same village.

Rambla A broad thoroughfare, usually a dried-up river bed.

Silla Montar Saddle. In this case, a geographical feature where a ridge swoops down between two peaks.

Sol y sombre Sun and shade. A potentially lethal mixture of brandy and anis, typically drunk alongside coffee at break-fast.

Teniente Lieutenant.

Tinao A balcony, often connecting two buildings on a narrow street.

Tocino White ham. Like lard which someone has traced with a thin line of red biro.

Toreador A handler who prepares the bull for the kill. Dressed in similar fashion to a matador.